Wolf Tales 11

Wolf Tales 11

KATE DOUGLAS

𝒜

APHRODISIA

KENSINGTON PUBLISHING CORP.

http://www.kensingtonbooks.com

APHRODISIA BOOKS are published by

Kensington Publishing Corp.
119 West 40th Street
New York, NY 10018

Aphrodisia and the A logo Reg. U.S. Pat & TM Off.

ISBN-13: **978-1-61129-074-5**

Acknowledgments

Wolf Tales 11 marks the twentieth story in my ongoing tales of the Chanku shapeshifters. During the course of the past five years since this series was first conceived, the characters have ceased to be creatures of my imagination. They've taken on lives of their own since that very first story when Alexandria Olanet ran her little car off the road and ended up in the arms of a most amazing gentleman.

When I write them now, each character speaks to me in his or her own voice, so that I actually hear them as I write their lines of dialogue—Anton Cheval with his amazing self-confidence and superior air, Oliver and his clipped British accent that's never quite faded away, Keisha's warm self-assurance, Mei's cockiness, Manda's soft yet unyielding strength—I hear them telling me what to write as if they're living, breathing creatures, which makes it all the more important that I get their stories right.

And that's where my amazing beta readers come in—those wonderfully diligent women who are willing to find time in their own busy schedules to read my stories, find my mistakes, and keep me on track. On this book, my sincere thanks go to Ann Jacobs, Jan Takane, Rhonda Wilson, and Rose Toubbeh, who, because I was late meeting my deadline (yes, life does occasionally get in the way), jumped in at a moment's notice to give my manuscript a very careful read and make excellent suggestions that vastly improved the story.

Producing a book—especially one that's part of a series—is truly a community effort. My thanks, as always, to my terrific agent, Jessica Faust of BookEnds, LLC, my wonderful editor, Audrey LaFehr, and her amazingly efficient assistant, Martin Biro.

And last—but always first in my heart—my sincere gratitude to the world's most patient husband. Sweetie . . . I can't imagine doing this without you . . . so I won't.

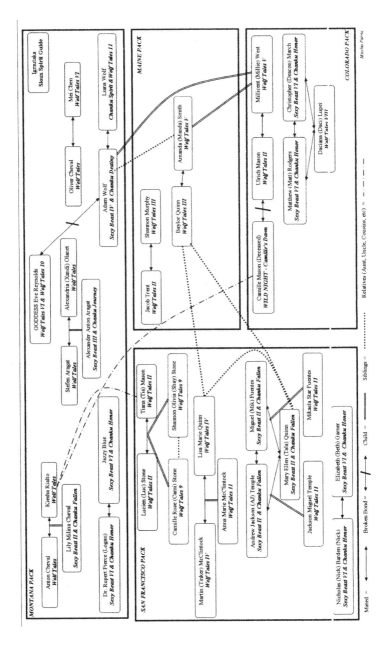

MONTANA PACK

Igmutaka
Sioux Spirit Guide

Mei Chen
Wolf Tales VI

Liana Wolf
Chanka Spirit & Wolf Tales II

Anton Cheval
Wolf Tales

Kiesha Rialto
Wolf Tales

Oliver Cheval
Wolf Tales

GODDESS Eve Reynolds
Wolf Tales VI & Wolf Tales 10

Lily Milina Cheval
Sexy Beast II & Chanka Fallen

Alexandria (Xandi) Olanet
Wolf Tales

Adam Wolf
Sexy Beast IV & Chanka Destiny

Dr. Rupert Pierce (Logan)
Sexy Beast VI & Chanka Honor

Stefan Aragat
Wolf Tales

Amanda (Manda) Smith
Wolf Tales V

Jazzy Blue
Sexy Beast VI & Chanka Honor

Alexander Anton Aragat
Sexy Beast III & Chanka Journey

MAINE PACK

Shannon Murphy
Wolf Tales III

Tiana (Tia) Mason
Wolf Tales 9

Baylor Quinn
Wolf Tales III

Millicent (Millie) West
Sexy Beast V & Chanka March

SAN FRANCISCO PACK

Lucien (Luc) Stone
Wolf Tales II

Shannon Olivia (Shay) Stone
Wolf Tales 9

Jacob Trent
Wolf Tales II

Ulrich Mason
Wolf Tales II

Christopher (Deacon) March
Sexy Beast V & Chanka Honor

Camille Rose (Cami) Stone
Wolf Tales 9

Lisa Marie Quinn
Wolf Tales V

Camille Mason (Deceased)
WILD NIGHT - Camille's Dawn

Matthew (Matt) Rodgers
Sexy Beast VI & Chanka Honor

Daciana (Daci) Lupei
Wolf Tales VIII

Martin (Tinker) McClintock
Wolf Tales IV

Anna Marie McClintock
Wolf Tales II

Miguel (Mik) Fuentes
Sexy Beast II & Chanka Fallen

Andrew Jackson (AJ) Temple
Sexy Beast II & Chanka Fallen

Mary Ellen (Tala) Quinn
Sexy Beast II & Chanka Fallen

Mikaela Star Fuentes
Wolf Tales II

Jackson Miguel Temple
Wolf Tales II

Elizabeth (Beth) Garner
Sexy Beast VI & Chanka Honor

Nicholas (Nick) Barden (Nick)
Sexy Beast VI & Chanka Honor

COLORADO PACK

Mated = ⟷ Broken Bond = ╫ Child = ━ Siblings = ══ Relatives (Aunt, Uncle, Cousins, etc) = ─ ∙ ─ ∙ ─

Mated Pairs

Chapter 1

Tiny motes of dust sparkled in shimmering beams of morning sunlight, stirred by the silent departure of the man who'd joined with them throughout a most enjoyable night of sexual excess—as if sex with his lady love and one of his dearest friends could ever be considered excessive.

Smiling at such a ridiculous idea, Adam Wolf stretched out on his left side and rested his right arm over the smooth curve of Liana's hip. He gazed at the brilliant sunbeams and thought of Igmutaka and the night just past as he softly stroked Liana's warm skin. The spirit guide generally left before the morning sun touched the windows of their small apartment, returning to his cougar form and the freedom of the Montana mountains.

Igmutaka knew he was always welcome in their bed, desired as much by Adam as he was by Liana. With memories of the night fresh in his mind, Adam leaned over and placed a soft kiss on Liana's shoulder. She tasted of salt and glistened with the soft dew of perspiration; her fair skin showed the subtle marks of sucking mouths and grasping fingers, even a few reddish nips from sharp, wolven teeth.

Marks Liana would wear with pride. She was, after all, a powerful and much loved Chanku bitch. She sighed in her sleep and turned to him. Her lips pressed against his chest in a sleepy kiss, reminding Adam of the convoluted twists and turns that had led him to this time, this place, this perfect moment.

If anyone had told him just a couple of months ago that he would love this woman who now held his heart, Adam would have cursed them as a liar. If someone had suggested that the cougar prowling the huge Montana estate Anton Cheval and his Chanku pack called home would manifest himself as an absolutely beautiful, albeit somewhat androgynous male, and insinuate himself into Adam's life—and his bed—he would have laughed outright.

But Liana, once a goddess and the woman responsible for his mate's death, had claimed Adam as thoroughly as Eve had once held his love. And Igmutaka, that son of a bitch, had not only unveiled his human side, he'd revealed an affinity for sex matched only by Adam's own.

Laughter bubbled up out of his chest. He rolled to his back, body shaking and eyes tearing with the effort to keep himself quiet.

Liana rolled over, opened her eyes, and stared balefully at him. "What, my love, is so damned funny?"

Still fighting the laughter that wouldn't die, Adam shook his head. "Us. This." He leaned close and kissed her. "Igmutaka and that damned Louisville Slugger of his."

Obviously biting back a grin, she raised a very expressive eyebrow and dryly offered, "He is quite impressive."

"A little more than impressive when it's shoved up my ass."

Liana shrugged daintily. Then she raised her arms over her head and stretched her lithe body along his full length. "As I recall," she whispered, "you were the one who introduced him to the pleasures of the flesh."

He grunted, nuzzling her neck. "The son of a bitch took to those pleasures pretty damned fast, if you ask me."

"Something for which I will be forever grateful."

Chuckling softly, Adam inhaled her seductive scent. He couldn't possibly be getting hard again. Not after the night they'd just spent—one that had involved very little sleep. Kissing his way along the smooth line of Liana's throat, he took another deep breath. "Actually," he grumbled, "you were the one who suggested he join us in a little ménage à trois. If you'll recall, Ig didn't have a clue what was coming next."

Laughing softly, Liana rubbed against Adam. "I do recall. One of my better suggestions, don't you think? I wouldn't worry about Igmutaka. He handled himself beautifully."

"Handled himself? I don't think so. More like he was handling *you* and *me*!" Adam snorted, and then both of them were laughing and touching and kissing. Somehow Liana managed to slide her body over Adam's full length with an almost sinuous grace, until she covered him like a living, breathing blanket.

The hard tips of her taut nipples tickled his chest. The tuft of tightly curled blond hair between her thighs brushed the ridge of his now swollen cock and tangled with his own damp thatch of hair. Laughter died and thoughts of Igmutaka fled as Adam's erection rose between Liana's slightly parted thighs and she slowly arched her spine, sliding her damp heat along his full length.

Groaning, he wrapped his arms around her back and rolled her beneath him, slipped the thick length of his erect penis between her buttery folds, and thrust hard into her hot, sleek channel. Her muscular vaginal walls rippled along his cock as she adjusted to his length and girth. Both of them shuddered deliciously when the sensitive tip of his penis brushed across the hard mouth of her womb.

Adam closed his eyes, fighting for control. He knew he must look like a man in pain as the cords in his neck tightened and his lips stretched into a flat grimace from his efforts. He arched his back and flexed his arms to keep from flattening Liana's slight frame with his weight.

She sighed and shifted her hips, tilting just right to accommodate his size. Adam took a deep breath, then another until he felt he could hold on, but damn it felt good, the heat and the life of her, the free and loving welcome he felt whenever he entered her body.

The body of a goddess. She'd been the one he prayed to, the one the packs had looked to for help and guidance. The one who had proven herself to have feet of clay—she had failed her beloved Chanku too many times to count.

Failed in many ways, yet been reborn in others.

She'd been cast out of her immortal office and into Adam's arms. Now Eve, once his mate, excelled in Liana's old role. Eve ruled now, with a firm hand and a vigilant yet loving eye. She answered prayers and worried and watched over the Chanku from that other dimension where gods toyed with the lives of men.

While here, on this plane, a man made love to a goddess.

Slowing his deep thrusts, finding a deliberate, measured rhythm he could sustain, Adam gazed at the woman whose neglect had almost ended him, yet whose uncompromising love had healed his heart. She opened her wide gray eyes and smiled up at him.

A smile that flashed straight to his heart like a bolt of lightning, taking his breath, branding him. It was time. Doubts and baseless concerns disappeared. She was his, the woman meant to stand by his side, to bear his children, to share his thoughts. He took a deep breath, aware of the pounding in his chest, the rush of blood in his veins. He wanted that most intimate of bonds, forever. Connected as only Chanku could be.

"Bond with me tonight, Liana. Be my mate, for now and forever."

Her vaginal muscles rippled over his shaft in a subtle reaction to his soft request. Her fingers brushed the rough stubble covering his jaw. "Are you certain, Adam? Have you truly forgiven me? Will you ever be able to forget my failures?"

He shook his head. "I can't forget what happened. I don't want to, because it's led to this time, this moment. It's led me to you, Liana. I loved Eve with all my heart, but I never realized my love wasn't enough for her. She has what she needs, now." He kissed Liana's mouth, sliding his lips over the softness of hers. "And me? I have what I need, Liana. What I want. The question is, can I be enough for you? A woman who was once a goddess, who has been loved by men much better than I'll ever be, for more centuries than I can imagine?"

She laughed against his mouth and teased his lips with her tongue while her body held him deep inside, clenching and pulsing around his erection. "Adam, you are such a rogue! You know there's no lover better than you. More important, there's no man who could possibly put up with me. I love you. I can imagine no other for my mate. I would be . . ."

Her body jerked and then went rigid in his arms. Her eyes flashed wide and bright.

"Liana? What's wrong?" Adam shoved himself away from her. His cock slipped free of her warmth as he gathered her up in his arms, held her against his chest. He tried to link but her mind was closed to him. Blocked. "Liana? What's happening?"

She blinked. Shook her head, frowning. Then she stared at him, frightened and wild-eyed. "No, Adam. No." She clutched at his shoulders and her fingers dug into his flesh. "This is terrible." The words rushed out on a whispered breath of fear.

"Absolutely terrible."

Baylor Quinn checked to make certain the big SUV wasn't overlapping a parking space on either end of the one he'd just managed to squeeze into. Then he turned in his seat and grinned at the two women in the back. "Okay, ladies. We're here—downtown Freeport, Maine, and all the shopping your hearts desire."

His beloved Manda laughed and rolled her eyes. "It's only taken us a year to convince you guys to bring us up here, so don't act like it's all your idea."

Shannon Murphy jabbed her lightly in the ribs. "Careful. Jake's still not certain he wants to be here at all. It's taken me ages to drag that man out of the woods. Don't blow it now. My credit cards are burning a hole in my handbag."

Jacob Trent merely snorted.

"See?" Shannon shook her head as she reached for the door handle. "What did I say? He is such a Neanderthal."

"Now that's an interesting concept." Jake climbed out and opened Manda's door. "A shapeshifting Neanderthal. Wonder if he'd shift into a dire wolf? Those suckers were big."

"You're plenty big enough for me, sweetheart." Shannon winked at him. Then she shut her door and met the others on the curb. Her eyes were twinkling when she kissed Jake. "Why don't you and Bay grab a cup of coffee and pursue the concept of shapeshifting dire wolves. Manda and I have shopping to do and a whole town full of stores waiting just for us . . . and your money."

Laughing, Manda and Shannon linked arms and headed toward the long row of shops along the main street. Baylor stood beside Jake, watching the smooth sway of Manda's slim hips as she walked away from him. Then he sighed and turned to Jake—his lover and truest male friend. "We'll be lucky if we hear from them for hours. Coffee or a cold beer?"

Jake laughed. "We'd better wait until later this afternoon for that beer. I think it's going to be a long day. Coffee for me."

Bay followed him into a small coffee shop not far from where they'd parked. Manda and Shannon had been arguing for a weekend away from home and a chance to shop in the little town of Freeport for months now, but it was still difficult for Bay to relax in unfamiliar territory.

"It's okay, you know." Jake set two coffees down on the small table Bay'd found near the front window and took the seat across from him. "We haven't had any threats for a long time. The girls are both sharp and they're well trained. They can take care of themselves."

Bay shrugged. He picked up the cup and stared at the dark brew. "I wish I could relax, Jake. I can't. I've been inside Manda's memories and I know the nightmare she lived."

Held captive by a man who was driven to learn her secrets, Manda had spent twenty-five years as his prisoner, subjected to horrendous experiments and vicious sexual attacks. She'd lost her childhood, and only now seemed to be recovering the sense of herself, her confidence as a free woman.

The image of her, crippled by her body's inability to complete a shift one way or the other, trapped for years in a deformed shell that was half human and half wolf, would haunt Baylor until his dying day. With thoughts of Manda's life before she'd discovered her true heritage much too clear in his mind, he gazed into Jake's amber eyes. "Think how your life would be if you hadn't gotten to Shannon in time when those bastards tried to snatch her. We've been damned lucky so far. Some day that luck's gonna run out."

Jake planted both hands on the tabletop and stood up. "We can't live our lives in fear, bro. Think the way you do when you're the wolf, about letting go and living for the moment." He took a swallow of coffee. "It works for me. See? Right now, at this moment, I gotta take a leak."

Bay chuckled, shaking his head as Jake sauntered across

the small shop. Curious eyes of interested women at nearby tables followed him as he headed to the back where the restrooms were located. Bay couldn't blame them for looking. Jake had an aura of sexuality about him that couldn't be denied, as well as a devil-may-care attitude that buried a much deeper persona. The combination of sensual aura, rugged good looks, personality, and intelligence was definitely seductive.

Still, Bay had to admit that Jake was right. Sometimes Bay spent so much time reliving the past and worrying about the future he forgot to relish the present.

Maybe he needed to work on that.

A shift in air currents caught his attention. A large man wearing a dark suit and tie slid into Jake's empty chair. Bay's head snapped up as recognition slammed into him. He hadn't seen his old partner since he'd left government service. "Rolf? What the hell are you doing here?"

"I was gonna ask you the same thing." The man glanced toward the door, then in the direction Jake had gone. "It's been a while, Bay. We've missed you."

Baylor shook his head. "It was time to get out. The last job left a bad taste in my mouth."

"It also left a lot of good men missing and presumed dead. What happened?"

"Can't talk about it. Still classified." So classified that even his superiors in the service had no idea what had happened the day he'd been sent to kill Jacob Trent and kidnap the woman who was now Jake's mate. "What brings you to Freeport, Rolf? You're still with the service, right?"

Rolf nodded. "Officially? Recruiting."

Bay sipped his coffee. "Unofficially?"

"Still looking for the missing agents. We've followed their trail as far as Bangor, but they seemed to just disappear off the face of the Earth at that point."

Bay set his cup down and sent a questioning thought in

Jake's direction. He wondered what was taking his buddy so long, wondered why he'd run into Rolf here and now. It was much too unsettling to be mere coincidence.

As far as Bay knew, Rolf had no idea he'd been assigned to work that final job with the missing agents. No idea Bay had been part of the team that had, as Rolf said and for all intents and purposes, *disappeared off the face of the Earth.*

Bay's addition to the team that was sent to kidnap Shannon Murphy had been a last-minute change ordered directly by Milton Bosworth, the late Secretary of Homeland Security—a change in personnel that never made it to the books.

Even Bosworth hadn't known that the bodies of those agents would rest forever at the bottom of a flooded, abandoned quarry deep in the wilds of northwestern Maine. Even if he had, Bosworth was dead now, a fact that filled Bay with a quiet sense of satisfaction since the discovery that Bosworth had been the one responsible for Manda's cruel treatment, for the horrible acts committed against an innocent child.

But, what if the service knew more than he realized? Bay frowned and stared at Rolf through the steam from his cup of coffee. "I want the truth. Are you following me?"

"No. Should we be?" Rolf shook his head as if answering his own question. Then he glanced about the room again and lowered his voice. "Bay, when I saw you, I knew I had to say something. We've got history, man. You kept me alive on more than one occasion. Listen up . . . you're working for that hotshot California agency now, Pack Dynamics, right?"

When Bay nodded, he continued. "I overheard a conversation yesterday I probably should have missed, but when I saw you and that other guy walk in here . . . well, let's just say it was too fucking weird. Coincidence like that doesn't just happen, and I knew I had to say something. Look, there's talk that our people tried to get Pack Dynamics to pick up a job. PD refused. The guys at the top weren't happy and they're looking for leverage."

Again, he glanced around as if he feared someone might be watching. His unease made Bay uncomfortable, but before he could comment or question Rolf, the man focused on him once again.

"They were talking about the fact that a couple of wives of PD agents are pregnant. About how vulnerable that made the agency. Word is, someone's going to try and kidnap them, hold them until PD agrees to do the job. I don't have any dates or any idea what the job entails, but whatever it is, our guys are willing to take some desperate and totally unethical measures."

Before Bay could respond, Rolf glanced over his shoulder again. He must have seen Jake as soon as Bay did, because he practically lunged out of the chair. "Look, Bay . . . I don't have any details, but you were someone I could trust when you were still with the service. There's no one there like that. Not anymore. Be careful. Things have changed. Not in a good way."

He was out the front door before Jake slipped into the vacant seat.

"Who was that?"

"Give me a minute." Bay dialed Lucien Stone's private line in San Francisco. Luc answered immediately.

"Luc, I just got a very strange warning that members of the agency I used to work for might be after Tala and Lisa. Keep them under guard until we can figure this out, okay?"

Luc's terse answer chilled his blood. Bay listened a moment and ended the connection. He felt Jake in his mind and merely filled in the details. "It's too late. Someone grabbed Tia, Tala, and Lisa less than an hour ago. Their mental connections disappeared at the same moment. No one can reach them."

Jake stood up. "Let's find our girls. I don't like this a bit. We need to get to San Francisco."

"You find the girls. I need to talk to Rolf."

"The guy who was just here?"

Bay nodded. "Yeah. We worked together a few years back. He just showed up and told me about the threat against Pack Dynamics, that Tala and Lisa might be in danger."

"He came all the way up here to tell you that? How the hell did he know you'd be in Freeport?"

Bay shook his head. "He claims he was surprised to see me but that he felt he owed it to me to tell what he'd heard. Says he's up here on the trail of some missing agents."

Jake's head snapped around. "Our missing agents?"

Again Bay nodded. "Same. Go find the girls."

Jake nodded and took off down the street. Bay cast his thoughts out for Manda as he scanned the busy street in search of the agent. Manda's sweet presence slipped into his mind. He sent her a quick warning, told her to watch for Jake.

Something made him turn just as a man in a dark suit stepped off the curb onto the crosswalk at the corner. Baylor recognized Rolf immediately and started forward. A black SUV swerved off a side road and accelerated up the narrow street. Bay barely had time to cry out a warning before the heavy-duty grill connected with the lone pedestrian in the crosswalk.

Rolf's body flipped over the hood, cracked the windshield, and spun across the top of the SUV. He caught for a moment on the luggage rack and then tumbled to the ground in a mangled heap of broken bones and torn flesh. There was no sign of movement, no sense of life. Bay glanced once at the retreating SUV and raced down the sidewalk, running for all he was worth in the direction of Manda's horrified mental cry.

* * *

Mik Fuentes and AJ Temple stormed into Luc's office as he hung up the phone. With all his heart, Luc wished he had something positive to tell the guys, but Baylor's call had merely confirmed what he already knew, what he'd learned for certain only moments before.

He'd been uneasy all morning, but he hadn't figured out why. Now he knew. Tinker McClintock muscled his way past Mik and AJ. "What the fuck's happened?" He leaned over Luc's desk, his chest heaving with each breath he took. "I can't reach Lisa. Her thoughts are gone. Flat out gone."

"Same with Tala." AJ grasped Mik's arm, holding on to him as if he needed the support. "Neither one of us had tried to contact her all morning. I mean, it's just a fucking shopping trip, right? But when we tried, we couldn't raise her. No mental signature . . ."

"No answer on her cell. Nothing." Mik stared at Luc. "Not a damned thing."

Shaking his head, Luc said, "They've got Tia, too. At least I think they do." He ran his hand across his eyes and took a deep breath. "I can't reach her, either."

"Who's got her? What the fuck's going on?" Tinker looked as if he might leap across the desk and go for Luc's throat. Mik slung an arm over his broad shoulders and gave him a quick hug.

"Give Luc a chance, Tink. We're all in this together. Luc?"

"Shit. I never expected anything like this. It didn't seem like that big a deal." Luc turned away and struggled to gather his racing thoughts. None of this felt real. It was too horrible a nightmare to be real. He took a deep breath and faced his packmates. "They've been kidnapped."

"Fuck." Tinker's entire body sagged. Mik tightened his hold on the big man.

AJ grabbed the desk for support. "Who? What do you know?"

Luc hardly knew where to begin. "I turned down a job a couple of days ago. Very few details, but I didn't like what I heard. I've never trusted the bastard who wanted to hire us. Honestly? I think he's nuts, like certifiable, and what little he told me—and he told me damned little—didn't make sense. That alone made me wary. I said Pack Dynamics wasn't interested, especially without details. He insisted. I declined, told him he'd have to find someone else. Thought that was the end of it."

"Who the hell's behind this?" Tinker's voice pulsed with anger. "How much do you know?"

"Not nearly enough. Not yet. The guy who called? He was once part of Bosworth's team." Luc walked over to the cabinet against the back wall and opened the cupboard. He pulled out an unopened bottle of Hennessy cognac. Their pack leader, Anton Cheval, had given the bottle to him almost exactly three years ago. The events of that time—when they'd rescued Tia's father from kidnappers—felt like a fresh wound as he removed the stopper with shaking hands and poured a glass of the rich amber liquor for each of them.

Obviously confused by his actions, the other men took the glasses he handed to them. Then Luc held his glass up and faced Tinker, AJ, and Mik—three men he loved more than he'd ever imagined possible. "A promise, gentlemen. Anton Cheval gave this to me after we'd successfully brought Ulrich Mason home when he was kidnapped. We will bring our women home safely. There are no alternatives, no other possibilities. We will bring them home and the ones who took them will pay. I swear this to you."

He sensed their joint resolve as each one took a sip of the smooth liquor, and he relished the heat as it slipped down his throat. Then he walked to the window and stared out at the traffic passing by on Marina. He kept his thoughts open for any sign of Tia and felt the anger within him build. No more. He'd had it with constantly being on the defensive. It was time to take the offense.

"We need to go over everything. Every single detail. What have you got so far?" AJ stepped up beside him. His voice was steady now, and though Luc knew it had to be killing him, AJ obviously had his temper and his anger under control.

He stared into the liquor in his glass. "I got a call about twenty minutes ago. Same voice as the guy who'd wanted to hire us, telling me he had Lisa and Tala. No word on my wife, but he gave me details for the job. The president and First Lady are scheduled to attend a concert at the Civic Auditorium tonight at eight. Our job is to make certain the president doesn't leave the building alive."

"What the fuck?" Mik grabbed Luc's shoulder and spun him around. "Are you fucking nuts? Assassinate the president? You're fucking kidding me. This dick thinks he can hire us to . . ."

Luc nodded. "I didn't know what the job was, originally. Only that I don't like the politics of the man behind it, and when he came to me with a supposedly top-secret project, I knew I wasn't comfortable taking orders from him. I had no idea in the beginning what he was proposing, but from the obscene amount of money he offered, I just . . ."

Shaking his head, he sighed and turned away from the window. "Once they snagged the women, I got the details, along with their promise that the minute the job is carried out, Tala and Lisa are free. No mention of Tia. Not a word."

He glanced at the three men. "I called Anton first. I wanted him involved immediately, but Liana had already warned him. She sensed the kidnapping when it happened. I'd barely hung up the phone when Baylor called from some small town on the Maine coast. He'd run into a guy from the agency he used to work for. The man warned him of a plan to kidnap your women. He'd heard mention of it within his agency. From the way he talked, Bay thought they were in on the deal, but he's not positive. For all we know, they were offered the job and turned it down as well, but Bay didn't think so. He thinks it's their hit."

Tinker softly asked him the question that had Luc close to breaking. "I don't get it. Why no word of Tia?"

Luc shook his head. "The guy who called didn't mention her. Neither did Bay. I can only assume they've got Tala and Lisa. I have no idea where my wife is. No idea if she's even alive."

"The babies?" AJ rubbed his shoulder, offering comfort.

He felt his voice break and cleared his throat. "Beth and Nick were babysitting the girls over at their apartment. I reached them mentally, the minute I got the call. Right now, they're on their way here. I figure this is the safest place we've got. Better than the compound where you guys all live. The security's not as good there. They've got orders to stay here, inside, out of sight until we get the women home safely."

Mik stood close against his other side. "Did Anton have any ideas?"

Luc swallowed and nodded his head. "He does. He's got a suggestion, but he wants me to run it by the three of you first. We know your women and babies are at risk. Obviously, there's no way we can give in to these bastards. We don't do jobs like this. We work for good, not against it. Hell, even if we hated the man leading our country, we don't work that way. The problem is, if we don't take the assignment, the women die. Anton has a plan. He's still working out the details, but it sounds risky."

Mik chuckled, but there was no humor behind his laughter. "Has Anton Cheval ever had a plan that wasn't?"

* * *

Keisha Rialto stood in the doorway to her mate's office. The wind howled outside. Part of her thoughts were with their sleeping daughter. Lily'd been fussy all morning, and Keisha hoped the blustering storm wouldn't wake their little one from her nap. Her focus, though, her worry, and her love were for the man seated at the large oak desk near the big window.

Something had drawn her to him, a powerful sense of need she could no more ignore than she could her daughter's cries. Anton raised his head, and the anguish in his eyes pulled Keisha across the room and into his arms in a heartbeat.

"What is it? I can't see your thoughts, my love. There's nothing but darkness and so much pain. What's wrong?"

He pulled her into his lap and held her close. She felt his heart racing, sensed the subtle opening of his mind to hers, as if a dark cloud slowly faded away and allowed the light to pass.

But there was no light in this knowledge. Keisha gasped. "All three of them? Even Tia? But what of her babies? And Tala and Lisa? They're both so close to their due dates. I don't understand. Who? Why?"

Anton shook his head. "Tia's little ones are safe with Nick and Beth. As far as who and why? We have an idea— a good idea, but it's one that makes me sick inside." He sighed and very softly kissed her cheek. "It appears I need to make a call. I've been searching for another way to help—our low profile is the most important thing we've got to keep us safe, but there's no way around it. I have to share the knowledge of our existence and hope it goes no further than this one man, but it's the only hope we have if we're to prevent a terrible tragedy." He chuckled. "At least I think the man's trustworthy."

He wrapped an arm about Keisha's waist and held her close as he bent down and reached for a small panel in the side of his desk, one hidden beside his right leg. Keisha felt her own heart race to match the pace of Anton's. She'd known the panel existed—even knowledge as closely guarded as this was shared in the mating bond—but she'd never known Anton to release the secret catch, nor to remove the small box contained within.

He took what appeared to be a slim cell phone out of the box, plugged in a power cord, and attached it to a strip on the underside of his desk. There were no numbers on the phone—nothing more than a series of buttons across the top.

He pressed the red one and held the phone to his ear. Keisha heard it ring twice. A man answered. His voice was familiar, one she'd heard often on the nightly news. She'd even seen him once, in person at a distance, when she and Anton had attended an event in Washington, DC, many months ago.

Wind buffeted their sturdy home, yet even above the roar Keisha caught the sound of her daughter's restless cry. She slipped off of Anton's lap and headed for the door. As she closed it softly behind her, she heard her mate's deep and steady voice.

"Yes, Mr. President," he said. "My name is Anton Cheval. I had hoped never to have to call this number."

Chapter 2

Perfume filled the air, cloying and thick. Tia's first thought was that it was a good thing she was in the bathroom, because she really felt as if she had to throw up right now, and that sickening sweet smell wasn't helping her roiling stomach.

She blinked and the walls so close around her spun and shifted in and out of her blurred vision. The nausea went from bad to worse, but she was on the floor beside the toilet, thank goodness, and it was fairly easy to lean over the porcelain bowl and vomit the acidic contents of her stomach.

Oh, Goddess! The pain was overwhelming. She cried out and pressed her hands to her belly. Forcing herself not to whimper, she took a few deep, calming breaths.

The nausea passed, but not the pain. Tia reached overhead, grabbed toilet tissue from the dispenser, and wiped her face. Then she blinked stupidly at the sticky tissue, confused by the crimson stains on the paper. She hadn't vomited blood. No, there'd been nothing but bile, so obviously she hadn't eaten in a while, but there was blood everywhere.

Her hands were covered. She must have smeared it

across her face. Blood was all over the toilet seat where she'd held on when she puked. Her jeans were soaked, as was the lower half of her shirt. Thank Goddess the pain had receded just a bit. Now it was a manageable throb in her lower right side, the same place that seemed to be the source of the coagulating blood.

Forcing herself to think, Tia leaned her head back against the metal wall and tried to remember how she'd gotten here. Then she realized she had no idea where *here* actually was. She studied her surroundings and saw pale green metal walls, a white toilet. The tile floor beneath her was clean, thank goodness, since she was obviously sitting on the floor in the stall of a public restroom somewhere.

The mall. The big one in Corte Madera. She'd gone to the mall with Tala and Lisa, one last shopping trip before the babies arrived. Babies? Dear Goddess, were her little ones okay?

Panic lent her strength. She reached out with her mind and tried to find Luc. *Shit.* Pain knifed through her head, a blinding, agonizing headache that pulsed directly behind her eyes. Had blood loss and shock screwed up her mindtalking? There was no sense of Luc at all.

No sense of anyone. Where were Lisa and Tala?

Slowly, bits and pieces of the day filtered into coherency, until the pattern of the morning began to take shape. They'd been planning this shopping trip for days. Christmas was less than a month away and Tala and Lisa were almost eight months pregnant. Tia's twins had come early—they'd agreed they were running out of time to do any shopping.

Tala had been determined to get at least one more trip in before she had two little ones to care for. Conversation filtered through Tia's memories—Lisa teasing Tala, something about already having two big ones who were high maintenance.

Mik and AJ. Dear Goddess . . . did they know their mates were missing? Or were they okay and was she the only one not found?

Tia's nausea ebbed and flowed with her memories—the beautiful drive across the Golden Gate, coffee at that neat little shop in Sausalito, arriving at the mall early.

Tala'd been so thrilled to get out of the city. Lisa, too. Tia and Luc had made a few trips to the mountains with the babies, so Tia hadn't been nearly as frantic to escape, but she'd still been excited about a day with her girlfriends, especially knowing the twins were safely in Nick and Beth's capable hands. They'd decided to shop at the big open-air mall just off the freeway, the one with the trees and fresh air between stores.

Poor Tala. She was big as a house from carrying twins fathered by Mik and AJ. This pregnancy had been a lot more difficult than she'd expected, but nothing would stop Tala.

Nothing stops Tala. Nothing. Fading in and out of reality, Tia leaned her head back against the metal wall. Should she try reaching out for Luc again? *Damn. It hurts. Everything hurts.*

Something terrible happened. *What?* She couldn't recall much after they'd locked the car and walked to the mall. Lisa holding on to Tala's arm, both of them cracking pregnant lady jokes. Tia prancing ahead of them, showing off her slim, trim, eight-months-post-baby self. Laughing about whether or not Tala would ever get her tiny waist back, or if Mik and AJ were really going to change diapers.

No one doubted Tinker. Lisa sounded so smug when she talked about her mate, but she had a right to. Tink was a gem. How many guys would willingly take on a woman's labor pains? Tinker had, when Tia had her twins. Then he'd helped care for her babies once they got home to San Francisco, and they weren't even his.

He'd been there for every second of Lisa's pregnancy, whether she was hanging over the toilet puking her guts out or worried about peeing her pants when Tink's unborn daughter practiced her soccer kicks.

Of course, Mik and AJ were just as terrific. Not quite as comfortable in the caretaking role as Tinker, but still wonderful and loving. No one could be like Tink—he was a natural. Still, the guys were there for Tala, worried and afraid, yet always supportive. As Luc had been for Tia.

Luc. She really needed to reach Luc, not lie here on the floor of a public restroom with her mind wandering and her body bleeding, but she couldn't seem to organize her thoughts. What the hell happened? She ran her fingers along her lower abdomen, gently probing for the source of the pain.

Holy shit! There. At the sharp curve of her hipbone. A tear in her jeans and a fiery wound that must have come from either a knife or a bullet.

Bullet? That's what it was. She knew this, but when? How?

Tia closed her eyes, drifting in and out of consciousness, catching herself in memories. Walking along the open pavilions of the mall, too early, arriving before most of the stores opened for business. A few other people wandering about—not too many, considering how close they were to Christmas.

Still, the stores were quiet, the weather was cold and clear—a good day for two very pregnant ladies to shop, for one harried mother of twins to enjoy getting away.

Tia pictured the metal gates guarding the doorways into stores that hadn't opened yet, turning the chic little shops into prison cells. That's what they'd looked like.

Prison cells.

She pushed herself, searching for those missing moments. Lisa and Tala behind her, laughing. People beginning to fill the area, the sound of laughter, of voices.

Voices. Men's voices. Low, threatening. Lisa's terrified mental shout, a silent warning that spun Tia around. She remembered now. They wore dark suits, neatly trimmed hair. Two had their arms around Lisa and Tala. Tia recalled the flash of hypodermic needles, the glazed looks on the girls' faces. A thick arm latched on, catching Tia around her waist. She'd struggled, even after the sting of a needle in her neck, she'd fought him.

His hand covering her mouth. Biting down, hard. The deadly *thump* of a silenced handgun, searing pain.

Then nothing. *Okay.* She'd been drugged and shot. Left unconscious, but for how long? Where? Why?

Lisa? Tala? Where are you?

Nothing. No sense of either of them. Head pounding, her side hurting like hell, she struggled to her feet, slapped her palms against the walls to keep from falling over. Gathered what strength she could, ignored the threat of that blinding pain through her skull, and sent out a mental shout.

If she was still in the mall in Corte Madera, and Luc was miles away in San Francisco, he might not hear her.

She called him anyway. Her purse was missing. Her cell phone. She felt something warm and sticky running along her thigh. Her wound was bleeding again. Black spots danced in front of her eyes and she knew, without any doubt, she was losing consciousness once more.

Luc! Luc, help me! Please help me.

There was nothing. No response. No loving voice in her mind. Her legs quivered and refused to hold her weight. *Luc? I love you, Luc. Can't you hear me? Cami? Shay? Mommy loves you. Mommy will always love you.*

She was sliding . . . slipping down smooth metal, caged in by the small bathroom stall, falling into a pool of blood on the tile floor. *So much blood . . .*

Slipping away from the light, away from consciousness.

Away from Luc. Darkness descended. Called to her, and pulled Tia into its welcoming arms, even as Luc's shout echoed distantly in her pounding skull.

Tia? Where are you? Tia!

"Luc? Are you okay?" Mik grabbed his arm as Luc collapsed into the big chair behind his desk.

"Tia. I heard her voice. Faint . . . far away. She's hurting. I felt pain. Sensed an injury, smelled blood. Hers? Someone else? I don't know for sure, but there's blood and some kind of weird perfume." He shook his head. "I can't identify it, but it's really familiar. Damn. Tia."

"Share it." AJ filled his vision, looming over him. "Share the smell, the perfume. Maybe one of us will recognize it."

Luc opened his mind, remembering, pulling up the cloying scent until the smell seemed to fill his office. Perfume and blood. It made him want to retch.

Tia's blood.

"I know what that is." Tinker stared toward the window, frowning. "It's that gross perfume they use in public restrooms. Sort of a combination disinfectant, hide the stink smell."

"You're right." Luc concentrated again. Nothing. "I think she was somewhere north of us, but . . ."

"That makes sense." Mik glanced at AJ. "Didn't Tala say something about going to that big mall north of Sausalito? The one with Nordstrom and Macy's. It's got a lot of outdoor pavilions, big stores, lots of little boutiques . . ."

AJ nodded. "It doesn't make any sense. Why would they still be there if someone's kidnapped them?"

Tinker reached for the door. "Maybe they're not all there. Maybe just Tia." He stared at Luc. "Luc? You come with me. AJ and Mik? Stay here. Keep your cell phones handy. Listen for our girls. I've got a link with Tia that's almost as tight as Luc's. If we can find her, maybe she can lead us to Lisa and Tala."

Luc nodded. He reached inside the drawer on his desk, pulled out a dark, zippered bag, and removed a small handgun. As he checked to make certain it was loaded, he glanced at AJ and Mik. "Get in touch with Jake and Bay. Baylor mentioned coming out here—he's frantic with both his sisters missing—but I think they can do us more good if they can get to Washington. Have them go to Anton's apartment in DC. We'll let them know what's going on as soon as we know anything."

Mik glanced at the phone on the desk. "What if you get a call from the kidnappers?"

"The guy's using my cell. He told me to keep it close. It might be the only number he's got." He paused a moment after slipping the pistol into his pants pocket and put out another mental call for Tia. Silence mocked him.

With one last look at Mik and AJ, Luc followed Tinker through the house to the garage.

Keisha tucked Lily into her crib and waited in the doorway until the eighteen-month-old settled back into sleep. It wouldn't be long now before they moved her into a regular bed, but at least as long as she was still in the crib, Keisha could think of her perfect daughter as a baby.

A baby with a powerful mental voice and the ability to understand well beyond her years.

"Is she asleep?"

Keisha had sensed Anton's approach. She always knew where he was, often what he was thinking. Now, though, his thoughts were a tangled mess. So unlike him—he was generally so cool and unaffected by the emotions swirling about him. There something especially touching about this unusual vulnerability she sensed in a man always so self-assured. She turned slowly, caught the questions in his amber eyes, and nodded. Then she took him by the hand and tugged.

Frowning, not speaking, he followed her.

"How long do we have?" she asked.

A sexy smile spread slowly across his face. "The plane won't be ready for a couple of hours. Logan's still gathering his medical supplies." He stopped, draped his arms over her shoulders, and pressed his forehead to hers. "We have time for whatever's on your mind."

Keisha sighed. Talk about your typical male one-track mind. If she weren't thinking exactly the same thing, if the situation weren't so dire, she might have laughed. Instead, she said, "I need to know what's going on, but I need you even more. Lily's asleep now. I still have to pack my own bags. I'm coming with you, you know. I've already asked Stefan and Xandi to watch Lily for us."

"You're willing to leave her?" He raised his head, his expression nothing short of incredulous.

"I am. Tia will need me. Luc needs you. We have to go. But first, we need each other."

She crossed the hall to their larger room, walked past the big bed, and stepped up to the sliding glass door. Sunlight glistened on fresh snow and the dark forest beckoned. The wind had died down to a gentle breeze. She turned and cocked an eyebrow in Anton's direction. He frowned. Obviously he'd thought she merely wanted sex— as if making love with Anton could ever be described as *merely sex*.

Keisha rested a hand on her hip and smiled softly at him. "Unless you intend to shift while fully dressed, I'd suggest you lose the clothes."

His eyes lit up. He ripped his sweater off over his head, slipped out of his jeans, and kicked everything into a pile on the floor. So unlike her tidy, organized lover, but it was obvious he had too many thoughts crowding his mind, too many worries bedeviling him.

Too many to share now, as he was—as a man.

"Xandi and Stefan know we're going to run. They'll keep an eye on Lily for us. Come." Keisha slipped her robe off her shoulders, opened the door, and stepped out onto the icy deck, but before she'd even begun to shiver, she shifted. Anton was right behind her, following her as she leapt over the railing to the frozen snow.

They'd had heavy snow, then freezing rain. Then the temperature had dropped and left a frozen crust atop the thick snowpack. Keisha's paws slipped on the hard surface and she almost skidded ingloriously across the ice, but she managed to catch herself and stay in motion. Anton was right behind her.

She felt his hot breath across her flank as she gathered her feet beneath her, dug her claws into the ice, and raced away from the house, away from all that linked them both to their often fragile humanity—raced with all her might toward the freedom of the forest.

Much of the woods had burned during a huge fire just a few weeks ago, but the thick blanket of fresh snow hid the devastation the fire had wrought. Once they slipped between the trees and found the trail, the going was easier, the surroundings almost surrealistic in their monochromatic beauty. Stark, black branches encased in silvery ice, pale shoots from willows and dark fir needles and pine trapped within their glittering, icy shells. The frozen snow crunched and crackled beneath their paws and puffs of steam burst from warm muzzles.

Keisha listened for the sound of life and heard only the harsh breaths of the wolf behind her. She opened her mind to his thoughts and found nothing beyond the feral processes of a wolf running through a frozen forest. He searched for game, listened for threats, followed the scent of the female ahead.

It was as she had hoped. She'd recognized the overload, knew that Anton had reached a point where processing all that he knew, all that he needed to do to save lives, had overwhelmed his brilliant mind. She'd never seen him this way, but then there'd never been so much at stake before.

Not only the lives of the missing women, but the three unborn children they carried. And, as if their desperate situation wasn't enough, a threat against the leader of their country, the man they'd sworn to uphold and protect. Who did they save? Which lives were theirs to protect?

Mere hours from now, it was all due to come together.

There wasn't enough time to gather other Chanku from all their various homes across the country, and yet Keisha knew that Anton drew his strength from the power of the pack. Knew his abilities were limited only by his connections to the energy each of them could share.

But how, when they were scattered so far and wide? Baylor, Jake, Manda, and Shannon, even now on their way to Washington, DC, where they would keep an eye on a few very questionable members of Baylor's old secret service agency as well as their handlers.

Poor Baylor. She'd hardly given him a thought, but Lisa and Tala were his sisters! He was such a good and loving man. How was he handling this, knowing both of his sisters were the targets, his unborn nieces and nephew's lives at risk?

Ulrich, Millie, Daciana, Matt, and Deacon were all in Colorado, awaiting direction from Anton, information from Luc, reassurance that all would be well, that lives would be saved. Were they close enough to share their energy with the one they'd all accepted as the pack's leader?

She and Anton would be boarding a plane in a couple of hours and flying to San Francisco. At least if he got closer to the action, he had a better chance of controlling the outcome, but Adam and Liana, Stefan, Xandi, Oliver, and Mei would remain behind, watching the babies, sharing energy, waiting to offer whatever help they could from a distance.

Logan and Jazzy . . . Keisha sighed as she thought of the young doctor and his mate. They would be flying to San Francisco, too. Adam had offered, but if Lisa and Tala ended up in a hospital, a certified physician would have a better chance of getting access to them for care.

If it came to that. Keisha's feet pounded the frozen snow and the wolf behind her kept a steady pace just off her left flank. If only she could lose her thoughts to the feral world of the wolf! It was not to be today, not with her worries about Anton paramount in her mind, drowning out the beast. Though she would love to run forever, run fast enough and far enough to leave all their troubles behind, there was no time. Not if she wanted to make this run through the forest truly count.

She dipped and spun to the right, slipping between frozen branches, finding a trail barely wide enough for one wolf to pass, yet she hardly broke stride, turning and twisting along the narrow path, with Anton following close behind.

She didn't want to exhaust him, but she knew he needed this run, the chance to leave the world of men behind and bond more tightly with the feral instincts resting so close beneath his terribly civilized human skin.

He would need contact with his wolven self more than he'd ever needed it before. Somehow, even when he shifted, she hoped he'd hold on to the powerful instinct that allowed the wolf to kill without remorse, to use whatever tools he had to protect the pack.

There was no doubt in Keisha's mind that they might be called on to take lives tonight. But it would not be the life of the president that was at risk, nor would it be the innocent females and their unborn young. No, the ones who had set this terrible plan in motion might need to die.

Keisha had no problem with killing to protect those she loved, those she honored and respected.

Her mate, though, often allowed his human conscience

too much free rein. He'd weigh the options, consider all the possibilities, often taking the greatest risk himself in order to keep others safe. Not this time. The risk was too great.

Somehow, they had to end this constant threat to their beloved packmates, to their children, to themselves. If killing was justified, if it was the only choice he could make, Anton needed the strength to make it. The support of his pack, and most of all, the support of his mate.

Bursting into a small, frozen meadow, Keisha twisted about and planted her front feet hard against the ground. She lowered her head and snarled, challenging Anton, daring him to take her.

He skidded to a halt, teeth bared, hackles raised. Searching his mind, she found only the wolf, his thoughts as pure and basic as the frozen world around them.

Mate. Conquer. Control. Dominate.

If she'd been in her human form, Keisha would have laughed. She'd not taken him to this bestial level for far too long. They'd been so caught up in Lily's amazing growth, in the dynamics of everyday life within the diverse personalities of their pack, that this side of their lives had often been put aside, this need to run as the wolf, to hunt, to howl at the moon, to mate beneath a frozen sky.

Anton snarled again. His amber eyes shimmered and his bared teeth glistened beneath the curl of his lips. Dark whiskers quivered along his muzzle. Tiny drops of condensation sparkled on a couple of the stiff hairs. Keisha yipped, and then she bowed her head, turning and showing her throat as she deferred to his superior size and strength.

Suddenly he lunged at her, nipping unexpectedly at the thick fur protecting her throat and rolling her over into the snow. She scrambled to her feet, shocked and surprised by his attack. What the hell was he doing? Anton was never violent with her. Shaking her head, Keisha backed away.

His behavior left her confused, even afraid. She'd not expected such overt aggression, not from her mate, but he charged again, snarling and growling now, and she yipped in surprise. Frantically she struggled to break free of his hold.

He snarled his satisfaction. She was trapped—his teeth clamped down on the loose skin of her throat held her tightly in place.

She could pull free, but not without injury. Truly frightened now, she opened her thoughts, called out to him as he loosed his grip and lunged closer, biting hard against her neck, forcing her to her belly in the snow.

Anton? Anton, why?

There was no reply. She searched his thoughts and saw nothing beyond the feral needs of a wild wolf, a haze of lust so thick it almost blinded her. So be it. This, at least, she understood. This was what he wanted, what both of them obviously needed, or she never would have led him on this chase. She stopped her struggle, dipped her head until her muzzle scraped the frozen snow.

Her capitulation was complete. His attack ended as quickly as it had begun.

Now he licked the place where he'd bitten, and covered her with his body. She felt the heat of his belly against her back, the powerful grasp of his forelegs as he mounted her, the sharp bite of claws as he anchored himself close to her body. His breath was hot and sweet against her ears, but even though this was all familiar, all a perfect fit to her own desires, she whimpered, still a little afraid and unsure.

It felt so unusual, mating without their usual loving connection. His human mind stayed closed to her—his thoughts were tightly locked into the basic instincts of the mating wolf, a swirling maelstrom of scent and sensation, lust and need.

Keisha struggled to her feet, lifting Anton as she rose up, and planted all four legs to hold his greater weight. His hips thrust hard and fast. She grunted as the hot length of his wolven cock parted her vulva and slipped inside. She felt the pressure of his knot forcing entry between her folds, locking their straining bodies together.

Then, even she was lost. Lost in a haze of passion, of lust so basic, so entirely bestial that humanity was thrust aside with each powerful drive of his hips, each harsh breath in her ear. She lowered her head, braced her legs, and lost herself to the hunger, the driving need that had carried her on this fool's mission in the first place.

And once more, sense intruded. Who the hell did she think she was, that she could influence her mate? He was stronger than she, mentally more powerful, magically more adept. He had talents even their mating bond hadn't explained for her, abilities so far beyond human, beyond wolf, that he was something else altogether, a creature of the gods, one who had consorted with a goddess.

Isn't that same goddess now Adam's flesh-and-blood mate?

The knowledge grounded her. Liana had once been a goddess, their Goddess. Eve—now their Goddess—had once shared their bed. They were all linked, all a part of the same pack, the same species, sharing the same convoluted threads of destiny. Each of them with their separate abilities, their individual skills, yet all dependent, one upon the other, Goddess and Chanku alike.

Anton needed her even as she needed him. And with that thought rising to the surface, Keisha opened her mind. Drew her mate in, not merely to link during the sexual act, but to bond once again, to share on that unbelievable level that connected them, tied them more closely than the physical mating itself.

She opened her thoughts, felt him enter her mind, and just as easily, Keisha entered his.

In the past, she'd been impressed by the orderliness of Anton's mind, the memories so neatly catalogued, the knowledge so unbelievably precise. Now, though, she sensed a certain amount of chaos, as if he'd gone searching through a closet and left shirts and pants and shoes scattered about the floor.

She might have smiled to find this evidence of his humanity, but in many ways it frightened her to see Anton as less than he was. Somehow, she'd always held him so far above the common man—above herself. It made her uneasy to see that he had as many questions as answers, as many fears as she felt.

And his greatest fear was failure. He saw himself as the only one capable of saving Lisa and Tala and their babies, of finding Tia. He took on the responsibilities his packmates shared with him—took them and tried to shoulder them entirely on his own. He felt a sense of duty to protect them. He loved the pack, depended on their energy to power his own strength, but still he saw himself standing alone.

Idiot. She would have laughed if her climax weren't hovering right on a knife's edge of sensation. Completion first, then she fully intended to give him hell. When was he ever going to accept the fact that a matriarchal society was just that?

He might have powers she'd never understand, an intelligence she couldn't hope to equal, and a heart as big as the sun, but when it came right down to it, he was not the boss.

With that thought in mind and a smile in her heart, Keisha set herself free to sensation. She felt the slick heat of his shaft riding hard against her womb, tightened around the hard knot of flesh and blood stretching her vaginal muscles, and let herself fly. Her climax ripped through her even as Anton's caught him in its powerful grasp.

Together they tumbled into freefall, locked body and mind in a mating as powerful as that very first time so long ago. Only this mating didn't occur beneath redwood trees as old as life. She wasn't a frightened young woman with a damaged soul.

No, Keisha soared with the knowledge she was strong now, and self-assured. An alpha bitch making love with her mate, taking from him and giving in equal shares. A woman who knew her own strengths, who finally understood the healing power of love and the beauty of finding her one true mate.

The pack was threatened once again. Tia, Tala, and Lisa were missing and their mates were frantic, but the solution to their horrible situation didn't lie with one man alone. She gave that assurance to her mate as her body pulsed and tightened around him. Shared her strength and her confidence not only in Anton, but in the power of the pack.

They would bring their women home safely. They would protect their unborn young.

And the ones who threatened not only the members of the pack but the leader of the free world would never threaten anyone, ever again.

Chapter 3

Luc? Luc, where are you?

Tia? We're crossing the Golden Gate, honey. Are you okay? Luc shot a quick glance at Tinker. "Punch it, Tink. I've got Tia." Then he focused entirely on Tia's voice. At least she sounded stronger, proof they were getting closer to her.

Tinker nodded and passed the vehicle on his right. Traffic was heavy going north—typical for a Friday morning—but at least it was moving. Luc waited impatiently for Tia's answer. It took less than a heartbeat but felt like forever.

I'm okay. The bleeding's slowed, but it hurts.

Bleeding? You? What the hell happened?

Men. At least three. Black suits, short hair. Agency types. Used needles on all three of us. Drug worked really fast. Took Lisa and Tala. Shot me. Small caliber with a silencer.

Shit. Where? How badly? How are you?

Hurts like hell, but the hole's not too big. Bullet's still in me, I think. I'm really pissed, so guess I'll be all right. Luc? Are the babies okay? Have you talked to Beth and Nick?

Cami and Shay are fine. They're all at the house on Marina with AJ and Mik for added protection. Honey, where are you?

In a bathroom at the mall. We were near Nordstrom when they attacked. I can't raise Lisa or Tala. I don't know how long I've been out. I keep waiting for someone to come in to use the restroom, but there's been no one.

We're north of Sausalito. Less than ten minutes. Hang on, babe. We're almost there.

I love you, Luc. I'm so sorry.

You know I love you. But why are you sorry?

I didn't protect Tala and Lisa. We were laughing and having fun. We didn't pay attention. You're always warning me to be careful. I wasn't . . .

Don't even go there. This is not your fault. Hang on, honey. Again he turned to his packmate. "Tink? Can you go any faster?"

Tinker grunted. "Not unless you want the cops involved. I'm thinking that's the last thing we need."

Luc nodded. Tink was right, but it felt like they were crawling up the 101. He dialed Ulrich Mason's number in Colorado. Ulrich's mate answered. "Millie? I've made contact with Tia. Tinker and I are on our way to Corte Madera right now. We should be there in a couple of minutes. Let Ulrich know she's alive. She's been injured, but it doesn't sound too serious. We'll call as soon as we reach her."

Millie's soft prayer of relief was drowned out by Ulrich's rough curse. Luc filled him in and then ended the call. He didn't even want to think what Ulrich was going through right now. Tia was his only child and he loved her desperately. Luc tried to imagine what it would be like, knowing one of his daughters was in danger.

No. He couldn't go there. Not and continue to function.

Tinker pulled into the parking lot behind Nordstrom.

Luc was out of the vehicle before it even stopped rolling. *Tia? We're at the mall. Talk to me, sweetheart. Tink's with me. Talk to both of us so we can find you.*

Okay. I've got to be somewhere near Nordstrom. I

*don't think they could have taken us too far without at-
tracting attention. We were in the area right in front of the
store. It hadn't opened yet when we got here.*

*I hear you, sweetheart. Your voice is stronger. Keep
talking.* He glanced at Tinker as the two of them jogged
across the parking lot. The urge to shift, to race as a wolf
to his mate's side was overpowering. He fought it, concentrated on Tia. "What do you think? That way?"

Tink nodded. He headed through the open pavilion between the stores, moving quickly for all his size. Luc noticed that people automatically got out of the man's way.
There was something feral about Tink, a sense of danger
radiating from his powerful frame.

Suddenly Tinker changed course. He walked across the
open area toward one of the public restrooms. Tia's mental signature worked like a beacon, drawing both men.
Luc stopped in front of the door to the women's restroom.
"Shit. That's got to be her."

There was a hastily scribbled OUT OF ORDER sign taped
to the door. Luc tried the handle. It was locked. Tink didn't
say a word. He merely elbowed Luc out of the way, put his
big shoulder to the door, and shoved.

It took a moment before the lock gave. The door
popped open. Rubbing his shoulder, Tinker held the door
and let Luc through. Immediately, he spotted the pool of
blood beneath the stall at the far end. "Tia! Honey, are
you . . . ?"

"I'm here, Luc. I'm here." The door jiggled and swung
free.

Luc carefully pulled it open. Tia leaned against the wall,
holding herself up with both hands braced on the tissue
dispenser, but her usual bronzed complexion was an un-
healthy shade of pale. "Goddess, sweetheart. What the
fuck did those bastards do to you?" Luc swung her into
his arms and carefully carried her out of the bathroom.

Tinker waited by the open door. He slipped his jacket

off his shoulders and draped it over Tia, hiding her blood-soaked clothing. "Let's get her to the car. We really don't need security finding us here. Keep your head down. They've got cameras everywhere."

Luc nodded. He walked quickly. Tia'd wrapped her arms around his neck and had her lips buried against his throat. He felt her warmth through the layers of clothing, and in spite of her injury, he wanted to shout to the rooftops that he loved her, that she was alive. Then he glanced toward Tinker.

Worry radiated from the man. Lisa and Tala were still out there, somewhere. More vulnerable than Tia with both of them in the late stages of pregnancy. They were possibly hurt, probably terrified. Guilt washed through him. Guilt that he should be rejoicing while Tinker, AJ, and Mik had to be worried sick.

Tia raised her head and touched the side of his jaw with her fingertips. *They'll be okay,* she said. *You'll find them.*

He nodded, a short, sharp jerk of his head, and held his woman close. A few people gave them curious glances, but no one tried to stop them. By the time Luc reached the SUV, Tinker had the door to the back open and the engine running.

He turned in his seat and watched as Luc settled her in the backseat. Then, his voice low and rough, he sighed. "Sweetie, any idea what the bastards did with Tala and Lisa?"

She shook her head. "I don't know, Tink. They came up behind us and jabbed needles in all three of us. Whatever they used worked really fast. They got Tala and Lisa a few seconds before me, but they both went unconscious immediately. I felt the needle hit my throat and tried to get away. That's when the guy shot me, but I think I deflected his pistol. He was aiming higher, but got me in the hip. I guess I was expendable."

"Not in my book you're not." Tinker shot Luc a sharp glance that spoke volumes.

Luc met his glance with one of his own. "We'll find them, Tink. We'll get Lisa back."

"Damned straight we'll get her back. And those bastards will pay."

Tinker watched quietly while Luc helped Tia lie down in back. Then he quickly backed out of the parking space and headed south to the city.

Luc leaned against the door and pillowed Tia's head in his lap. "Logan told me once that if we ever got shot and there was still a bullet inside, to shift as soon as we were able. The bullet should fall out."

Tia's soft chuckle surprised him. "Sort of like Tala's IUD?"

Luc smiled, though he really wanted to howl with relief. "Yeah. Just like that." He fished his cell phone out of his pocket. "Here. If you're up to it, call your dad. Tell him you're okay. The poor man's frantic."

Tia cocked one very expressive eyebrow at him. "And you weren't?"

He shrugged and wondered if she could see the tears threatening to spill. "I knew you could take care of yourself," he teased. He struggled to swallow back the lump in his throat. "Shit, sweetheart. Don't ever scare me like this again."

"Trust me. This was not on my list of things to do. I think I'm bleeding again." She tried to sit up to get a better look.

Luc put a restraining hand on her shoulder. He wadded up Tink's jacket and held it against the slowly seeping wound over her left hipbone. "Tink, looks like you just donated a jacket to the cause."

Tinker didn't say a word. His focus was on the road ahead. Luc knew exactly how his friend felt. He gazed steadily at Tia, so pale and quiet lying across the seat with her head resting in his lap, and sent a word of thanks to

Eve for Tia's safe return. He hoped their new goddess listened. Hoped she watched over Lisa and Tala. Fear and frustration practically overwhelmed him.

He handed the cell phone to Tia. Then, as she made the connection with her dad, he sent another soft prayer to the Goddess, this one for the two missing women. Damn, he hoped that Eve was watching over her Chanku. There was no way they were going to get through this without a little divine intervention.

The sky was steel gray over Washington, DC, when Baylor, Jake, Manda, and Shannon reached the capital city. By the time they'd driven the few miles from Freeport to Portland, Maine, Stefan Aragat had a private jet waiting to fly them to Reagan International. The moment they'd landed, a limo driver had met them with an envelope containing the keys to Anton's apartment.

Everything had gone seamlessly—almost too easy after the harrowing morning they'd had. The connections and properties Stefan and Anton had never failed to amaze Bay—or anyone who knew the men. The comfortable flight had certainly made a trip that would have taken them long hours by car into a fairly simple jaunt, though after the events of the day he still felt slightly off balance.

He'd hardly had time to mourn the sudden death of his old friend and associate. Rolf and he had never been all that close, but they'd worked well together during Bay's years at the agency, and the man's last act had been one of kindness when he passed on the warning about Tala and Lisa.

A kindness that had obviously cost him his life, but it had also provided a link that just might help save Lisa and Tala's lives. His warning suggested who was behind the kidnapping and who wanted a hit on the president. His death was an even more powerful warning—that these people would stop at nothing.

It was all so far out, so bizarre, that Bay couldn't help but wonder if somehow the Goddess had intervened. Why else would Rolf have been in that tiny town in Maine at the same time as Bay and the rest? How could everything have come together so that Rolf would have been the one man to overhear such a horrible plot? That he and Bay would cross paths?

Bay sighed as he exited the elevator on the fourth floor. Would he ever understand the serendipitous ways of fate? Most likely not, so he might as well get over it and accept that Rolf was dead, the clock was ticking, and all they had going for them was Anton's *yet-to-be-disclosed* plan.

He stepped into the vestibule, unlocked the door into Anton's apartment, and held it open while Jake and the girls entered. He followed them inside, staring at the spacious rooms spread out before them.

He'd never been here before, though he'd been aware Anton kept a place in Washington for anyone in the pack, should they need a comfortable place to stay. Comfortable was the key word—the apartment was huge—it took up the entire fourth floor of the building, with a view of the thickly forested grounds of the National Zoo just across the road.

Jake stared through a window and then glanced over his shoulder at Bay. "It's certainly not Maine, but at least it's better than looking at high-rises."

Bay noted that many of the trees were bare of leaves in the winter chill, but evergreens still gave the entire area a wild and protected look. "It's a far cry from Montana, too." He checked out the kitchen and the big brick fireplace that took up one whole wall in the main room. There were lots of windows, but the apartment had obviously been closed up for months. The air was stale, and it was cold inside.

Manda found the thermostat and turned the heat up while Shannon cracked open a couple of windows to let in some fresh air. "How long's it been since anyone's stayed here?" She glanced around the spacious room with its fashionable furnishings and tasteful decorations. "It looks so sterile. Like no one's ever lived in it."

"No one has. At least not since Anton bought it." Jake poked his head into one of the bedrooms and tossed their travel bags on the bed. "He uses it for business trips on occasion. He and Keisha were here a couple of months ago, but I don't think anyone's actually lived here for any length of time." He stepped back into the main room and stared at Bay.

Baylor felt Jake's concern rolling off him in waves, but he knew it was worry about him more than for Tala and Lisa. He'd been blocking everyone since this morning. He couldn't handle sharing all the crap in his head, not this.

How could he possibly explain the convoluted relationship he had with his sisters? Sisters who'd grown up as strangers to him in a home as dysfunctional as a home could be. Helplessly, he glanced at Manda. She was his strength, the only one who truly understood the way his mind worked, the way his past had scarred him, yet even she had never quite figured out the confused feelings he had for Lisa and Tala.

He'd been the oldest, the one who felt responsible for their safety, yet he'd failed them in every way possible. His guilt remained, even now that they'd all found their home within the pack, their rightful place as Chanku shapeshifters. Guilt lay alongside that special bond as packmates—a bond even stronger than flesh and blood.

And now they were missing, kidnapped and held hostage somewhere on the opposite side of the country, while he was stuck here in the nation's capital without a clue what he should be doing to help them. As usual, he was keeping everything bottled up inside to the point it was making him physically ill.

Manda caught his eye and he felt her love. He opened to her voice and sighed at her soft reprimand.

At least she was smiling. *My love. When has hiding your fears ever done you any good? Share the burden. It's so much lighter that way.*

He took a deep breath, let it out, and nodded in agreement. Then he met Jake's steady gaze. It wasn't easy, but slowly he lowered his barriers and opened his thoughts. Shared his fear and his convoluted feelings for the two women who were part of his pathetic history, one that still left him feeling shamed.

Chuckling softly, Jake grinned at him. Bay felt the warm flush spreading over his face as he realized his lover had so quickly picked up all his twisted thoughts and memories the moment they'd been set free.

"There's no need for shame, bro. Not over things we couldn't control." Jake shook his head, smiling at something he didn't share with Baylor. "When we were kids, we all did our best to survive. You, Lisa, and Tala are no different from any of the rest of us, no better, no worse. For what it's worth, you must have made the right choices because you've all found love with really good people. More love than you ever got as kids."

He walked across the room and stopped right in front of Bay. His amber eyes crinkled and his lips quirked up in a devilish grin. "Hell, we all had screwed-up lives, but we're all still here, all with someone who loves us in spite of ourselves. Think about the night Tia had her babies, about the stories we all shared. Was yours so much different than anyone else's? So much worse? Did you fail more than anyone else?" He laughed out loud and planted a wet kiss on Bay's mouth.

Before Bay could return the kiss, Jake backed away. "Nope," he said. "You're no better, no worse than the rest of us. We are who we are because of what we are. Get over it."

Manda stepped up close behind Baylor, wrapped her arms around his waist, and rested her cheek against his back. "He's right, you know. Not at all subtle, but still right." She kissed the back of Bay's neck and sent shivers down his spine. "And you know how much I hate to agree with Jake. He'll never let me live it down."

Shannon laid her head on Bay's shoulder, but she was holding Jake's hand. "Isn't that the truth? Nothing worse than agreeing with Jake. He'll just throw it back in our faces at some point, but when he's right, it's hard to argue." She kissed Bay's cheek. "They'll be okay, Bay," she said. "Anton's on it, and he's got contacts in very high places. Luc's got Tia back, and she should be able to help find your sisters."

Baylor turned and planted a kiss on Shannon's lips. "Thank you. All of you. Sometimes I get so caught up in crap that really doesn't matter anymore, I forget about the good things in my life now. You three are the best of them."

His cell phone chimed. Manda fished it out of his back pocket and handed it to him. Bay took the call while Jake and Shannon grabbed Manda and left to explore the rest of the apartment.

A few minutes later, Bay caught up with them. They'd found what must have been designated as the master bedroom. It was elegant and absolutely huge, with windows looking out over the forested zoo grounds. Bay stood in the doorway and watched as Jake teased both Shannon and Manda about their abbreviated shopping trip and all the stores that were waiting for them here in the nation's capital.

He reminded Bay of Stefan Aragat in a lot of ways. Jake had learned long ago to use humor to diffuse just about any situation, but the man was much deeper than a lot of folks gave him credit for. Now Jake's eyes were twinkling and Shannon's smile lit up the room. Manda, always the quiet one, sat on the edge of the big bed, laughing at Jake's antics.

Bay felt as if he might burst with the love filling his heart. It was a moment in time to hold close—one to remember.

Love and hope, and the assurance that all would be well, his sisters would be rescued, and the perpetrators caught. At least now, after his phone conversation with Anton, they had a mission—something tangible they could do to help.

"That was Anton," he said, stepping into the room.

And as he expected, at the mention of the alpha's name, all eyes turned in Bay's direction. He felt a renewed sense of hope in each one of them as he sat down on the edge of the bed beside Manda. "I don't know how he does it, but the man's contacts are amazing. He's got a job for us. At seven tonight he wants us to have dinner at a restaurant over near the capitol. I've got the directions. Anton's already made reservations.

"There are some guys scheduled to have dinner there tonight who should be at a table close to ours. I remember a couple of them from my years with the agency, but I doubt they knew who I was. Even if they recognize me, there shouldn't be a problem. Anton wants us to listen to what they say, make note of any names we might hear. We're to take no action and stay as low-key as possible. If we hear anything, he wants us to get back to him. Then tonight, before nine, we have to be on the zoo grounds as wolves, thinking about sex and not worrying about anything that's happening in San Francisco. He says there's more than enough cover for us, but the hit against the president is supposed to go down at exactly eight fifty-five, Pacific time, tonight. Anton wants us to get enough of a run in our feral state to build up as much sexual energy as we can, and then find a protected area."

He chuckled and tightened his hold on Manda. "Orders are for us to mate. Anton wants us to hit our sexual peak and climax at precisely eleven fifty-five." He rolled his eyes and grinned at Manda. "Think you can orgasm on schedule?"

Grinning broadly, she kissed his nose. "I don't know, but it sounds like something I'd love to try."

Shannon shook her head, laughing. "And this is supposed to help Anton how? I mean, c'mon, Bay! We're clear across the continent. It's not like he can pull in our sexual energy from this far."

Baylor thought of what Anton had said, thought of how the pack leader had shot down the arguments Bay'd thrown back at him. "He says it will work. He said Eve's going to help transfer our energy. I don't know exactly what his plans are, but I figure we have to trust him, and Eve."

"Eve?" Manda's look of disbelief made perfect sense. More than Anton's phone call had. "But she's a goddess. She doesn't take directions from Anton. Does she?"

"I don't know. I only know what Anton asked us to do. He never asks for anything without a good reason." He shrugged and wished once more they were closer to San Francisco. "I can't think of a better reason than helping get Lisa and Tala back safely. I'm willing to do whatever he wants."

Jake stared at him a moment. Then he nodded. "He's asking because he knows he can do it. He's done it before—the first time our packs got together, those of us from San Francisco and Anton's group in Montana. It happened a few years ago, before any of you even knew you were Chanku. Ulrich was kidnapped in San Francisco and taken to an old farmhouse about an hour outside of Reston, Virginia, so it wasn't all that far from here. I stayed in San Francisco, so I wasn't with them, but a bunch of the pack—Luc, Tinker, Tia, Stefan, Xandi, and Keisha—combined their mental forces in Montana and were able to reach Ulrich in Virginia. Somehow Anton piggybacked on their energy stream across country and actually took over the consciousness of a crow so he could fly over the area where Ulrich was held, in preparation for their rescue attempt. Then they flew out here—in a plane," he added as the others gaped at him, "and rescued Ulrich."

"Glad you clarified that." Shannon punched Jake's shoulder, laughing. "I remember when Tia told me about it. It happened just before I was kidnapped." She grabbed Jake's hand. "Just before you rescued me."

Jake kissed Shannon, but then he smiled at Bay. "Right. And that's when we met Baylor."

"Yeah, when he showed up to kill you." Manda leaned against Bay. "Amazing how that all worked out."

"It is, actually." Bay thought of all the things that had come together over the course of those few days, but the man who'd been behind the kidnappings, the one he'd worked for, was dead now. Milton Bosworth had died of a stroke, though all of them suspected Ulrich Mason had somehow been behind the bastard's death.

Two of the men they were to watch tonight had worked under Bosworth.

"I wish I'd been in Montana when they first linked like that, but if I'd been there, I might not have been sent to rescue Shannon." Jake kissed her again. He wasn't laughing, and his voice had gone gravelly with emotion. "Babe, I know I drive you nuts, but I don't know where I'd be without you."

Shannon faked a light punch to his chin. "Driving me nuts is part of your charm."

Manda nodded. "So that's what she's calling it, now? Charm?"

Jake laughed and tugged Shannon's hand. "If you're gonna pick on me, I'm leaving. C'mon. We've got time for a shower before we leave for dinner. I think we need to work on building up that sexual energy Anton's so fond of using."

* * *

Bay leaned back on the bed and stretched. "Thank goodness he's gotten strong enough on his own that we don't need to be celibate for his plans to work. That used to make me nuts. Celibacy is not a good thing when you're wired for sex."

Manda stood up and grabbed his hand. "If you're so wired, you can join me in the shower. I need someone to wash my back."

She tugged. Bay stood and followed her to the room where she'd left their luggage. Thank goodness they'd packed for a long weekend in Freeport. He tried to put his worries for Lisa and Tala out of his mind. It was easier, now that they had a job to do. He wondered what they might learn from the men they were supposed to spy on tonight.

Wondered if their luck would hold when they sneaked onto the grounds of the National Zoo, and how Anton intended to use whatever energy they were able to share.

Then he thought about mating later tonight, the fact they'd be in the heart of Washington, DC, mating as wolves and hoping like hell they wouldn't get caught. Why the hell did he find that so arousing?

And why was he even worrying about it when his mate was stripping her clothes off that perfect body of hers and gazing impatiently over her shoulder because he was moving so damned slow?

Grinning like a complete idiot, Bay kicked off his shoes. He managed to lose the jeans and shirt in record time, but Manda was already in the shower, waiting impatiently for him. She stared at him through spiky lashes with her long blond hair plastered to her head and her lips full and inviting. As always, the sight of her was more than he could handle, and he was lost.

He'd loved her before she was beautiful. Loved her when he'd first found her alone in that small apartment in upstate New York where she'd been hiding out from the rest of the world.

She'd startled him at first, a misshapen creature beyond anything his nightmares could have envisioned. Half wolf, half woman, with twisted limbs and a perpetual snarl deforming her hideous face, but she'd still been Manda. Loving, beautiful on the inside, an intelligent young woman trapped in the body of an impossible monster.

He'd loved her more than he'd believed himself capable of loving anyone, ever. And when she'd finally shifted after so many years of pain, the woman inside had proved to have a body as perfect on the outside as the beautiful soul inside.

Like a moth escaping from its chrysalis, she'd spread her wings and flown.

Thank the Goddess, she'd chosen to fly into his arms. He'd loved her. He loved her now. No matter how she looked, he would always love her. Bay stepped under the spray and held Manda close, remembering what it was like when he'd found her, when he'd first realized she was meant to be his.

It wasn't sex he thought of. It wasn't the perfect fit of her body to his.

No, he was thinking of Tinker. Of Mik and AJ, and what they must be feeling right now, loving their women the way he loved Manda. He didn't want to imagine their pain. Selfishly, he tried to ignore it, but he couldn't help himself.

He held Manda in his arms, safe and whole and perfect, and felt guilty for the perfection of this moment with his bonded mate. He opened his mind and found her there with him, sharing her thoughts from his sisters' point of view. How frightened they must be right now, how worried about their unborn babies.

He pressed his forehead to hers. "We're too much alike, you know?" Then he slipped into mindtalking, needing the intimacy of their mental connection. *I love you, Manda. I love you more than I can possibly express, but I am so worried about Lisa and Tala. I feel sick for AJ and Mik and Tinker, for what they must be feeling.*

I know, Bay. I know. Just hold me. Share your thoughts with me and hold me. They're going to be okay. We have to believe that. Anton's always come through before.

He nodded, thankful for the streaming shower that hid tears he couldn't control. Thankful for the woman who held him every bit as tightly as he clung to her.

All those years he'd been estranged from his sisters came back to haunt him. They had to survive. As Anton had said, there were no other options.

But damn, he wished they weren't so far away.

Chapter 4

Keisha waited until they were both back in their room, both in human form and heading for the shower before she stopped Anton with the slightest of touches. Stroking his forearm with her fingertips, she waited for him to stop, to raise his head and look into her eyes. She met his with all the honesty in her heart. "This isn't about you," she said, smiling to take the sting from her words. "It's not all your responsibility. Not your burden to shoulder alone."

He blinked and frowned at her. "What do you mean? What's not about me?"

"Lisa, Tala. What happened to Tia. Thank the Goddess Luc's got her home, but I was in your head today. You see yourself as the only one capable of fixing this mess. My love, we are a pack. You might be the alpha male and a wizard beyond compare, but I'm your mate. Don't cut me out. Don't think you have to handle this on your own. We are a team. We, all of us who are Chanku, are a pack. We solve our problems together. We share our strengths even as we share our fears and our weaknesses."

He closed his eyes and lowered his head, but he couldn't hide his smile. "You know me much too well." Sighing, he gazed at her once again. "Old habits die hard. There was a time when I was so entirely alone . . ."

"Well, you're not now. Not anymore. Try to remember that."

He brushed her tangled hair back from her forehead. "Keep reminding me, would you?" Then he leaned close and kissed her. "We need to hurry. I want to shower and then go talk to Liana and Adam. Liana sensed the moment the girls were attacked. I'm not sure how that happened or how much she knows, but I want to see if she can help us with anything at all."

They were in Liana and Adam's small apartment atop the garage within twenty minutes. Keisha had pulled on a comfortable pantsuit for travel and tied her long, wet hair back in a tight ponytail. Her bags were already in the car.

She'd not been up here for a while, and the change in the once sterile little room was amazing. The big bed was still the largest piece of furniture, but Liana had added a comfortable couch and a work desk and two chairs. The walls were painted a soft, mossy green, and the bedspread had all the colors of the forest in an intricate pattern of geometric shapes.

Liana was on the couch surrounded by rolls of yarn in all shades of pink, busy crocheting what appeared to be a crib blanket. When Keisha raised an eyebrow, the woman who was once a goddess merely laughed.

"Not for me, Keisha! This one's for Lisa's little girl. I've already finished blankets for Tala's son and daughter."

"I wondered. That's beautiful."

Liana sighed. "I'm still learning. Don't look too closely. Xandi's been teaching me but I still make mistakes." She dug into her work bag and pulled out two neatly folded blankets. One pink, one blue.

Keisha took a moment to admire her work. "Definitely traditional, I see. Lisa and Tala are going to love them."

Liana sighed. "I hope so. I've been so worried. I keep listening for the sense of their life force and I can't find anything. It's scary. I've been praying to Eve since this morning when I first heard their cries."

Keisha sat next to her on the couch. "Does she answer you?"

Liana shook her head. "Not really, though I know she hears." She flashed Keisha an open, honest smile. "Eve's a much better goddess than I ever was. I don't expect answers, but I have complete faith she'll do what she can."

Keisha wrapped an arm around her shoulders and hugged her close. "We always had faith in you, Liana. You didn't fail us."

"I failed Eve."

Anton sat on the other side of her. "Not necessarily. I think Eve's happier in her life as Goddess than she ever was as a mortal. And aren't you better suited to this life, as a mortal woman?"

The door opened and Adam stepped into the apartment. That's when Keisha realized that the best thing about this small room was the amazing change in Adam.

He smiled at Anton and Keisha, walked across the room, and planted a big kiss on Liana's mouth. "She'd better be suited to this life, because I'm not turning her loose. What's up? Any word on Lisa and Tala?"

Anton stood. Keisha had a feeling he was too tense to sit still. "Not a word. That's why we came by, to see if there was anything Liana could recall from her vision this morning that might help us. We honestly expected some kind of word, some proof by now that they were alive." He paced, crossing the room, staring out the window toward the forest, then walking back to the couch, where he stopped and shoved his hands in his pockets.

Liana shook her head. "I wasn't even thinking of them when I suddenly felt Tia's cry of pain and saw Lisa and Tala through her eyes. Two large men in dark suits grabbed them from behind and jabbed needles into their necks. It looked like they went for the big artery." She touched her neck, just over her carotid, as if she'd felt the sharp prick of the needle herself.

"My vision was very brief—mere seconds. Lisa and Tala immediately went limp, but the men were holding them up, encircling their waists so that it looked natural, as if they were walking close together. I couldn't see Tia's attacker. He grabbed her from behind. She struggled. The needle went into her neck, but I think he missed the large artery because she didn't fall unconscious immediately, the way Lisa and Tala had. I heard the gun, felt the bullet pierce her body, here."

She touched herself, over the jut of her hipbone. "Then the drug must have taken effect. Her vision and my sense of her disappeared."

"Damn. Could the drug have killed them? I don't want to think that, but . . ." Anton ran his long fingers through his hair.

Liana gave a sharp, determined jerk of her head. "I don't think so. Tia came out of it, though she said it affected her ability to mindtalk and gave her a huge headache. I've been wondering if they're still unconscious, though. If the dose was too high, or went directly into the artery. If whatever they used reacts differently to Chanku metabolism. Do we know if the ones who kidnapped them are aware they're shapeshifters?"

Keisha shook her head. "Luc doesn't think so. Very few people know of our existence. They might know of Pack Dynamics and that we work with wolves, but that's about it."

"Then I'm guessing they're still unconscious." Anton glanced at Keisha. "And they can't shift to escape, so . . ."

Liana frowned at him. "Why not? Unless they're tightly collared, they should be able to shift."

Adam was the one who interrupted her. "Not if they're eight months pregnant." He glanced at Keisha. "Didn't you say you couldn't shift after about the middle of your term?"

Keisha shrugged, remembering how awkward and big she'd grown during her pregnancy. "After my second trimester, I was afraid to. I didn't think it was safe for the developing fetus."

"But why?" Liana glanced from Anton to Adam and then focused her attention on Keisha. "A Chanku bitch can shift up until she delivers. During delivery, if she's in wolf form, she will have no control over a shift to human when birth is imminent, but until that moment, she can shift and the baby will shift with her. The connection is total between mother and child. Whatever her form, that is her unborn child's form."

"I had no idea. I worried so much about shifting, even in the very early months." Keisha glanced at Anton. "This is knowledge that Lisa and Tala don't have. It's something that could make a difference."

"I agree." Anton ran his fingers over his forehead. "We need to get down there." Keisha wrapped her fingers around his outstretched hand. He pulled her to her feet.

"Liana," he said, wrapping his arm around Keisha's waist, "when this crisis has ended and the women are safe, you and I need to sit down for a long talk." He laughed, leaned over, and kissed the woman who'd once been their Goddess, and long ago, his lover. "I've been afraid to bother you with all my many questions, but it's time to put that consideration aside."

Keisha jabbed him in the ribs with her elbow. "Actually, I think the girls and I need to spend some time with Liana and see what kinds of misconceptions we might have. I'd hate to discover we're not really a matriarchal society." She tugged Anton toward the door. "Because if we're not, I don't want the men to know."

Liana and Adam walked them to the door. "No worry there, Keisha." Liana's laughter was contagious. "Female Chanku will always have the last word. It's not only bred into us, it's part of the males' physiology as well."

"I was afraid of that." Adam kissed Liana's cheek. "I knew there was a reason she wins every argument."

"It's because I'm smarter and faster than you, my love."

"There is that." Adam opened the door and stood back. "Be safe, both of you. Get the women back, and make those bastards pay. If there's anything at all we can do to help . . ."

Anton grasped Adam's wrist. "There is. I need your energy—whatever you've got, tonight at precisely five minutes to ten." At least he had the good sense to look embarrassed when he turned to Liana and added, "If you can time your orgasm for that precise moment, it would be most helpful."

Liana raised both eyebrows, but at least she was smiling. "Is that all?" She swung around and gazed at Adam, then she nodded, as if in agreement. She touched Anton's fingers, where they wrapped around her mate's arm. "Would the power of our mating bond give you added strength?"

"Liana!" Keisha grabbed her in a big hug, but her eyes were on Adam. "Tonight? You were planning to bond tonight?"

Adam answered. "We were, but then this happened. We thought maybe we should put it off until we knew how things were going, but if the energy from our mating bond would help, I imagine we can time things about right."

Anton looked absolutely shocked. "That's more than generous of both of you."

He stepped back, but Keisha could feel his roiling emotions. Not only that Adam and Liana would choose to share such a private moment, but that Adam's emotional pain had healed enough to allow him to accept a bond with another mate. That was more than any of them could hope for. He'd been horribly grief-stricken over Eve's death.

Adam seemed aware of their thoughts. He hugged Liana close. "I will always treasure my time with Eve, but she's found her place, the life she was meant for. It's not one I can, or would even want to share. Liana has shown me a future I never imagined for myself. We have a love, already, that's more powerful than I dreamed possible. I'm not letting her go."

Anton gazed from Adam to Liana, then back at Adam. "I can feel it, Adam. The link you and Liana have forged is already strong. Our best wishes to both of you. You have no idea how this makes me feel. There are no words to express how very happy I am for both of you."

Adam was the one who reached out and drew Anton into a tight hug. Adam, a man who rarely showed his emotions, who never exposed himself this openly. "Thank you," he said. "It's all good, Anton. Now go and do whatever it is you need to do to help bring Lisa and Tala home to their men. I don't know that any of them would survive a loss like that." He gazed down at Liana, tucked tightly against his side. "They wouldn't have Liana to save them." Then he sighed deeply and turned to Keisha. "They're going to need both of you. Stefan asked me to give you a lift to the airport, so I'll meet you in front of the house in fifteen minutes. Now go."

A gust of wind caught the door and almost pulled it from Adam's hand. He held it until Keisha and Anton were headed down the stairs. Then he shut it quietly behind them. Keisha squeezed Anton's fingers. "I didn't see this coming. Not this soon."

Anton smiled and wrapped his arm around her waist as they walked across the driveway. "Neither did I, but I can't imagine anything that could make me happier." He stared at the winter sun, riding low above the snow-covered mountains. "Anything, except for bringing Tala and Lisa home alive and well."

Keisha slipped out of his grasp and tugged his hand. "Let's go check on Lily and then find Logan and Jazzy. We need to get moving."

Anton nodded. Together they went to bid their little girl good-bye.

Keisha followed Anton down the hallway to the front door. It was a lot harder to walk away from Lily than she'd expected, and when that perfect little girl stood up in the crib, stretched her arms out, and cried, "Mama!" she'd almost changed her mind and told Anton to go without her.

Almost. Until Xandi grabbed her by the arm and turned her toward the door with a reminder that Tia needed her more than Lily did right now.

As they reached the front door, Anton turned and grabbed Keisha's hand. She flashed him a quick smile. Thank goodness he understood how difficult this was. Clutching his fingers tightly, she walked quickly through the house beside him. He pulled the front door open and they walked down the wide stairs to the big SUV waiting in the driveway.

Adam stood in front of the vehicle, talking to Igmutaka.

The spirit guide was dressed in worn blue jeans and a flannel shirt, with his hair neatly braided in two long braids on either side of his face. He had a pair of Mik's old hiking boots on his feet, something that caught Keisha's eye. She didn't think she'd ever seen him wearing shoes before. Generally he kept to his puma form when he was outdoors. As far as she knew, he only appeared as a man when he joined Adam and Liana in their bed, or showed up on occasion with the rest of the pack for breakfast.

He'd taken human form for the first time just a couple of weeks before. Keisha was still getting used to his androgynous beauty. Definitely of Native American blood, he would have been considered beautiful as either a man or a woman, but there was no doubt in anyone's mind that Igmutaka was all male.

She'd never forget the first morning he'd appeared in the kitchen for breakfast. He'd been badly injured in his cougar form, but Liana had found and healed him. He'd hung around to thank her, but he'd done it as a man.

He'd fit right into the pack, and Keisha knew it hadn't taken long for him to share Liana and Adam's bed. She wondered how the spirit guide felt about the two of them bonding as mates. Would he feel left out of the relationship? Or would he continue on as their sometimes lover, spending more time in his animal form than human?

No matter. That was something for Adam, Liana, and Igmutaka to work out on their own.

Anton stopped beside the car. Keisha thought he looked as if he was trying really hard not to laugh. "Going somewhere, Igmutaka?"

The spirit guide nodded. "With you." He held up a small travel bag.

Anton shot a quick glance at Keisha, then shook his head. "It's a four-passenger plane. All I could get on such short notice. Room for payload, but not extra passengers. Logan and Jazzy have the other seats."

Igmutaka bowed his head. "Then I will be payload. I will travel as the cat and shift when we arrive. I must go with you."

Anton nodded. "Okay. We can do that. What do you know? Have you been in contact with the little one?"

Igmutaka let out a deep breath. "In a way. Not true speech as you would understand. I sense danger. I know the baby is aware her mother is frightened. Tala is a woman of honor and she carries a child I must protect. You will take me to her."

"That's all we need to know. You're welcome to come with us, but you'll need to wear a collar and a leash so you don't scare the crap out of the pilot." He chuckled. "A loose cougar on board might be a bit much for the poor guy. If you're ready, let's go. You can shift in the car."

Anton gazed at the house, in the direction of Logan's clinic on the second floor. After a moment, he nodded. "I've asked Logan to bring an extra bag for your clothes and boots, along with a leash and collar. The collar's designed to break away should you need to shift in a hurry. It's for looks, not restraint, the same kind the Pack Dynamics wolves wear."

Igmutaka nodded and climbed into the seat at the very back. Anton sat beside him. Jazzy and Logan came out of the house a minute later and handed over the leash, collar, and extra travel bag. Logan rode shotgun, Jazzy sat in the middle seat beside Keisha. Once they were settled, Adam drove away from the house and headed for town.

It was a quiet ride to the airport in Kalispell. When they arrived, Anton climbed out of the back with a large puma on the end of a leash and extra bags thrown over his shoulder.

He shook Adam's hand. Whatever passed between the men remained private. There were some things Keisha realized she really didn't want to know.

Keisha tightened her seat belt and tried to relax in the small jet Anton had chartered for the flight. He'd never replaced the one that had crashed on the way to Tia and Luc's wedding, and Keisha wondered if she'd ever enjoy flying again.

Anton sat across from her. Jazzy and Logan were in the seats behind them, and Igmutaka sprawled in the narrow aisle between the seats. Considering the fact he'd never been in an airplane before, he seemed terribly calm, but then he'd been alive for thousands of years. Maybe he'd just learned to accept change easier than most.

Once the pilot got past the idea of an uncaged mountain lion traveling on his jet, he'd turned his attention to the business at hand. Keisha listened as he and his co-pilot went through their checklists, readying the plane for take-off.

She watched the men for a moment, remembering. Wishing she could get past the memories of the flight they'd taken along this same route just eighteen short months ago.

Instead, fear tightened her lungs and had her clenching the armrests as the small jet rolled down the runway. Most of the baggage she carried with her on this journey was all in her head, and it wasn't merely Lisa and Tala that had her worried. Tension had her strung tight as a bow, but she forced herself to lean back and close her eyes as they gained altitude.

To help herself relax, she filled her head with details. The flight to San Francisco International would last about two hours with at least half an hour travel time from the airport to Luc's place in the Marina district. Then she remembered that with the difference between Mountain and Pacific time, they'd gain an hour, which should put them on Luc's doorstep by three thirty. Lisa and Tala had been taken captive just before nine in the morning, and the hit was supposed to take place just before nine tonight, which meant that . . .

Anton turned to Keisha and raised one very expressive eyebrow. "Any reason you're sitting there doing all the math and time zones in your head?"

Keisha laughed, covering her eyes with her hand and then peeking between her fingers. "You know me too well. I'm trying not to think of what happened when we flew to Tia's wedding. At least I'm not pregnant this time."

Anton reached across the aisle and clasped her hand. "You're not in danger, either. I know the pilot and co-pilot personally. They've flown for Stefan and me on numerous occasions. We will not end up in a swamp this trip. I promise."

"That's certainly a comforting thought."

Jazzy's dry comment struck Keisha as absolutely hilarious. "You don't know the half of it," she said. "That's where I delivered Lily—lying in a swamp somewhere in North Dakota with the aromatic scent of jet fuel perfuming the air."

Frowning, Logan looked up from the medical journal he'd been reading. "Well, let's just hope we don't end up delivering Tala or Lisa's babies on this trip. They're pretty early yet, and the trauma they've got to be experiencing can't be good. I'm worried about them. Especially Tala, with the problems she had earlier."

Anton shot a quick glance at Keisha. "We all are, Logan. That's why Igmutaka's along. He's got a mental link to Mik's daughter. He told me he can sense her fear, so we know they're still alive, and that means we'll get them back. The problem is, Luc hasn't had any word at all from either of the women yet, so we don't know any details of their condition."

Keisha squeezed Anton's hand. *I'm worried. Shouldn't the kidnappers have let Lisa and Tala make contact by now, something to prove they're alive? Tia told Luc the drug interfered with her mindtalking, so that could explain why the girls haven't contacted their men directly, but you'd think they'd have been allowed a call by now. That's the only way those men can possibly think Pack Dynamics would carry out their plan.*

You'd think so, Anton said. *I'm worried, too, but we have to trust Igmutaka. If he says they're alive, I prefer to believe he knows what he's talking about.*

"Why the hell haven't we heard anything?" Mik paced the small area in Luc's office. Tinker and AJ sat on the couch near the window. Tinker stared straight ahead, but AJ was all hunched over, elbows resting on his knees, his head in his hands. Mik wanted to offer him comfort, wanted to go to him and tell him everything would be okay, but he'd run out of lies. How could he say something like that when he didn't believe it himself?

Luc had gone back to the bedroom to check on Tia. She'd shifted and managed to get rid of the bullet, but the shift had opened up the wound again. Damn but she was a tough little thing. Every bit as tough as Tala. Even though she'd lost a lot of blood, Tia had refused medical care. Her argument that Logan was just an hour away now wasn't easing anyone's mind, even though it made the most sense. She absolutely refused to go to a hospital where doctors were required to report a gunshot wound.

Involving the police could screw up any chance they had of saving Lisa and Tala. But why the fuck hadn't they heard from the women? Unless they'd been taken entirely out of mindtalking range, they should have made contact by now. Tia'd said the drug screwed up her head, but she'd reached Luc hours ago. Where the hell were Lisa and Tala?

He was certain Tala would have called out to them by now if she could. Mik couldn't allow himself to think of the alternative. Couldn't even touch on that. If anything happened to Tala, if anyone harmed the babies she carried . . . No. He couldn't do it. No way in hell could he let his thoughts go there.

Not if he wanted to be in any shape to help her.

Mik stared at the cell phone Luc had left sitting on his desk and willed the damned thing to ring.

It sat there like a piece of worthless shit. He wanted to pick it up and throw it through the window. Throw it so hard it splashed down in the middle of San Francisco Bay. He pictured himself reaching for it, grasping the useless piece of crap in his fist, hauling back for a long throw . . .

And then it rang.

Millie West stepped out on the deck and paused quietly for a moment, watching her mate. Ulrich stood at the back railing, elbows resting on the rough-hewn wood, his gaze fastened on the snow-covered forest. After a moment, Millie crossed the short distance and stood beside him. As much as she wanted to wrap her arms around him, she held back. Instead, she wrapped them around her own waist. Held tightly to herself and prayed for calm, for an end to this horror.

At least they'd gotten word Tia was all right. "She'll be okay, Ric. Luc said the wound's not too serious, that they got the bullet when she shifted."

Ulrich didn't move. He did nothing to acknowledge what Millie'd said. Impatiently patient, she waited. Finally, his head dipped and his voice broke when he answered her.

"Yeah, but Luc said she started bleeding again. That he's worried the bullet might have nicked an artery."

"But they have the bleeding under control. Logan will be there in less than an hour. He's good, Ric. He'll make sure she's okay. They can't risk involving the police until Lisa and Tala are safe. Not at this point."

Ulrich still didn't look her way, but he nodded his head. "I know. I just wish we were closer. I wish I could be there and see for my own eyes that she's all right." Finally he turned and leaned his butt against the railing. Gave Millie that crooked little grin she'd grown to love. "I know what you're thinking, Millie m'love. You're thinking I'm an overprotective old man."

Shaking her head, she laughed softly. "Never. I don't think you can ever worry too much about your children. I've had Manda and Adam on my mind all day, ever since Luc called, thinking how I would feel if it were one of them in this position. I know what it was like when Adam lost his mate and he was hurting so terribly, and there was nothing I could do to help him. And when Manda told me what it was like all those years she was held prisoner, treated so horribly by a man she'd thought was rescuing her. My heart bled for my children, even though they're grown now. I bled because I wasn't there for them when they needed me. I'm still their mother, just as you're still Tia's father."

She laughed softly. "And you, my love, are most certainly not old. Besides, Luc might be her mate, but he's there with her now and can see she's safe. Plus, it's different for him. He sees her as an adult, as his mate. Unlike you, he didn't change her diapers. He doesn't see her as a helpless baby."

Laughing, Ulrich rested his arms on her shoulders. "He almost did. He came into our family when she was just six years old. I often wonder if he remembers what she was like at that age, now that she's the grown woman he loves."

Millie kissed his chin and then brushed her lips over his. "Do you think he had any idea then that they'd end up together?"

"Hard to say what he thought. Poor guy was so traumatized by what he'd done. I question if he's ever really forgiven himself for killing Tia's mother. Camille forgave him, and so did Tia, but I've always wondered if Luc has forgiven himself."

"He's a good man, Ric, but even good men can have their own demons. He's learned to deal with it, and that's what counts. I worry more about Tia, if anything happens to Tala and Lisa. She was there with them when they were taken. She's okay. Hurting and injured, but she's safe and we know she'll heal. I don't want to think what it could do to her, to have two women she loves so dearly end up injured or worse. I hope Anton's plan works, as much as I hope Eve's paying attention to the mess our girls are in."

"Hey, guys! Any word?"

"Sheesh, Matt." Millie slapped her hand over her chest. "You scared me half to death."

"Sorry about that, Millie. I thought you heard us coming."

Matt Rodgers led his bonded mates, Deacon March and Daciana Lupei, through the powdery snow around the side of the cabin. "We've got the pens cleaned and everything's under control with the wolves. They've all been fed. We had the volunteers close up early today so they could get home before dark. It's going to be really cold and icy." He glanced at his mates. "We didn't want anyone driving home late. I hope that's okay with you."

Millie nodded her approval. "Thanks, Matt. You guys made a good decision. I'm sorry I haven't been around, but things have just been so unsettled."

"Plus, there's no word yet," Ulrich said, answering his question. "Nothing beyond the fact that Tia's with Luc and they got the bullet out of her hip. Anton, Keisha, Logan, and Jazzy should be there shortly."

"And Igmutaka," Millie added.

"The spirit guide?" Ulrich folded his arms across his chest. "Why's he going?"

"Stefan called just a few minutes ago. That's what I came out here to tell you. He said Igmutaka has a link with Mik's daughter. He can sense the baby's fear and the connection with Tala, proof she's still alive. Igmutaka showed up in human form at the house and informed Anton he was going to San Francisco with them. With a powerful link like that, there was no way Anton was going to turn him down."

"Wow." Daci climbed the steps and took a seat on the porch swing. "He must be Mik's baby's spirit guide, just like he was Mik's grandfather's. That's pretty cool." She cocked an eyebrow at Ulrich. "We still on for tonight? All five of us together?"

Ulrich shrugged and focused on Millie. "It's entirely up to Millie. Anton wants all the sexual energy we can create. Do you think there'll be more if we're together, or would you be better off with just a couple of us. Or the two of us?"

Millie let her gaze slide over Ric's rugged features. She'd heard all about Anton's plan, and she'd taken his directions to heart—to let the ones in San Francisco worry about saving the girls while the various packmates around the country worried about powering up the operation.

Thank goodness sexual energy was something all of them appeared to posses in excess. She winked as she moved beyond Ric to give Matt a very careful perusal. He boldly returned her smile, proof he was definitely gaining more confidence. Millie took a lot of the credit for Matt's amazing transformation.

She shifted her gaze from Matt to Deacon. At six and a half feet tall with a wide, bony frame, Deacon, aka Christopher March, still needed to fill out all his angles and edges. He'd definitely gained some weight and muscle since settling here in Colorado, but Millie suspected it would be a few more years before he finally reached his prime.

Still, he was one big, sexy young man, and the look he gave Millie told her he was just as interested in what five of them could figure out to do together as Matt was.

Of course, Matt and Millie had been lovers for months, now, an arrangement Ulrich had set up when Matt was still so shy he could barely look at Millie without blushing. That certainly wasn't a problem any longer, but Millie had never been with Deacon, and she'd definitely not made love with Daci. She'd been much too inhibited for that.

Now, though, Daci boldly challenged her with an open smile and the subtle suggestion of what they might be able to discover. She hadn't been with women all that much, either, as far as Millie knew. One thing they all seemed to agree on was the excitement of discovery.

Sometimes the learning process generated more heat than anyone expected. This might be the night to see where their imaginations—and their libidos—took them.

Knowing they were working toward a common goal added an extra level of arousal to the idea of group sex.

Millie glanced over her shoulder and caught Ric grinning at her like a damned fool. "So, it appears you've been hitchhiking along on my thoughts. Like what you see?"

He laughed out loud, the first real laughter she'd heard from him all day. "I love what I see. Might I suggest we go for a run later, come back and shower, and meet over at Daci, Matt, and Deacon's cabin for a glass of wine . . . or two. They might have less space overall, but they've definitely got a bigger bed."

Daci stood up and grabbed both her guys' hands. "Works for me, but guess that means we need to go change the sheets and clean house a bit." She leaned close, stood on her toes, and planted a big kiss on Ulrich. "Your suggestion, so you get to bring the wine."

"I promise to bring one you like, Ms. Lupei. We'll meet all of you out here at six. That should give us time to shift, run, hunt, eat, and shower." He chuckled, and Millie couldn't wait to get him alone and see what he had in mind. The man never seemed to run out of ideas.

"Anton's got us on a pretty tight schedule," he said, and there was no denying the challenge in his voice. "So, after we run, we need time to build up enough good, healthy lust to produce one large, simultaneous orgasm, minds open and broadcasting, at nine fifty-five Mountain time tonight. Timing is everything. Well, timing and skill. You kids up to it?"

Instead of answering outright, Matt sauntered across the deck. He was about an inch shorter than Ulrich, but he carried himself tall and straight and his broad shoulders and lean, muscular build made him appear larger than he actually was. He stopped in front of Ric, but he flashed a big wink at Millie. Then he looped an arm around Ulrich's shoulders and pulled him close for a kiss.

Ric's surprise at Matt's uncharacteristically bold move quickly gave way to arousal. Millie felt his response all the way to her toes, and when Matt cupped her mate's genitals through the soft denim jeans he was wearing, she almost climaxed on the spot. Ric's arms went around Matt's waist and he thrust his hips forward, pressing against the younger man's big hand and long fingers gripping his crotch.

Suddenly Matt broke the kiss and stepped away from Ric. Both men were breathing hard, though Matt tried to disguise his own arousal. "See you at six," he said, as if they'd just made a date to play golf. Then without another word, he and his mates turned and clattered down the steps. The three of them disappeared around the corner of the cabin.

Ric turned to Millie with a stunned smile on his face. "Shit," he said. "How could we ever think that kid was a beta?"

Millie reached up on her toes and kissed him softly on lips still damp from Matt's mouth. "He was. I think he outgrew it."

"Shit again." Laughing, Ric slowly shook his head. "You're not kidding." He gazed toward the kids' cabin, barely visible through the trees. "I think Anton might get more than he expected."

Millie grabbed Ric's hand to drag him inside. "Well, I don't know about Anton, but I can almost guarantee we're going to get more than we expected." She flashed him a wink. "I'm definitely looking forward to tonight."

Chapter 5

It felt as if someone had a jackhammer working right between her eyes. The pain, the noise, the total disorientation were terrifying. Tala didn't move. She couldn't. Her arms and legs felt weighted down with lead, her eyes must have been glued shut, and nothing worked right.

Nothing except her kidneys, obviously. Damn but she had to pee. How long had she been like this? Questions. So damned many questions, and her brain too muggy to answer any of them. She tried to figure out where she was, why she couldn't move, what day, week, year, place she could possibly be.

Memories rushed into her mind—memories she immediately recognized as old history, no matter how clear they were. She wasn't still a whore working a cheap town in New Mexico. She didn't live in fear of her pimp.

No. She was not Mary Ellen Quinn. She was Tala, mated to Mik, to AJ. Carrying their babies.

Dear Goddess. The babies! She searched for the bright mental signatures she already recognized as her unborn son and daughter. AJ's little boy. Mik's daughter, and damn but she felt sorry for that little girl, because Mik probably wouldn't let her date until she was at least forty.

There! Sleepy but okay. She breathed softly, unwilling

to make any moves, unsure why, but knowing somehow that she needed to continue the façade of unconsciousness. She concentrated on the babies. Felt their thoughts, both of them curious and wondering what had happened, why they felt so strange.

Well, hell. She wondered the same thing. She tried to reach out for AJ and Mik, but a sharp, knife-edged pain in her head put a quick stop to that. Maybe if she tried something close and used the family link she had with her sister? Maybe Lisa was nearby. Maybe she could hear and explain.

First Tala reassured her babies. Everything would be fine, she told them. As soon as she figured out what was going on.

She sensed them, stronger now. Her son was nervous, but her daughter seemed amazingly calm.

Why? What makes you so brave, little one?

Igmutaka.

What the . . . ? *The spirit guide? You know him?* Tala bit back a smile. She'd known that old spirit guide a lot better than she'd wanted when he'd taken over her body and tried to keep her as his own, but that wasn't anything she had to share with her baby girl. Not yet, anyway.

Of course I know him. He is my guide. He watches over me. He's coming to protect us all.

Interesting. Definitely interesting, but in a good way, or bad? She was going to have to keep tabs on this, obviously, but she reassured her babies and promised them all would be well.

Now, where the hell was Lisa?

She sent out a light, questing thought.

Tala? Oh Goddess, Tala. I thought you were dead.

I'm okay. I think. Where are we?

I'm not sure. A hotel somewhere, in the city, I think. I tried reaching Tinker but the pain was excruciating. We must have been drugged. Are you tied? I think I have those plastic restraints on my ankles and wrists. It's hard to know for sure. I'm afraid to open my eyes or move. I don't want anyone to know I'm conscious.

I know. I couldn't reach Mik or AJ, either. Is anyone guarding us?

At least one man. I heard him cough a little while ago. I thought I heard voices, but it's just the television in another room.

Lisa, I'm going to have to let someone know I'm awake pretty soon. I've got two sets of feet playing soccer with my bladder. I've really got to pee.

Okay. I have no idea how long we've been here, but I think it's been a few hours at least.

She almost laughed at how ridiculous it felt, worrying about bodily functions at a time like this, but, *If you can hold it, let me go first. I'll open my thoughts so you can see what I see, but I'd really hate to wet the bed.*

When Lisa agreed, Tala blinked slowly, as if coming out of a deep sleep. *Are you with me?*

I am. Just forget I'm even here.

Tala glanced slowly around the room. She and Lisa were lying beside each other on a king-size bed. Lisa still looked unconscious. Tala gazed at her sister a moment, checking for injuries, but she seemed to be okay, and she'd guessed right. Both of them had their wrists and ankles restrained with those plastic ties the police used in place of regular handcuffs.

She slowly checked out their surroundings. It looked like a really nice hotel. The room was large, furnishings upscale. She thought she heard the sound of trolleys passing nearby, which meant they were back in San Francisco.

It was obviously a suite, since the sound of the television came from another room. She picked up the soft voices of men talking. Cuing Lisa to listen with her, Tala strained to hear what they were saying.

"I don't know. Shit. I thought they'd come around within

an hour. It's after two. The boss said that stuff would wear off really fast."

"Yeah, but they're both pregnant. Maybe it affects them differently. The one's really tiny. I'm worried it was too big a dose."

"Idiot. It was obviously too big a dose, or they'd both be awake by now. Fuck. If they can't contact their husbands, how the hell do we get PD to do the job?"

"You hear back from the boss? He got any kind of antidote we can give them?"

"I asked. There's nothing. You know what he's going to tell us."

"Kill 'em and dump the bodies."

"I'm not killing any pregnant ladies."

"I'll do it. Hey. Don't look so surprised. It's us or them."

Lisa? Looks like it's time to wake up and hope we can contact the guys later. I wonder where Tia is?

I don't know, but I think you're right. Besides, now since you brought up the subject, I have to pee really bad, too.

"Hey? Anyone here?"

Tala slurred her words and kept her expression as blank and doped up as she could. The rush of footsteps startled her. She wasn't sure what she expected, but three well-dressed young men hadn't even been on the radar.

They wore dark suits and they looked like they all went to the same high-end hairdresser. It was freaky, yet in a weird way, she was reminded of pictures she'd seen of her brother when Baylor'd worked for some government agency. He'd had the same slick, uptight look.

"What's going on?" She held up her manacled hands. "Where are we? What's wrong with Lisa? Where's Tia, our friend? What have you done with her?"

"That one's just taking longer to come out of the drug than you. It's about time. The third one's dead. No more questions." The dark-haired kid who spoke glanced over his shoulder. "Grab the phone, would you? She needs to make a call."

"She needs to pee, first." Tala refused to accept what he'd said. Tia wasn't dead. She'd just figure he was lying until she knew better, so she ignored him and tried to swing her legs over the edge of the bed.

One of the men stopped her. "You're not going anywhere until you make a call."

"Oh, yes, I am, unless you want me to pee on the bed. You don't drug a pregnant lady carrying twins and tell her she can't use the bathroom." She held her hands up and glared at the kid.

He glanced nervously at his companions.

The oldest in the group cursed. "Okay. Let her use the bathroom, but tie her again when she's out."

Tala kept her mouth shut while the youngest-looking one used a very sharp knife to cut the plastic restraints around her ankles. He left her hands tied. She shook her bound wrists under the guy's nose.

He glared at her. "That's all. You're going to have to figure it out on your own." He leaned close and leered at her. "Unless you need my help."

"Fuck you." For just a moment, she imagined shifting and tearing his throat open, but she was almost eight months pregnant, and shifting was out of the question. She stood up with all the dignity she could muster. Her mouth felt full of cotton and she hoped she could make it across the room to the bathroom without wetting her pants.

She did. Barely, though getting her slacks down with her hands restrained wasn't easy. After she relieved herself, she managed to wash her hands and face in spite of the restraints, but the cold water helped clear her head. There were glasses still wrapped in plastic, with the name of the hotel clearly printed in a band around each glass. She fumbled around with one long enough to open the wrapper and fill it out of the tap. Two glasses of cold water helped her even more. She felt Lisa in her mind and wished she could share the cool drink with her sister, but that was beyond her abilities.

"Hurry up in there."

She glared at the closed door. "I'm hurrying. Give me a minute." There was no window, so escape was out, even if they could shift. For now it appeared they'd have to play along with these bozos. She wished she knew what they wanted, what they knew.

So far, there'd been no sign at all they were aware she and Lisa were Chanku shapeshifters, that they had telepathic abilities. No hint of why they'd been kidnapped. She had to find out about Tia, but that would have to wait because they'd probably just keep lying.

She opened the door and walked back across the room. Lisa was blinking her eyes, pretending to come awake. Tala crawled up on the bed beside her. "Lisa? Honey, are you okay?"

"Head hurts. Really bad." She frowned. "Where are we?" She shot a quick, confused glance at Tala. "Who are those guys?"

"I don't know." Tala tucked her legs under her and hoped no one would think to restrain her ankles again. She looked at the men in the room and tried to make eye contact. No one met her gaze. "Who are you?" she demanded. "What do you want with us?"

No one answered. One of the guys shoved a cell phone into her hand. "I want you to call Pack Dynamics. Tell them you're alive, that your pregnant friend is alive. That's all. Say anything else, and neither of you will stay alive for long."

Tala glanced at Lisa and then at the man. She nodded and took the phone. Dialed the number for Luc Stone's cell phone, the one they used for their business calls, and hoped like hell he had the damned thing turned on.

Mik answered on the first ring.

"Mik? Sweetheart! It's Tala. I'm okay. So is Lisa, but—"

The older guy ripped the phone out of her hand. "You heard the bitch. She's alive. You want to keep her that way, want to keep the other one alive, you know what to do. You'll find a packet on the front seat of the black SUV parked in the driveway of your headquarters on Marina. Everything you need is inside the envelope. Screw up and you'll never see either one of these women again." He paused a moment and then stared at Tala. His eyes were such a pale blue they didn't look real when he snarled, "You might find the babies, but they'll be in pieces."

He ended the call and turned a truly ugly smile on Lisa and Tala. "Okay. Now it's up to them. The ball's in their court."

Quietly, as if she was afraid to speak aloud, Lisa asked for permission to use the restroom. The young kid clipped the restraints around her ankles and she hurried across the room. As soon as she returned, the older man gestured to his companion and they left the room. The one who stayed, the youngest one, glanced nervously at Tala and then at Lisa. Then he sat in a chair in the corner of the room and pulled out a pocket video game.

Lisa turned to Tala. Her amber eyes were wide and frightened, but Tala knew it wasn't her own safety she worried about. No, it was the little girl she carried. Tinker's daughter. The ugly threat the bastard had made was much too graphic for either of them.

She and Lisa still had no idea what Pack Dynamics had been asked to do, but whatever it was, it obviously went against everything any of them would consider.

Even with their women held hostage.

Honor and integrity could not be bought. It could not be compromised, ever. No matter the risk. No matter the threat.

Dear Goddess, she hoped Tia was okay.

Tala returned Lisa's stare with a look of grim determination. *We know our men. They will do everything in their power to protect us. By now, they'll have everyone, every single Chanku across the country, involved in our rescue, but we have to be ready to save ourselves and our babies.*

I agree. Lisa glanced at the one guard who'd been left to watch them. He sat in the corner, engrossed in his video game. Obviously he didn't see two pregnant women as much of a threat. *I have an idea that might help us contact the guys. We have to bust through whatever that drug is still doing to us. I think if we combine our energy when we reach out, it might help buffer the pain.*

Tala nodded and scooted closer to Lisa. She opened her thoughts to her sister, connecting at an even deeper level with their familial bond. Lisa's energy poured into her mind, powered by anger and her sense of resolve.

Tala pushed outward, reaching for Mik, for AJ. She felt Lisa drawing on her, reaching for Tinker. There was some pain, but it was manageable now, sharing it this way. Buffering the sensation, one to the other.

The link between them grew, and they reached out, together. Searching for the familiar mental signatures of their bonded mates. Tinker. AJ. Mik.

Tala? Is that you?

Mik's voice. His familiar beloved voice, so frightened, so filled with emotion she wanted to weep. She glanced at Lisa and saw the soft smile on her face, knew she'd reached Tinker.

AJ's words tumbled into her mind. *Where are you? Are you okay? Dear Goddess, we've been worried sick.*

Tia? They said she was dead? Is she . . . ?

She's fine. We've got her here. She was shot and drugged, but she's okay. Don't let them know. Any idea where you are?

The Four Seasons. I saw it on the wrapping on the water glass in the bathroom.

Okay. If you can figure out what room, let me know.

I will. No idea what the room number is, though it's a big suite. I think those are only on the upper floors. What do they want with us? Why'd they kidnap us? They don't seem to know we're Chanku, so . . .

Mik broke in. *It's bad. They want us to assassinate the president. You're our incentive to do the job right.*

It took Tala a moment to assimilate what her mate had just said. Assassinate the president? Who were they kidding? *Never.*

Don't worry. Mik sounded almost lighthearted, considering. It must be relief at finally making contact. *We're not even thinking of it, sweetheart. Everything will be fine, especially now that we have you and Lisa in our minds. It's all going to be okay. Anton's almost here. He's got a plan.*

Tala bit back a bubble of laughter and kept her features totally blank. It wasn't easy. *Oh, shit. Anton's always got a plan, hasn't he? I feel better already.*

AJ interrupted. *You should. And he's coming with Igmutaka. It appears the spirit guide is in contact with our daughter. He's her spirit guide as well.*

Tala leaned back against the headboard. Despite her restraints, she managed to turn and grab Lisa's hands in both of hers. Lisa squeezed her fingers, but she was obviously still deep in conversation with Tinker.

Our daughter informed me of that fact a little while ago. She's frightened, Mik. Get us out of here, please. I'm okay, but I hate that our babies are afraid. These are not very nice men.

That's an understatement, Mik said. *Hang tight. Keep the link open. As soon as Anton gets here, we'll fill you both in on what's going to happen.*

Okay. We'll be fine. I mean, what can possibly go wrong? Anton's got a plan.

* * *

Mik, AJ, Tinker, and Luc sat around the big oak table in the dining room and looked over the packet of materials that had been left in the SUV out in front. Nick had discovered the package shortly before the phone call, when he'd left to pick up the Montana pack at the airport.

The silence in the room was unnerving as they studied the maps and diagrams describing the president's route for the evening. Paperwork and badges giving them status as official security with top-level clearances, a complete schematic of the huge auditorium and every step the president would make, as well as a tightly defined timetable that was all spelled out were also included in the package.

All culminating in the death of the president.

Mik raised his head and looked at the others. "Anyone else notice what's missing here?"

AJ chuckled. "You mean the lack of an escape plan for after the killing? Maybe they just forgot."

"Look." Tinker slapped his big hands down on the table. "We have contact. We can find our women, get to them before anyone hurts them. Kill the bastards that kidnapped them. We can save them now, before we go through with this fucking charade."

Luc glanced up at Tinker. "You're right, Tink. We could, but we'd only be getting the worker bees. We wouldn't be getting the ones at the top. The ones who planned this. Lisa and Tala understand. Neither one of them wants out yet. The minute they feel as if they're in danger, we pull them out, but not yet. Not if we want to get these bastards."

Tinker sat quietly, but he was trembling with rage and frustration as he stared at the scattered papers spread across the dining room table. "She's so fucking brave," he said. His voice was hardly above a whisper. "Lisa keeps checking in with me, telling me not to worry. She's calm, she's got it all together." He raised his head and looked directly at Mik. "Our women are trusting us to save them. If anything goes wrong, if Lisa or our baby gets hurt, I . . ." He shook his head and pushed his chair away from the table. Walked across the room and stared out the front window.

The clear skies of the morning had given away to low, dark, ominous-looking clouds. Rain was forecast for later tonight, but now, with the barometer dropping as the storm moved on shore, the pressure change was affecting all of them, making it harder to concentrate. Increasing the tension in what was already a tense situation.

Mik stood up and followed Tinker, stopped just behind him and hung his arm over Tink's broad shoulders. "Lisa and Tala come from tough stock. They're survivors. I have to believe they'll be all right, that our babies will be all right. Tink, you can't let yourself go anywhere else. Not if you're going to be there for your mate, for your daughter."

Tinker shook his head. "I'm just so fucking tired of this, Mik. So tired. I want to live with my woman, raise our babies, have a normal life without constantly worrying about some bastard trying to hurt us. Lisa deserves better. We all do."

"I agree." Mik leaned against the wall beside the window and folded his arms across his chest. "Which is why we have to do more than just rescue them. We have to find out who's behind this and take them down. I don't care who it is, how high up they might be, even if it's military or the government, but whoever they are, we need them gone. We go after the girls now . . . yeah, we can get them out, no problem. You know that, I know that, so do they. But what then? The ones who plan this start planning something else. They might do more research, find out stuff we don't want anyone to know. They could make things even more dangerous for our children. I don't want that. I don't think you do, either, and you know Lisa doesn't."

Tinker turned away from the window and gave Mik a

lopsided grin. "You're preaching to the choir, Mik. I agree with everything you say. Doesn't mean I have to like it, and I don't. I don't like it one bit. I know where my woman is and I want her out of there, now. I don't want those slimy bastards in the same state with her, much less the same hotel room."

"Sucks, don't it?" Mik punched Tinker's shoulder and turned away from the window just as Tala's voice whispered in his mind. His gaze automatically flew to AJ to confirm he was in on the link. Then he concentrated on Tala.

One of the guys just ordered room service. I heard him give the room number. Eighteen-ten. I think that's an executive suite. Two men are out in the living area. Lisa and I are in the bedroom with one distracted guard. He's heavy into his video games.

Okay. Are you and Lisa okay with what we're doing? With going along with this until we can catch the ones at the top?

Damn straight we are. Lisa agrees. We're okay for now.

Good. He glanced at AJ, caught his lover's hesitant nod. *I love you. It's killing me to leave you stuck over there.*

I know. I'm okay. AJ? You all right with this?

AJ's stricken glance told Mik volumes more than he knew AJ would ever think of sharing with Tala. *Yeah,* AJ said, after a long pause. *But only because you're okay with it. My gut is telling me to come get you now, but my head's reminding me what we have to do to keep everyone safe in the long run. I'll listen to my head, for now.*

Don't worry, AJ. We'll be okay. Besides, everything will work out perfectly. Don't forget, Anton's got a plan.

Oh, fuck.

Luc stepped into the main room, glanced at the door, and said, "They're here. Anton just contacted me."

"How's Tia?" Mik realized he was drumming his fingers on the arm of the chair and quickly folded his hand into a fist. This waiting was killing him, but they'd decided to hold off on anything until Anton and the rest of the Montana group had arrived.

Luc shook his head. He looked as if he'd aged a hundred years over the course of the day. "She's sleeping. Pale. She's lost too much blood." He stared at the closed front door. "I hope I'm not putting too much faith in Logan. He's a doctor, but Adam's the one with the healing powers that . . ."

AJ slung an arm over Luc's shoulders. "Adam's taught Logan what he knows. She'll be okay."

Luc raised stricken eyes to AJ. "How can you be so calm? Those bastards have Tala and . . ."

AJ sighed and glanced at Mik. His jaw tightened. "Mik and I are in constant communication with her. She's okay, we know where she is, and they're not going to try anything until tonight. And I have the satisfaction of knowing I'm going to personally destroy every single person who's hurt our women."

Luc's smile was strained. "Yeah. There's that."

Tinker opened the door before anyone even heard a step on the porch. Nick was just reaching for the handle. "Thanks, Tink." He stepped aside. Keisha was the first one into the room.

She drew Luc into a tight hug, flashed a quick hello to the group, and headed down the hallway to Tia. Anton, Logan, and Jazzy entered, but it was the last man, tall, unmistakably Native American, and preternaturally beautiful, who caught Mik's eye.

He stood up and held out his hand. "Igmutaka?"

"Yes." He moved close and drew Mik into a warm embrace, then stepped back, still clasping his shoulders. "You are your grandfather. I feel his spirit in you, just as he exists in your daughter. I did not feel his presence before now. I find that curious."

Bemused, Mik stared at the human form of the guide he had known as spirit and then wildcat. He'd heard the man's human manifestation was unusual—the body he wore so comfortably was tall and strong and powerfully shaped, with lean muscle and a stark yet almost feminine beauty, with his long, dark hair, dark skin, and dark eyes.

This was the man who had linked with his daughter, who would guide her to adulthood along with Mik, Tala, and AJ. Suddenly, the whole of his little girl's life flashed before him. Mik burst into laughter.

The others in the room looked at him as if he were nuts. Maybe he was. Maybe he was losing it, standing here in a loose embrace with a man who couldn't possibly exist, a man who'd walked the ancient world as a mountain lion, survived as spirit to guide many generations of Sioux warriors, and now stood here in this San Francisco home wearing faded Levis, a red plaid flannel shirt, and a pair of Mik's old hiking boots.

"You find me funny?" Igmutaka frowned.

Mik just shook his head. "I'm thinking of something Tala said the other day, how it's going to be almost impossible for our daughter to ever go out on a date with me and AJ looming over her. Now she's going to have you, too? The poor little girl won't have a chance."

Igmutaka slowly shook his head from side to side. "I disagree. She will have every chance." He glanced over his shoulder at Anton.

Mik realized Logan and Jazzy were no longer in the room. They must have gone immediately to Tia's room with Luc and Keisha, but he noticed that Anton observed the dynamics between him and Igmutaka with a thoughtful smile on his face.

After a moment, Anton turned and focused directly on Mik.

"Igmutaka's right. She'll have every chance because she will survive today, healthy and alive, with memories of her mother's bravery, two fathers who love her, and the spirit guide who protects her. As will your son, AJ, and Tink, your daughter. And your mates. I applaud your bravery, yours and your mates, for not taking the easy way out and going for the quick rescue. You're giving us a chance to end this threat here and now."

Mik crossed his arms over his chest. He felt Tala's presence in his thoughts along with AJ, knew Tinker was linked to Lisa. "So, Anton." He cocked one eyebrow. "What do you propose?"

Chapter 6

Baylor stepped out of the shower, dried off, and wrapped a towel around his waist. He dug around in his overnight kit, in search of his razor. "Son of a bitch." He jerked his hand out of the bag and glared at the perfect little parallel slices on his fingertip. Hopefully Manda wouldn't notice. She was always telling him to put the stupid plastic cover on the blades, which seemed like a fucking waste of time.

Grumbling, he set the razor on the counter and stuck his bloody finger in his mouth. Damn but he hated it when she was right, though it was almost worth admitting he'd screwed up, just to see her gloat. She really loved the occasional gloat.

He glanced at the bathroom door, comforted by the fact she slept just on the other side of it. He didn't even want to think about what Mik and AJ were going through right now. And Tinker? How was he handling things? Tinker lived and breathed for Lisa, and he was so fucking excited about the baby.

His sisters had found damned good men and he was glad for them. They'd lived lives of pure hell. They sure didn't deserve what had happened. None of them did.

Bay stared at the mirror and lathered up his face, but it was Tala's smile he saw, Lisa's soft laughter that he heard.

He hated feeling as if he was too far away to help, and even though they had their instructions from Anton, he couldn't see what good they could do. Not from clear across the country.

He'd failed them when they were little, when their parents had done their best to screw up their kids' lives. He couldn't handle it if he failed them now. Didn't know if he could survive if anything happened to either Lisa or Tala or the babies they carried. It was too much. Too fucking much.

He glanced at a small clock on the counter. It was almost six—their dinner reservations were for seven, and then they needed to be on the zoo grounds by nine or so. For what? So they could overhear something from someone without knowing what they were supposed to be listening for, and then go off in the trees and fuck like bunnies?

"Crap." He stared at his image, dark amber eyes rimmed with red from worry and the lower half of his face covered in white foam, and wondered what the fuck Anton was trying to do. None of what he wanted made sense. Thank the Goddess the girls had been able to tell their mates they were all right, at least for now. Knowing they'd finally made contact had taken some of the worry off his mind.

Now if his stupid finger would stop bleeding . . .

Double crap. He'd feel a lot better if the guys would just go in and free the girls and worry about their damned plans after everyone was safe. Instead they were all dicking around with some convoluted plan that required him and Jake and their women to fuck their brains out while someone tried to kill the president of the United States. Stupid. Just plain stupid.

Except he didn't have any other ideas. Nothing at all that would help them figure out who the hell was after them this time. Why someone in his old agency would be plotting against the commander in chief. Bay whipped the blade across his chin and then caught the last few whiskers under his nose, rinsed himself clean, and ran his hand over his smooth jaw.

Cursing under his breath, he dried his face and tossed the towel in the hamper. He was still silently seething when he stepped out of the bathroom and saw Manda, curled up under the heavy down comforter. One shoulder peeked out from beneath the thick blanket. Her hair, still damp from her shower, lay in tangled streaks of gold and honey across the pillow.

He stared at her, loving her so much he ached, and all the fight went out of him.

Those poor bastards, *Mik and AJ. Tinker.* How the hell were they coping with this nightmare? He didn't know if he could handle it if something were to happen to his mate. They'd had a few close calls, times when guys had come after Manda, and thinking of those times still made his blood run cold.

She rolled over and opened her eyes, those beautiful amber eyes that sometimes looked as if they'd seen more pain than any one person should ever have to witness. She didn't say a word. She just lifted the covers, held out her hand, and reached for him with a smile on her perfect mouth.

Groaning, not even trying to explain the emotions twisting him apart, Bay clasped her fingers and let her tug him lightly into bed.

He stopped his fall forward, supporting himself over her body. Close, but not nearly close enough. Looking down at her, he kissed her quickly on the end of the nose, keeping things light. Holding his body in check even as his cock rose hard and ready against his belly. "We don't have time. It's late. We have to . . ."

"Shush." Smiling, she pressed her fingertips to his mouth. "I need you. Now. I can't do what Anton wants of us if I'm as tied in knots as I feel right now. Make love to me, Bay. Just you and me, making love as if there's not a care in the world. The way we'd planned to when we left for Freeport this morning. Remember those separate hotel rooms we had waiting?"

He chuckled and kissed her again, though he still held his body above hers. He was so afraid to turn himself free, to let the need for her take over, take him. What she said was so true, though. He loved Jake and Shannon, but they'd fallen into such a comfortable routine with them, all sleeping together in that big bed of theirs, sharing thoughts and hearts and minds without really concentrating on the one they loved most.

He'd actually been lusting after his mate, wanting her to himself, all by himself. The way he wanted her now. And she was right. There was time if he'd just quit wasting it.

He lowered his hips until the towel tangled between them.

"That's cold!" Laughing, sucking her belly in close and curling up against his chest, Manda ripped the wet towel off his hips. Then she eased back against the sheets, looped her arms over his shoulders, and drew him close.

The tight curls between her legs brushed the sensitive underside of his cock, and he sighed, nestling against her. She looped one long leg around his hips and rested her thigh on his butt, and it was such a simple thing to slide between her damp folds as she opened for him.

Such a simple thing, and yet rife with so much emotion, so much meaning, that every time they loved, it seemed more intense than the time before, every time they touched, it felt as if they conveyed a deeper meaning.

He propped himself up on his elbows and stretched his fingertips out to brush the tangled hair back from her beautiful eyes. Jerked his hand back and stuck his bloody finger in his mouth.

She grabbed his hand and looked at the tiny cuts. Eyes twinkling, she kissed the small wound. It had finally stopped bleeding. "Did it to yourself, did you? Again?"

He nuzzled the soft skin where her shoulder curved into her smooth neck. "Go ahead. Gloat." He kissed her smile. "I know you want to."

She licked her lips. "Later, maybe. Now I'd rather make love. Hot, nasty sex in the afternoon."

He gazed into her sparkling eyes and fell for her all over again. "I will never, if I live to be a hundred, get enough of you. Of this. I love you, Manda. It scares the crap out of me when I think how much I love you, what it would do to me if anything were to ever happen to you."

Her lips curved in a slow smile. "I promise to be very, very careful." She wriggled her hips. "Now, are you just going to lie there, worrying about things that aren't going to happen, and wasting what little time we've got, or do you think you could get this show on the road?"

He rubbed his nose against hers. "Bossy little thing, aren't you?"

"Someone has to occasionally light a fire under your delicious butt." She encircled his neck and pulled him close for a long, slow kiss. Her lips roved over his, teasing, tasting, nipping. He ran his tongue along the seam, slowly breached it with the very tip until he could brush across the smooth surface of her teeth, inhale her breath, absorb her into himself.

Manda. His. From the moment he'd first seen her, misshapen and frightened and yet alight with her own special inner beauty, somehow he'd known.

He rolled his hips, thrusting deep and smooth, in, out, and filling her again. Her body rippled around his, the sleek muscles holding him, reluctantly giving way as he withdrew only to plunge deep inside again. He kept the rhythm slow, easy and loving, a mere prelude to what they saved for later this night.

Anton wanted their power, their energy. The pack alpha knew it would be stronger if they mated as wolves, knew that the call of the night would throb within their veins if they were beneath the naked branches of trees stripped bare for winter. The sound and scent of wild creatures, even though they lived within the confines of pens and cages, would add another level of arousal to the mating of the four Chanku.

Baylor had no doubt Anton could tap into their energy. He'd sensed the man in his mind on more than one occasion, a subtle connection of one alpha to another. Bay had never once resented the fact Anton checked in on them on occasion without announcing himself. No, he saw it as the über-alpha's right, his duty to protect and monitor his pack.

None of them had ever denied Anton's leadership of the packs. They certainly weren't going to start now. Bay thought of the man, of the pressure he took so willingly on to himself. He wore the mantle of leadership well, and he'd proved himself capable on many occasions.

But this time was different. This time the lives at risk were special—Lisa and Tala. The sisters Bay had known since their births, the young women with whom he shared a convoluted bond of flesh and blood and Chanku heritage. Only Manda was closer. She was his heart, his soul, the very breath that kept him alive.

He gazed into her slumberous amber eyes and sensed the climax hovering so close. He opened his thoughts and found her waiting, wondering why he'd not joined with her on this more intimate level.

A level only one mate could share with another. Not merely sensations, not just the sense of muscles contracting and blood rushing, of need growing and expanding, of making love through two sets of eyes, two minds, two hearts. No, this was something more, something deeper, a spiritual sharing that went beyond anything either Manda or Bay could ever explain.

Why should they? There was no reason to wonder, merely to accept. They not only made love, they *were* love. A single entity ripe with power, two bodies so closely linked they had become one soul, one single organism.

Bay blinked and tried to focus. He wanted to watch her, his Manda, his love. Wanted to see the faraway look in her eyes as all her focus centered on the crescendo building slowly and surely within their bodies. He blinked, tried so hard to focus on her eyes, but she swam in a sea of tears.

His? Hers? Emotions surged, so raw, so close to the surface he knew a momentary panic, that he should be so entirely naked to anyone, even himself.

Then she smiled and touched his cheek with her fingertip, carried a glistening tear from his face to her lips. The pink tip of her tongue slipped out and she tasted him, tasted the tears on his cheek, but it felt to Bay as if she'd licked the length of his cock. Lightning raced from her sweet mouth to his balls and forced a groan out of him.

He tilted his hips and drove deep inside, parting her sensitive folds, sliding over the hard mouth of her womb. Manda's lips parted, startled into a smile as he thrust again, so hard, so fast. He never wanted this to end. If only he could find that perfect moment of completion and hold it forever. He wanted . . . more. Always more, always Manda.

He groaned and gave over to sensation, gave in to the rush of orgasm, the almost painful sweetness of his climax. Manda's sleek thighs tightened across his buttocks, her strong arms wrapped around his neck, and she lifted her hips, seeking him, forcing him deeper until there was no sense of separation, no way anything or anyone could ever part them.

His cock jerked, his seed spilled, and her sleek muscles contracted and milked him, holding him deep, taking everything he had to offer. Her lips were close against his ear, and even though their minds were linked and their thoughts shared as one, he smiled with the words she whispered, over and over, a promise that bound them both.

"I love you forever, forever mine. I will always love you."

He wanted to keep her like this for all time—connected, bodies damp with sweat, muscles clenching, his balls aching from the powerful blast of orgasm. Never ending . . . if only they could stay this way forever.

But there was a dinner to attend, secrets to learn, and a run to be made through a wild tangle of woods. Tonight they would make love as feral creatures—wild and tumultuous sex beneath a dark winter's sky, and they would share their energy, the very essence of who and what they were, in order to protect the pack. It would be wonderful and he knew his body would feel replete when the last tremors of his climax subsided.

But it couldn't compare. Could never compare to what they'd shared over these last few moments—the sense that they were the only two people in the world, making love, being love, existing solely to love one another.

His ragged breathing began to slow, his heartbeat found a steady cadence once again, and Baylor Quinn tucked the memory of these past few moments deep within his heart. He nuzzled Manda's slim throat and reluctantly separated his body from hers.

She reached for him, a wordless plea that had him bending close, kissing her once more. She closed her eyes and sighed, but when he searched her thoughts, there were barriers where none had been before.

He frowned. "You're blocking me. Why? Did I hurt you?"

She blushed. Shook her head. "No. I didn't want you to see."

He tilted her chin up with his fingers. "See what?"

"It's silly." She glanced away, then, after a long moment, looked him in the eye. Finally, she smiled and shrugged. "I didn't want you to see how much that affected me. Making love, just the two of us. Nothing fancy, nothing out of the ordinary. Just you and me and it was . . . it was perfect, okay?" She bit her lip, almost as if she expected him to laugh at her.

"You're kidding, right? You'd hide that from me?" He leaned close and kissed her sweetly, deeply. Then he tugged her fingers and pulled her to her feet. "We need another shower, I think. And then we have to get moving. And while you're scrubbing my back and telling me what a wonderful lover I am, I'll remind you that, yes, it was perfect. Because you're perfect."

She laughed and he swatted her behind. Then he followed her into the shower, feeling lighter, more hopeful, than he'd felt since this morning when a man from his past had totally upended the present.

"You're sure? Liana was absolutely positive they could shift even at this point in their pregnancies?" Mik shot a glance at Tinker and AJ. "If she's wrong . . ."

Anton glanced at the sheets of paper in front of him. He'd been taking notes only he could read, but Mik often wondered if he wrote things down more to organize his thoughts than to actually refer to the illegible notes. "She's been our Goddess since time began. Maybe not the best, according to Liana, but she's been around long enough to know more about our physiology than anyone else. I don't think we should set any plan in motion that requires the girls shift, but I do want them to know that, should their lives be in danger, it's a viable option."

AJ nodded. "I can agree with that. Damn. I just want Tala out of this mess."

Anton raised his head. "AJ, I wasn't kidding when I told you we can abort at any time. Just go in and get them out. It's entirely up to you. And to the women, obviously, since they're the ones at risk."

Mik shook his head. "Tala'd kill us if we pulled the plug right now. She's more concerned about the threat to the president than she is about her and Lisa. As much as I hate leaving them with those bastards, I have to agree that we need to find out who's behind this."

Anton glanced at Tinker. "Tink, you've been pretty quiet. What's your honest feeling about what we're doing?"

"Honestly? You sure you want the truth, Anton?"

The menace in Tinker's softly growled question had Mik's feral senses leaping to attention. He noticed that everyone in the room had suddenly gone on alert. Only Anton remained entirely calm and at ease. He nodded his head. "I always want the truth, Martin. Don't ever doubt that."

Tink gave a sharp jerk of his head. "I'd like to rip your throat out for even suggesting that we leave them with those sons a' bitches, but like Mik says—I know if we pulled the girls now, they'd never forgive us." He brushed his hand over his eyes and stared at the tabletop, slowly shaking his head. Anton rested his hand on Tinker's shoulder when Tink slowly added, "Lisa and Tala . . . they've got more balls than any of us, but damn, that doesn't mean I have to like what we're planning."

"What, exactly, are we planning?" Luc walked in with Tia and Logan. Jazzy and Keisha followed behind.

"Tia!" Anton stood up and drew her into a hug. "How are you? Did Logan manage to repair the damage?"

"Logan is absolutely brilliant. Remember, though, I already knew that since he's the one who delivered my babies." She kissed Anton and then leaned over and gave Tinker a kiss as well. She smiled ruefully at Mik and AJ. "I'm sorry, Tink, guys. We should have been paying closer attention. We weren't at all prepared for anything like what happened."

Tinker patted her fingers where they rested on his shoulder and tilted his head so he could see Tia standing behind him. "Don't be sorry. It wasn't your fault. I'm just glad you're okay. We'll get the girls. Don't worry."

Anton shuffled his stack of notes. "Luc, you asked what we're planning. I've been waiting to give everyone a rundown until you got here, since the original information comes from you and I want to be sure I've got it right."

He glanced around the table, making eye contact with each of them. "Here's what we know. The president and First Lady are due at the Civic Auditorium at eight tonight. The kidnappers want us on site at seven thirty. They requested two human and wolf teams. Their plan is remarkably simple. They want the wolves to lose control and attack the president. If his wife gets in the way . . . too bad."

"What? That's absolutely . . ."

"Think of it." Anton shook his head. "We've guarded them before and the president was really impressed with how well trained the wolves were. In fact, Mik, wasn't that a job where Tala was the handler and both you and AJ stood guard?"

"That's right. Six months ago when he was giving a talk at an auto plant that was reopening. Wolves are amazingly effective for crowd control." He shook his head. "But we'd never lose control and attack anyone. What do those idiots think we are?"

"Killers. They know we've killed while on assignment. The deaths have always been laid on the wolves doing their job, but in this case, since it would be obvious that the animals had gone totally out of control, they would be put down, the whole thing chalked up to a horrible accident, maybe something the president was wearing, a perfume the First Lady has on. Point being, dead president, maybe even dead First Lady. No one to blame but dumb animals. Of course, our business would be irreparably harmed and a couple of you would have to die, but what the hell, right?"

When he gazed at all of them, Anton's expression was totally at odds with his flip comments. "There's one good thing about this—they don't know that we are the wolves. They're still thinking we work with highly trained animals, so our unique abilities are unknown. Now, obviously, what they expect is not going to happen, but the ones behind this plan can't know until the last minute that we're not following orders. So here's what we're going to do."

He glanced at Keisha. She shoved her long hair over her shoulder. Then she rolled it up and slipped on a wig. Her long black curls were hidden beneath a shorter, straightened style. When she subtly altered her stance and expression, even Luc gasped.

"Eerie, isn't it?" Anton folded his arms across his chest and stared at his mate. "My love, you look almost exactly like the president's wife." He glanced about the room. "Keisha will be attending tonight's concert on the president's arm as his wife, who will be safely stashed until the evening is over. He is aware of, and approves of the plan. AJ, I want you in uniform as a guard with Nick and Luc on leashes with breakaway collars. I'm going to take the second position with Tinker on leash."

He glanced at Keisha and smiled. "Lose the wig, sweetheart. You're really freaking me out."

She laughed and some of the tension in the room melted away. Anton shuffled his notes again and looked up. "What's interesting, after looking through the paperwork Luc got today, is that all of our clearances to work as guards for tonight are in perfect order. I've checked with the White House staff, and absolutely nothing is out of the ordinary, which means this has all been approved. It's gone through the proper channels. Whoever is behind this is close to the top."

He let them think about that as he focused on Mik. "I want you and Logan at the Four Seasons. We've reserved

the suite next to the one where the women are being held."
He glanced at Tinker. "Tink, I know you want to be there
to pick up Lisa, but I need you to guard the president. If
things get ugly, we may have to depend on your physical
strength. You and Mik are equals when it comes to muscle, and the one thing we don't know for sure is if we're
the only hit that's planned."

Mik glanced at AJ and Tink. "What are you getting at?"

"I've got Baylor and Jake and their women checking
out some men, including a current White House staffer
and two guys from Bay's old agency. They're dining in a
very public place tonight in Washington, DC. Bay's orders
are to observe, eavesdrop, and let me know if they hear
anything at all suspicious. I've got a very strong hunch that
there might be a backup plan in place in case we fail—or
maybe we're the backup if someone else fails. I wish I could
be certain, but I'm not, so we all need to be alert. Jazzy has
offered to stay here with Tia and the babies."

Mik caught Igmutaka's eye. The spirit guide stood
against the wall, apart from the rest of the pack, yet obviously paying very close attention to what was going on.
He nodded at Mik but said nothing, so Mik asked the
question for him. "What about Igmutaka? What's the plan
for him?"

Anton glanced at Igmutaka and smiled. "He and Beth
will be checking into the room next to the one where the
girls are being held. Igmutaka is visiting royalty from a
small but very wealthy country. Beth is his assistant. With
her darker coloring and dark hair, she and Igmutaka will
have to pass for residents of an obscure island nation.
They're traveling with a pair of wolves—Mik, you and
Logan will be acting the part of very large, extremely pro-
tective watchdogs."

Mik glanced at Logan. "Woof," he said.

Logan merely shook his head. "I want to make sure my

medical bag is included with whatever luggage Beth and Ig might have with them."

AJ stared at Logan. "Why? Is there a problem we don't know about?"

Smiling, Logan held up both hands and shook his head. "No. Nothing to worry about. I just want to be prepared. We have two perfectly healthy young women, each going into her eighth month of pregnancy. They were both given an unknown drug when they were kidnapped. They've been under highly stressful conditions all day. I'm going to want to check blood pressure, heart rate of both of them and their babies . . . just the basics. AJ, I'm a doctor. I don't go anywhere without my bag."

AJ glared at him a moment. "Okay then. I just wanted to be sure."

Mik took his partner's hand and squeezed. "We've both been in touch with Tala. She's fine. If I didn't know better, I'd almost think she's enjoying the excitement."

AJ snorted. "I know better and she is enjoying the excitement. She's making me crazy and scarin' the crap out of me."

Shrugging, Mik leaned back in the chair. "See? Just the usual thing with Tala." Everyone laughed, but he squeezed AJ's hand a second time and glanced his way. *I'm worried, too, man, but she'll be okay. She has to be. We'll get her out, and Lisa, too. Just hang in there.*

AJ nodded, but his tension was a palpable force in the room. The only one who appeared even remotely relaxed was Anton.

Sitting on a tall stool at his worktable, Adam rubbed a soft, oiled rag over the old Philco he'd finished repairing for Stefan, a 1930s-era wooden radio that had been working perfectly until eighteen-month-old Alex decided to explore the inner mechanism. The tubes were now back in place and the wires that had fallen victim to a toddler's busy fingers had been repaired or replaced.

He almost wished it hadn't been so easy to fix. He loved to bury himself in a project like this, whether it was something under the hood of a car or the intricate workings of Anton's Rolex. Each represented a challenge and gave him an immense sense of satisfaction when he was able to return an item to its owner, completely restored and perfectly repaired.

Working on Stefan's old radio had helped the afternoon pass quickly. It had taken his mind off the horrible situation with Tala and Lisa—but even more important, it had buried his apprehension over the night ahead and the fact he was actually going to bond with the woman he loved.

Now the evening stretched out ahead and the hands of the clock crawled toward the time they would leave to run as wolves.

To mate as wolves. With Liana.

No, it wasn't apprehension at all. It was impatience. This waiting was making him crazy. Adam looked out the window at the long shadows stretching across the meadow and then glanced over his shoulder at Liana. "It's already getting dark." The expectant grin he shot at her was met with a soft laugh.

"It's barely five, sweetheart. Relax. We have hours yet." She leaned close and kissed him behind his right ear. The touch of her lips sent shivers racing along his spine.

Damn, he was definitely ready. "Well, if Anton expects an orgasm at precisely five minutes to ten, we're going to have to start a whole lot earlier." He tilted his head back and smiled at her. "Hours earlier. We certainly don't want to rush anything."

He breathed in the sweet scent of her, and at the same time opened his thoughts and listened in to the other voices nearby.

Mei and Oliver were on their way to the main house.

He sensed them crossing the driveway below his apartment. They'd planned dinner with Stefan and Xandi and an early evening wearing the kids out so the adults could have the night to themselves.

Adam chuckled. Mei had her toys. Lots of toys, and a slew of fresh batteries. Obviously she and Xandi were looking forward to building up as much sexual energy as they could.

Adam? Is that you? How's my radio?

Hey, Stef. It's ready to go. You need to have a talk with Alex. He's not quite ready for the Philco. Not yet.

Stefan's snort might have been telepathic, but Adam swore he actually heard it. *Try explaining that to the mobile monster from hell.*

Your perfect son?

Yeah, right. Perfect in every way. You and Liana going to join us tonight?

Adam glanced at Liana and thought of their plans for the evening. *No. Not tonight. We're going to run, but we plan to keep to Anton's timetable. Besides, it appears the girls have specific plans for you and Oliver.*

He sensed Stefan's laughter. *They're taking Anton's request for a nine fifty-five orgasm as a challenge, and you know how Mei and Xandi are when someone challenges them to do anything.*

Adam thought about the evening ahead. He hadn't intended to, but he went ahead and shared his intentions with Stefan, a man he honored as much as he did Anton.

Good, Adam. It's time. You and Liana have a connection that's greater than I ever saw between you and Eve. In this particular instance, I have to agree with Anton. Some events, some relationships, are fated. The two of you are meant to be bonded mates. There was a pause. A moment later, Stefan was back. *I hear Mei and Oliver. We'll talk later, after Lisa and Tala are home safe.*

That's a promise. Adam blinked, pulling himself out of

Stefan's mind. He realized Liana now stood in front of him with a soft smile on her lips. She ran her fingertips along his jaw. He tilted his chin and caught three fingers between his teeth for a gentle nip.

She sighed softly and brushed them over his lower lip. "The girls will be fine, my love. Tala and Lisa and the babies have so much yet ahead of them. They have full lives to live. Not only Anton, but all of us will see to it that they survive."

He thought about her words for a moment, and wondered once again just how much Liana remembered from her life as their Goddess. Eve had most of Liana's knowledge now, but Liana still seemed to know more than she should, more than the rest of them.

Did she have knowledge of Lisa and Tala that the rest of them didn't? Would he discover that information when they bonded? Would he learn things from Liana's life as their Goddess before she'd gained mortality? The thought was exhilarating, but a little frightening, too. Did he really want to know of things to come? Did he want to share knowledge better left to gods and goddesses?

She'd promised him that the memories that might have been dangerous to him were gone, that a total bond was physically safe, but what of his emotions? Could he handle it? He could be such a jerk sometimes. What of her memories that stretched into prehistory, the men she'd loved, the mistakes she'd made, the amazing things she'd experienced? Would he be strong enough to accept all those many parts that made up the woman he loved?

Would she be strong enough to accept him and his failings? He knew his had been greater than most. So many mistakes he'd made, so many promises unfulfilled, and yet Liana loved him. She loved him even more than Eve had.

Unlike Eve, Liana had every intention of staying with him. No, that wasn't fair. He couldn't blame Eve for anything. She was blameless . . . actually, all of them were. Who could control the vagaries of fate?

He gazed into Liana's luminous gray-green eyes and knew he was falling harder each moment he spent with her. He still thought of Eve, still remembered the way they'd loved, the times they'd shared, but in many ways their life together had been so brief and his time with Liana so much more intense that he felt he'd known this woman forever.

Her soft whisper in his ear dragged Adam away from his swirling thoughts. She stood behind him once again.

"There's something I want to do tonight." Liana pressed against his back and draped her arms over his shoulders. She rested her cheek on top of his head.

He turned his head and kissed her. "And that is?"

"I want to ask Eve to bless our bond. Are you okay with that?"

He never would've thought of such a thing, but if that was what Liana wanted . . . "Of course. If you like. But why?"

He felt Liana's sigh against his back. "I owe her so much, Adam. My chance at a mortal life, the freedom to be the woman I never thought I'd be. You. If she hadn't made you promise to watch out for me, do you honestly think we would be here, on this day, loving each other? Planning to bond as mates?"

He chuckled. "I guess I was pretty stubborn. And I wasn't very nice to you." He reached behind, caught her in his arms, and tugged her around his side and into his lap.

She snuggled against his chest, a petite yet terribly womanly armful of warmth and life. "We both had so much to learn," she said. "I worry, though, what you'll feel when you see what's in my mind. My memories of so many men, so many lovers, so many terrible mistakes stretching over hundreds of lifetimes. When Eve took my knowledge, she left those memories intact. I wasn't a very nice goddess, Adam. I like to think I'm better than I was, that I've left my selfish ways behind, but will you see who I was and think less of me?"

He nuzzled the soft fall of her hair and laughed. They even worried alike. "Never, my love. We are two very flawed people with a lifetime of mistakes behind us. This step we're taking? It's forward, not backward, and it's not a mistake. I imagine we're perfect for each other."

Chapter 7

As Bay ran a comb through his hair, he caught Manda's reflection in the dressing-room mirror. She was slipping into a dress, covering up all those perfect curves with something soft and dark. Not black. No, as she smoothed the soft fabric over her slim hips he realized it was a bluish green so dark it almost looked black, but it shimmered with blue fire when she turned beneath the overhead light, and it clung to all those perfect curves and valleys as if it were her second skin.

She raised her head and smiled at him, and just like that, he was hard as a post. She blinked, and he knew she'd caught the sense of his desire, maybe even scented the arousal she caused in him.

"Baylor Quinn!" She laughed and sauntered across the room, kissed him teasingly on the nose. "No. Absolutely not." Then she palmed him, running her warm hand lightly over the erection straining to life beneath his dark slacks. "Down, boy! Behave. I can't take you out like this."

He leaned close and kissed her. "We could always stay in."

The laughter went out of her eyes. Bay felt like a jerk for what he'd said. "I didn't mean . . ."

Manda shook her head. "I know. I wish we could, but

we have to do this for Lisa and Tala." She sighed and leaned against his chest. "It's for all of us. It has to end, this constant threat against us. What happens to one of us, happens to all of us."

He swallowed back a lump in his throat and tasted fear. Unwelcome, terrifying fear. "If something were to happen to you, I . . ." No. He really couldn't go there. Couldn't allow himself to even imagine anything happening to Manda. To his one, true love.

"I want your child, Bay. I want a baby."

Stunned, he frowned at her. Now? With the threat still out there? With Lisa and Tala in such jeopardy? "Manda . . . sweetheart. It's so dangerous right now. We don't even know who's after us this time. Not for sure. Are you certain?"

She nodded and held his gaze with hers. Steady. Unwavering. He wished he could be half as brave as Manda. Even half as sure of himself.

"I've been thinking of it for a long time, ever since Tia and Luc had their twins, but I didn't want it to be a decision driven by holding those gorgeous babies." She blinked. Her eyes were suspiciously shiny.

He tried to see her thoughts, but she was blocking him as she turned away and grabbed her coat off the bed. Slipped the strap of her purse over her shoulder.

She fiddled with the clasp on the purse and didn't meet his eyes. "I won't force the issue. It's not one any woman should make on her own, but I want you to think about it. Maybe try and get used to the idea." She glanced up and gave him a tentative smile, one that let him know how uncertain she'd been of his reaction.

He hadn't reacted very well. It made him feel like a selfish jerk. Neither of them was getting any younger, and she'd already lost more than half her life. Had it stolen from her, while he . . . he'd always just worried about himself. He hadn't even worried about his sisters.

Lisa and Tala. Beautiful women now. In danger again, through no fault of their own. In many ways, their lives hadn't been a whole lot better than Manda's. They'd each lived in their own hell. Trapped in a nightmare childhood that no child should have to endure.

The decision was much simpler than it might have been if he'd really let himself agonize over all the potential problems. He was good at that—agonizing. Dissecting. Creating problems where none should exist. Instead, he stepped forward, drew Manda into his arms, and rested his chin atop her head. Her smooth hair felt like silk. She smelled amazing, like fresh air and clean woman and sex. She always made him think of sex, of losing himself within her heat, of loving her.

"When's your next heat? How soon can we . . . ?"

She pushed herself away, far enough to look into his eyes. The surprise, the happiness on her face reaffirmed everything he was feeling. He brushed his palm over the soft curve of her belly. "You're sure you want to mess with perfection? Goddess, but I love this body." Laughing, he leaned close and kissed her. "Are you going to tell me when, or make me guess?"

"Tonight," she said. "I should be fertile tonight." A small frown puckered her eyebrows. She cupped his jaw with her palm. "Bay? Are you sure? I know you've had doubts. It's not like we both had ideal childhoods."

"No doubts. We can give a baby something we never had. Unconditional love, a stable home, two parents who want the very best for their child." His arms were actually shaking when he drew her close against him again. Kissed her gently, then deeper as the emotions swamped him. "Damn it, Amanda Smith. I love you so much. Will you marry me? I know we're mated, that our mating is forever, but I want the world to know you're mine. And, yes, I want a baby."

Shaken, he kissed her again. In his mind's eye, he saw

her body change, growing ripe with his child, and he realized it was true. He had no doubts. None where Manda was concerned.

It was only his own ability he worried about, but he'd done okay as this amazing woman's mate. Because of Manda. Always because of her.

She traced his cheek and showed him her fingertip. It glistened with his tears. Damn. She had the ability to unman him with a word, with a thought, with the slightest possible touch.

"Bay, you'll be a perfect father. Absolutely perfect. And I would be honored to be your wife."

Manda snuggled against his chest and he held her close. Her thoughts were open to him now. They mirrored his own. Thinking of the night ahead, imagining the two of them as parents. Trying to picture their child, a combination of the two of them. Each of them wondering about the child they would be bringing into their lives, of the vows they'd so quickly and easily agreed to make in front of family and friends.

She had no fears for the future. None at all, but he guessed that was because she'd already lived through hell and survived. What more was there to be afraid of? He would never be that sure of himself, not the way Manda was. Never that certain of the future. It made him ache, and yet, at the same time, the thought of his baby growing inside the woman he loved made him whole.

A sharp knock on the door snapped them both out of their thoughts. Jake's voice, impatient as he could so often be. "You guys ready to go? I called a cab. It'll be here in ten minutes."

"Coming right out." Bay glanced at Manda. "You okay?"

Smiling, she nodded and touched another damp spot on his cheek. "What about you, big guy? Are you okay?"

He nodded, grabbed a damp washcloth off the counter,

and ran it over his face. "I've got you, haven't I? I'm better than okay." He took her hand, and they left the room.

She tightened her fingers around his and flashed him a saucy wink. For some reason, he felt light, almost free—and very much like laughing.

As the maitre d' led them to their table, Bay heard Jake's voice slipping into his head. *Will you look at this place? Hope you've got plenty of room left on your credit card.*

Chuckling, Bay actually looked around and paid some attention to their surroundings. He'd been so focused on Manda he hardly remembered the ride from the apartment to this fancy restaurant across from the capitol. *Anton's picking up the tab tonight. You can order off the grownup side of the menu.*

Gee, Dad? You sure that's okay?

Bay jerked his gaze to Jake, but Jake was busy seating Shannon at the table and missed his surprise. *Dad.* He glanced at Manda and quickly pulled her chair back for her before the waiter could help her to her seat. *Daddy.*

The thick wave of emotion that washed over him from Jake's teasing comment kept him shaken, even as he took his own seat beside Manda. Shannon and Manda talked quietly. Jake selected an eight-year-old bottle of Jordan cabernet sauvignon and sent the sommelier away smiling. The four of them looked over their menus, but it wasn't easy for Bay to pull his thoughts back to the reason they were sitting here in this pricey restaurant near the nation's capitol.

He glanced up as two men took the table beside theirs, both wearing dark suits with neatly trimmed hair and that overall manicured look he associated with life inside the Beltway. One was older, sort of heavyset. The other man was younger, with the hungry look of a guy who seriously wanted to move up the food chain. The table was set for four. Obviously the others hadn't arrived yet.

He thought he recognized the older man, but he couldn't recall his name or department. The other guy was an unknown, but he had that buttoned-down, freshly trimmed look that practically screamed *government employee*. Bay had once looked the same. He'd loosened up a bit since his years with the agency, though he still wore his hair short. Turning away from the table beside him, Bay glanced at his lover.

Jake's hair was long enough to curl around his collar, and no matter how often he combed it, he still managed to look like he'd just crawled out of a warm bed with a willing woman . . . or an equally willing man.

Bay never denied he was willing any time Jake wanted him. Couldn't recall a time when he'd ever turned him away.

What was it about the guy? Bay didn't think he could look that sexy if his life depended on it. Maybe Jacob Trent just had overdeveloped pheromones. That had to be it. Whatever it was, Bay was getting hot just looking at him.

Jake glanced up, caught his gaze, and grinned. *You're broadcasting, bro. Put a lid on it. You're giving me a boner.*

And just like that, he lost it. Laughing, Bay picked up his wineglass and quickly changed the subject. "I'd like to propose a toast."

Shannon cocked an eyebrow and looked at Manda. Then a huge smile spread across her face and her green eyes twinkled. Bay raised his eyebrows and glared at Manda. "No talking out of turn, my love."

"Yes, dear." She dipped her head in a blatantly subservient manner, but he heard her snort.

Jake frowned. "What's up?"

"I have asked Manda to marry me. Fool that she is, she has agreed. Wish the poor woman luck."

Jake's eyes went wide. "Marriage? You're getting married?"

"We are." This time when Manda gazed at him, she wasn't teasing. "I love Bay. He loves me. And . . ." She tipped her glass to his, smiling his way. The crystal rang like a bell.

Bay finished her sentence. "And we decided that if we want to start a family, the least we can do is bring a child into a traditional home with two married parents."

"Wow." Shannon's smile kept growing wider, but now her eyes were on Jake.

He blushed. He actually blushed. Bay chuckled as he sipped his wine. He didn't think Jake had it in him to blush, but the proof was right there in front of them. "Okay, Jake. What's got you so befuddled?"

"We've got to quit taking these weekends away. All they do is get a man into trouble."

Bay cocked an eyebrow.

Jake reached across the table and took Shannon's hand. Bay noticed that he studied his mate's fingers with an unusually pensive expression on his face. "I proposed to Shannon tonight, too." He grinned then and looked directly into his mate's eyes. "I'm not really sure what got into me. Maybe it was making love in a bed without Bay's ugly mug beside me, but I know it's the right thing to do. We're still trying for that baby—we have been for a long time. It hasn't happened yet, but we're not giving up hope. At least she's agreed to marry me."

"I'm not worried." Shannon squeezed his fingers.

"About what?" Jake asked, dryly. "Me or the baby?"

"About any of it. You. Me. The baby we will have some day. I refuse to worry about . . ." She shrugged and added in mindspeak, *Lisa and Tala. It's all going to work. I have to believe that.*

Bay tightened his grasp on Manda's hand. They all knew Shannon had been rendered sterile by an infection before she'd become Chanku, knew that her body had begun to heal once she'd made her first shift. Whether or not it would ever heal enough to allow her to conceive was something else altogether.

The waiter brought their first course just as two more men joined the two sitting at the table next to them. They could have been clones of the first two in their dark suits, with neatly trimmed hair and bland, nondescript faces.

Bay kept his face averted. *I worked with the two who just came in, though they were in a separate division and may not recognize me. If they do, just go with it.* He winked at Jake. *We're celebrating, right?*

That we are. "So, have you two decided when you want this wedding to take place? Shannon and I haven't set a date yet."

Manda picked up the conversation, chattering away as if wedding plans were the only thing on her mind. Shannon and Jake added a few comments, but Bay sat quietly, closest to the four men with his back to their table. Listening.

He never really thought much about the fact his hearing had become so much more acute after his first shift. Even in human form he clearly heard conversations and sounds he never would have noticed before.

The four men spoke quietly, but he might as well have been sitting with them. From what he heard, he was thankful he was not part of their group.

Names, dates, information he could pass on to Anton later, once they left the restaurant. There was so much anger, but something else he hadn't expected, something he felt with his Chanku senses, was the touch of insanity. The mental and emotional imbalance of the older man and the Machiavellian control he appeared to have over the others. It was chilling, the way they celebrated, all of them buoyed by the crazed plans of one man.

Celebrating because of what they knew would happen

in a few short hours. Toasting one another and referring to events by such foolish code names that Bay had no problem at all understanding their intent.

Dinner passed quickly. The four men completed their meal and left without ever noting Baylor. But what was there to notice? Four good friends, both couples newly engaged, celebrating their happiness. No reason to note their presence, nothing at all to draw attention.

But the four drew Manda's eyes. Or at least one of them appeared to. As the older gentleman passed by their table, she glanced up, gasped, and clumsily knocked her wineglass over.

Red wine spilled across the pristine tablecloth. Bay grabbed his napkin to blot at the spill before it spread any farther. "Sweetheart? Are you okay?"

Slowly, Manda shook her head. She clasped her hands on the table in front of her. He saw that she held them together to keep from shaking. *Manda! What's wrong?*

That older man? I know him. He was Milton Bosworth's assistant. One of the men who kept me caged all those years.

Shit. That's the connection.

Just then the waiter arrived to clean up the spilled wine. Manda blinked, composed herself, and apologized for making such a mess. Baylor took her hand and wrapped his fingers around her smaller ones. "We're going to skip dessert. If you don't mind bringing us our tab . . ."

The waiter smiled and bowed. "You are guests of one of the owners of the restaurant. Mr. Cheval asked me to convey his deep congratulations on your recent engagements. He said he looks forward to hearing from you as soon as you have the opportunity to call."

Jake laughed out loud. Shaking his head in obvious amazement, he turned to Bay and said, "How the hell does he do that?"

Bay shrugged. "I don't know, nor do I want to know.

Nothing gets past him. Ever." Then he stood up, left a large tip on the table, and helped Manda to her feet. She still trembled. He collected her coat, wrapped her in its warm folds, and the four of them left the restaurant.

Silently, he filled Jake and Shannon in on Manda's discovery as they stepped outside, effectively killing the mood. With his arm around Manda, Bay glanced back at the beautiful façade—probably one of the nicest restaurants in all of Washington, DC. "Is there anything, anywhere, Cheval's not involved in?"

No one answered him. Jake signaled to a nearby cab. Silently, they headed back to the apartment.

Darkness had descended by the time Ulrich and Millie met the rest of the pack and headed into the woods, though it wasn't entirely dark. The moon rising above the mountain was already throwing a silvery glimmer across the snow. Daci led off with Matt and Deacon following, tails high, ears up, alert to danger, to prey, to the scents and sounds of the night.

It was impossible to ignore the added sense of expectation and excitement. Ric didn't even try. While they often ran together, they always separated when they returned to the cabins—Daci and her two mates to theirs, he and Millie to their own larger cabin. Sometimes Matt joined them, but more often than not it was just the two of them. Aroused after running, loving each other, needing so damned much to lose themselves in the overwhelming passion that followed shifting and racing through the night.

It was always good, always fresh and exciting.

But tonight was different. Ulrich couldn't ignore the thrumming in his blood, the arousal simmering at a level just barely under his control. It wasn't so much the fact they'd be doing something different tonight, something they hadn't, for whatever reason, done on any other night. No. It was more, the fact they'd discussed their plans, scheduled their time, organized a sexual gathering as if it were some sort of fucking business meeting.

For some reason, the whole idea left him feeling practically giddy, filled his head with visuals and his libido with all sorts of wild expectations. Uppermost was the image of his beloved Millie, naked and aroused, tangled up with Daci, Matt, and Deacon.

She was so utterly perfect, so beautiful, and still, in many ways, such an innocent. Yet in her innocence was a carnality so powerful, so addictive that Ric knew he'd never get enough of her, enough of seeing her lost in passion, her body open, giving, awakening to each new experience.

He just hoped he didn't embarrass himself before they finally got together, as aroused as he was already. He had to stop thinking of later. He needed to center himself in his feral presence and live for the moment.

Damned easy to say, almost impossible to achieve. For now, he and Millie followed the younger group, trotting along at that steady, ground-covering pace that could easily carry them up to fifty or more miles over the course of a night. With any luck, the physical effort of the run would keep his raging lust under control. He could only hope.

They'd decided ahead of time not to run as far as usual—not with the schedule they needed to keep. That damned schedule that somehow set his blood to boiling, made his body tighten and his balls ache. He almost wished they could pick up the pace enough to take his mind off their plans, but they kept things steady—racing smoothly along the narrow trail over hard-packed snow.

At least half an hour passed before Matt pulled to the right and led them through a narrow break in the trees. Slipping through barren, leafless brush, they finally broke through into a small meadow covered in snow and bathed in moonlight. Matt took the lead, circling the meadow, sniffing trees and bushes until he finally yipped sharply to let them all know it was safe. Then he nipped Daci's flank and urged her into the center.

Ric glanced at Millie and caught her confused stare. *What?*

Just watch and follow. Ric nudged her forward, into the moonlight. Millie glanced his way and he knew the moment she understood Matt's intent as the five of them came together in this perfect setting, beneath a silver moon, flanked by tall pines and cedars, with the soundless night all around.

Once gathered, they raised their muzzles to the moonlit sky and howled. Wolves in the pens at the sanctuary added their howls to the chorus. Their many voices echoed against the hills, rebounding over and over again until the cacophony took on a pulse-pounding rhythm all its own.

Shivers raced along Ulrich's spine as he watched his mate. Whatever Millie did, she did with her full heart and soul. Now her muzzle pointed skyward, her sharp canines glistened, and steam billowed out around her beautiful wolven face.

Love such as he'd never experienced swept through his veins, thrummed with the steady thunder of his heart. His Millie, his mate, the woman who knew him even better than he knew himself, and loved him still.

So serendipitous, the steps that had brought them together, yet he guessed it was more an act of fate ruled by the hand of the Goddess. To think Liana might have had a part in this. One of these days, he really needed to sit down with the ex-goddess and find out just what she knew.

Because of her, with Anton's intercession, he'd had that final night with Camille, the night that had freed him to love again. It had freed him to find Millie and make her his own.

To help Millie fulfill her own destiny as Chanku, to find the children that had been taken from her, to find love with a man desperate for exactly what she had to offer.

Yes, she was here because of him, but she had been the one to save him. His mate, his closest friend, the one he would always love. What a tangled web their lives had become, all of them in some odd way connected. He never would have guessed, that afternoon when he'd stood in Golden Gate Park and watched his lovely niece Keisha at the dedication to the garden she'd designed, where that chance meeting would lead.

Now, he studied Millie as she, in turn, watched Matt, and Ulrich shared his mate's pride that this young wolf was already showing the qualities of leadership none of them had suspected in him before.

Showing those qualities because Millie had helped him find the alpha character he'd been hiding all his life. The howls faded into the night and Ric opened his convoluted thoughts to Millie. *He's going to be a fine leader some day, my love. Because of you. You are the one who helped him find himself.*

Millie turned and studied Ric for a long moment. *Only because you helped me find myself. If not for you, Ric, I have no idea where I would be tonight.*

He wished wolves could laugh out loud. *Certainly not sitting on your butt in the snow in ten-degree weather, howling at the moon.*

You're probably right. He sensed the dry laughter behind her pithy reply.

Then Matt whirled about and nipped Deacon's flank, spun once more, and took off in a whirl of flying snow and playful yips. Daci and Deacon tumbled after him, scrambling like pups in the fresh powder.

Ric and Millie followed, a bit more sedately, but Ric noticed how Millie watched Matt, how she studied Deacon, and even followed Daci's graceful moves along the moonlit trail with a new sense of interest.

His body tightened once again with a surge of arousal, and he wondered about stopping here and now, of taking her as a wolf beneath the shimmering moon, thrusting hard and fast into her always willing body. Sometimes it happened like this, where his need for Millie rushed through him like a damned tsunami at the most inappropriate times. Running with the pack, knowing they should be saving their building sexual need until later, meant he could think what he liked, as long as he didn't act on it.

Not easy, with his blood running hot, his damned prick clamoring for a warm, wet home within his beautiful mate. But it wasn't going to happen. Not now, when their energy was needed later, when lives might depend on their timing, their level of arousal, their ability to project the power generated by their Chanku passion so that Anton could have it all, could take every last bit and work it at the precise moment in time when he had need of it.

Ric had no idea what Anton planned, but the wizard had never once failed them, and damned if Ric was going to let his need to screw his mate interfere with tonight's plans. He was an adult, for crying out loud! The elder in this group. The one who should be in control, not worried about losing it.

With that thought in mind, Ric followed Millie, watched Matt and Deacon and Daci, and let his desire build for each member of the pack. It was easier this way, to concentrate on all of them.

If he thought only of Millie, he'd lose it for sure.

The snow crunched beneath his big paws and steam billowed out about his muzzle. They ran with a purpose, now. Searching for game, for their meal for the night. Hunting always fueled their sexual desire—their need for blood seemed tightly connected to their need for release—but the night was cold and so far there'd been nothing to catch their attention.

Not until Deacon suddenly paused, raised his nose in the air, and slipped off the trail through a thick tangle of brush.

How he managed to find a trail through such a maze of brambles and poison oak amazed Ric. As big and ungainly as Deacon was in his human form, he was amazingly graceful as a wolf on the hunt. Moving silent as a wraith, he pressed his belly to the snow and slowly worked through the edge of the bramble patch and up on top of a pile of large boulders.

The others followed, practicing the same stealth, circling to Deacon's left and right as they closed in on an unsuspecting doe hiding in a thick patch of windblown willows near a frozen creek.

She was thin and crippled, her right rear leg twisted and unable to bear her weight. Deacon didn't even hesitate. Lips curled in a silent snarl, he sailed off the slick boulder with a powerful leap and caught the back of the doe's neck in his strong jaws.

She was dead before they hit the ground, her neck cleanly broken by Deacon's lightning attack. He backed away, snarling, and turned on Matt, but Matt's low growl had Deacon backing away from his own kill—backing away and waiting until Daci and Millie had approached the still warm body and settled in to feed.

Only then did Matt step aside and let Deacon at the fresh kill. He'd easily kept his own mate—the one who'd made the kill—under control until the females had begun to feed.

Ric stayed back and waited until Matt approached the deer. It wasn't until all four wolves were busy feeding that he finally found a spot near the doe's haunch and tore into the thick hide with razor-sharp teeth. The taste of warm blood and hot meat filled his mouth and fired his feral nature, but it was pride in Matt that made his heart race.

Pride in the young man who showed more qualities of leadership each day, who had once been unable to meet Ric's eyes without blushing and stammering and turning away in an overt display of submission.

Ric raised his head and caught Millie looking at him. Thick blood streaked her muzzle and chest and her eyes glittered with the thrill of the hunt. Caught up in the scent of the fresh kill, the hungry wolves beside her gorging on the meat, she was every bit the wild wolf, her feral nature captured by the purity of their bloodlust, her human side buried beneath the instinctive drive to gorge herself and feed while there was plenty to eat.

Then he saw it, a glimmer of her humanity as her long pink tongue came out and cleaned the blood from the stiff hairs around her muzzle. In that moment, Ric opened the link between them, opened to Millie's soft mental voice.

I love you, she said. *I love you more than life itself.*

As I love you. He took in the three younger wolves, still eating, but slower now as their bellies filled, and then returned to gaze once again at his mate. *But it's a damned good life, don't you think, Millie, m'love? Damned good.*

Laughter filled his mind. Millie's laughter, followed by her very soft, extremely seductive voice. *I agree. And I have a feeling tonight's going to be even better.*

Suddenly his head filled with images—Millie's images, the fantasies she'd been having while they ran. Matt and Deacon dominating Ric, Daci between her legs in her wolven form, exploring Millie with sharp teeth and her long, mobile tongue. Then as a woman, with fingers and lips and no inhibitions.

Millie taking both Deacon and Matt, and Ric . . . dear Goddess, what she saw him doing with all of them and some very inventive use of soft rope and well-placed knots.

He swallowed, his appetite for the deer suddenly gone,

his desire now to get back to the cabin, to shower and see just how many of Millie's ideas the five of them could accomplish before the deadline Anton had given them.

Millie stood up, shifted for merely a second to cleanse the blood from her fur, and quickly returned to her wolf form. Shifting so easily, so naturally, as if she'd been Chanku forever, a shapeshifter all of her life. The others did the same, and Ric almost sighed with the beauty of the shift, the instantaneous change from wolf to human and once again to wolf. Such a simple thing for each of them, now.

Life altering, to embrace that amazing destiny that could have so easily been denied each of them . . . but for a twist of fate, or a goddess's intervention.

Then Daci flashed Millie a knowing grin that looked almost dangerous coming from the jaws of a wolf. Ric snapped out of his uncharacteristic contemplation. He'd been a wolf longer than any of them. Why, then, should he be worrying and wondering about the *what ifs* and *might have beens*?

The thought was lost as they turned away from the half-eaten doe and headed back toward the main trail. Already Ric could hear the rustling in the brush as coyotes and other scavengers waited impatiently for the wolves to leave.

There'd been one death in the forest tonight. One old and injured doe that would not have survived the winter. Ric was glad Deacon's sensitive nose had picked up her scent. They'd fed well and now others would eat, and the doe had died a clean and merciful death.

Life went on in the forest in the way it was meant to. Predators taking what they needed and nothing more, prey surviving only if they were fast enough or smart enough to avoid wolves or cougars or any other of the many large carnivores in these vast mountainous areas.

Unlike the situation in San Francisco. There, the predators seemed to have all the advantages. For now.

He sent a prayer to Eve, to the Goddess who watched over them, and hoped like hell she was keeping a close eye on Lisa and Tala. And then, almost as an afterthought, he suggested Eve stay close to Anton, just in case anything went wrong.

Chapter 8

Do you think they ever intend to feed us? I'm starving! Lisa shot a quick glance at Tala and then went back to staring at the crappy artwork on the wall in front of her. Her stomach growled.

Not if we don't ask. "Hey! Jerkface! You guys planning to let us starve? Pregnant ladies here . . . we're eating for extras, remember?"

"Shut up, bitch. You'll eat when the boss says you can eat."

"Fuck you."

Leave it to you, Mary Ellen. Lisa bit back a grin. *Subtlety never was your strong suit, sister mine. We need to talk.*

Tala didn't answer for a long time. Lisa heard her sigh, then her soft reply. *Mary Ellen died a long time ago, Lisa. Tala's a survivor. She has to be. And I promise you, we will get out of this alive. There's no acceptable alternative.*

Lisa merely nodded. Tala was right. Mary Ellen had died one night, long ago in a dirty little New Mexico town, beaten half to death by her johns. Then she'd shifted and killed both men. When Tala rose like a phoenix from the ashes, she'd been a new woman—stronger, more self-assured. Capable of surviving anything. Lisa'd never been that brave, no matter what people told her. Not like Mary Ellen . . . like Tala.

Even with her wrists restrained, Lisa still managed to squeeze her sister's hands and hold on. Then she connected again with Tinker. She needed to hear his voice and let his warm words of love calm her racing heart.

Except, what he told her sent her heart rate into overdrive. They could safely shift? They'd always figured that was something they needed to give up after the fifth or sixth month, but according to Liana, and she should know, damn it, they could shift up until they went into labor.

Liana'd been a goddess for more years than any of them could count, so there was no reason to doubt her. According to Tinker she was surprised none of them realized their unborn babies would shift right along with their mothers.

They'd still be pregnant, still awkward and slower than usual, but it was an option.

The only downside, obviously, was that if they shifted, they'd better be prepared to kill everyone in the room. No way did they want these idiots knowing about Chanku shapeshifters.

She squeezed Tala's hands again. Her sister had just gotten the same information from Mik and AJ. And the same warning. She turned and gazed at Lisa, and the half smile on Tala's lips spoke volumes.

Obviously, Tala wouldn't have any problem killing the bastards who held them. Not at all.

Not that they planned to. With any luck, Anton's plan would get them out of here without resorting to shifting or killing. But it was certainly nice to know the option existed.

Lisa's stomach growled again. This time she ignored it.

Beth hoped like hell she could carry this off, but even with both Mik and Logan stalking ahead on all fours and

Igmutaka walking beside her with all his royal attitude, her knees still shook like crazy. They'd arrived by limousine with a ton of luggage—very nice designer suitcases loaded with all kinds of clothing and blankets to give the bags weight. All their stuff was piled neatly on a cart pushed by a young man in uniform, who followed them at a safe distance as they walked across the huge marble and brass foyer.

At least the wolves and Igmutaka were appropriately intimidating. Beth knew there wasn't a darned thing scary about her. Wiping her hands on her dark slacks was out of the question, but her palms were sweaty. Maybe no one would notice.

She shot a quick, sideways glance at Igmutaka. Thank goodness for the spirit guide, because he sure had it all together. Plus, he was so damned gorgeous, everyone would be looking at him, not her.

She hoped.

With that thought in mind, Beth strode as confidently as she could across the hotel lobby to the registration desk. Igmutaka walked beside her and Mik and Logan surged ahead on leashes—two solid black wolves with glinting amber eyes, doing their best to look like large, well-trained guard dogs.

Their nails clicked noisily across the marble floor and Beth felt as if every eye on the place must be on them. With Igmutaka's beauty and two huge, black beasts, it was going to be hard to escape notice.

She'd worn a navy blue tailored suit of Tia's that made her look totally professional, and Igmutaka had borrowed a suit from one of the guys. He looked like royalty with his piercing emerald green eyes and that black hair neatly plaited in dozens of long braids and tied back in a queue hanging almost to his waist. The suit fit him perfectly, and the man had such an air of superiority about him, it was easy to imagine him as the ruler of a nation.

Unfortunately, it was also really easy for Beth to imagine him in her bed. Nick had had the same reaction the first time he'd seen the man. With an almost mystical, androgynous beauty, Igmutaka not only appealed to both sexes, he epitomized sex, and the dark suit only added to his allure.

As they drew closer to the reservation counter, Beth noticed the concierge signaling to security. It looked as if two burly guys in dark suits were going to intercept them before they got to the front desk.

Taking a deep breath, she continued walking as if she and the sexy guy beside her owned the place. From the way Anton had joked around, it sounded as if he'd practically had to buy the hotel to get permission for them to bring Logan and Mik in as guard dogs, so it was probably a pretty close analogy.

She hadn't had the nerve to ask Anton how much extra it had cost to register with animals in a fancy hotel like this, but with any luck and Anton's credit, they'd get through without any problem.

The guys in suits planted themselves in front of Igmutaka and Beth. Both wolves growled low in their throats. The larger of the two men paled a bit and glanced at the animals. Then he stepped forward and addressed Igmutaka.

"I'm sorry, sir, but you can't bring animals into the hotel. Regulations prohibit . . ."

"Excuse me." Another man, another suit, but this one was nodding with deference toward Igmutaka, though he spoke directly to Beth. "My apologies, Ms. Garner. Welcome to the Four Seasons. Your reservation is just now being processed. I'm so sorry. We haven't had a chance to inform personnel"—he flashed a quelling glance at the two men—"of your impending visit. Your Majesty." Smiling, he bowed slightly to Igmutaka, who maintained his aloof and kingly air as if people bowed to him all the time.

He was a spirit guide. Maybe they did. Beth bit back a grin and avoided making eye contact with either Mik or Logan. "Thank you," she said, nodding to the manager. "I'd like to check in and take the beasts up to our rooms. I imagine you'd prefer not to have them here in the lobby any longer than necessary."

It never hurt to be as accommodating as possible. She smiled, the man smiled back and led them quickly to the reservation desk. Igmutaka never said a word, though his eyes followed the movement of everyone around them. Beth had a feeling very little got past the man. Ever.

She signed in under her real name, as Anton had instructed. There was no need to create any more confusion, in case she had to show her identification. As Anton had explained, he was good, but not that good, and there'd been no time to secure counterfeit paperwork for Beth or Igmutaka.

He said he'd described her as the royal's assistant and explained to the hotel manager that she was stationed here in San Francisco, a city the royal family had only recently begun to visit in hopes of securing business for their developing nation. He had, of course, neglected to give a name to said nation, and Beth hoped no one asked.

If they did, she'd bluff, but she signed in and no one said a thing when they handed over the key cards to the room. She checked the number and quickly linked with Igmutaka.

We're in. The room is next door to the one where Tala and Lisa are being held.

Igmutaka nodded imperceptibly in reply. Beth smiled at the bellboy, gave him the room number, and then she and her little band followed him to the elevator.

"They're in." Anton smiled at Luc and the rest of the pack. "I just heard from Beth. They're in their room, next to the one where the girls are being held. Mik's actually picked up Tala's scent, so there's no mistaking they've got the correct location."

"Good." AJ slouched back in his seat. "I feel better just knowing Mik's close by." He glanced in Tinker's direction. "They'll be okay. Mik won't let anything happen to either of our ladies."

Tink nodded, but he kept his eyes on the window as if he expected Lisa to come walking up the front steps at any time. Then he checked his watch. "What time should we get ready?"

"After you eat." Tia stepped out of the kitchen and waved her spatula. "It's nothing fancy. I'm just making hamburgers for everyone, but I don't want you going off without food in your bellies. The last thing we need is a bunch of hungry wolves who can't concentrate on the job."

She smiled, but Anton sent her a quick *thank you* for thinking of food. He tended to forget the practical side of things when faced with a problem, and Tia was right. As wolves, they were more easily distracted when they hadn't eaten in a while. He stood up and obediently headed to the dining room.

The others followed. Keisha went on ahead and helped Tia get the plates on the table. Luc stood beside the double baby swing and teased his daughters. Anton had been in Luc's head earlier, but he'd left as quietly as he'd entered.

Luc's emotions were a mess, his thoughts so twisted up with relief for his wife's safety, his fears for his daughters' future, and his concern for Tala and Lisa, that Anton had backed out as much in self-preservation as to give the man privacy.

The weight of the entire pack rested on Luc's shoulders, much as it often did on Anton's. He didn't envy the young man the job ahead. Once again he sent a prayer to Eve.

Anton felt a sense of calm settle over him and realized it was getting easier all the time to pray to her, a woman who had shared his bed on more than one occasion. Of course, as Keisha had reminded him, he'd also shared Liana's bed, and that had been while she was a goddess.

And afterward, as well. Goddess or woman, they all had the same needs, the same perfectly beautiful bodies. He glanced at Keisha and realized he didn't want to think of the night ahead. Not with the role his mate would be playing and the danger she could be in. Luckily the president appreciated the need for secrecy and understood how important it was, not only for his own safety, but the safety of the Chanku, that they find the one responsible for this latest threat.

This could not go on. They'd been persecuted long enough. It was time to end it—tonight, here and now. *Eve?* He found himself gazing skyward, though he knew she wasn't actually in any sort of heaven overhead. No, she was on the astral plane, in her own *where,* her own *when,* but still he glanced up as he sent his thoughts her way. *Watch over us, Eve. Please. Give Luc the strength he needs to hang on, give Mik and AJ and Tinker the fortitude to get through the night ahead, to be strong for their mates and their unborn children. Watch over the women and their babies, and please, be with me.*

He sighed and turned to Keisha. She watched him with so much love in her eyes it was almost his undoing. *Be with me, Eve . . . and please, don't let me fail any of them, especially my beloved mate.*

Eve didn't answer him. He really didn't expect her to, but he could have sworn he felt a soft breath of wind touch the side of his face. Somehow, that light caress filled him with the strength to accept the danger, the resolve to face the risks they would all be taking.

All of them depending on one another. He reached out and touched the minds of the others spread about the country.

Adam and Liana preparing to shift and run in Montana,

and farther to the east, to Colorado, where the pack had already made a kill and fed. He sensed their growing power, their unity.

Ulrich. The man amazed him. He'd accomplished so much in his sixty-odd years, and yet he was still a young man, not only in body, but at heart as well, ripe with the love of his mate, generous with his support for the younger members of his pack.

Stretching farther, expanding his mental abilities to their limits, he touched on Baylor's mind, on Jake's. They were already back at the apartment, preparing to shift and run as wolves. Baylor was thinking of calling him, but he wanted to be certain the phone line was secure.

Anton stepped out of the busy front room and found a quiet spot in the hallway where he could concentrate on Bay. The link strengthened, and with it he sensed Bay's surprise and then his quick acceptance of Anton contacting him mentally from so many miles away.

Cheaper than a phone call, eh, Bay?

Definitely. Thank you for a wonderful dinner. The meal was perfect, and the wine was excellent. Jake chose a good Sonoma cabernet. We did raise a toast to you and Keisha.

Anton grinned. Leave it to Jake to go for the best. *How were the seating arrangements?*

Baylor's satisfaction was clear, even through the distant link. *They couldn't have been better. It was a productive evening. Hard on Manda, though. She recognized one of the men. He was Milton Bosworth's assistant.* While Anton was still assimilating that shocking news, Bay gave Anton the name of the other young man, a current White House staffer, and possibly the source of their authorizations.

I confirmed his name online, Bay said. *They mentioned names that link them to people I remember. Should help me follow up on others, see if they're actually involved or not. The second two worked for my old agency, which re-*

ported directly to Bosworth. They didn't notice me. They were too busy celebrating the evening's plans.

Anton pinched the bridge of his nose and sighed. The idea of anyone celebrating an assassination attempt made him physically ill. Just as bad, how could they celebrate the kidnapping of two innocent, pregnant women? Wrong. It was just wrong.

Baylor's report was concise and factual. He passed on the names he'd heard, the contacts, even the silly code names he'd picked up at dinner. Then he severed the contact. His pack was waiting.

Tia called them all to dinner. Anton took a moment to compose himself. Food was the last thing on his mind, but Tia was right. They couldn't go into the evening ahead on empty stomachs. It was already after six. They needed to be at the Civic Auditorium by seven thirty.

He sensed his mate and raised his head. Keisha stood in the entrance to the hallway. Her eyes sparkled with mischief as she reached for him.

"I sense you in here thinking of all the things that can go wrong tonight, my love. Don't borrow trouble."

He laughed and linked his fingers with hers. Grumbling, he let her tug him toward the dining room. "You just think you know so much about me."

She pointed him to an empty chair. "Sit. And I do. I know everything about you." She took the seat beside his, leaned over, and kissed his cheek. "So count your blessings, because in spite of all I know, I still love you."

Anton merely rolled his eyes and commented to no one in particular, "And here I thought she was an intelligent woman."

A few laughed. Keisha snorted and passed the plate of hamburgers. Anton took one and glanced at the pack members sitting at the long table, each of them worried about the night to come, and realized what a blessed existence he had. These were his friends, many of them his lovers. They believed in him and trusted him, and they loved one another unconditionally.

Keisha was right. It wasn't all on his shoulders. Each person in this room carried part of the burden. Together they could handle it.

"I just talked to Baylor," he said, focusing on Luc.

Lucien Stone—the leader of the San Francisco pack, the undisputed heir to Ulrich's reign as the San Francisco pack's alpha—nodded, silently urging him to continue.

"We now know who's behind this whole mess." When he mentioned the aide, no one seemed at all surprised. So many of the problems they dealt with went back to the era of Milton Bosworth and his cohorts in Washington. A man verging on insanity, for all intents and purposes, who had been a cog in the political machine in Washington, DC, for far too many years.

Now it appeared that one of his associates had filled the vacuum Bosworth's death had left. A man who took fanaticism to a whole new level, according to Baylor Quinn.

And he was the one behind this entire ridiculous yet deadly plan. Caught up in the frenetic power plays rife in Washington politics, he appeared to have lost touch entirely with reality, and yet he had managed to hang on to enough power to control and direct the remnants of Bosworth's secret agency.

Anton glanced at the clock. "We'll leave for the auditorium after dinner. Igmutaka, Mik, Logan, and Beth are already in place at the hotel. Lisa and Tala know they're close by. They're in contact and okay for now. Our people will make their move to free the women at precisely eight fifty-three. Early enough to get them out quickly, and too late for anyone to get a warning to abort other plans. At that moment, Keisha will be covering the president, and AJ with Nick and Luc as wolves will move into position just behind the presidential box."

He took a bite of his hamburger and chewed thoughtfully. It was such a simple idea—if it worked. "Tinker and I will stick close to the president. Tinker, you'll be in wolf form, but if we need your human strength, I want you ready to shift. All of you will have your standard break-away collars."

Tinker's bark of laughter caught him by surprise. Anton cocked one eyebrow and stared at him.

"You don't think folks'll notice a big naked black guy chasing after the president and his wife?"

AJ snorted. "Hell, this is San Francisco. Why would anyone notice something like that?"

Everyone around the table cracked up. Anton chuckled. "Note to self. Pack extra pants for Tink." He smiled serenely at Tinker. "All taken care of."

Tinker merely shook his head, but the laughter had eased some of the tension in the room. "Just what I've always dreamed of doing," he said mournfully. "Meeting the president bare ass and buck naked with my balls hanging and prick dangling."

Anton shot him a quick grin, but he shook his head. "Hopefully it won't come to that. Besides, I don't think that prick of yours knows how to dangle. I've only seen it at attention."

Luc's mumbled, "You ain't kiddin'," brought more laughs.

Anton continued. "If you have to shift, it means we've got problems, so hopefully, you won't need those spare pants. The wolves are supposed to attack the president at exactly eight fifty-five. This is where it gets dicey. We don't know if there's a second plan in motion or if we're it, but I can't believe they're counting entirely on us. I've got a feeling we're there for our ability to distract and divert attention, not actually to complete the mission they've given us."

"So what do you plan to do?" Luc sat back in his chair and gazed at the others at the table. "Other than not kill the president when we're supposed to, what can you do that will draw the others out?"

"There will be a complete blackout in the Civic Auditorium at precisely eight fifty-five. All lighting, all power, down to individual cell phones and radios. The generator will not work, the emergency lights will fail. It will be a complete and total power failure, at which time we will move the president to safety and hopefully snag whoever is trying to kill him. We need the ones involved, and we need them alive."

It wasn't quite the reaction he'd expected. The room had gone absolutely silent. Every single person stared at him as if he'd lost his mind. Anton frowned and his gaze connected with Keisha's. She had the strangest expression on her face. Almost as if she were going to . . .

Keisha burst into laughter. "They're all convinced you're absolutely nuts, m'love."

He shrugged and smiled at her. "I get the same feeling." Flattening both palms on the table, he gazed at the others and said, "Any questions?"

There was no humor in AJ's voice when he said, "Yeah. I've got a bunch, but the main one is, how the fuck do you intend to carry off this oh-so-critical power failure?"

"Sex."

"What?" Tia had started clearing the table. She stopped with her hands full of plates and stared at him.

"More precisely, sex magic. The power of sex. We've done it before. Luc, the time we saved Ulrich, that was nothing but combining our sexual energy. When you guys got together and saved my life, it was your energy, your sexual energy, that gave you the strength to share your life force with me. I'm going to be drawing from the pack in Montana, Ulrich's group in Colorado, and Baylor and his pack in Maine. All of them, reaching orgasm at precisely eight fifty-five Pacific time, minds open and sharing their energy with me. I will harness that energy and use it to shut down the auditorium. Trust me. It can be done."

Tinker glanced at AJ, then at Luc. His disbelief warred with his obvious anger, but both emotions were right there on the surface, for everyone to see.

Including Anton. He'd expected disbelief, but not this intense level of angry frustration. Tinker looked ready to take a swing at him.

"Anton, have you ever done anything like this before? How do you know you can shut down a place as big as the Civic Auditorium? How the hell do you expect to grab energy from DC, Colorado, and Montana when you're here in San Francisco?"

Anton caught Tink's angry glare and held it without flinching as he stood up. "Tia? Jazzy? Can you come in here please? I don't want to leave you in the dark."

The women stepped out of the kitchen. Anton closed his eyes, held his hands together beneath his chin, and the entire house plunged into darkness.

"Holy shit."

Tinker's soft exclamation brought an answering chuckle from Luc. "And to think he did that without sex. Impressive. But, can you turn them back on again?"

The lights flashed back on. The hum from the kitchen announced that the refrigerator had been off as well. Now it was back up and running.

Everyone applauded, which was a good thing. Anton really didn't want any of them to hear his sigh of relief. He hadn't been entirely certain he could carry this off without the added burst of energy from the others.

He took a deep breath, calming as he felt Keisha's thoughts melding with his, soothing his nerves, reminding him of her unwavering love. He nodded in her direction and once again took his seat at the table.

"Remember, my friends. I am a wizard as well as Chanku,

and I constantly work to keep my powers strong, to improve my abilities. I have to believe that with the power our packmates will share with me tonight, and with our Goddess, a woman we all knew and loved when she was one of us, standing beside me, that I can do as I have promised. If I'm unable to darken the entire auditorium, I know that I can at least kill the area where the president will be sitting, enough that we should be able to get him to safety."

This time Tinker's gaze was level and filled with respect. Anton knew how worried the man was. He wanted to tell him everything was going to be fine, that they'd be entirely successful and no blood would be spilled tonight. He couldn't promise him a thing. Not in good faith. "Tink, for what it's worth, when I say we've got Eve with us, I'm not speaking in a metaphorical sense. She's here, aware and part of everything we do. She takes her role seriously. She knows what's going on, and I trust her, as our Goddess, and as our friend."

Tinker nodded. "Believe me, Anton, I've been praying to her since the minute Lisa and Tala got nabbed. But I'm counting on you, too." He flattened his hands on the table and shoved himself to his feet. Six feet, six inches tall, with hands that could palm a basketball and shoulders so broad he barely fit through some doors. Physically powerful with a brilliant, logical mind, and yet he was willing to put his faith in a goddess he couldn't see and a wizard he didn't always trust.

Humbled, Anton watched as Tinker headed into the kitchen to help Tia and Jazzy with the cleanup before they left tonight. He was like that. Martin "Tinker" McClintock. A good man who loved his mate more than life, who couldn't wait for the daughter Lisa carried to finally make her appearance.

In a lot of ways, Anton saw Tinker as the backbone of this entire operation. If he had Tink on his side, believing he could do what he set out to do, then Anton knew they'd succeed.

He carried his plate into the kitchen. Baylor's mental voice touched his mind, surprisingly powerful considering the immense distance. Generally Anton had to initiate contact with the ones in Maine. He stopped, plate in hand, and listened.

We're on the zoo grounds, ready to run. The night's clear, the ground is frozen. We'll do our best. I wanted you to know we can feel the link, feel your mind as if you're much closer. For some reason, it's clear and strong tonight. Good luck, Anton. Let us know the moment Lisa and Tala are free and all is right.

His voice faded away, but the connection remained, the sense of Bay and Manda, Shannon and Jake, as if they were only a few blocks away, not almost three thousand miles. He was still marveling at the strength of their mind-speaking when Ulrich's voice rolled softly through his thoughts.

We had a hell of a run tonight. Millie's eyeing Deacon and Matt with a look I would describe as dangerously speculative. Daci's got her eye on everyone. His soft laughter sounded relaxed and so upbeat Anton felt himself relax just a bit more as Ulrich continued in a quiet, conversational manner.

Just wanted to let you know we can feel you like you're right here with us. We'll be ready. Good luck, Anton. Be safe. We'll want the details when this is over.

You'll have them.

Details. So damned many details, and each dependent upon the success of another. Anton frowned. He caught Keisha smiling at him.

"I'm going in to get my things together," she said. "We'll be ready to leave shortly, whenever you are."

He nodded. Both he and AJ would be wearing dark suits—the Washington, DC, Beltway look, Baylor called it.

He'd slick his hair back, tie it neatly at his nape, but AJ insisted this was San Francisco. Short hair wasn't necessary to create the look.

Suddenly, Adam's voice in his mind shocked him with its clarity and stopped him in his tracks. *Liana and I want to wish you well tonight. We're all going to be ready when you need us. Just wanted to confirm that the link was strong and you should be able to grab whatever we can send.*

Voices from such a distance had never been so clear, which meant that whatever energy they shared should be even stronger than he'd hoped. Anton headed down the hallway to the guestroom Luc had given to him and Keisha. He caught up to her at the doorway, grabbed her around the waist, and pulled her close.

"I love you. Be careful tonight." He kissed her soundly, feeling almost carefree. She kissed him back, but it was obvious she wondered what had gotten into him.

"The connection." He couldn't have stopped grinning if he'd had to. "I've been worried about the distance, about taking power from such a long way away, but the connections are all strong and clear. Baylor and Jake could have been in the next room. The same with Adam and even Ulrich. Ric's usually not that powerful—he could have been sitting beside me and speaking."

Keisha leaned back so she could look into his eyes. He loved that little frown between her brows. It made him want to kiss her until she laughed, until she felt the same confidence that he was feeling.

And then Stefan's voice touched him. The beloved voice of the man who was like a brother to him, one he loved above all other men—his lover, his closest friend. Keisha's eyes danced and Anton knew she heard him as well.

We're with you in spirit, Anton, though about now I think I'd rather be with you in person. Xandi and Mei have Oliver and me cuffed to the bed. And you know that scary look Mei gets in her eyes?

Anton swore he heard Mei and Xandi laughing, but that was impossible, wasn't it?

Well, she's got it now, and so does Xandi. We'll do our best to hold out, but if you get a blast a few minutes early, I sure hope you can use it. Oh, shit . . .

Anton raised his eyes and caught Keisha's grin. Then all they could hear was Stefan's aroused moan before the connection ended. "I've never had such clear mental connections when we're this far apart." He shook his head. "I don't understand."

Keisha covered his hand with hers. "I do. Accept the fact Eve's helping. Don't you think that's a sign she's with us?"

He'd hoped Eve would be able to do something, but he realized now he really hadn't counted on it. Not on anything as visible, as real as this, but Keisha was right.

She had to be right.

He stepped into the bedroom and closed the door. The voices in the rest of the house faded as he shut the two of them inside the small room. He felt as if he should be doing something—anything more than taking a quick shower and merely dressing in his good black suit, but there was nothing else. Nothing at all.

His thoughts drifted to Bay and the others in DC. What was it like, running as wolves in the midst of the nation's capital? Were they at risk? Able to find the privacy they needed? He thought of connecting, and just as quickly extinguished the link before it opened.

He had to trust his pack. They'd not failed him before, and he couldn't micromanage the whole evening. He could only play the role he'd given himself. With that thought in mind, Anton stripped out of his clothes and headed for the shower.

Chapter 9

Bare branches rattled with the stiff evening breeze. Snow lay in a few bare patches, though the ground was mostly clear. Frozen, coated with ice, but clear.

Steam billowed from their warm muzzles as Bay and the small pack raced through the parklands of the National Zoo. Their feet pounded on the hard-packed earth and paved pathways, and the sounds of the city were muted by the trees and shrubs, the buildings and pens and cages. It had only been two days since their last shift, their last run through the frozen forests of their Maine home, but Bay couldn't get over how good this felt, how much he'd missed the connection with the natural world around him.

As natural as it could be, running through a zoo in the midst of the nation's capital with the scent of alien animals all about. And, with his good Rolex strapped to his upper left leg. Manda had gotten a little bit hysterical, laughing so hard she could barely fasten the expensive wristwatch to a wolf, and Jake had certainly managed his share of jokes at Bay's expense, but they had that frickin' timetable of Anton's to stick to.

It would definitely be a story for their children one day. Would one of those as yet unknown children be conceived tonight? He put the thought from his mind and tried to lose himself in the run, in the sensation of his broad paws striking the ground, in the chill air rushing past his muzzle and rippling over his dark coat. He scented the animals in the cages they passed, relieved that they didn't seem overly stressed by their confinement. Still he sensed their curiosity, even their territorial displays as he and his small pack ran past.

And then he wondered—when had he begun to think of this as his pack? Jake was the one who owned the property in Maine, the one who had helped Bay embrace his Chanku birthright, and Shannon was definitely an alpha bitch. Manda would always defer to the others, but that was her nature. She could be tough when tough was needed, had even killed when it had been called for, but she was essentially softer, sweeter. Exactly what Baylor needed. What he wanted.

And she wanted his child. He still couldn't believe she was willing, even excited about a baby. The whole concept scared the crap out of him. Neither of them had known a normal childhood. How could they possibly figure out how to raise a baby without totally screwing up?

Not only that, Manda had agreed to be his wife. When he'd asked her, for some reason he'd expected a negative response, but she loved him. She wanted him as her legal husband even as she'd already claimed him as her mate. He wanted to raise his nose to the heavens and howl, but that wouldn't do. Not here, in the midst of the grounds of the National Zoo. So he put his nose down and ran. Ran with his mate beside him, his packmates up ahead. His pack. Jake's pack. Did it matter? They loved one another, needed one another. That was what counted.

There were others he could count on. After always thinking of himself as a loner, he wasn't alone anymore. It was good, and it was scary. Frightening when he thought of the responsibility tonight, the idea that whatever energy they could create would help to save his sisters' lives. He'd always avoided that sort of responsibility for Lisa and Tala.

They'd been of his blood, but not really kin. Not until he discovered the amazing heritage they shared. All of them, Chanku shapeshifters. Little Lisa and Mary Ellen, now known as Tala.

Shapeshifters. United by a heritage that was more powerful than any other blood link.

And tonight, they were in terrible trouble.

Thank the Goddess, Anton had given him a way to help. Now that he had a connection to his sisters, he understood their worth, their value. How his life, his happiness, depended on their lives and their happiness. Their safety.

That was the way of the pack. They looked out for one another. Loved one another. Knew they could count on every single member should they ever need help.

And so he ran, with thoughts of Lisa and Tala in the forefront of his mind, and his love for his mate, for Jake and Shannon, filling his heart.

The night seemed to grow darker in spite of the lighting that illuminated trails and cast strange shadows. They ran deeper into the small forest that made up the zoo grounds, running as they would in the woods near their home. The smells here were at once alien and yet familiar. Prey, yet not, as they raced past pens of zebra and gazelle and some kind of goat, and predators that would have had him pausing in the wild to check for danger.

Lions and tigers and bears. His nose couldn't stop twitching. He sensed the curiosity of those behind bars as the four of them ran, slipping in and out of the forested parkland, skirting pens and cages and even scaring up the occasional wild critter running free on the grounds.

They would not hunt tonight. Not after that amazing meal they'd had earlier. What a day, to go from a weekend getaway to a flight into Washington, DC, to dinner at one of the finest restaurants within the entire capital city, and now to running as wolves in the presence of creatures from all over the world.

And then he thought of Rolf, the old friend who had set off the madness of their day with his warning, and he wondered if the man's soul had found rest. There was no doubt in his mind that Rolf had died today because he'd warned Baylor.

So much to think of, which was unusual. Generally when he ran as the wolf, his mind was free of the worries of men. Under normal circumstances, he'd be thinking of the scents on the night air, the way his mate looked as she raced through the darkness.

Under normal circumstances. But there was nothing normal about tonight. He hoped Anton had been able to use the information they'd gathered. Hoped he could harness the energy Baylor and the others would be sharing tonight.

Manda paused and glanced his way. Her sides heaved in and out with each breath she took, and the glittering light in her amber eyes stopped him dead in his tracks. Bay's nose went up and he sniffed the air, nose twitching, ears forward in heady anticipation. The rich aroma of Manda's heat tickled his sensitive nostrils. He growled deep—the low rumble rolled out of his chest.

He noticed Jake sniffing at Shannon and realized she was in heat as well. Both females, receptive and potentially fertile, though he knew of Shannon's difficulty trying to conceive. Jake had shared their frustration with him, how her body had healed, but she'd not had any luck yet on the occasions when they had tried to fertilize an egg. Jake had feared that the problem could be his, had wondered if his years of excess might have harmed his own ability to reproduce.

Jake said they had talked of seeing Logan about it, now that they had a doctor who truly understood Chanku physiology, but not yet. Not until they'd tried at least one more time. Bay watched as Jake drew closer to Shannon, as his dark muzzle disappeared beneath her tail. She snarled and shifted away.

It was too early in the evening.

He glanced at the watch strapped to his leg. It had one of those stretchy metal bands, so he knew it wouldn't damage his arm should he have to shift into his human form in a hurry, but according to his spiffy Rolex, they had almost half an hour before Anton needed their energy.

Mating as wolves took less time than they spent as humans, and yet the intensity of their orgasm was more powerful. It lasted longer, coiled deeper within the heart and mind, and that was what Anton needed tonight. What Lisa and Tala needed.

No matter what any of them wanted, they had a purpose to fulfill. Which made him wonder about getting his mate with child when he knew how much Jake and Shannon wanted one of their own. His thoughts were spinning and he wished for that feral state, the forgetfulness that usually accompanied his wolven self. Why the hell was he worrying so much about his human issues?

Then he glanced at Manda and caught her watching him with an intensity that brought him up short.

Our choice to have a child is not dependent on Shannon's ability to conceive. It's our choice, Bay. What we want, what we are able to do. Can you agree with me on that?

He felt the tension ease from his limbs. Damn, there was something so sexy about Manda when she stepped up to her role as his bitch. *I can agree with whatever you want,* he said. *You are my mate. The one who matters, who counts. The only one.*

She spun about and took off running. With his nose still twitching, Bay followed close behind.

* * *

Adam watched closely as Liana slipped out of her warm sweats and stood beside the door, waiting on him. He disrobed, crossed the room, and placed one very chaste kiss on her shoulder.

His cock didn't think it was all that chaste and rose to attention. He ignored the rush of arousal, the need he felt to pull her close and hold her, to make love to her. The afternoon had crawled so slowly as he'd waited to run with her, finally to mate with her, but now that the time had come, he felt as if everything had gone into fast forward. He didn't want to rush anything, but they had that damned timetable to adhere to.

Did he want to have his mating with Liana linked to a stupid clock? He frowned at her as she cupped his cheek in her palm. "It's not a stupid clock we're linking our mating to, my love. It's saving the lives of two women we love, saving their babies. You're a healer. You have to understand that."

He practically snorted. "I understand it, and logically I think it's great, but damn it all, Liana, I want you. Now. I always want you. I never seem to get enough of you. Will this need ease at all once we're mated?"

Her laughter shivered over him like a cooling breeze, though it didn't cool his desire for her at all.

"No. I think it's going to be even stronger, this desire we have for each other. That's a good thing. Now come. I want time to speak with Eve, if she'll hear me."

She handed a necklace to him, and it took a moment before he realized what he was holding—a beautiful little timepiece on a silver chain. Anton and his damned timetable! Now what the hell was he supposed to do with this?

Liana opened the door and stepped out onto the icy step. Adam was right behind her. She shifted and glanced at him. *Put it around my neck. Make sure it's tight. We'll need it later.*

Laughing softly, Adam fastened the chain around her neck. No way was he going to admit how impressed he was—he hadn't even thought about how they were going to stay on time. Liana yipped once and raced down the stairs. Adam shut the door, shifted, and followed close behind. The snow was packed hard leading from their steps to the woods, and they practically flew across the surface, with Liana holding the lead. He wasn't certain where she was headed, though he had his suspicions.

He was right. They raced through the woods, climbing higher up the mountain until they reached Eve's meadow. The place where her ashes were scattered, where he'd tried to kill himself.

Where Liana and Eve, now their Goddess, had saved his life in spite of himself. He stared across the smooth expanse, at the untouched snow reflecting the cold light of the winter's moon, the bare branches ringing the edge, and he felt a welcoming sense of peace.

This place should haunt him. It should hold nothing but sadness for him, but Adam recognized it for what it was. This meadow and what it represented had saved him. He'd come here to die, but he'd been reborn.

Because of Eve. Because of Liana and the love of his pack. So many who cared for him, who loved him in spite of himself, had come together to save his life. In so doing, they'd managed to save his soul. He paused a moment longer and sniffed the air, curious to see if he could sense Eve in this place, but there was nothing more than the chill night air, the spicy scent of pine and cedar . . . and the rich, seductive scent of his mate.

He turned his gaze on Liana for a moment, appreciating her beauty, her regal stance, her gray coat shining silvery in the moonlight. She watched him carefully, as if weighing his reaction to the place she'd led him.

I wondered if this was where you wanted to come, he said. *It's a good choice.*

It's the only choice.

Liana gazed at him with such pure and absolute love that Adam felt an ache in his heart. To think he'd been so lucky, so blessed, that he could have two such amazing women love him. *I'm one lucky bastard, Liana. You and Eve have both changed my life.*

There was a soft *pop*, as if the pressure had changed, and suddenly Eve was standing there, bathed in moonlight, gowned in a flowing white dress that swirled about her ankles. Her eyes swirled from gray to green to blue, and her blond hair blew about her shoulders, carried by some ethereal breeze Adam neither sensed nor felt.

Her laughter sent shivers across his spine, but there was no sense of arousal, no need to reach for her. She was Eve, his Goddess. The woman he had once loved. She flashed him a saucy wink, reminding him of that woman.

"You are that, Adam," she said. "One very lucky bastard."

She waved her hand. Immediately, a clear bubble encased the three of them. The snow disappeared and the two wolves stood in knee-deep grass with wild primroses blooming all about. Adam was the first to shift. Liana followed suit, grabbing for the chain that miraculously remained around her neck. He reached for her hand and squeezed her fingers.

She dipped her head, bowing slightly to Eve. "We wanted to ask your blessing, Eve. It seemed only right."

Eve's smile widened. "Ah, Liana. I owe you much, and you and Adam already have my blessing. You were meant for this life, Liana. Meant to be a flesh and blood woman, to mate with one man, to bear his children." She shook her head and smiled again at Adam. "Remember how I fought you in the beginning? How I ran from your love? I should have listened to my heart, Adam. I was not meant to be mated. I know that now. I loved you, but not enough. Not ever enough."

Her gaze rested on Liana again. "All those men you took to your bed, Liana. Remember? Across the ages, so many men as you searched for power through their energy. That wasn't it at all. You were searching for the love you've found with Adam. I can see it so clearly, now. I've had no need to call any man to my bed. My power comes from the love all of you share, one with the other, each of you with the pack. It's enough. It's more than enough, and it makes me almost complete."

Adam cocked his head to one side. "Almost?"

"Almost. There is one thing I ask of you, when you mate tonight. Liana, I want you to conceive. I want you both to create a baby with this mating. Please tell me it's not too much to ask." She smiled at Liana and then turned to Adam.

He sensed her hesitancy, as if she feared she'd overstepped her bounds, but her request went straight to his heart. Before she could explain herself, Adam reached for Eve's hand, so that he now held on to both women he loved, who loved him. "It's Liana's choice to have a child, just as it was yours. But, if we have a little girl . . ." He turned to Liana and saw hope in her eyes. "If we have a girl, I would like to call her Eve."

Tears sparkled in Eve's swirling eyes and there was sadness in her smile. Had he made a mistake in speaking his heart?

Eve shook her head. "Not a mistake, Adam. I would be honored. But Liana, Adam's right. If you're not ready . . ."

Liana stepped forward and drew Eve into a warm embrace. "I am more than ready. I just never . . ." She choked back a sob. "All those years, I never once dreamed motherhood could be mine. Even when Adam and I've talked about children, it hasn't felt real. Adam? Are you sure?"

He nodded. Then, before he had time to think of what he was doing, Adam pulled Eve into his arms and kissed her. Her lips felt warm and alive against his, her body molded against his as if she'd never left him, and yet he felt none of the arousal, none of the heat her touch had once fired in his blood.

Still, he loved her. He would always love her, though that love had changed from one of passion to admiration, from desire to friendship. "Thank you," he said, leaning away from her lush mouth, yet still holding her in his embrace. "For the love you gave me so unselfishly when you lived, for the care you give all of us now. Please, watch over us, but tonight, I beg of you, be with Anton. With Luc and Tinker, Mik and AJ. All of them. Keep Lisa and Tala safe."

Eve grinned at him. There was nothing goddesslike at all about the smile she flashed first at Adam and then Liana. "Don't worry. I'm all over that mess down in San Francisco, which is why I'm leaving the two of you now."

She touched the tiny clock hanging at Liana's throat. "This will remain with you as you shift. It reminds me that time is drawing short and we've got quite a fight ahead of us. Shift so you don't get cold when I pull the protection away. Blessings on your mating, and on the two of you as you live your lives. On your children, and especially on the child you conceive tonight." Then once again she gave Adam a very ungoddess-like wink. "This is the little one I didn't get to have, Adam. The child you and I might have created if I'd lived."

Liana's stricken glance tugged at Adam's heart, and her regrets filled his mind, but Eve shook her head and squeezed Liana's fingers. "No regrets. I have none. Neither should you nor Adam. This is all as it should be. For all the angry words I hurled at you, I don't believe now that what happened was your fault. The Mother has a greater hand in our lives than any of us realize. Keep that in mind as the hours unfold. I have to go now. Take care, and love one another always."

She waved her hand, the clear bubble winked out with

an audible *pop*. Adam and Liana, wolves once again, stood motionless in the meadow, knee deep in the thick green grass, surrounded by a magical circle of pale pink primroses.

AJ met Anton in the front room. Dressed in a black suit almost identical to the one Anton wore, he was so devastatingly handsome, Anton worried he might have erred in choosing AJ Temple as the one to keep his human form.

They wanted to avoid attention, not beg for it, and there was no way in hell that AJ could walk into a room and not have the eyes of everyone there, male and female, watching him.

Just then Nick, Luc, and Tinker trotted into the room. Entirely black, Luc would blend easily with the shadows, as would Nick with his dark brown and black coat. Tinker's gold highlights within the heavy black fur would help draw attention away from the smaller, reddish brown wolf trotting into the room behind him. At least that was Anton's fervent hope.

Keisha. Dear Goddess, she was beautiful, and so damned courageous Anton felt like cheering. For now, though, he merely grabbed up the small bag of clothing he'd packed, nodded to AJ, and then put the breakaway collars on Keisha and Tinker. AJ did the same for Luc and Nick. If by chance any of them needed to shift, the collars wouldn't stop them.

Jazzy and Tia stood together in the doorway to the kitchen, holding tightly to each other's hands. Tia's babies slept and the house was quiet. Without a doubt, they had the most difficult job, waiting here until the night was over, Lisa and Tala were freed, and everyone was home safely.

Anton went to Tia and kissed her soundly. "I will keep your man safe, Tia. Trust me. And Jazzy, I've been in constant contact with Logan and, as much as I hate to say it, I think he's having fun."

Jazzy's laughter seemed to have a calming effect on everyone. "Don't worry about us. Tia and I will be fine, and if, by chance, the terrible twins are asleep at five minutes to nine, you can count on us adding our own burst of power to your project."

Biting back unexpected laughter, he nodded deferentially to both young women. "You are most generous. Damn. Almost makes me wish I was hanging out here with you two."

"Go." Tia leaned over, kissed his cheek, and shoved him. Then she turned her attention to the black wolf, and Anton carefully blocked the words she spoke to Luc.

There were some things even a wizard accepted as private.

AJ drove carefully through heavy traffic toward the center of town. Gazing out the window, thinking of the night ahead, Anton felt the soft vibration of his cell phone in his coat pocket and immediately took the call.

Already there were changes in his plans, but he had to agree, this might just make things easier in the long run. "AJ, we need to go directly to the Fairmont. The president has asked us to accompany him to the Civic Auditorium. He wants us with him instead of the assigned security detail."

AJ didn't question him. He merely caught a left on California and headed east toward the hotel. Finally he glanced at Anton and asked, "Any idea why the change in plans?"

Anton shook his head. "He's got new security assigned to him tonight. Doesn't recognize any of them, and he doesn't want his wife anywhere near them or the auditorium. He wants Keisha to take the First Lady's position before they leave the hotel so his wife can remain in the penthouse. He thinks she'll be safer there. It's bad when the man can't trust his own people."

When no one made any comment, he added, "And he wants me to leave one of you there, to safeguard her." He glanced at the four wolves in the open back of the SUV. "Nick? Are you comfortable with guarding the president's wife? I know it's a lot to ask, to leave you on your own, but . . ."

I'm okay with it. Just leave me a pair of pants.

Laughing, Anton turned around in his seat. "What is it with you guys and this sudden modesty? I don't understand."

AJ glanced his way and winked at him. Then he made a left on Mason Street and pulled up in front of the luxurious Fairmont Hotel.

Anton leashed all four wolves and got out of the vehicle, while AJ informed the valet that it was to remain here, in front of the hotel, until they returned with the president and First Lady.

They showed their paperwork and got inside the tightly secured lobby without any problem. Anton nodded to the young man in military dress who was there to lead them to the presidential suite.

There was an impromptu press conference with the president's press secretary, quickly arranged by the president for just this purpose, going on near the far side of the huge lobby. As hoped, Anton's small pack managed to cross behind the gathering without attracting notice. Within minutes their guide was knocking on the door to the penthouse, the door opened, and Anton and his group entered.

The security guard who answered the door did not appear pleased by their presence. He turned, nodded stiffly to someone just out of sight, and left the penthouse. He moved too quickly for Anton to get a good look at his thoughts, though the sense of anger and frustration was clear.

The president stepped into the main room as soon as the door had closed. "Mr. Cheval?" He smiled and held out his hand. "It's a pleasure finally to meet you, sir." As he shook Anton's hand, he looked wonderingly at the four wolves sitting patiently behind Anton and AJ. "All of you." Then he turned, smiling even broader. "My wife, gentlemen."

The resemblance was striking. Anton bowed over her hand, but he couldn't quiet the soft chuckle. "This will work even better than I had hoped," he said. He turned to his mate. Her ears pricked forward, and he heard her laughter in his head.

Here, my love? Or should we do this privately?

"Has the room been swept for cameras, listening devices, anything that might record what we say or do?"

The president shook his head. "I can't guarantee anything." He turned away, took a seat on the couch, and pulled his wife down beside him. "Everything has felt off this evening. My regular security team was switched out for all new men about half an hour ago. I'm not certain, but I had the feeling our luggage had been searched. This room does not feel secure, which is why I asked that you leave one of your . . ." He shook his head, grinning. "One of your *associates* behind."

Luc's voice slipped into Anton's mind. *Tink and I will make a quick check around the premises. Listening devices of any kind, cameras, anything that doesn't belong.*

AJ unleashed both of them. Tinker headed for the bedrooms, while Luc did a sweep of the living area and the terrace. AJ followed Tinker first, then met up with Luc. Within minutes they were all back in the sitting room. AJ handed a small, black bag to Anton.

He dumped the contents out on the coffee table—a collection of various electronic snooping devices.

AJ said, "They're all here. The guys found cameras in each room, six listening devices spaced to pick up the entire apartment. I've disabled all of them. It shouldn't make anyone suspicious. Clearing stuff like this out of a room is a standard procedure, so I doubt anyone's going to suspect us for finding it." He turned to the president. "Sir, you had a good reason for not feeling secure."

The president glanced at his wife. "Our new security people said they did a complete sweep of the room. I wonder if they're the ones who planted this crap?"

Instead of replying, Anton glanced at his watch. "We need to hurry. Keisha? Sweetheart, why don't you go with the First Lady and get ready. I want your hair, makeup, everything the same." He leaned over and unfastened her collar. She glanced at the president's wife and winked, much to the lady's obvious surprise. Then Keisha trotted in the direction of the bedroom.

Anton stayed in her head. *Be gentle. She knows what to expect, but until you've actually seen someone shift . . .*

Keisha's soft laughter echoed in his mind, and they all heard the First Lady's gasp of shock. Anton grinned. "It appears my wife just shifted." He reached into the bag and grabbed a pair of sweatpants and a T-shirt. "Nick, why don't you go ahead and shift. At least you can keep the president's wife company while you wait here." AJ removed Nick's collar, and the young man rose from four paws on the ground to two human feet.

Tall and slim, he still had a youthful build, with broad, bony shoulders, dark olive skin, and long, dark hair. His high cheekbones and dark coloring could have been Middle Eastern or Native American, but he was beautiful no matter what his race. He nodded his head in respect as he quickly dressed.

The president shook his head slowly, obviously bemused. "I know what you told me, but if I hadn't seen that, I never would have believed it." As soon as Nick slipped into his sweats, the president shook his hand. "I am trusting you with the safety of the most important woman in my life."

"I'll keep her safe. You have my promise."

"Well? What do you think?"

Keisha—at least he thought it was his mate—stood in the open doorway wearing a dark teal blue gown. With heels, she stood almost as tall as the president, and with the subtle use of makeup and her long hair tucked up under the shorter wig, she no longer looked anything like herself.

Grinning broadly, the First Lady stepped up beside her. Instead of showcasing their differences, her proximity only made their similarities more profound. Other than her slightly lighter complexion, they could have been twins.

Anton checked his watch once again. "Ma'am. Meet Nick Barden. Nick will stay with you this evening. He'll be in mental contact with me at all times and can keep you informed on what's happening. His mate is involved in the rescue of our two kidnapped pack members, so he's got a link to that action as well. He'll shift into his wolf form if anyone comes to the room. This floor is supposed to be secure, but we really can't know for certain. Don't allow anyone in. Remember, you're not supposed to be here. Don't answer the door unless it's one of us—Nick will know since we can all communicate telepathically."

The president kissed his wife, a long, slow kiss that reminded all of them how serious the night had just become. Then he held his arm out to Keisha. She wrapped her fingers around his arm, and with all the grace of a queen—or the wife of a president—allowed him to escort her from the room.

Anton glanced back in time to see the First Lady fold her hands as if in prayer. Nick stood beside her, but she seemed totally unaware of his presence. Her eyes were on her husband as he stepped swiftly out of the room. Then her glance flashed to Anton.

Once again he dipped his head in respect. "We'll keep him safe. I promise. Nick will watch over you. If you have any questions, ask him." He shrugged. "Very few know of our existence, but I'm sure Nick can answer whatever concerns you have. It might help you pass the time a bit faster."

"Thank you."

Her surprisingly calm smile was the last thing he saw as he quietly shut the door and followed the others to the waiting elevator.

Keisha smiled and acknowledged greetings and shouts from the people pressing close against the ropes separating the president's small entourage from the huge crowd. She clung to the president's arm, laughing and obviously enjoying herself while Anton and AJ scanned the hundreds of people surrounding them. Luc and Tinker pulled just hard enough against their leashes, baring teeth and managing to make eye contact with almost everyone straining for a closer look.

It had the effect of forcing the crowd back, as if a subliminal fear of the huge beasts controlled their desire to draw close to the president and his wife. His press secretary had put out a statement about the special security teams guarding the president tonight, the fact that they were helping to promote new legislation for the protection of endangered species, which, of course, had brought in an entirely new group of protestors for the evening's event.

And then there was AJ. Tall and gorgeous, with his perfect features and powerful build, he looked more like a professional model than a security guard—or wolf handler. Except Luc's black wolven coat was a perfect match to AJ in his dark suit—two powerful animals, both intelligent and in complete control. Anton wished he had AJ's charisma, his confidence when all eyes were on him. Only when he was dealing with magic did Anton feel some semblance of control.

This was not one of those moments, and he hoped he looked a lot calmer than he felt. Of course, he could blame most of his nerves on his fear for Keisha. He'd never asked her to play such a pivotal part in any of his dealings outside family before. Everything tonight, every step they took, every minute detail they had planned, scared the crap out of him.

It took an act of will, but he kept his nervousness locked deep inside and stayed close to the president, with Tinker keeping the tension tight on the leash. Anton's pride in Keisha gave him the strength and presence that was so natural to him with his pack or his business dealings, and yet sorely lacking tonight, with so many depending on him for their safety.

But Keisha? She was magnificent. She *was* the First Lady.

In what felt like hours but was merely a couple of minutes, they'd reached the roped-off area front and center in the auditorium where Keisha and the president took their seats. A few other couples were already there and waiting, people carefully chosen who were familiar to the president but had never met his wife.

So far, so good. Anton and Tinker took up their position standing just below the stage in front of the sectioned-off area. AJ and Luc stood to one side but still close enough to respond quickly, and while everything was quiet, for now, anyway, Anton took a moment to check in on the various members around the city and across the country.

It was already after eight. Everything was scheduled to come together in a little over half an hour. He cast his thoughts far and wide, sensed the pack in Montana, the ones in Colorado, the four from Maine now racing through a forested park in Washington, DC.

And then, to ease the tension building inside, he thought about Eve and wondered if she might be near.

The soft brush of a summer breeze across his cheek told him their Goddess had not forgotten just how much her Chanku needed her and how very much Anton counted on her to stand beside him tonight.

Chapter 10

Ulrich stepped out of the shower. As he reached for a towel, he caught Millie staring at herself in the bathroom mirror. He didn't say anything as he dried himself off with the big towel she'd left for him. He loved watching her, especially when she wasn't paying any attention to him at all.

Like now. He grinned, enjoying the view of her trim, naked ass, tight little waist, and the perfect swell of her breasts. He even liked that little wrinkle between her eyebrows that she got as she frowned at her cloudy image in the steamy mirror

After a bit she planted her hands on her hips and jerked her head in his direction, glaring at him. "Look at us," she demanded. "What do you see?"

He stepped up behind her and wrapped his arms around her sleek body. Her skin felt like warm, living silk. She was still damp from her shower and her scent, a mix of shampoo and soap and clean, warm woman, filled his nostrils when he pulled her close against his chest. His cock immediately went from parade rest to full attention, and the first thing he thought was, if they didn't step apart really fast, they'd never make it to the kids' cabin.

Of course, stepping away from her was the furthest thing from his mind, until he palmed her breasts and caught her nipples between his fingers. Instead of reacting the way he had hoped, Millie raised her head and glared at his reflection. "Ric. I asked you a question. What do you see?"

He chuckled at the minor setback, nuzzled the sensitive skin beneath her left ear, and ran his tongue around the shell-like curve. "I see the most beautiful woman I've ever known. I see the woman I love, the one I call my mate. She is also a very sexy grandma. What did you expect?"

Shaking her head, she laughed softly. "Ah, Ric. You do know what to say, but you're not answering my question." She turned to face him and tapped the end of his nose. "If you didn't have white hair, you'd look like a thirty-year-old. I'm almost sixty. If I were human, I'd be all through menopause and well on my way to being an old woman."

"You are most definitely not an old woman."

"Exactly. That's what I'm getting at. All evening long, I've been freaking out about getting naked with three young kids, when I suddenly realized we're not old. We don't look old. No wrinkles or age spots. We don't act our ages. Your body is muscular and mature, but it's not the body of an old man. You look like a man in your prime."

Ric chuckled, not at Millie's vehement declarations, so much, but at himself. He'd subconsciously sucked in his belly when she'd started talking about how he looked, but Millie didn't even notice. No, she was definitely on a roll.

"Matt and Deacon aren't even thirty yet." She was still frowning, still busy making her point. "In fact, they still need to grow into their bones, but Daci and I could be the same age. We look like contemporaries." She shook her head, obviously frustrated by something she couldn't explain. "Ric, I didn't look this good when I was thirty. I've started going into heat again, like a young woman. For all I know, heaven forbid, I could get pregnant if I wanted.

Which I don't, so don't even go there. What's happening to me?"

He coughed, almost choking on the laugh he couldn't dare turn loose, but it wasn't easy when she got going like this. Still, it was more than obvious she wasn't kidding, and since everything she said was true, he figured she had a right to be concerned, so he merely shook his head and sighed. "I don't know, Millie. Anton and I've talked about it. At first, we wondered if our aging stopped once we started shifting. Now, all of us realize we actually look younger, but we don't know why, not for sure. I honestly can say I haven't aged a bit since my first shift with Camille, so many years ago." He laughed. "I have to admit, though, it really hasn't been a priority, worrying about why we're not getting old. Not with all that's been happening over the past couple of years."

"It's just weird. I don't like questions without answers." She turned around and stared at herself, looking closer now that the steam was dissolving away. "Not that I'm complaining, you understand, but I certainly never expected to look like a young woman again." She palmed her breasts and laughed. "Perky tits! Never in my wildest dreams did I . . ."

Ric wrapped his big hands over hers, covering her breasts. "Do not make fun of the world's most perfect breasts. Come on. We have to get moving. There's that simultaneous orgasm we need to work on."

Laughing now, frowns and worries obviously set aside for the moment, Millie gave him a quick kiss and left the bathroom. Ulrich stayed behind a little longer, staring at the young man in the mirror. White hair notwithstanding, Millie was right. He didn't look like a guy in his sixties. Even his skin, a telltale sign of aging, was supple and smooth like that of a young man. If not for the white hair, he could have passed for thirty.

And she was worried about this, why? He shook his head, chuckling softly. *Not bad for an old fart.* With one last glance, he turned away, followed Millie into the bedroom, and pulled a comfortable pair of sweats out of the closet. He wasn't going to worry about something as fantastic as not looking or feeling his age. Just like he wasn't going to dress with too many layers in spite of the cold outside. What was the point—not when they'd be undressing in a matter of minutes.

At least, according to his lovely mate, he didn't have to worry about looking old and worn out next to the young guys. He grabbed a couple of bottles of good wine on the way through the kitchen. Daci had excellent taste in wine, and she was doing her best to educate the rest of them. He was just as happy with a cold beer or a good glass of brandy, but he stuck the bottles in a tote bag and followed Millie out the back door and along the snow-covered path that linked their two cabins.

A wolf howled from the enclosures at the sanctuary. Another joined in, and another. The air was crisp and cold, the path lit by moonlight, and the song of the wolves felt and sounded like a benediction. His body thrummed with arousal, with need for the woman walking just ahead, with desire for the packmates awaiting their arrival.

He sent a quick thought to Eve. Not a request so much, beyond his fervent desire that Tala and Lisa would soon be free, but to give thanks for this night. He thought of all he'd been through to reach this moment, this perfect slice of time when he walked with the woman he loved beneath a moonlit sky.

He thought of Lisa and Tala, of their bravery and their selfless decision to remain captive until the entire operation could unfold and, with any luck, lead Anton and Luc to the leaders. Something the average woman would never consider, especially a woman in her final months of pregnancy.

There was nothing average about a Chanku bitch. Alphas, every one. Brave, honorable, and proud. Very, very proud. Ric had no doubt the Pack Dynamics crew would prevail tonight. He'd trained them well. There was no finer man than Lucien Stone, and Anton Cheval wasn't a man to fail at anything he set out to do.

Neither, for that matter was Ric. He glanced at his watch and realized they were cutting it close. The five of them had never spent a night together, so the dynamics of sex with the whole group would be new. Matt often joined him and Millie, but Deacon and Daci had always remained behind. Of course, they all acknowledged that the relationship Matt had with Millie was special. The fact the two of them often included Ric always reminded him just how special.

The boy was something else, no doubt about that. Matt had grown in so many ways, and it was all because of Millie's love. Her encouragement, her ability to make a man feel confident and strong. Hell, she'd made Ulrich feel as if he could move mountains. It was no wonder she had Matt finally believing in himself. She'd given him the courage he needed, the strength of his character he'd not recognized on his own. Millie had given that to him, that sense of who and what he was. Not a beta, not an omega—no, Matt was truly an alpha, with leadership abilities that continued to develop more depth and intensity every single day.

Millie had shown him the strength that was his, and Matt had proven himself worthy of that strength, even if it meant defying a goddess.

Of course, he'd had Daci and Deacon watching his back, but it wasn't often when a goddess backed down to a mere mortal.

Deacon opened the door when Millie knocked. He wore

sweatpants but no shirt, and a big grin on his face. He'd added some muscle since arriving in Colorado, though he was still lanky and lean.

Deacon reached for Millie, grabbed her hand, and drew her into the shadowed interior of the small cabin. There were no electric lights burning inside—nothing beyond a few strategically placed candles that made the pitch on the beautiful old logs sparkle like diamonds and threw the finely drawn planes of Deacon's face in sharp relief.

Drawing himself up to his impressive height, he looked Ric up and down, as if judging him and finding him less than impressive. "So you showed up, too, eh? Damn. After everything Matt's said about Millie, I was sort of hoping that . . ."

Ric growled. Laughing, Deacon bowed and stepped back, sweeping an arm wide in greeting. "Sorry, boss. I'll behave."

Ric nudged him none too gently with an elbow as he stepped through the door. Deacon grunted dramatically. Throwing a dirty look at Deacon, Daci reached around him, grabbed the wine from Ric, and set it on the tiny counter in their small kitchen. She looked freshly showered and just a little flustered, with her long hair curling in damp tangles past her shoulders and her brilliant amber eyes sparkling.

"Later for the wine, okay?" she said. "We're running out of time, and I really do not want to rush anything."

She was practically fluttering, moving about the tiny area in such nervous haste. He rarely saw her like this. She was usually so self-assured, so comfortable with her two big mates, that it was sort of endearing to see a more vulnerable side to Daciana Lupei. Endearing, and somehow very arousing. He wasn't quite certain why, but his libido didn't seem to care. It was responding more than appropriately, considering the reason for their visit.

He wondered if that was it, if Daci was feeling a bit uncertain bringing him and Millie into her home. They were both, after all, lovers to one of her mates.

Matt didn't appear at all nervous. He lounged on the big bed, leaning comfortably against a stack of pillows piled against the headboard. He held a can of beer in his hand, but he set it aside as Millie and Ric stepped far enough into the room for Deacon to close the door.

There really wasn't much room for any of them to move around. The big bed took up almost the entire space. Larger than a king, it was hard to ignore the visual that popped into Ric's head of how the five of them would actually fit on that huge mattress. He glanced about the small cabin with open curiosity. It had been an old rental, built almost a hundred years ago, according to Millie, and updated back in the early sixties, which meant the updates were already antique, but it definitely had its own charm, and it suited the three kids.

Kids. Hell, they were all in their mid-twenties, and after the tough lives each of them had lived, more mature than their years would normally indicate. Mature, intelligent, and absolutely gorgeous, each in their own way. It was strange to think he and Millie had never come here before like this, with nothing but sex on the schedule.

Maybe, after tonight, that would change. Whenever Matt had come to their cabin, sex was generally the only thing he had in mind, but it had never happened with Daci or Deacon. Not there. Not here. Now, though, after that fantastic run, after a successful hunt and an entire evening knowing what lay ahead, his libido was in fine form. He was ready for just about anything, but what about Daci, Deacon, and Matt? This was still fairly new to them— they'd not been aware of their Chanku heritage for all that long, though they'd definitely adapted well. But the open sexuality—sometimes that took a while for someone to grow used to. Millie was still adjusting.

With that in mind, Ric expected at least a little awkwardness before things got going. Then Millie kissed his cheek, slipped out of her boots, and crawled across the bed to Matt. She straddled his hips, leaned close, and gave him a kiss that lifted the temperature in the room by more than a few degrees.

Maybe she'd adjusted faster than he realized.

Ric was still thinking along those lines when Daci gave him an impish grin and knelt down in front of him. Carefully she removed both his boots. Then she took his hand and tugged him toward the bed. Ric didn't hesitate, so caught up in the vision of Millie straddling Matt, of Daci's fingers wrapped around his big hand.

When he was close to the bed, Daci gave him a small shove and he toppled backward, laughing. Deacon followed close behind, stripping his clothing off as he moved. In the shadows and flickering candlelight, everything quickly took on a surrealistic quality as Ric stretched out on the bed beside Matt and Millie. Daci stripped her shirt off and shucked her pants.

Her mound was bare, her sex entirely free of any hair at all. He hadn't expected that, for some reason, but he liked it. A lot. So much the better for a man who loved to use his mouth and lips and tongue, and, on occasion, his teeth.

Before he could complete the thought and share it with Daci, she leaned close and tugged his shirt up over his torso. He'd expected, as the older male and pack alpha, to take the lead, but Daci, Matt, and Deacon appeared to have other ideas.

Now that they'd gotten started, there was no hesitation from any of them, but Daci's aggressive moves caught him by surprise. Again, unexpected, but he loved it. There was something amazingly sensual about this beautiful young woman stripping his shirt over his head and then tugging his pants down over his hips while his mate was slowly disrobing atop another man.

He glanced at Millie just in time to see her lift her sweatshirt over her head and bare those amazingly perky breasts of hers. Biting back a laugh, he returned his attention to Daci, and the fact he was totally undressed and hadn't even realized she'd gotten his pants off him. They were gone.

He glanced over the edge of the bed and would have laughed at the tangled pile of clothing on the floor, except Daci was shocking him once again, sliding that perfect body of hers beneath him, tugging gently to pull him over her so that he covered her from toes to breasts.

Her eyes were already heavy lidded as she arched her back and pressed her breasts against his chest. Parting her legs, she invited him to enter, but it was much too soon. Besides, he'd given up more than enough control, and it was his turn to show Daci how things were done, no matter how aroused she might be from her run. He glanced at the clock on the wall beside the bed. They still had half an hour, and Anton was counting on them.

The impatience of youth. Leave it to the youngsters to try and rush things. Ric scooted down and knelt between Daci's legs, slipped his big hands beneath her firm little butt, and lifted her high. Her legs spread wide and she opened to him, her labia shimmering like pink petals covered in dew. He nuzzled her bare mound, nipping at the smooth expanse of skin. Then he touched his tongue to her center and tasted her spicy flavors—so unlike Millie, and yet every bit as seductive.

He noticed her hands clutching the thick comforter and sent the simple thought to her, that he was glad she'd anchored herself so well, since he intended to make her fly.

Shivers ran across her legs and the skin over her abdomen rippled in reaction to his provocative thoughts. He showed her what he was thinking, how he would take her with his mouth and his fingers, his tongue and teeth until she couldn't stand it anymore, teasing and tormenting until her arousal was a living, breathing entity, another soul sharing this big bed.

She quivered and her sex seemed to pulse in reaction. He sent a warm puff of air over her buttery folds and smoothly shorn mound. Then he touched his tongue to that tiny bundle of nerves. She jerked in response. He wrapped his thumbs over her hipbones and held her tightly so she couldn't move. Then he circled her clit with the very tip of his tongue, around and around until she was panting and moaning, struggling against his tight hold.

He used the flat of his tongue to bring her back down from the heights he'd led her to, then he deftly wrapped his lips around the sensitive nub and suckled her softly.

She shuddered in his grasp and he licked her again, delving deeper this time between her folds, spearing her with his tongue, curling the tip against her inner walls until she moaned and twisted her hips. Writhing against his powerful hands, she tried to force him to lick harder, thrust deeper, take her further with his tongue, with his lips.

Laughing, he sat up and grinned at her. "We have almost half an hour, Daciana, m'dear. Be patient. I've just begun."

She opened her eyes and glared at him. "Fuck you," she said, but the laughter in her voice gave her away.

"I intend to. Eventually." He grinned at her and dipped his head between her legs once more. This time he suckled her labia, drawing first one full lip and then the other into his mouth. He licked slowly from her perineum to her navel, long, slow sweeps of his tongue that barely touched on all her most sensitive points, yet teased her enough to set her legs to trembling and her heart soaring. He heard it thundering, sensed it with the connection that was steadily growing between them. Pounding out a cadence of lust and need, of desire and almost unbearable arousal.

It was good. So good to feel what Daci felt, to absorb her need and make it his own. He wondered about Deacon. Where had he gone and what was he doing? Matt was suckling Millie's breasts, moving from one to the next as she arched her back and writhed against the thickened shaft still covered in his sweats, but Deacon was . . . *ah*. Deacon was behind him. Ric shivered, wondering what the young man had in mind.

Hoping it was the same thing he was thinking.

He'd heard stories about Deacon. Taller than most at six and a half feet, his large hands and feet merely hinted at the size he'd finally reach when he eventually filled out. They were also supposed to be indicative of some of his other attributes.

At the moment, he was running those big hands over Ric's shoulders, caressing his back, following the line of his vertebrae and trailing down the crease between his cheeks.

Lost for a moment in Deacon's gentle exploration of his ass, Ric didn't realize Daci had turned beneath him so that her head was now between his thighs, her tongue reaching out to lick first the underside of his balls and then his sensitive glans. He rose up on his knees, well aware of what he was offering Deacon, and wondering if what he'd heard was true, that Deacon was hung even bigger than Matt.

He thought of looking and then decided against it. There were some things a man was better off not knowing. Instead, he concentrated on Daci, on the smooth curve of her belly, the even smoother mound between her thighs. Her clit was swollen now, distended from his play, and he focused on that glistening nub. He leaned forward and wrapped his lips around it, suckling as if it were a tiny nipple.

Daci moaned and lifted her hips, pressing herself against his mouth, but he backed away and blew a small puff of air against her heated flesh. She was close. He sensed her frustration and checked the clock.

Ten more minutes. Could he last that long? Build the energy among the three of them until they gave it all to Anton? And what of Millie and Matt? Before he could check on his mate's progress, Deacon's fingers caressed his ass and thoughts of Millie fled. How could he think of anything else when Deacon was slowly rubbing something slick and cool along the crease between his cheeks, over that tightly puckered hole back there?

Impossible, especially when Deacon pressed with one thick finger just as Daci sucked Ric's cock deep into her warm mouth. Deacon's finger breached the taut muscle and speared him deep just as Daci's tongue swirled over the underside of his cock.

Dear Goddess! He wasn't ready. It was too soon and he didn't want to lose it. Not now.

He opened his mind and caught Deacon's thoughts, his vivid images as he pictured filling Ric's ass, of coming at exactly the right moment to give Anton the full thrust of energy he needed, but Deacon knew his limits, knew he wouldn't be able to last long at all once he got inside Ric.

No, not long at all. He'd wanted to do this for months now, but he hadn't had the nerve to approach the pack alpha. Regretted the fact he'd been too cowardly, too afraid of rejection. There was no chance of rejection now, and he planned to make up for any missed opportunities tonight.

Ric let Deacon know he was eavesdropping. Told him he'd been just as curious about Deacon as Deacon had been about him. Once they got that cleared up, Deacon's moves became more forceful, less tentative. He slipped one long finger deep inside Ric, and then he added another. Two fingers, slipping in and out, stretching him, sliding over his prostate and sending shivers of arousal racing along his spine.

Millie moaned. Ric's head snapped up just in time to see her pull away from Matt. She rolled over to her belly and rose up on her hands and knees, facing Ric. Matt knelt between her parted legs and palmed his huge cock, stroking himself slowly from tip to groin. Then he rolled his hips forward and entered Millie from behind, sliding in slow and deep with his big hands planted on her hips.

Sharing her sensations with Ric, Millie licked her lips and sighed as Matt's groin pressed against her buttocks. She shared the fullness, the way it felt when Matt's thick cock bumped over her cervix and filled the small space behind, the rasp of his coarse pubic hair grinding against her buttocks when he pressed even deeper, twisting his hips and filling her completely.

Then Millie did something she'd never done before. She dipped her head and put her mouth between Daci's legs, sharing tastes and visuals, sharing the excitement of doing this to another woman for the very first time.

As Ric watched his beautiful mate sweep her tongue through Daci's dark pink folds, as he experienced everything exactly as she did, he felt Deacon's thick cock replace his fingers, felt the pressure and the burn as Deacon buried himself fully inside.

A low groan burst out of him, along with every bit of breath in his lungs. Damn but the kid was huge, but for all his size, he was gentle, entering Ric with such care that the pain was minimal.

At least as minimal as it could be, considering what he was shoving inside a part of Ric's anatomy clearly not designed for anything quite that big. Ric held on, barely. They still had at least five more minutes and he was hanging on by his toenails.

So close, now, he was afraid of coming too soon, of wasting energy Anton was counting on. Deacon drove deep and slowly withdrew. Went deep again, rubbing his thick length along Ric's prostate in agonizingly slow motion, sending shivers of arousal sparking across his nerve endings, taking him to the edge and hanging him out there without a damned thing to anchor to.

Franticly, barely in control, Ric took a chance. He opened his thoughts wide and found Matt, straining to hold on just a little bit longer, found Daci and discovered exactly how his cock tasted, the way it felt sliding over her tongue, scraping along her teeth, bumping the back of her throat.

She wanted to swallow him, but not now. Not yet. It was too soon and just thinking about what she wanted to do had him harder than he'd been a moment before—if that were even possible. Even harder to deal with was Daci's sense of Millie's tongue teasing her folds, the way it felt when Millie nibbled and licked and sucked. Too much. The visuals, the tactile sensations shared from mind to mind were too much, too powerful—too soon.

Quickly, he slipped out of Daci's mind and found himself caught in Deacon's. His was a swirling mass of sensations. Ric was tight and hotter than he'd expected. Deacon knew he was hung like a damned bull and it felt way too good, sliding in and out of that tight, tight channel, slipping through wet heat and muscles that rippled and pulsed around him, but he could do it. He could hold on just a little bit longer.

He had to. No way was he going to go first when Matt and Ric were still in control. It was a matter of pride, now, as much as arousal, more than desire, stronger than lust.

Ric knew when Deacon glanced at the clock, knew they had only minutes more to go, but they'd caught their rhythm now, all five of them thrusting and sighing, clenching and slipping, licking, touching, and tasting. Each of them on the edge, struggling not to slip past a point of no return.

With a huge act of will, Ric captured their thoughts and drew each mind into a single space, connecting all, sharing everything.

Every heartbeat, every breath, every shiver and touch and taste. Sensation grew and spread, exploding from one mind to the next, spiraling upward from one body to the next and on to each of the others. They were drawing close, so damned close, until Ric felt as if he grasped powerful threads of energy tying each of them together, united each of the five until they were one, and that one breathed and pulsed and needed.

And it loved. Loved with a fierce loyalty connecting each heart, each mind—holding each one in stasis as the seconds ticked slowly by, as bodies strained for that ultimate release. Part of the cumulative mind watched the second hand, while the rest hovered, poised for flight, straining against the powerful drive as climax beckoned and the seconds passed like hours.

Lisa'd been lying here on the bed beside her sister, thinking of every scenario possible when it was finally time for Beth, Mik, Logan, and maybe even Igmutaka, to break down the doors and rescue them. Most of the time she saw everything turning out great, but what if . . . ?

And, for some reason, that *what if* kept looming larger. There were currently three men guarding them, but two of the guys were in the main room, and the one who had no compunction whatsoever against killing pregnant ladies was sitting guard in their room—and he was armed.

But, if they could somehow get everyone in here at once, and if their packmates knew all the men were in the same room, it might make things easier—and the outcome not quite so chancy.

They needed a plan. Something that would tip the scales just a bit more in their direction. Something none of these bozos would suspect. Two alpha bitches had to be smarter than three total idiots. A lot smarter.

Lisa squeezed Tala's fingers. She had an idea . . .

And maybe—just maybe—it would work.

Chapter 11

Liana broke through the thick brush, caught her front foot on a twisted root, and tumbled ungracefully across the shimmering meadow just ahead of Adam. Plowing to a stop in newly fallen snow, she snorted ice crystals from her nose as he playfully nipped at her heels. Finally getting her feet beneath her, she spun about and jumped him, tumbling the powerful wolf over, rolling with him through the fresh powder until both of them were covered in white and panting from the exertion.

Adam lay on his belly with his chest heaving. They'd run hard as the snow fell, chased after game and drunk from ice-encrusted streams, but the small silver timepiece hanging around Liana's neck reminded him it was growing late.

The sky had cleared, the moon glowed overhead once again. He stood and shook himself, sending snow crystals cascading in all directions. Liana shook her coat clean as well. She stood as if poised to flee, watching him. Waiting.

Adam searched for her thoughts but found a solid wall blocking him. *Typical female.* She wanted to bond, and now she locked him out, but it was all part of the ritual, part of the challenge she offered him.

It appeared he must prove himself worthy of her. He

only hoped he could. She was, after all, once a goddess, but he loved her. She loved him. It was time, and challenges be damned.

He pawed her shoulder and she growled. He hoped it was an instinctive response, not a sign of temper, but with her thoughts closed to him, how could he be sure? He gazed into her eyes, those amazing gray-green eyes of hers and knew this was the one, the only woman, the Chanku bitch he wanted for all time. There was no doubt in his mind. In truth, at this point, there was nothing more than need and the overwhelming sense that he must have her. She was his to protect, his to love, his to worship. This female, this time, was right.

And that, he realized, was the difference between what he'd felt for Eve and how he felt about Liana. Where he'd needed Eve in the physical sense, where he'd loved her and cherished the woman she'd been, the need had not been this great, this all-consuming. Her loss and the pain he'd felt had been selfish in comparison—she'd left without his permission. He'd grieved his loss more than he'd mourned her death.

She'd abandoned him without reason, and he'd missed her horribly, needed the affirmation of her love, and yet he'd moved on. Very quickly, in fact. Looking back, he realized he'd moved on from Eve without guilt, without regret. She had her new life. He had his—except, he knew, on some intangible level, that he needed Liana to survive. He would always need her, and he would always love her.

Her mind was still blocked, but he shared those thoughts, the depth of his desire and the power of his love. He hoped she was at least listening, if not broadcasting.

She said nothing. She stared at him for the longest time, and he would have given anything to know what was going on in that brilliant mind of hers. Then she trotted across the small meadow to the circle of fresh grass and primroses still blooming, the spot where they'd stood with

Eve just a short time ago. There, in the circle blessed by their Goddess, Liana planted her feet and gazed back over her shoulder, inviting Adam to mount her.

A wave of absolute relief washed over him. He hadn't realized just how worried he was. What if she'd changed her mind? No matter. This was as plain an invitation as he was going to get.

He stepped from frozen snow to soft grass, from winter into spring. He could have sworn the frozen air felt warmer the moment he crossed into that blessed circle. Once again he raked Liana's shoulder with his paw. She didn't growl this time. Instead, she braced her legs. Turning her head to gaze over her shoulder, she watched him, bearing his weight as he mounted her.

He and Eve had mated only a few times in their wolven form. This was Liana's first time as a wolf. It took Adam a moment to settle into the change in his shape, the altered perceptions, even longer to find the proper position for penetration. He braced himself, clasping her body between his front legs and burying his nose in her thick fur. A low whimper sounded deep in his throat as he inhaled her rich, wolven scent and smelled the powerful perfume of her heat.

His hips had begun thrusting the moment he mounted her, an instinctive act of mating that he barely controlled with the remnants of his human senses. Then his feral needs took command. His spine curled as he hugged her close, plunging and thrusting until his sharp thrusts finally found their target.

Liana's eyes never left his as he buried himself in her warm sheath, as the knot at the base of his cock swelled to full size, filling her, tying the two of them together.

Adam felt a momentary disconnect. Even though he'd done this before when he mated with Eve, this was Liana. This was the woman who had agreed to be his mate, the one he would bond to tonight and for the rest of his life.

He planted his hind legs firmly in the thick grass as Liana's inner muscles clenched and pulsed, holding him tightly within her channel.

His thoughts were still open, still searching. His mental barriers were completely down as he consciously searched for Liana. Still, there was the slightest sense of fear he had to force aside. Fear tempered by trust as he opened himself to her amazingly brilliant mind.

The mind of a woman who had once been a goddess. A mind with enough power, at one time, to kill any mere mortal foolish enough to attempt a link. Trusting Liana, loving her, Adam reached into the heart of her thoughts, reached for whatever she offered.

Her barriers dissolved and her mental pathways blossomed, opening entirely to him. She offered everything, a link as full and complete as two minds could achieve. She gave him answers to questions he'd not even known he had.

He felt as if he'd tumbled into another space, a different world, and in so many ways, he had. Her mind was like a time machine, a trip through memories of a life before recorded history, of people who were culturally different, yet physically the same as those who walked the Earth today. He saw creatures that no longer existed—huge, mountainous mastodons with gleaming tusks, and powerful dire wolves with their heavy bodies and powerful jaws. Small, shaggy horses moved in herds across vast grasslands, and hunters trailed after, primitive men from an ancient time.

Fast-forwarding through her memories and knowledge, he saw the rise and fall of tribes he recognized as the earliest years of ancient Chanku on the Tibetan steppe. Shapeshifters from the beginning, yet they appeared to be more civilized in many ways, a more advanced people than their neighbors, but why?

He walked her paths of knowledge and discovered small

secrets of their kind, even the largest one, the one she'd not thought important enough to share. He might have laughed if not for the constant onslaught of information—so much information he knew it would fill his brain, that his mind might explode with all the amazing things Liana knew and remembered.

Eve hadn't stolen her memories after all. No, it appeared she'd merely taken what she needed as Goddess. Liana's mind was filled with knowledge and so many lifetimes of memories that Adam wondered if he'd remember it all.

He saw everything, felt everything, shared everything. The way Liana did her healing, how she'd felt when she first realized she had been cast out of her role as Goddess, the things she'd done for which she would always feel shame.

He was with her when she took a younger Anton to her bed, when she sent the wizard on his unexpected journey of discovery to the monastery that still held their history within its magically protected walls. Adam shared her shame over those long weeks when she'd held Matthew Rodgers against his will in a fruitless attempt to make him her consort.

He saw that for what it was, that she'd been desperately searching for the kind of love she'd only discovered now, here, with him. She'd spent hundreds of lifetimes searching—a search that ended with Adam. That knowledge made it easier to absorb the memories of every man she'd bedded over the ages, the hundreds of men she'd taken without permission or even their conscious knowledge, though Adam couldn't help but notice every single one of them, except for Matt, had gone to her willingly.

He could have stayed there in her memories forever. He knew he would return, again and again, to learn from this amazing woman, but tonight they had a purpose in their bonding, and goals yet to accomplish.

He knew the moment the mating link was complete. While he hated the thought of leaving this wondrous treasure trove of memory, Adam sensed Liana's desire to move forward.

She was almost childishly anxious for the next step. He realized why when she shared the moment with him, releasing an egg, the one that would become their child.

One egg. Memories of Tia Mason's frightening delivery swept through him, but he brushed worry aside. This was Liana's experience. Their child. Each of them was an individual with his or her own path to follow—their own risks, their own success. He would not borrow trouble. Instead he concentrated on the sense of their future in that unseen ovum.

Powerful waves of emotion crested in and about his mind, his heart, and his soul. Liana's emotion, as she realized this act would change both of their lives forever.

Just as their mating would change them. Her desire for a girl child, the daughter Eve had not been able to bear, was a powerful force, and it made him love Liana even more. She might have been a selfish and self-centered goddess, but she was a generous and giving mate.

Time passed in the small circle of spring. The grass was cool against his paws, the flowers dipped their heads to the moonlight, and he held a sense of timelessness, the feeling that they'd somehow slipped earthly bonds and floated outside of the cares of their world. He blinked and glanced about, afraid, but he'd not separated from his body and neither had Liana.

They were still tied, their bodies linked physically and emotionally. Now though, instead of the driving need he'd experienced earlier, Adam knew a contentment unlike anything he'd felt before. He and Liana so perfectly united, their wolven bodies aligned, their human hearts linked, their thoughts one.

It was all good. So much better than he'd ever dreamed,

this sense of becoming one with a woman he'd once thought he hated. Amazing, what time and love could accomplish, which brought him full circle, to think of the time, and the fact there were people counting on him tonight, counting on Liana, on the power of their mating and the energy their bodies and minds could provide.

He had no idea how much actual time had passed. He didn't know if they were anywhere close to Anton's schedule, if they'd missed the deadline or hadn't reached it yet, but he felt his climax growing, knew he couldn't hold back any longer.

Liana's tight sheath contracted around his thrusting cock, squeezing him in a pounding rhythm that left him no other recourse. Praying it wasn't too soon, hoping like hell they'd gotten this right, Adam tightened his forelegs to better grasp his bonded mate.

It's time, she said, and Adam knew she was right. Sensed Anton's mind linking with his, synching with others about the country. *I love you, Liana. Now and forever.*

Her laughter brushed his thoughts, the first powerful shocks of her impending climax almost brought him to his knees.

Now!

The big wall clock loomed large in the bedroom, an alien and only partially welcome presence ticking down the seconds and the minutes to the long-awaited moment when the women might finally let them find release. Groaning with the combined pleasure and pain he'd been trapped in for what felt like forever, Stefan Aragat checked the handcuffs holding him bound to the thick, iron railing on the bed. He glanced once more at the big clock Xandi had hung on the wall just for tonight, and sighed. He wasn't going anywhere, any time soon.

Not that he particularly wanted to leave.

He rolled his head to one side and caught Oliver grinning at him. The look of absolute bliss on Ollie's face had Stefan biting back a laugh and sending his partner in bondage a private message.

Nothing worse than a damned submissive getting exactly what he wants.

Oliver managed a big wink and a grin, in spite of the fact his dark skin was beaded with sweat and he had a death grip on the chains holding him so tightly bound. No doubt, he was exactly where he wanted to be and loving every minute.

Stefan tried flexing his shoulders. It wasn't easy, as tight as his loving spouse and her cohort in crime had tied him. Oliver was restrained even more, if that was at all possible, but the damned guy loved this stuff.

The vote was still out as far as Stef was concerned, though he had to admit, when the girls finally let them come, it was going to be amazing. No doubts there. In the meantime, though, he was having a hard time finding the humor in the whole situation.

He'd been ready to blow for at least the last half hour, and that was after using amazing control for the hour before. He hadn't expected so much creativity from Xandi and Mei, but it appeared that when the two of them got together with a bottle of Anton's best wine, their imaginations went beyond inventive.

He looked at the clock. Again. The hands must be stuck, because he was almost sure they weren't moving. They still had a good fifteen minutes before the girls took them over the edge.

He stared at the second hand. It *was* moving. Barely. Why was it, the closer they got, the slower time crawled? Stefan wasn't sure he'd be able to last. Not with that damned vibrator in his ass, pressed way too close to the magic button. Thank goodness his prostate was practically numb from such continual attention, but it still felt way too good. The weirdest thing was the way the subtle vibrations in his ass made the nipple clamps vibrate exactly enough to drive him nuts.

Hands and feet restrained, an anal vibrator with batteries that showed no sign of failing, and nipple clamps just tight enough to keep him on the edge between wanting to scream and wishing someone would tug on them. Just a little? He glanced at Mei and thought of suggesting it, but she was too busy with her own vibrator.

Watching her slide that big pink phallus between her legs, seeing it disappear deep inside her pussy, had him licking his lips and wondering what she had planned for him next.

So far, their plans had worked perfectly. Switching mates for the night didn't seem like that big a deal. All of them switched around on a regular basis, but having Mei's total concentration for an entire evening while his mate serviced Oliver had definitely had a weird effect on Stefan.

He glanced at Oliver and decided it had been pretty effective on him, too. Xandi was doing her best to take Oliver to the edge without letting him go over. She appeared to have found new levels of torture for Oliver.

He wasn't complaining a bit.

In fact, the plan was working much too well on both men, as far as Stefan could tell. At least it was working on him, and from all the whimpering, moaning and groaning coming from Oliver, Xandi must be learning a lot of Mei's tricks—and learning them well.

He thought about that a moment. Xandi learning from Mei could be interesting—especially if she decided to try out her new skills on Anton. She was certainly learning from the master—or mistress, to be more specific.

Mei was devilishly inventive with all her toys and weird implements. She'd outdone herself tonight, but then, there was a goal in mind, one they all intended to meet.

Stefan's mind snapped back to the present as Mei crawled up on the bed, knelt between his widely spread legs, and slowly pushed the vibrator deeper inside his ass. She cupped his balls in her left hand but totally ignored his lonely prick. He tried not reacting, but there was no way.

Groaning, Stefan bucked his hips. No way could a red-blooded male hold still, not with that slow slide of vibrating heat impaling him and those long fingers carefully massaging his painfully stretched balls. His cock ached from standing at attention for so long, but the leather restraint Mei had skillfully woven around his ball sac and the base of his cock would probably keep him from climaxing for at least a month.

At least it felt that way, though he wasn't anywhere near as trussed up as Oliver. Xandi had locked the poor guy's package in a shiny chrome cage that glistened with reflected light. A ring trapped his balls and the bars of the cage encased his cock so tightly that it had to hurt. Ollie was so damned hard his cock looked unnaturally dark and swollen, with the thick metal bands pressed tightly into his flesh. Stef figured it probably bothered him more looking at it than it did Oliver experiencing it. Of course, Oliver, as usual, was loving every bit of whatever toys the girls chose to use.

"Mei, where in the hell do you find this stuff?" Stefan rattled his handcuffs and lifted his butt off the mattress as high as he could. It wasn't easy—not with his ankles tied to opposing bedposts. One of his legs was crossed over Oliver's so that both men were trussed, connected, and totally helpless.

Mei stretched out along Stefan's naked body, forcing his erect cock against his belly. She rubbed her nipples over the clamps on his. He clenched his teeth to keep from cursing her, but he had to admit, the pain was exquisite.

"I love the Internet and home delivery, don't you? Research, shopping . . . whatever a girl needs." She kissed him, tracing the contours of his lips with her tongue. Dragged her nipples over his, making him groan again. "The world is my marketplace," she whispered.

Stefan chuckled. At least she'd left the floggers at home. "Mei, I am convinced your mind must be a very, scary place."

Oliver snorted and made choking sounds. Finally he seemed to catch his breath. "Stef, you really don't want to know. I've been inside her mind. It's beyond scary."

"I was afraid of that."

Xandi leaned over the end of the bed and glared at both men in mock ferocity. "Mei, I think they're much too talkative. For two men who are supposed to be undergoing intense sexual torture, they don't sound as if they're in nearly enough distress."

Mei flashed her a big grin. "I agree. What do you think we should do about it? We've got . . ." She glanced at the clock. "Oh. Wow, we still have almost ten minutes. Sweetie, I've got a whole box of new toys we haven't even gotten to yet."

She crawled off Stefan. He rolled his head until he could see Oliver. "Quit grinning, stud muffin. I'm the one who signed for that new box of toys the day they were delivered, and I know what's in there."

Oliver sighed. "I know. Isn't it great?"

Snorting in disgust, Stefan lay his head back down on the pillow as Mei pulled a huge blue dildo out of the box. She held it up for his perusal.

"What do you think?" she said, turning it this way and that to show off the shape and dimensions. "It's anatomically correct."

Stefan raised his head, stared at the dildo, and flopped his head back on the pillow. "Yeah. Right, Mei. Anatomically correct if your name is Paul Bunyan."

Or Babe the Blue Ox. Stefan stared at the clock, willing the hands to pass faster. Mei pulled the vibrating dildo out of his butt, the one toy he'd almost gotten used to, and slowly began feeding him the new one.

His body really wasn't designed for this. He was absolutely sure Mei's confidence that the thing would fit was a bit misplaced. He closed his eyes and concentrated on relaxing, on not fighting the size and the length and how much it hurt, stretching that tight little ring of muscle.

Anton, damn it all. You're going to owe me big time. Except he doubted Anton would ever believe exactly what the girls had put them through tonight.

Some day, he really needed to think about writing a book.

Beside him, Oliver grunted as Xandi removed his chastity cage and began slowly applying something like little alligator clips to his cock and balls. Stefan watched, fascinated, but shit, those had to hurt. He cringed when Xandi fastened one to that sensitive spot just beneath Oliver's glans. Oliver's breath hitched in his throat. Stefan realized he was clenching his own jaw in sympathy.

The vibrator stretched his asshole and slid deeper.

Seven more minutes to go.

Mei twisted and turned the thing. Whatever she was doing took away any semblance of pain and felt way too good. His nipples ached. His balls ached. His cock was lonely, all trussed up and tied, and it ached.

His ass tightened around this new intruder. The pain faded as he adjusted to the size. At least one part of him was happy.

Then Mei twisted the damned thing, turning it on. Vibrations coursed through Stefan's balls and up his cock as if he'd been struck by lightning. He felt that coil of heat at the base of his spine that told him he was going to come. Now.

Except he couldn't. He'd forgotten all about the straps tied tightly around the base of his cock, forgotten that Mei could keep this up for hours. She shoved the dildo in as far as she could, so deep he could have sworn it made his molars vibrate. Then she slowly, sinuously, crawled back up his body.

She pulled both the nipple clamps off at the same time. "Shit! Ouch! Son of a bitch!"

Laughing, Mei put a finger to her lips. "Tone it down, big guy. We don't want to wake the kids."

He glared at her. Blood rushed to his tits. After that first blast of pain, they throbbed in painful counterpoint to the vibrations in his ass. Grinning like the devil's spawn, Mei straddled his belly and rocked her pussy against his chest.

Dear Goddess, he really wanted to come. But he couldn't. Not until it was time. Not until Mei undid the damned straps holding him prisoner. She'd wrapped one tightly around the base of his dick that was linked to the one wrapped around his balls. Another part of the strap ran the full length of his shaft and put pressure just beneath the glans.

The pain the straps caused was a combination both absolutely excruciating and unbelievably erotic. He jerked at the manacles for no reason other than the fact he just couldn't seem to help himself. But, sick as it sounded, he didn't want to be free. Didn't really want this to end.

He'd never spent a night like this in his life. Aroused beyond belief, in more pain than he'd thought himself capable of enduring—it was such an intimately carnal experience, the sensations by themselves overwhelming, and yet when combined, they created a symphony of pain, a full orchestra playing over his body's erogenous zones.

Why did he keep waiting for the cymbals?

He looked at the clock again. Four more minutes. Somehow he had to hang on for four more minutes. Mei ran her long, slim fingers through the dark mat of hair on his chest, leaned over, and licked first one nipple and then the other. Then she sucked the one over his heart between her lips and tugged.

Every muscle in his body tensed. His hips lifted involuntarily and he thrust against nothing but air with a cock that needed a warm, wet place to call home.

Three minutes. Moaning, he clenched his butt around the giant dildo and lost himself in the combination of vibrations, warm woman, and a whole lot of exquisitely frustrating pain.

They'd explored the entire area that housed the National Zoo. Had run through forested woodlands as wild as anything back home in Maine, and then trotted between perfectly placed pens and cages and observed all types of creatures housed here.

The scents on the night air alone were invigorating, fascinating, and in many ways, so amazingly foreign. Bay had never been in a zoo before in his wolven form, not with his sense of smell so sharp and his hearing this acute. His nostrils twitched and on occasion his hackles rose. He'd salivated unashamedly when they'd trotted by pens holding potential prey.

Jake's silly comments about hunting zebra and chasing down a wildebeest had them all in high form as they circled the park once again and finally reached a thick copse of trees hidden entirely from glaring lights. Even the sounds of the city were muted by thick branches and the open spaces beyond.

It was easy to imagine they ran wild in the forests of Maine, not within a park in the middle of Washington, DC. That the open spaces were broad meadows, not vast, empty parking lots.

Now, though, time was growing short and Bay was more than ready to mate. From the intense look in Jake's amber eyes, he was just as primed. Following two sexy bitches in heat had driven them both so far inside the feral state that it was hard to concentrate on anything beyond the physical act of sex.

Shannon trotted over to a shadowed area beneath a large evergreen. Jake followed her, walking stiff-legged with his ears flat to his head. Baylor might have laughed if he'd been in human form, but it was hard to deny the fact he wasn't in much better shape than Jake.

He wanted Manda. Now. Anton's plans be damned, for all he cared. Lisa and Tala's needs weren't even on the radar. All he could think of was Manda and the rich scent of her heat. His human intelligence was muted by the thick wash of pheromones that wrapped him in their silken trap and drew him closer, held him tighter with every moment that passed.

His vision narrowed until all he saw was Manda. All he wanted was his mate. Now.

She waited in the shadows, a dark figure almost lost in the night except for the reflected gleam in her eyes. Bay crossed the area slowly, stalking her as if she were prey. Manda braced her front legs, lowered her head and laid her ears flat against her broad skull. Growling low in her throat, she teased him.

Dared him.

Tempted him.

He drew closer and the hair along his spine rose up on end. Finally, he was close enough to touch her, but her head was down, her ears flat. He'd checked the time moments ago and knew he needed to take her now, but still she dared him.

A sharp *yip* behind Bay told him Jake and Shannon had tied. That was all the incentive he needed. He leapt over Manda, shocking her with the unexpected move. She flexed her shoulder muscles to spin around, but he caught her, clamping down on the thick ruff of fur at the back of her neck. Holding her in place, Bay quickly mounted her, thrust hard and deep, and penetrated on his first attempt.

She whimpered and braced her legs, taking his weight,

taking him. And then her mind opened, her thoughts so clear it was as if they both experienced the depth of the mating bond once again.

He'd not expected that. Hadn't really prepared himself for the emotional burst of Manda's memories, of the past she'd worked so hard to put behind her. Painful as those memories were, he shared them willingly, proud to know she trusted him enough to feel her terrible fears, to experience her years of imprisonment at the hands of people who saw her as nothing more than a lab animal.

Seeing that man tonight, the one who had worked with Milton Bosworth during the years he'd imprisoned Manda, had to be weighing on her mind, sparking the memories, but her reasoning was crystal clear. Fear would not be their child's way. She wanted this baby with everything in her heart, with all of her soul. Wanted the chance to relive a better childhood than her own, this time through the innocent eyes of their much loved offspring.

Baylor buried his muzzle in the thick fur on Manda's shoulders and clasped her body tightly with his forelegs. For a moment he wished he were human, wished for the understanding his human form would have. They would talk about this, later. Now, the needs of the wolf were more powerful than the expectations of the man. The wolf needed completion.

And his body responded. He felt the thick knot at the base of his penis slip between Manda's tight folds, felt the clenching, squeezing muscles within her slick channel ripple and tighten around him. Locked now, their minds in sync, hearts beating the same rhythm, lungs billowing at the same pace, they slipped naturally into the deepest level of the mating bond.

So tightly connected that when Manda released an egg for fertilization, Baylor sensed the promise of life within the ovum. So much a part of his mate that when she asked the Goddess for her blessing, he was almost certain he heard Eve's soft Southern drawl in reply.

His hips continued their rhythmic rock and sway, and the power between them grew. Manda's joy, his body's response, until they hovered there, building the power and sensing the same growing level of arousal from Jake and Shannon. Sharing their joy that this time, for the first time, Shannon's prayers were answered—finally there would be a child.

It was time. It had to be time. He had that stupid watch on his foreleg and he couldn't really see it all that well, didn't really give a shit at this point. He couldn't contain the sensations any longer. Could no longer hold back the amazing rush of energy that told him their climax was going to happen, no matter what.

Manda! Manda, my love, I can't wait.

Chapter 12

Jazzy wandered in to check on the babies while Tia locked the doors and looked carefully through every room in the house to make sure all the windows were latched as well. No way was she going to take any chances. Not while the guys were gone and it was just her and Jazzy and the babies.

Thank goodness Jazzy was the one to stay home with her. She'd liked her from the first moment they met, and it wasn't just the fact their chocolate au lait skin color was so close they could have been sisters. Besides, her blond curls were nothing like Jazzy's long, straight black hair, but then Jazzy's Asian background had beat out the black genes when it came to hair.

Of course, in Tia's case, her dad's blond color had beat out her mom's black curly hair, though she'd definitely gotten her mom's curls. They were softer now, from shifting, but nothing like Jazzy's board-straight locks.

No, it wasn't looks that made her love Jazzy so much. It was attitude. Jazzy had it in spades. Maybe, if Tia was lucky, a little might rub off. Not that she was a wuss, but this morning's attack had left her badly shaken.

Well, she'd just have to get over it. No way was Shay and Cami's mama going to set a bad example. Those girls were going to grow up with a mother who loved them and wanted them to be tough and brave and self-confident.

Everything it had taken Tia ages to figure out on her own.

With that thought in mind, she grabbed a bottle of chardonnay out of the refrigerator and a couple of glasses, flipped out the lights, and met Jazzy in the family room. A group of candles burned in the corner and another flickered from atop the bookcase, but otherwise the room was dark. Jazzy was curled up in the shadows at one end of the big leather couch. Luc's Enya CD was still playing. Tia thought about switching to something else—the same music had been on early this morning when she'd left to go shopping with Lisa and Tala—but she loved the sound and it fit her pensive mood.

She poured a glass of wine for Jazzy and one for herself and then flopped down beside Jazzy on the comfortable couch. "They're asleep?"

"Finally." Jazzy laughed and took a sip of her wine. "I love babysitting those two. It's like birth control. Spend a few hours with a couple of live wires like your girls and I know for sure I'm not ready for motherhood."

Tia chuckled, remembering how ambivalent she'd been. Thank goodness Luc had wanted children or she might still be wondering if the time was right. Now she couldn't imagine life without Cami and Shay. "When it's time, if you don't know, Logan will tell you." Laughing softly, she curled her feet under her and turned toward Jazzy. "Have you heard from Logan?"

Jazzy sipped and nodded. "Yeah. While you were checking the locks. He said Lisa and Tala are fine, but they're getting impatient. Logan and the others are almost ready to go in." She grabbed Tia's hand and squeezed. "Stuff's going to start happening in just a few more minutes."

Tia nodded. "I've stayed out of Luc's head. I'd hate to think my curiosity screwed up his concentration and endangered the president. Can you imagine what the guys are thinking right now? I mean, this is so far beyond a kidnapping. It's huge."

Jazzy gazed at Tia over the rim of her wineglass. She stared for so long, Tia almost squirmed in her seat. Then Jazzy's full lips tilted up in a big smile. "I have an idea how we can take our minds off things." She shrugged. The wide neck of her sweater slipped off one rounded shoulder.

Tia realized she was imagining Jazzy losing the sweater altogether. She took another sip of her wine. "Well, Anton did say he could use all the energy he can get."

Jazzy's grin spread slowly across her face. "And those two little monsters you call daughters are sound asleep."

"Out for the count." Tia took one more swallow and set her wineglass aside. Slowly she leaned over, took Jazzy's glass out of her hand, and put it on the table beside her own.

"We don't have very long," Jazzy said, reaching for the hem of her sweater. She peeled it quickly up her slim torso and tugged it over her head. She wasn't wearing a bra. Her dark nipples beaded up as the cool air touched them.

Tia was already unzipping her jeans. "Then we'd better not waste any time." She glanced at the clock, laughing. "How hot can you get in seven minutes?"

Laughing, Jazzy rushed through the rest of her clothes, peeling her tight jeans and panties down her long legs while Tia stripped off her sweatshirt and bra. Within seconds they were both naked and giggling on the couch.

Caught for a moment in the pure eroticism of a night alone with a young woman she loved so dearly, Tia took a deep breath, let it out, and took one more. She'd fantasized about this before, but the time had never been right. Maybe the timing tonight wasn't perfect, but that didn't seem to matter to her libido. She felt a warm pulse between her legs, and a slow, even clenching that seemed to start deep in her womb.

Jazzy leaned close and pulled Tia into her arms. Breasts met, nipples aligned perfectly. When Jazzy's lips touched hers, Tia didn't even try to stop the soft moan from escaping. Jazzy took control. Tia relaxed entirely and let it happen. Warm lips moved along her jaw, down the side of her neck, over her chest. A tongue flicked across her left nipple, and then the right.

Jazzy suckled each of her breasts, moving slowly and yet surely from left to right to left again before she slipped off the couch and knelt on the floor. Then she helped Tia turn and slide forward until her butt hung off the edge of the seat and her legs sprawled ingloriously over Jazzy's shoulders.

As ready as she thought she was, when Jazzy's tongue swept between her labia, Tia cried out and jerked her hips. Closer? Away? She had no idea what she wanted, but the sensation of warm tongue and full lips, of teeth and breath and Jazzy's soft hum of pleasure took her very quickly to the top.

After a couple of minutes, Tia forced herself to scoot away. That damned clock on the wall was just too easy to see. Panting, she cupped Jazzy's shoulders in both her hands. "You. Me. Sixty-nine now."

Laughing, Jazzy glanced at the clock. Just a few minutes to go. Since she was the tallest, she stretched out on the bottom with her legs hooked over the arm of the couch. Tia straddled her, held her long legs apart, and dipped her tongue between the buttery folds.

Jazzy cried out and then did the same for Tia. It was a race now, one both of them intended to win. With the big clock ticking steadily and the seconds passing by, Tia went to work on Jazzy Blue. It was so hard to concentrate, with Jazzy's tongue exploring Tia's folds, with her long fingers probing and stroking, but Tia found her rhythm just as Jazzy found hers, each of them sucking and licking, tasting and touching.

Racing the clock to the finish, minds open, ready to give whatever Anton asked, but taking all the pleasure they could, each from the other. Aware of the energy building between them, Tia put her fears for Lisa and Tala aside. She concentrated on her arousal, on Jazzy Blue, and gave herself over to sensation.

Lost as she was, her body so perfectly in tune with Jazzy's, with her touch, her taste, her loving heart, Tia was aware of the power building, of the massive burst of energy just the two of them made.

It was good. All of it good, and all of it for Anton.

Tala? I'm linked with Beth and the guys. Can you pick them up?

Yeah, sis. I'm ready when they are.

Good. Our guard just left the room. He's talking to the other two guys and telling them we're asleep. He wants to stay out there and watch the game with them.

Lisa listened a moment longer and then she squeezed Tala's hand, but she was including Beth, Mik, and Logan in her mindtalking. She wasn't certain about Igmutaka. You never knew quite what the spirit guide was thinking, or how much he was paying attention.

I am here, Lisa. And I am most definitely paying attention.

Oh, shit. She heard Tala snort in her ear. *Shush! We don't want them to know we're awake. Okay. Our guard is staying out there. I'm going to shift and find a place in the room to hide.*

Mik's strong voice filled Lisa's mind. *Don't take any chances, Tala, but if you can get all three of them in there at the same time, and Lisa can freak them out by disappearing, it's going to give us an edge. Two minutes, ladies.*

I love you, Tala Quinn. Be safe or I'll make you regret it. Are you ready?

Tala answered him. *Damn but I love you, Miguel Fuentes. In exactly two minutes, I'm gonna start screamin' and cussin' and askin' what they did with my sister.*

Lisa heard Tala silently counting off the seconds in her head. She shifted, relieved when the plastic ties holding her wrists snapped and broke. Silently she slipped over the edge of the bed and crawled out of the baggy maternity clothes tangled on her wolven frame. Using her nose she pushed the wrinkled but undamaged clothing under the bed. Silently she padded across the floor and found a dark corner behind an overstuffed chair on the far side of the room.

She could still hear Tala's silent count as the seconds slowly passed. The men in the other room talked softly, too quiet for her to hear what they said. She made herself as small as she possibly could and hoped like hell they wouldn't spot her. Her baby kicked. She almost sighed in relief.

She'd not let herself think of the fact she was eight months pregnant and had just shifted, contrary to everything they'd believed in the past. It looked like Liana really did know what she was talking about. One of these days, they all needed to sit down with the ex-goddess and get a few lessons in female Chanku physiology. Some day, when things settled . . .

"Hey, damn it! What'd you do with Lisa? Where's my sister? What the fuck did you do with her? Bastards!"

Tala was sitting up in the bed, screaming for all she was worth. Cursing and the sound of heavy footsteps. The lights went on and Tala kept on screaming holy hell.

"Shut up, bitch! What the fuck? Where the hell'd the other one go?" The sharp sound of his hand connecting with Tala's face and her shriek of anger covered up the sound of the door in the other room bursting open.

Before any of the three men had time to react, a huge mountain lion leapt through the open door into the bedroom. Two wolves followed close behind.

Igmutaka took out the one man who was holding a gun in his hand. The automatic pistol clattered across the floor. Lisa charged out of her hiding place and raced after it. She grabbed the thing up in her jaws as Mik and Logan flattened the men they'd each gone after.

Within seconds, Igmutaka sat on one terrified man and Mik and Logan each held down another. Beth stood in the doorway with a frown on her face and a faraway look in her eyes. After a moment, she stepped into the bedroom, grabbed Lisa's clothes out from under the bed, and took them into the bathroom. Lisa slipped in behind her, dropped the automatic pistol into Beth's outstretched hand, and watched as Beth left the bathroom, shutting the door behind her.

Within a couple of minutes, Lisa stepped out of the bathroom, fully dressed, as if she'd been in there all along. Beth had all three men restrained with the same kind of plastic ties they'd used on her and Tala, but none of them paid her any attention at all. They were so focused on the snarling cougar and growling wolves, they hadn't noticed her as a wolf. Didn't take note of her now that she was here in the room when they'd thought she was missing. Tala was free, sitting beside the big, black wolf who was her mate, her arms wrapped around his neck.

She was crying. Tala never cried. Not ever. Lisa knelt beside her. "Sweetie, it's okay. Everything's going to be okay."

Tala shook her head. "I don't know if it is or not. None of us know." She glanced at Beth and then leaned her head against Lisa's shoulder. *You know how Beth can read minds really well? She picked up that older guy's thoughts. Not enough details, but she learned that our guys at the auditorium are a diversion. There's a bigger plan, a scarier one. She's warned Anton, but she doesn't know enough. She's trying to get what she can out of these bastards before the police get here.*

And there wasn't a damned thing any of them could do. Whatever plan Anton had was already in motion. So was the enemy's.

Lisa glanced at the clock on the wall. It was almost nine.

The first band hit the stage hard with a loud set, heavy on the drums, with a lot of bass guitar. Beth's first warning caught Anton by surprise. He'd been so certain he was keeping an eye on the right people that she literally knocked the pins out from under him. What she told him now had him stunned. He acted immediately, mentally shouting orders.

Thank goodness everyone was in position. *Keisha, protect the president! Get down, now! AJ! Grab the guy behind him, the man to his right. He's armed. Get the gun. Luc, cover me.*

Anton pressed his back to the wall of the stage, opened his mind, and reached out. He'd felt the power building, knew the energy was there, waiting for him, growing stronger, reaching its climax.

He called it to him, holding his hands high, acting as a lightning rod, a conduit pulling the shared energy into himself. Calling on each member of the pack, demanding their power.

Seconds felt like hours. Everything around him slowed. His focus expanded, and the members of the pack heeded his call across the miles.

It wasn't Manda's voice that sent Baylor over the top, wasn't his mate's permission that sent him soaring into his own climax to drag the others right along with him. No, it was Anton's voice, his powerful voice, there in his mind as clear and close as if the man stood beside them.

Anton, asking his Chanku for what they'd promised. Calling to each of them, demanding their power, now.

Knowing he and Manda weren't alone, aware, suddenly, that they were but one cylinder in Anton's huge engine, Bay set himself free. His orgasm slammed into him. He knew and accepted that part of it was Anton's doing, that somehow the climax each of them felt was shared, and sharing the sensations made them all the more powerful.

He'd not imagined such an amazing link. He'd expected to share Jake and Shannon's arousal, and yet he sensed Stefan, Oliver, Xandi, and Mei, Adam and Liana, all the Chanku still in Montana. Ulrich and Millie, Daci, Deacon, and Matt joined them from Colorado, and in San Francisco, even Jazzy and Tia added their own potent jolt of sexual energy. Each of them reaching their sexual peak, sharing the sensations, the joy, and the absolute love, one for the other and each for the pack.

The power expanded in waves, a visual, physical burst of brilliant energy that blossomed about the four of them in the shadows, then suddenly compressed, tighter and tighter until an intense flash of pure power winked out and disappeared entirely.

Bay collapsed over Manda's back. Unable to support his weight, her legs folded beneath her. They lay there, enervated, as weak as a couple of day-old kittens on the cold, hard ground.

Groaning, Stefan stared at the second hand as it suddenly seemed to pick up speed. With a flick of her wrist, Mei straddled his hips and released the leather restraints holding his cock and balls. Blood rushed through his cock in a burst of pain and pleasure so intense, the climax he'd been denied for too long wrapped his body into one, huge orgasmic convulsion.

He grasped Mei's slim hips and held her against him, thrusting up hard inside the tight, hot sheath of her vagina. Her muscles clamped down on him, squeezing him, pulling him deeper yet. And there, calling Stefan, calling on his energy and all that he could give, all that Mei and Xandi and Oliver were capable of sharing, was Anton.

Dear Goddess, but he loved the man. Hearing his beloved voice, knowing it was Anton who needed him, who needed all of them, made this all the more powerful.

Only Anton could do this, and do it so well—bring all of them together, combining their climaxes, sharing the power of each and every member of the pack. Anton opened each of them up to the others. Stefan felt Liana and Adam as they came together, shared Baylor, Jake, Shannon, and Manda's energy even as he gave all of his own. The group in Colorado, even Tia and Jazzy in San Francisco. All together, shared, multiplied, freely given.

And, long moments later, when Mei lay across his body, barely conscious, and Xandi and Oliver gasped for breath beside him, Stefan marveled, once again, at the immense power of the man he loved.

Wave after wave of sensation washed over Adam as their orgasm continued to grow and expand. It was unique, unlike anything he'd ever imagined. He lost all control of his wolven form. His legs collapsed, and so did Liana's. As they tumbled to the ground, Adam shifted so that he could pull out without hurting her. He rolled to one side in the deep grass, aware Liana had shifted at the same time.

His muscles twitched and rippled as if he still responded to Anton's desperate call. His cock remained hard. He sensed Anton, knew he'd succeeded in connecting with each and every one of them. Adam hoped it had been enough. It had to be. For now, though, he lay in the grass, barely conscious, yet still aware of the shared sense of connection, the fact he and Liana had climaxed with the entire pack, all of them, together.

"How the fuck does he do that?" He reached for Liana and caught her hand. Turned and looked into those gorgeous gray-green eyes of hers. "The man is scary powerful." He took a deep breath and blinked through a sudden sheen of tears. "I love you, Liana. I will always love you. And that has got to be the most amazing thing I've ever experienced in my life."

"Are you okay?" Liana's eyes were wide with worry.

Worried about him? He nodded without getting up. He wasn't even sure he could get up. Not yet. "I'm good, my love. What about you?"

She smiled. A slow, sexy smile that made him want her again. "Never better. As long as I don't have to move."

Adam nodded. "Good. Then we'll just lie here awhile longer." He laughed softly. "It's a good thing Eve left us a spot without snow."

He felt Liana's fingers tighten around his, but she didn't answer. There really wasn't anything either of them needed to say. Not right now. Holding his mate's hand, Adam lay in the circle of grass amid the pink primroses and finally remembered to hope like hell Lisa and Tala were safe.

Ric felt as if he'd been holding on to all of them forever, like fragile threads attached to balloons, each of them ready to fly away. Arousal pulsed, alive and growing as the seconds ticked by, until suddenly Anton was there, calling out to them, demanding their power, their energy. He needed it now.

All they could give. Whatever they had to share. And just like that, Ric turned loose of the threads and set the balloons free. The moment Anton asked, they delivered. Orgasm slammed into each one of them, a shared experience multiplied by the love each of them felt for the others.

Ric heard Millie's cry and Daci's short, sharp scream. Matt groaned and Deacon cursed and drove into Ric, taking him deeper, harder, fucking him to the point of pain and beyond. Then Daci swallowed his cock. Her throat convulsed around his full length, tipping all of them over the top.

It was a most amazing experience. Ric felt as if he watched from a distance—five bodies writhing together, linked in orgasmic excess, directed by a man hundreds of miles away. It took forever for the final convulsions to end, for their bodies to relax enough to consider the orgasm over. For long moments they lay there, unmoving, stripped of whatever energy they'd been able to produce.

Anton had grabbed all of it. He'd somehow managed to reach out at precisely the right moment and pull every last bit away from them, into himself.

Ric unclenched his fist and caught Millie's hand in his. She squeezed his fingers as the same thoughts united them—had Anton's plan worked? Was everyone safe?

Tia wanted to turn around so that she was facing Jazzy, but her body refused to obey. Ripples of pure pleasure still rolled across her skin and deep inside her body, as if her orgasm had become the sea and she was merely bobbing on the surface at the whim of the ebb and flow of the tide. The candles had burned almost completely down, the room was almost entirely dark.

Her cheek rested on Jazzy's groin. Jazzy's breasts were squished beneath her belly. She heard Jazzy's indrawn breath, felt a cool rush of air between her legs as Jazzy exhaled. "Logan says they've got Tala and Lisa. They're safe, but no one knows what's going on at the auditorium. Power just went out in the hotel."

"The hotel? I thought he was only shutting down the auditorium." Tia carefully rolled off Jazzy and landed with a thump on the floor in front of the couch. "I promised Luc I wouldn't try and contact him. I don't want to get in the way of whatever happens there."

"Well, we know Anton got everyone's energy. He sure sucked up all of mine. Damn. I feel like a wet noodle, but he definitely got it." Jazzy sat up and leaned against the couch. "Got it, shared it, and made it even stronger. The man's amazing."

Tia laughed as she hunted under the pile of magazines on the coffee table for the remote control. "Amazing and downright scary. Let's see what the local news says."

She aimed at the TV and pushed the button. Nothing happened. "Jazzy? Try the lamp next to the couch."

Jazzy pulled the chain. "Nothing. Didn't you have the CD player going earlier?" She stood up and walked over to the door into the kitchen and tried the light. "Power's out here, too. Crap. I wonder what's happening?"

Tia reached into a drawer beside the TV and pulled out a flashlight. "I'm going to check on the girls. Stay in contact with Logan. This is starting to make me nervous."

She was back within the minute. "They're both out, sort of like our lights. Any word from Logan?"

"Yeah. The power went out citywide at eight fifty-five. As far as he can tell, no cell phones, no regular phones, nothing. And no word from the auditorium. They've got the three guys who kidnapped Lisa and Tala tied up, and they're waiting at the hotel for the police. Mik's shifted and he's handling things in human form. Igmutaka and Beth are on their way to the auditorium to make sure Anton and the others are okay."

"Why aren't they just connecting mentally, the way you and Logan are?" Tia sat next to her on the couch.

Jazzy took her hand and squeezed. "No one wants to interrupt Anton or the guys. Be patient. They'll let us know as soon as they can."

AJ reacted. He didn't think, didn't question Anton's command. He launched himself into the air and leapt over the heads of the people sitting between him and the man Anton had told him to stop. What had simply been a rather large, well-built middle-aged man in a dark suit had suddenly become a target. A dangerous and threatening target.

He was aware of Keisha placing herself in front of the president and shoving him to the ground as the man rose and reached for something in his pocket. Then AJ was on him, knocking him to the floor, scattering chairs and bodies in all directions while the driving rhythm of heavy bass guitar and pounding drums masked the noise.

Startled screams, the sharp retort of gunfire, and the frenzied commotion of people scrambling out of the way played a discordant counterpoint to the rock band on stage. Then, as the band members suddenly realized they might be in danger, they scattered like ants.

The music faded away to the final notes of guitar, a loud squeal from the microphone. Gasps of shock and fear.

AJ's left arm whipped around the man's throat. He struggled for bare seconds before grabbing hold of the man's fist and the small automatic pistol he was holding in his right hand. AJ was bigger and stronger and the force of his attack gave him the advantage. He shoved the muzzle of the gun down, pointing it at the floor as the thing went off a second time.

The sound of the shot echoed. Everyone around him stopped moving, and every hair on his body suddenly stood on end. Once he had the senator trapped securely in a headlock, AJ glanced toward Anton. The wizard stood immobile in front of the stage, his arms raised high, his eyes wide and staring as he pulled in energy from all across the country.

He wasn't certain what made him do it, but AJ linked with Anton. Searing pain streaked through his head. A blast of immense power shattered the link and sent him tumbling out of Anton's mind, but he didn't let go of the man he held.

All the lights went out.

Screams and shouts filled the huge auditorium, but the darkness was absolute. Even the emergency lighting had failed.

AJ's prisoner stopped struggling. AJ loosened his hold on the man's throat and the body beneath his sagged, limp and unconscious. At least AJ hoped he was merely unconscious. He'd hit the man hard and fast.

Held on to him, maybe just a bit too long.

He couldn't see a thing. Not a glimmer of light, even with his Chanku senses revved up on high.

Keisha? You okay?

We're fine. I've got a death grip on the president's hand so I won't lose him in the dark. Tinker's staying close. The bullet grazed my shoulder. Hurts, but it's not too bad. Anton's unconscious. It must have been the power surge. He collapsed when the lights went out. Luc's with him. He thinks Anton's okay. We need to get the president out of here.

Can you go back to the hotel? I'll turn this guy over to the authorities as soon as I can. Then I'll take care of Anton.

We'll go as soon as we can get out of here safely.

He sensed that she spoke aloud to the president, but AJ couldn't hear her. The noise around them was growing as panic set in. Shouts, demands for light, for help, echoed in the huge building. A few cigarette lighters flamed to life and AJ worried about fire, but he worried more about his packmates.

About Anton. Dear Goddess! If that burst of power that burned through AJ's brain was just a fraction of what Anton had dealt with . . . He sent a quick prayer for the wizard's safety.

Keisha's voice was back in his mind. He sensed the

worry she tried to mask, but AJ knew she'd promised her mate that the president's safety would be her primary concern.

We're going now. The president wants to stay so I can be with Anton, but I've convinced him he should be with his wife. I can't carry this charade off if we're under any close scrutiny.

You've done great so far.

He sensed Keisha's tired laughter. *Thanks. I'm ready to go back to being Lily's mommy. Okay . . . we've made it over to Anton.*

AJ waited impatiently, still hanging on to his prisoner.

Anton's still unconscious, but I don't sense any serious injury. Luc's staying with him. Tinker's going with me and the president. Beth and Igmutaka are out in front with a vehicle. They'll take us to the Fairmont.

The man beneath AJ shifted and moved a bit. AJ tightened his hold, then stood up and pulled the guy with him. He held the man upright. He was conscious now. AJ smelled the man's fear, could hear his heavy breathing, but he was no longer struggling. He hadn't said a word since AJ had stopped him. AJ didn't loosen his hold. This guy wasn't going anywhere, not until the authorities arrived.

It was totally dark except for a few flashlights flickering among the crowd. AJ heard a shout and stared in the direction it had come from. Four large men with flashlights raced toward him. AJ recognized them as security personnel moving his way.

He'd thought of moving closer to Anton to protect the wizard in case these were some of the fake security forces they'd run into earlier. He decided against it as soon as he recognized the one guard in the front as someone he'd seen watching over the First Family before.

AJ kept his hold on his man and called out to the ones who were obviously headed to the president's defense. "Over here. In the roped-off section. My wallet and ID are in my left hip pocket." He wasn't about to turn his guy loose.

"Where's the . . . ?"

AJ interrupted. "He's safe. We've got him headed back to the Fairmont with the First Lady and extra security. This gentleman"—he shook the man none too gently—"pulled a gun and fired it twice. He may have wounded one of our security people. She left with the president."

He twisted the man's arm and showed the guard the handgun still clasped in the man's hand. Both hand and gun were entirely encased in AJ's big fist.

"Son of a . . ." The guard shook his head and grabbed the weapon with a clean handkerchief. One of the men behind him pulled out a small plastic bag. The gun went into the bag.

His prisoner cursed and twisted in AJ's strong grasp. AJ merely tightened his choke hold. Gasping for air, the man quit struggling.

It took them only a couple of minutes to cuff the guy and read him his rights. By then, lights were beginning to come back on—first the emergency lighting, and then, one by one, the overhead lights. People milled about, unsure exactly what had happened, but well aware something had gone horribly wrong. Members of the media headed en masse toward the place where the president should have been. Security guards blocked them and moved everyone away from the roped section.

The stage was littered with guitars and other musical paraphernalia left when the band had scattered at the first sound of trouble. Thank goodness Keisha and the president had escaped under cover of darkness. If there was anyone else after the man, they'd have a hard time finding him now.

AJ spun around when he heard Luc growl. One of the security guys was trying to check on Anton, who still lay unconscious in front of the stage. "Excuse me." AJ shoved through the crowd and went to Anton's side. He tapped the guard's shoulder. "Thanks for checking on him. He's one of ours. I'll take care of him."

The man nodded and returned to the others. Anton's eyes slowly opened, but he was obviously confused.

"Hey, boss. How are you?"

Anton blinked and stared at AJ. Then he slowly shook his head. "I don't know." He tried to sit up. AJ slipped an arm behind his back and helped him until he was able to lean against the stage. "Where's Keisha? Is she okay?" Slowly he shook his head. "I can't hear her voice. Can't hear any voices. Nothing. No links, no connections."

AJ squeezed his shoulder. "I think you might have fried a brain cell or two. I know you fried a few of mine. Beth said you shut down the entire city. It's just now beginning to come back up, but the president is safe. I stopped the bastard you told me to go after. Beth was right—he was armed and he got off a couple of shots. Keisha got nicked but she's okay. Lisa and Tala are safe. The babies are safe."

Anton's hand came up at the sound of Keisha's name. AJ grabbed it and held on. "She's fine," he said. "Bullet grazed her shoulder, but Logan will be with her shortly. By the time you see her, she'll be healed and probably madder than hell at you for scaring her like this."

Anton nodded and leaned his head against the wall. He closed his eyes, obviously still rattled from the huge burst of energy he'd handled.

"Stay with him Luc, okay?"

The black wolf dipped his head as AJ returned to the small group of men holding the assailant. This all felt so strange, for him to be taking charge, but Luc was in wolf form and obviously couldn't do his usual job, Anton was out of the picture for now, and that left AJ. He usually hung back, let others take over. He glanced around, hoping like hell he didn't screw up, but no one had planned for Anton being out of commission. It looked like he was their only choice.

Other security people arrived. They held the crowds back and kept the media entirely out of the area. Worried, AJ glanced at Anton. He appeared to have passed out again. The man would hate for anyone to see him this way, but AJ couldn't leave. Not yet. At least Luc was sticking close, guarding him from curious eyes as best he could. AJ grinned. Luc was a very large wolf. Anton was barely visible behind the huge beast.

AJ dealt with security as quickly as he could and set up a time to meet with the one leading the investigation. They'd go over everything tomorrow. By then he hoped Anton would have some way to explain the power outage, because AJ didn't have a clue how they were going to deal with that.

It appeared they'd been successful, though little had gone as planned. He still had a dull ache in his head from Anton's power surge. He hated to think what the wizard must be feeling right now. Damn. How long was all this going to take?

He needed to connect with the rest of his team and see what, exactly, had happened.

Then he really needed to connect with Tala.

Mik's terse message, that she was fine and they'd caught the three men holding the women, was a huge relief, but it wasn't enough.

Not nearly enough.

Chapter 13

AJ stretched out in the big bed, tucked Tala against his chest, and hugged her close. Then he reached across her waist and rested his hand on Mik's hip. It felt right, the way it was supposed to when they went to bed at night. He needed this sense of unity, of the three of them together, more than ever. He'd begun to wonder if they'd ever get home, but after what felt like hours of questioning, the feds had finally turned them loose to return to the renovated old mansion where all of them lived in the Sunset District.

This late in Tala's pregnancy, there was no talk of sex, though he and Mik often made love before falling asleep. Not tonight. Tonight all he and Mik wanted to do was hold Tala close and revel in the fact she was safe.

Igmutaka, glorious in his puma form, slept on the floor at the foot of their bed. He'd insisted on remaining close to Tala's daughter, but not as a man. He chose to guard her in the form where he felt strongest, and the big cat had remained an unobtrusive shadow once they'd gotten home.

Tinker and Lisa were just down the hall. Poor Tink had been a wreck until he finally held Lisa in his arms. AJ knew exactly how the big guy felt. Even after Mik had assured him that Tala was safe, he'd needed to see for himself. Then he'd insisted Logan check her to make sure she was really okay. Even Mik had teased him about that, but Mik had been with Tala for hours before AJ finally got to see for himself she hadn't been harmed.

He never, ever wanted to go through anything like tonight again. Not as long as they lived. He honestly didn't think his heart could take it. He still wasn't sure how well his mind had come through everything. His head still ached and he sensed weird echoes of the thoughts of others. Not enough to really disturb him, but something was different, and had been since he'd linked with Anton.

He wondered how Anton was doing. He still hadn't had a chance to talk with him. Logan and Jazzy had stayed at Tia and Luc's where Logan could keep an eye on the wizard. He'd been unconscious when Tinker picked him up out of the SUV and carried him like a child into the guest room. Keisha had been so calm that AJ worried about her, but she said she knew Anton would be fine, and then she sent them all on their way.

Keisha would know, wouldn't she? He took a deep breath, pulling in the scents of Tala and Mik. They were both so damned precious to him. If anything had gone wrong . . .

Tala pressed her face against his chest and practically burrowed into him, clinging as tightly as her huge belly would allow. Mik was curled around her back, his forehead touching AJ's.

"Guys?" There was a definite quiver to her voice.

"What's wrong, sweetie? Are we crowding you?" One of the babies kicked hard enough that AJ felt the pressure against his belly. An unexpected surge of emotion closed his throat and his eyes burned. They'd come so close today. So damned close. He ran his fingertips along the firm swell of her hip, then rested his fingers on Mik's waist. Damn, he'd been so afraid for her today.

She laughed, but it sounded like the beginning of a sob.

"Never. But today, when I thought about the chance I might never get to do this again, I realized how much I love you both."

Mik's arm went over Tala and he grabbed AJ close, squeezing them tightly together. "Don't even go there, baby. You're safe, the president is safe, and they caught the ones who planned this. You and Lisa were so damned brave today. I don't know any other women who would have taken risks like you girls did."

Tala sniffed.

AJ kissed the top of her head. "And if you ever scare either of us again like you did today, I swear we'll both paddle your butt."

She giggled, hiccupped, and sniffed. Then she yawned. "You'll have to wait until tomorrow. I'm really sleepy."

AJ chuckled. "Works for me."

Mik merely grunted. It was the last sound AJ heard as he drifted slowly off to sleep.

Anton felt as if he might be floating, but his head wouldn't stop pounding and there was a strange sense in the back of his battered mind, that maybe things hadn't quite gone as planned. He needed sleep to heal, but he couldn't relax. Not until he knew for sure that Keisha was all right.

What did AJ say? She'd been shot? No. That couldn't be. He would have known it. Their link was so powerful, so complete, he would have sensed her pain. Would have known if she was injured.

Wouldn't he? Then why couldn't he sense her now? He'd tried searching, but there was nothing. No sense of Keisha. No background noise of the other packmates who so often inhabited his mind. No, all was quiet. Calm, and very, very quiet.

"Anton? Ah, my love. What have you done this time?"

He blinked. The room was dark, but he wasn't in the

auditorium anymore. Strange. He didn't remember coming home, but . . . He wasn't home. He was in the guest room at Luc and Tia's house. "Keisha?" He tried to lift his hand, to touch her face, but it wouldn't move. It was much too heavy to lift.

Something warm, wet, touched his cheek. He frowned. Tears? "Why are you crying?" He reached for her mind. Nothing. "Why are you blocking me?"

She shook her head, sobbing openly now. The tears fell faster. "I'm not. I'm not blocking you. I'm wide open. I've been calling to you since I got back to the hotel with the president, but you weren't there. You weren't in my thoughts where you belong. I thought you were dead. I still can't feel you." Her palm swept along the side of his face. He turned and kissed her, nuzzling into her warmth, reveling in the fact she was here and alive and apparently unharmed.

"AJ said you were hurt?"

She nodded. "Just a graze across my shoulder." She laughed, but once again the sound ended on a sob.

"Keisha?"

Smiling, sniffing, she wiped her streaming eyes and then she kissed him. "I ruined the First Lady's dress. Hard for her to explain a bullet hole in the shoulder, and the bloodstains probably won't come out. She was very understanding."

"I certainly hope so." Incensed, he tried to sit up. Nothing. "What's wrong with me? I have nothing. No energy, nothing. My mind feels . . ." He blinked, trying to remember something terribly important. "AJ? He's okay?"

"He is. He caught the guy before he could get off a clear shot. The one that grazed my shoulder was meant for the president. AJ saved both our lives."

Anton blinked, remembering. "He saved mine, as well."

"How?"

"I called the energy to me. Too much." He tried to smile,

but it was halfhearted at best. "Once again I let my ego get in the way of common sense."

"You?" Keisha pressed her hand to her heart in a melodramatic gesture. "Never!"

"Cut it out." This time he knew his smile worked just fine, because his beloved mate returned it. "Our Chanku have no concept of their own strength. They not only created their own sexual energy, they somehow made it work through my link with them. All of them feeding off each other, making the energy grow exponentially. When I called it, I got more than I expected."

"So that's how you managed to shut down the entire city of San Francisco? I wondered about that."

The whole city? Now, that was something he'd need to think about. He had no idea he'd drawn that much power, no idea he could wield that kind of strength.

Because normally, he couldn't. It should have killed him. Might have, but AJ . . .

Keisha was nodding. "Yep. Streetlights, cell phones, land lines. Everything went dead for at least a couple of minutes. The nightly news is still trying to come up with a reason for the massive power failure. It's unprecedented to have everything fail. Even generators. Luckily, within about a minute, emergency procedures were able to override the failures around the city and no deaths have been attributed to the loss of power, but no one can explain it. It's making people crazy."

"I guess we'll just have to let them wonder. Is AJ here? I need to thank him. To ask him how he knew to save me."

"I don't understand. You told him to stop the shooter. How else would he know the guy had a gun?"

In spite of the tremendous pain, Anton shook his head. "No. Not that. When I called the power, AJ linked with me. How did he know I needed him? If he hadn't linked, hadn't been there to buffer the energy, I think it would have killed me."

Keisha sat back. Shook her head. "I don't know. He's in the other room, with Tala and Mik. They got here a while ago from their place over in the Sunset."

Anton squeezed her hand. "Call him, please? I would, but I can't seem to send or receive."

"I know." Her eyes sparkled, amber glowing through unshed tears. "I can't feel you at all, my love. It's as if you're lost to me." She leaned close and kissed him. "I want you back."

Then she left the room. Anton lay back against the pillows and once again tried to reconstruct the night he'd almost lost.

AJ kissed Tala and left her snuggling with Mik on the couch. It was hard to walk away and leave her, even though he knew everything was fine and she was in great shape this morning, but he couldn't help looking back as he followed Keisha to Anton's room. There was so damned much to do, when all he really wanted was to go back to their apartment, crawl back into bed with Mik and Tala, and hold both of them close.

Instead, he needed to spend a little time with Anton, and then he had to head over to the Fairmont. There was a meeting planned with the president and his regular security forces, as well as members of the local law enforcement agencies that had been involved in last night's attempted assassination.

The media was all over the story, but so far everything they reported was mere speculation. No one was saying anything specific, not until they cleared details with AJ and Luc. Thank goodness Luc was planning to go as the head of Pack Dynamics—though he couldn't offer any information. The fact he'd been there as a wolf was known only to the president and his wife.

AJ checked the time and hoped Anton wouldn't want him for long. He had to get moving. Beth and Nick were already at the Fairmont, but they'd stayed the night in the presidential suite.

No one was getting near the First Couple. Not with the two of them on watch.

Keisha stopped him at the doorway. "He's fallen asleep. My gut feeling is to let him rest for now. Why don't you come back after your meeting, when you're not as rushed?"

He leaned close and kissed her. "Perfect. I really do need to get over there."

Keisha stopped him with a light touch to his hand. "Thank you, AJ."

He frowned. "For what?"

"Anton says you saved his life. That if you hadn't linked with him at the moment he called the power, it would have killed him. He wasn't expecting such a huge burst of energy. He said you buffered it and that gave him the chance to work it."

Amazing. Shaking his head, he tried to recall exactly what had happened. He still had no idea. "I don't know why I did it. I just had a really strong feeling I should link with him. I didn't last more than a couple of seconds. The blast of power blew me right out of his mind." He rubbed the back of his head. "I've still got a headache. I can't even imagine how much pain Anton's in."

Keisha's mysterious smile caught him by surprise. "What?" he demanded. "You look like you know what's going on."

"I wonder if Eve had her hand in this? Why else would you have linked?"

He'd have to think about that. He hadn't actually sensed anyone else, but that would explain the sudden urge to do something he'd never done in his life.

Keisha glanced inside the room and then quietly shut the door behind her. "When you meet with the feds this morning, what are you going to say?"

He shrugged and followed Keisha down the hall. "The

truth, or at least as much of it as we can. Obviously we plan to avoid any mention of shapeshifting. The president appeared to agree with us on that, but that was last night. Luc's going with me and I'm hoping he'll do the talking. He's better at that sort of thing than I am. I'm not sure if Tinker's coming or not. He stayed in wolf form the whole evening, so there's no reason for him to make a statement. Besides, he really doesn't want to be away from Lisa right now."

"I don't blame him. Are you okay leaving Tala?"

Chuckling, he raised his eyebrows. "What do you think?" He shook his head. "No. Not really, but she's got Mik, so it's not like I'm leaving her alone. And don't forget Igmutaka. He hasn't left her side, either, though he's more interested in Mik's daughter. So long as the baby's inside Tala, she's got her own personal watchcat. Lisa's only got Tinker, and he knows she's dealing with the aftermath of all that happened yesterday. Plus, she had some spotting this morning. I think she's concerned shifting might have done some harm."

"What's Logan think?"

"That she's fine, but he wants to keep an eye on her, and if that's the case, I imagine Tink's going to want to keep an eye on Logan." He laughed. He and Mik were just as bad about Tala.

No, big guy. We're worse. Mik's voice resonated with laughter. *I have to admit, I sort of like having Igmutaka on our side. He's sticking to Tala like glue.*

Keisha'd obviously caught Mik's comment. She was grinning as they turned away from Anton's quiet room. "If you want my opinion, I think Mik just likes having another hot guy hanging around."

AJ was still thinking of Keisha's teasing comment as he and Luc left their car with the valet in front of the Fairmont. It was true that both he and Mik thought Igmutaka was a beautiful man, but neither of them had thought of him sexually, which was sort of odd, considering. They knew he was Adam and Liana's lover, but he was their unborn daughter's spirit guide.

For some reason, he couldn't look at the man as anything else. He wondered how Tala saw him, if she thought of him sexually. They'd accepted him as the baby's guide without question. Now he wondered if Igmutaka expected more of them. Of course, he was a shapeshifter, but not Chanku. Maybe Ig's libido didn't run his life the way Mik and AJ's did.

He was still wondering about the spirit guide when they got into the elevator that took them straight to the penthouse suite. Luc paused for a moment as they stepped out into the long hallway and studied AJ for a moment. "You okay? You seem really distracted for some reason." Then he laughed. "Shit. That sounds like the sort of question Tia would ask me."

AJ grinned and nodded. "Yeah. Still have a headache after last night, but I'm fine. Maybe a little spacier than usual."

Luc nodded, but he didn't pursue it. A sentry met them at the doorway to the president's suite. Luc pulled out his wallet. AJ did the same, they showed their identification to the man, and were ushered inside.

Keisha had given her statement the night before and it was surprisingly simple for AJ and Luc to fill in what they knew. No one mentioned the power outage, and AJ suddenly realized that no one suspected any of them. It was an anomaly that would probably drive people nuts, but even the president hadn't been aware of Anton's plans to shut down power.

Maybe it was better that way. If the question ever came up, he would tell the truth, but until then, Anton's part in the power outage was going to remain a secret.

Beth and Nick entered the room during the questioning. Luc glanced up and smiled. AJ noticed that Beth seemed quieter than usual, but Nick was more animated, practically buzzing with excitement. Luc was still discussing some of the night's events with the officer. AJ watched the two kids for a moment.

Their voices suddenly slipped into his mind. Voices he shouldn't have heard. They were mindtalking directly to each other, privately, and yet their conversation was as clear as if they spoke to him out loud.

Nick, I think it's really going to be hard to convince Luc. He's spent a lot of time training us.

This is such an amazing opportunity, Beth. Living in Washington, in the White House? Think of it. We would be part of the presidential family's security team. We'd travel all over the world. They want us, Beth. You and me. Think of it.

That's all I have thought of.

Beth glanced around, as if assuring herself their conversation was private. AJ focused on Luc as if he were involved in that conversation, but his mind was spinning. He'd never picked up private conversations before. The only one who could do that with ease was Anton.

Except Anton couldn't pick up anything at all since he'd gotten zapped last night. And now AJ could.

What the fuck is going on?

He focused on Beth and Nick, eavesdropping without shame as the two kids discussed this absolutely amazing opportunity they'd been offered.

If he ignored the pain, it didn't go away, but it didn't control him, either. That was good. He'd been struggling now for hours, hanging on to what little of himself there was that seemed to be functioning, but it was terrifying, this sense that he was no longer the man he'd always been.

Anton lay quietly with his eyes shut and wondered how he would go on from here. Wondered if he would ever feel whole again. He knew he was in the guest room at Luc and Tia's house, though he'd much rather be home in Montana. He missed the smell of pines and the fresh, clean air. He missed the quiet.

He missed Lily's laughter. Nothing quiet about Lily.

He really missed Stefan. Stefan would find something about this current mess that would make him laugh. Right now, Anton wondered if he'd ever laugh again.

At least his eyes still worked. He could speak, though it was exhausting, thinking about the words and forming them with a mouth that didn't feel quite attached to his body. He could hear, but it was such limited hearing. He hadn't realized how much a man missed when he heard only sound, not the thoughts of those around him.

He could no longer feel Keisha's love, even though she sat in a chair beside the bed. So close, yet she might have been a million miles away. And the constant buzz in the back of his mind, the thoughts and conversations of the other Chanku across the country that had become such a welcome companion to his thoughts—that buzz was gone as well.

He might have cried out in frustration, but that wouldn't do him any good at all. It would scare the hell out of Keisha and probably make Lisa and Tala feel bad. They would blame themselves for his strange disability. He was, after all, rescuing them when he apparently fried a few neurons too many.

It hurt to think about it, but he guessed he should be thankful he was at least alive. He had AJ to thank for that. Where in the hell was AJ? Hadn't Keisha gone to get him?

He thought of opening his eyes, asking Keisha where AJ was, but then he felt sleep overtaking him again. That seemed to be the one thing he was really good at. Sleeping.

If he was going to excel at something, sleep worked. With that thought in mind, Anton drifted away once again.

Then he blinked his eyes. Opened them wide and looked

around. Apparently, he'd drifted somewhere besides sleep. He sat alone in a grassy meadow. Naked, just the way he'd been in bed. Grass tickled his butt and a warm breeze caressed his shoulders. He gazed around, struck with the familiarity of the meadow. He'd been here before, but it wasn't the same.

Or was it? His memories felt as if they shifted, one within the other, and he rubbed his eyes with both hands. At least his head didn't hurt anymore. The relief was exquisite, and more than welcome.

"Hello, Anton."

He jerked his chin up and caught Eve looking at him, only it wasn't Eve as he remembered her. The last time he'd seen her had been when she'd come to take Liana's knowledge. Then she'd seemed every bit the powerful Goddess.

Now, she was more like the Eve he remembered, except for those strange eyes that seemed to swirl and pulse with various shades of color. He smiled at her. "Eve." He tried to stand, but his legs were still rubbery. He bowed his head, showing her the respect she deserved. She had, after all, come through for him.

Maybe even more than he'd needed. "The girls are safe," he said, fully aware she already knew. "With your help, we stopped the assassination attempt. Thank you."

She walked across the meadow and sat down in front of him. "You did. Lisa and Tala are safe, the perpetrators are in jail, and it appears that you, my friend, are the only casualty."

That didn't sound at all promising. He sighed. "Is there any hope my abilities will return?"

Eve glanced away. Her chest rose and fell with her deep breath. "I don't know. The Mother was very cryptic when I asked."

"I see." That really didn't sound good. "What did she say?"

Eve reached for his right hand with both of hers and squeezed his fingers. "That to achieve great things, sacrifices must be made."

He nodded. What could he say? Though he realized he had a new appreciation for Adam's suicide attempt just a few months ago. Some sacrifices were more painful than others.

Eve was nodding and smiling. "That's exactly what I was thinking. We've all made sacrifices to gain something else. Adam gave up his grief in order to find love again, and while it doesn't sound like much to give up, for Adam it was a very difficult thing. I gave up life to fill the role I was destined for. Liana gave up her life as a goddess in order to find love."

Anton gazed at her hands, so tightly wrapped about his big mitt. He was trying to imagine life without the mental abilities he'd taken for granted for so long.

It wasn't easy.

"Would you have done anything differently, if you had known the sacrifice you would be making? Would you have tried to free Lisa and Tala another way? Risked the death of your president?"

He thought about that for just seconds and realized that no, he wouldn't have done anything differently. "It was the only way I could see to rescue the girls and find out who was behind the whole plot. The girls are safe, the men who orchestrated it are all behind bars." He shook his head, hating the fact that he'd been forced to make such a choice, but at the same time realizing that, even knowing the outcome, he would do it again.

Smiling, Eve squeezed his hand. "I thought so. Go home to Montana. Rest. Let your mind heal. AJ has what you need. You'll know when you're ready to take it back."

"What I need? What do you mean? I don't understand."

"You will, my friend. Now rest."

His world spun and left him feeling dizzy and disoriented. He blinked, tried to focus, and rubbed his hands over his eyes. Keisha lay beside him on the bed. At first he thought she was asleep, but she blinked, opened her eyes wide, and smiled at him.

"You're awake. I was getting worried. You've slept so soundly. It felt like you were a million miles away."

"If you only knew." Smiling, he rolled to his side and kissed her. "I love you. I was so afraid for you last night, I couldn't even let myself think about the danger you were in."

She brushed his face with her fingers. "I saw you lying on the floor and I couldn't reach you. Your mind was shut down entirely and I wanted to go to you, but I'd promised to keep the president safe. I wanted to stay with you, but I couldn't."

"You did the right thing. Have they caught everyone? I should know more of what happened, but it's all so vague."

"It's going to get very ugly. Milton Bosworth's aide was the ringleader. It sounds like the guy's insane, as if Bosworth rubbed off on him a bit too much. He had help from a member of the White House staff and the director of the special service agency that Bosworth formed and Baylor once worked for. The whole agency appears infected with the same fanaticism that marked Bosworth—and they hate the president. Passionately."

Anton thought about the things Bosworth had done that had impacted the pack—Ulrich's kidnapping, Manda's twenty-five-year nightmare, Daciana's twisted upbringing. So many people hurt by his hatred and his twisted mind.

"Bay's going to be called to testify," Keisha said. "All about the meeting they observed at the restaurant as well as the death of Rolf Jurgens, the one who warned him of the plot."

"All of them were involved? All those people in a plot to assassinate our president?"

Keisha nodded. "The staff member switched the security guard watching over the president. He's the one who got our paperwork to get us into the venue. The man who shot me, who was trying to kill the president, is the long-time director of Bay's old agency and very close to Bosworth's aide. He has a terminal illness—only months to live, so he volunteered to be the shooter. The plan was, when the wolves attacked he'd shoot at them, only he was going to miss and hit the president. It would all be a terrible accident."

Anton tried to make sense of it. "But the wolves didn't attack. He fired anyway. He could have killed you." Just saying the words left him cold inside.

Keisha gently touched his hand. "It was five minutes to nine. The minute he knew we weren't going through with our part, he chose to act without us. He wanted the president dead. The aide had him convinced that if he succeeded, he'd die a hero."

"What about Bay's friend? They murdered him?"

Keisha nodded. "He was sent to Maine in search of the missing agents, as he'd told Bay, only he didn't realize the director of the agency no longer trusted him. That hit had nothing to do with his telling Baylor about the plot against the girls. He was already marked for death. It was pure coincidence he happened to see Baylor just before it happened."

Anton raised his eyebrows. Keisha frowned. Then she broke into a big grin when she realized what she'd said.

"Well, it could have been a coincidence!"

Anton chuckled. Right now, he missed Stef more than ever. Then he sobered. "It's just so hard to believe."

"But true." She sat up on the bed beside him. "Do you feel strong enough to sit up? I can help you."

"I need to get up." He tried to sit, but Keisha had to help him. "Why don't you call one of the guys to help me?

I want a shower, and I don't think you're strong enough to carry me."

Laughing at his dry comment, she kissed his cheek and slipped off the bed. Anton watched her go, and he wanted to curse, to rail against fate or the Goddess or anyone he could think of, but he had only himself to blame.

He'd thought he was strong enough to handle it all, but once again he'd screwed up. Only this time, it had cost him more than merely his pride. He'd lost the intimate connection with his pack, with his friends, and with the woman who meant more to him than anyone else in the world.

He couldn't connect with Keisha at all. It wasn't the fact she was blocking. She wasn't. He'd lost the ability to reach out with his own thoughts. He'd lost the single most important thing that connected him to his kind.

At least he managed to sit upright on the edge of the bed by the time Keisha returned to the room with AJ in tow.

"Good to see you looking so much better." AJ sat down on the bedside chair and began removing his shoes. "I'll just get in the shower with you. It's easier that way."

"How's Tala? Is she okay?"

AJ raised his head and smiled, and once again Anton was reminded what a beautiful man he was. Inside and out.

"She's great. She wasn't harmed at all. She was, however, pissed enough to do some damage on her own if she'd had a chance. Thank you, Anton. Everything worked perfectly." He shrugged. "Well, perfectly other than you doing your best to fry stuff you probably should be a little more careful with."

Laughing softly, Anton shook his head. "I owe you, ya know. When you linked with me, you took a huge brunt of the backlash from so much power. You probably saved my life."

AJ stood up, tugged his shirt off, and slipped out of his jeans. "Actually, it wasn't your life so much that I may have saved." He put an arm around Anton's waist and helped him stand.

His legs wobbled at first, but then he seemed to get his bearings and his balance. He straightened up, but he wasn't about to turn loose of AJ. "What do you mean?" He thought of Eve's cryptic words, that AJ had what he needed. Was that a dream? Had he really seen her, talked to her? Did he actually cross over into the astral plane?

AJ helped him across the bedroom to the bathroom. "Anton, something weird happened when you pulled all that power. I have no idea why I felt I needed to link with you at that precise moment, but I did. Keisha and I are both wondering if it was a nudge from Eve, but I got zapped with some kind of an energy explosion."

Anton leaned against the counter while AJ turned on the water. "I didn't realize that. Are you okay?"

AJ glanced over his shoulder. "That remains to be seen. I'm hearing voices, the private conversations of my pack-mates. I think I picked up Baylor and Jake mindtalking this morning while they were driving back to Maine. You tell me. Am I okay?"

He helped Anton into the shower, one barely large enough for the two of them, but with a sturdy bar bolted to the wall. AJ grabbed a washcloth and soap. Anton hung on to the bar.

He hated feeling this weak, but his mind was spinning and he was afraid if he didn't pay attention, he'd end up on his butt. The grab bar made a lot of sense. "Did Keisha tell you I can't use any telepathy at all? That my senses are completely dead? I can't read her, even when we're touching."

AJ nodded. "She did. Let's try something. I'm going to put my arms around you. I want you to see if you can feel any mental connection to me at all when we're physically connected."

Anton nodded. Terrified it would fail, expecting failure. AJ stood behind him and wrapped his arms around Anton's waist. He felt the broad expanse of AJ's chest, the thick length of AJ's erection pressed hard against his buttocks, and his own cock rose in response.

He almost laughed. He would have, if that hadn't been the only thing that worked. There was no sense of AJ. No connection at all. He tried reaching for him. No luck, except his headache returned. He gave up and sighed. "Nothing. I had hoped . . ."

"Me, too. Maybe it's just too soon. We'll try again, another time."

When I'm ready? Didn't Eve say I'd know when I'm ready?

AJ scrubbed Anton's back and shoulders, ran the cloth over his belly and chest. Then he knelt behind him and washed his legs and buttocks. Turned him so that he could still hang on to the bar and washed his growing erection, ran the washcloth over his balls and inner thighs.

Groaning, Anton leaned against the tile and hung on to the bar with both hands behind his back. AJ rinsed him off with the handheld shower head. Then, without any comment, he knelt once again and nuzzled Anton's groin with his lips.

Steam filled the small bathroom. Any other time, Anton would have been begging AJ to finish what he'd started, but for some reason, with his thoughts trapped within his own hard skull, he hesitated.

Thank the Goddess, AJ didn't. Anton bit back a groan as AJ ran his tongue over his sensitive glans. He gave up trying to stay quiet when AJ slowly wrapped his lips around the entire head. Using his tongue and his teeth, nibbling and sucking, slipping up and then down Anton's swollen cock, AJ drew a little more inside his mouth each time.

Each fraction of an inch felt incredible. Anton clung to the bar, thankful for something to hang on to. The hot water beat down on the two of them, cocooning them both within a thick cloud of steam and the sound of water against tile, of lips over hot flesh.

Anton arched his back as AJ's big hands grabbed hold of his buttocks, holding him in a powerful grasp he had no intention of fighting. His entire cock was engulfed in AJ's mouth, sliding down his throat. The sensation of throat muscles rippling and clenching around his full length almost took him over the edge.

Almost. He locked his knees to keep from falling and hung on to the bar for dear life. AJ's powerful shoulders flexed as he practically lifted Anton to his mouth, drawing him deep, sucking so hard it felt as if he drew the sperm right out of his balls. Anton trembled, fighting the desire to climax until AJ slipped one long, soapy finger through his tightly clenched ass and rubbed gently but firmly over his damned prostate gland.

Orgasm slammed into him. Anton doubled over, turning loose of the bar and grasping those strong, hard shoulders for support. His legs collapsed and only AJ's mouth, the strength of his back, and the grip of his powerful hands held Anton upright.

AJ kept sucking and licking, dragging the pleasure out for what felt like forever, swallowing every drop of ejaculate, squeezing and massaging the tense muscles of his buttocks until Anton felt as if he were floating, as if his body were nothing more than a single nerve pulsing with pleasure.

Finally AJ turned him loose. Anton's cock was entirely flaccid when it slipped out of AJ's mouth. AJ caught the broad crown between his lips and licked the tiny slit with the tip of his tongue. Anton jerked sharply in reaction. He laughed, an almost frantic bark of sound as AJ stood up, rinsed them both, and then grabbed a towel.

He dried Anton first and helped him sit on the closed lid of the toilet seat while he dried himself. "I'm going to find something for you to wear. It's cold tonight and you're pretty weak right now. I don't want you to get chilled."

Still trembling from his climax, Anton laughed. "You're treating me like a little kid, Mom. I'll be okay."

AJ leaned over and kissed him quickly on the mouth. Teasing, he said, "Maybe, but I'll bet Mom never sucked you dry before." Then he sighed. His smile slipped away. "I had hoped, if I could bring you to climax . . ." He looked away as he wrapped the towel around his waist. "I thought maybe, then you could link. That it might work." He couldn't seem to meet Anton's eyes, and he left him sitting alone in the steamy bathroom.

Anton stared as the door shut behind AJ. His body still vibrated from the force of his climax. AJ's blow job had been perfect, except for one thing. Anton had tried linking, too, at the height of climax, when his ability should be at its best.

AJ said he'd tried. So had Anton. It hadn't worked.

Both of them had failed.

There'd been no connection at all.

Chapter 14

Bay's heart actually felt as if it expanded as he pulled into the long driveway that led to the house. They'd only been gone for a few days, but it had felt like forever.

And it wasn't over. Not by a long shot. There would be trials ahead, and more questions, and the terrible risk of exposure. He glanced at Manda, sleeping peacefully in the passenger seat beside him, and knew he would do anything to protect her from the rest of the world.

They couldn't afford for their secret to get out. Especially now, when he was almost certain she carried their child.

He looked in the rearview mirror and caught Jake's amber eyes staring back at his. *Feels good to be home, doesn't it?*

Jake nodded and tightened his hold on Shannon. She slept soundly beside him with her head on his shoulder and the thick waves of her dark red hair flowing over his chest. *That it does. You'll never guess who I've been talking with, though.*

Before Bay had a chance to answer, Jake said, *AJ.*

AJ? But how? He can't mindtalk this far.

He can now. Ever since he caught that energy blast from Anton. And Anton can't project at all. Not even to

Keisha. AJ said he's really worried that somehow he got Anton's ability. Said he feels like he stole it. He chuckled softly. *He wondered if I had any idea how to give it back.*

Bay frowned as the house came into view. He wasn't seeing their home and the end of their journey. No, not now. His mind was filled with sympathy for Anton, for the isolation the man must be suffering.

He'd always been there, before. Always in the background of Bay's mind. At first it had bothered him, but now he knew how much he actually missed the connection. There'd been comfort in Anton's presence. A sense of belonging he'd not felt before he embraced his Chanku heritage.

How must it be for Anton Cheval, a man whose mind had always been his most powerful weapon? Would he ever heal? Bay pulled into the parking spot in front of the house, leaned over, and kissed Manda awake. He tried to imagine what life would be like without the unique Chanku link he shared with his mate.

Empty. Life would be empty and without purpose.

Ulrich poured himself a cup of coffee and joined the rest of the small pack at the breakfast table. They'd all ended up here this morning, probably to discuss the message Deacon had gotten from AJ yesterday.

From the smell of bacon and pancakes, it appeared Millie had already fed them. He glanced around, hoping there might be something left, but the kitchen was already clean and everything had been put away. That'd teach him to oversleep, but the damned pups had worn him out last night.

And the night before. It appeared he and Millie had created monsters. Very, very good monsters.

Millie smiled at him and pulled his chair out. "G'morning, sleepyhead. I wondered if you were going to crawl out of bed. I was thinking of coming after you."

He leaned over and kissed her, loving the sexy twinkle in her eyes. "If you'd come in to get me, we'd still be there."

Matt and Deacon laughed. Daci merely shook her head and snorted. "Men," she said. "You're all alike. Human, Chanku . . . it doesn't seem to matter." Then she cast a sly glance at Millie. "Not that I'm complaining, mind you."

Ric chuckled and raised his cup in salute. Then he sat in the chair beside Millie. "Good morning, brats." He took a sip of his coffee, studying each of the kids over the rim of his cup. Young, maybe, but they were all powerful Chanku, each with a strong sense of the pack.

They were good people. Honorable and loving, and as true as any man could ever hope to call his friends, his packmates. And, just like him, they worried about the wizard. "So, any news about Anton?"

Deacon sighed. "I called AJ last night. He's able to communicate long distances, but I get the feeling it's tiring for him. The phone was easier. He said Anton's planning to go back to Montana. He's had some dream or vision— something about the Goddess. He told AJ he might need him, that Eve told him he'd know when. Other than that, it's all just a waiting game."

Millie squeezed Ric's hand. "What about the girls? Are they okay?"

Deacon's smile changed his entire appearance. When Ric first met the kid, he'd known exactly where the nickname came from. Christopher March—otherwise known as Deacon—had looked like a dour, rather morose old-time preacher. His Goth style and penchant for wearing black hadn't helped. He'd lightened up a lot over the months he'd been here in Colorado, but he still wasn't one to smile a lot.

Now he was definitely smiling. "Yeah," he said. "Tala and Lisa are fine. They're trying to decide whether to go to Montana for their deliveries or stay in San Francisco. Logan said he'll do whatever they want, because Anton will have Adam and Liana for medical care. AJ said they're hoping the two of them might be able to help figure out what the problem is. Logan can't find anything to fix, so his hands are tied."

Ric squeezed Millie's hand and tried to imagine what it would be like not to have the link that kept them connected at all times. Not that he knew what she was thinking. That wasn't the most important thing. No, it was the sense of a part of her always connected to him. As if their souls were never separated.

He didn't want to think about it. The whole idea was much too painful, and for the wizard, a man who stayed connected to the entire pack most of the time, it must be devastating. He sent a quick prayer to Eve, asking her to keep an eye on Anton.

The whole pack needed Anton's mind in good order. Ric hadn't realized how much he'd come to depend on the wizard until that subtle presence was no longer in the back of his thoughts.

Ric searched for him. *Nothing.* It was hard to accept that he wasn't there, even harder to believe he might never feel that connection to Anton again. All of them accepted the wizard as the heart and soul of the entire pack. The glue that held them together and made them stronger as a whole than any one of them could ever hope to be alone. He did it without overt intrusion, without affecting their choices or their actions, yet he connected them in a way both powerful yet inexplicable.

The thought of going on without Anton's presence was more than a little unsettling. Ric sent another quiet prayer to Eve, and hoped like hell the Goddess was paying attention.

Stefan carried a big tray of sandwiches into the dining room. Normally, they'd just have lunch in the kitchen, but today seemed to call for a more formal setting. They had a lot to discuss, and he had a feeling it wasn't going to be easy.

Xandi glanced up and smiled at him, but her eyes were red from crying and he knew how hard this was. Before he could comment, she turned away to finish fastening Lily into the high chair next to Alex. Lily chattered and giggled, totally unaware of the disturbing currents around her.

Xandi tried to tie Lily's bib on. Giggling, Lily tugged it down. Alex reached across the small distance separating the two chairs and grabbed Lily's hand. She giggled louder and then squealed. Alex erupted into giggles.

Xandi burst into tears.

Stefan set the tray on the table and gathered his mate in his arms. She sobbed uncontrollably against his shoulder, and her mind swirled with frustration and pain, the shared pain she felt for Keisha.

She said it feels as if he's dead. She can't sense him at all. There's just nothing there when she reaches for him. He can't touch her, either.

"Sweetheart, Anton's tough. He's been through some really bad things before. He'll come through this. Have a little faith. No matter what happened, he's still Anton. He still loves us and we will always love him."

I know. She sniffed, took the cloth Stefan handed to her, and wiped her eyes and nose. Then she noticed the embroidered wolf in the corner. "Stefan! This isn't a handkerchief. It's one of Keisha's good linen napkins." She rolled her eyes.

He laughed. "Better Keisha's napkin than snot all over my shirt." When the corner of her mouth quirked up in a smile, he kissed her. Then he glanced at the kids. Both Alex and Lily stared at Xandi with wide, troubled eyes. "No more tears," he said. "You'll have both kids crying along with you."

She nodded. "That's all I need. I'm okay." She took a

deep breath. "Here." She handed the soiled cloth to him. "Throw this in the laundry and keep an eye on the kids. I'm going to get some iced tea for everyone."

He watched her go and tried to imagine life with Xandi without the connection, without her soft laughter in his mind, the sense of her love in his heart. It made him ache, an actual physical pain in his gut. How the hell was Anton going to handle it? His loss had to be devastating.

Liana and Adam came in through the kitchen. Just seeing the two of them together made the day brighter, especially after all Adam had been through. Not only bonded now, but possibly on his way to parenthood—it certainly appeared to agree with him.

And Liana positively glowed. She carried the pitcher of iced tea Xandi had gone after. Adam had a tray of glasses filled with ice cubes. Once Oliver and Mei arrived, Stef wanted to sit down and see if they could come up with any ideas, anything at all to help Anton recover. He had to get better, and this was the best place for it to happen, surrounded by his immediate family, the ones who loved him most, in the home he loved.

Stef opened his mouth to greet Adam and Liana when he heard voices. Mei and Oliver came in together. Mei was somber at best, but Oliver looked devastated. Of all of them, he'd known Anton the longest, had been with him through more shit than most men would have hung around for, but his loyalty and his love for the wizard had never wavered. If anyone should feel hope, Stefan figured it would be Oliver.

So why did he seem so hopeless now?

"You okay, Ollie?"

Oliver nodded. "It's tough. I'm not dealing with this as well as I should. I think I'm pissed off, more than anything. Anton did everything he set out to do, but it seems like one hell of a sacrifice."

Stefan forced a smile. "You of all people should know

he won't take this lying down. He'll heal, and we'll get him back. You have to believe that. Do you want to pick them up, or should I? Their plane's due in around four."

Oliver raised his head. There was a stricken look on his face. *I don't know if I can face him yet without losing it. Please, Stefan. I need to prepare myself. The last thing Anton needs at the airport is a blubbering idiot.*

Which was why Stefan found himself waiting at the hangar belonging to the charter company at quarter to four, where Anton's jet would deliver all of them. He stared at the empty sky, willing the small plane to arrive, anxious to see for himself how Anton was doing. He hated the emptiness in his mind that the wizard always filled.

Keisha had already contacted him, and the utter sadness in her mental voice had left him shaken. She'd said she felt horrible, like a terribly faithless wife, mourning her loss as if Anton were actually dead to her, even when he sat beside her, needing her love and her strength more than ever.

But, in so many ways, he truly was lost to her. He'd curled up in his seat on the plane and slept the entire way home. Usually he was curious about everything, talking to the pilot, discussing the trip with all of them, talking about what they'd done, where they'd been, who they'd seen.

Bragging about Lily.

He hadn't even mentioned their daughter. Not once. He hadn't asked about her, hadn't said her name. That alone had Keisha worried sick. That, and Anton's reaction to the events they'd all been part of—more specifically, his lack of reaction.

He'd been concerned about her injury until she showed him how well Logan had healed the deep gash where the bullet grazed her shoulder. Then he'd dismissed it entirely. Any other time, he would have been hovering about her for days.

He'd merely nodded when the feds had finally given

them the word they were free to go home, as if his part in saving the life of the most powerful man in the free world wasn't a huge event. That was so unlike the man she knew. He was a stranger to her. A stranger she didn't seem to understand at all anymore.

She was worried about AJ, too. He'd looked absolutely stricken as they'd boarded the plane. She wasn't exactly certain what had happened, but somehow, when he'd linked with Anton during the energy surge, he'd not only saved Anton's life, he'd ended up with some of his powers.

Powers AJ wanted no part of. He'd begged her to tell him the moment Anton was ready to take them back. He'd insisted, as if there was somehow going to be some miraculous way for him to return them to Anton, but she'd been too distraught to ask how in the hell he intended to do that, when Anton could no longer link with anyone. It made no sense.

And poor AJ had been too agitated to explain.

Now, with her thoughts still in turmoil and her heart broken, Keisha was bringing Anton home. Waiting on the tarmac, Stefan watched the small jet circle the airport and come in for a landing. Out of habit, he reached for Anton, for the man who always answered his mental call.

There was no one there. Not even the vaguest sense of the wizard as the plane touched down on the runway. Unsure of what was to come, how he should behave, Stefan shoved his hands in his pockets and waited disconsolately for the plane to taxi to the hangar so he could take its passengers home.

Anton hated everything about this. The way he felt cut off from the rest of the pack, the surreptitious glances the others made in his direction when they didn't think he was watching. He knew they worried about him, that they loved him and wanted him whole, but, for now at least, they couldn't do a damned thing to help him—and he sure as hell wasn't whole.

No, he was fractured, his mind scattered, his life in shambles. It was frightening, really, how quickly he'd been reduced to this state. Frightening and humiliating, when he thought about it, that such a minor disability could bring him down so quickly.

He'd escaped to his office the moment they'd arrived at the house. It hadn't been fast enough. He'd still had to walk what felt like a gauntlet of his packmates. Their loving concern had almost been his undoing. He didn't know if he'd be able to handle sitting at the big table with everyone. Acting as if everything was just fine.

The ride home had been bad enough. He'd sat in front with Stefan and told him what he remembered of the evening. He'd described what he could recall of AJ's sudden link and the way their minds had immediately synched. He still wasn't certain what had happened, though he fully believed Eve had her hand in the outcome. Somehow, AJ had become the key to his survival. Anton wasn't certain how, but AJ held something he needed. Something he couldn't yet retrieve.

Not until he was ready.

"Anton? Dinner's ready." He glanced up from the stack of mail he'd found waiting for him on his desk. Bills and statements and proposals. How the hell would he manage his work if he couldn't read the minds of the people around him? He'd learned to rely on that edge.

Of course, he could still rely on Stefan, but it wouldn't be the same. Not for a man who wanted control in all things. "I'll be there in a minute." He glanced away from Keisha's hopeful expression and shuffled the stacks of mail. When he raised his head a minute later, she was still there. Standing in the doorway with her arms crossed over her chest.

Obviously not very happy with him. "What? I said I'd come in a minute."

"Lily is awake. You haven't even given your daughter a hug since you got home. You've avoided your packmates and you're being rude to me. Feeling sorry for you only goes so far, Anton. Man up and deal with it. Is it so impossible for you to have a little patience with a mind that's still far better than the average member of the human population?"

He wasn't sure which was the more powerful emotion—anger or shame. He went with anger. He'd never been all that good about dealing with shame. He slowly rose and carefully planted his palms on the desk. "You forget, my love, that like you, I am no longer human, so don't put me in a category with humans. It has no bearing on what I can and cannot do. Like you, and like our daughter, I am Chanku, only I appear to have lost those special abilities that define our very existence."

Keisha took a quick step back, as if his anger had physically shoved her aside. Then she straightened her spine and glared at him. "You don't know that you've lost your abilities forever. You told me that Eve said for you to return to your home and heal. Well, my love, you are home. Give yourself time to get well, but in the meantime, act like a man. I will not allow you to punish me or our daughter because you can't deal with your perceived weakness."

She glared at him a moment longer, magnificent in her anger. He wanted to tell her how much he loved her, how much he admired the strength she'd shown throughout this past week. She'd been cool under pressure, unbelievably brave when faced with a madman with a gun. She'd been wounded, yet in spite of her pain, she'd gotten the president to safety and then stayed beside her mate while he hid away in the guest room at Luc and Tia's house.

She'd been spectacular. He'd been absolutely worthless. He still was, yet he, who always had an explanation for everything, had no words to explain his actions. None worthy of his mate. She waited a moment longer. Gave him every chance in the world to apologize, but when he didn't speak, she turned away in anger and left him standing there like a fool.

He was a fool. And he owed her an apology. More than that, he owed her his life. She'd saved him, time and time again, and now all he did was give her grief. She had a right to be angry.

He shoved the mail into a tray on his desk and followed Keisha to the dining room. Voices, laughter, Lily's squeal and Alex's funny giggles. Life waited in the other room.

He had to figure out a way to embrace it without giving in to despair. And he had to hope like hell that Eve was right, that he'd somehow get back to what he'd been, to the man he was supposed to be.

Keisha and Xandi took the babies in for play time in the tub before bed. Oliver, Mei, and Liana volunteered to clean up after dinner and that left Anton staring out the window in his office. The fact it was dark outside and there was nothing to see didn't really matter.

At least Keisha had accepted his apology, as lame as it had been, though she was still angry. He knew she didn't understand the depth of his grief. Hell, he didn't understand it himself. He'd never experienced anything like this, had no way to articulate his feelings. Telling her he was sorry for acting like such a bastard had been a step in the right direction, but not enough.

Not nearly enough.

He heard motion behind him and turned. Any other time, he would have sensed the intruder. He would have known it was Stefan, would have been just as aware of Adam coming through the door behind him.

He really didn't want company. Not tonight. Keisha was still pissed off in spite of what she'd said when he apologized—he didn't need to read her mind to know that. Stefan was disappointed in him, but not saying why, and he really wasn't up to Adam's quiet contentment. It was too damned much. He just wanted them to leave him alone.

Neither man said a word to him. He frowned, turned his head, and watched as Stefan went straight to the cabinet where he kept his liquor. He pulled out three glasses along with a bottle of the really expensive Hennessy, and poured shots in each glass. He handed one to Adam, took one for himself, and shoved the third into Anton's hand.

Stefan's eyes were blazing. He practically pulsed with his anger. Adam stood off to one side, but it was difficult to read his mood. He was difficult to understand even under the best of conditions, his mind often blocked to Anton's curious thoughts. Now, with his comfortable stance and serious expression, he was impossible to figure out.

So why even try? Anton took a swallow of the cognac and sighed as it burned a trail down his throat. He took another and turned his back on the two men. He wasn't trying to be rude, but they were the ones who had breached his sanctuary, who had interrupted his moment of reflection.

That thought almost made him laugh. Almost. The only reflection going on right now was his own sorry face staring back at him in the big window opening out to the back meadow.

He took another swallow of cognac and realized he'd emptied his glass. Before he could set it down, Stefan was tilting the bottle over it, filling it once again.

"Trying to get me drunk, Stefan?" He cocked one eyebrow in Stef's direction. "It won't work. I seem to have developed a tremendous tolerance for good liquor. Just about wiped out Ulrich's hidden stash at the Marina house. I imagine Luc was glad to see me go."

"Getting you drunk would be a waste of good booze." Stefan topped off his own glass and handed the bottle to Adam, who set it aside on top of the cabinet.

Anton chuckled, but he realized he was staring at the amber liquid in his glass, not looking into Stef's eyes. He wasn't sure he'd like what he saw there. Even so, he raised his head and asked, "Well, if getting me drunk isn't your purpose, what is on your agenda? You looked ready to take my head off when you walked in here."

Stefan shook his head. "Pissed at the situation, my friend. Not entirely at you, though you certainly need to consider your mate's feelings. Keisha's exhausted and scared and afraid for you. That half-assed apology you gave her needs some improvement."

Anton hung his head. "You're right. I tend to get a little too self-involved when things don't go my way."

Stefan laughed. "Ya think? Gee. I never would have guessed."

Anton shot him a sharp glance. "You've made your point. What else are you here for?"

"Figuring out what the fuck we're going to do about your little problem." He nodded at Adam. "I want you to let Adam take a look at you. If he can't find anything, then we're going to bring Liana in and let her have her way with you."

Anton winked at Adam. "I like the sound of that. Go on."

"Then if we can't figure out what's wrong, I thought maybe we'd all shift and go for a run, get away from the house and fuck like bunnies."

Only Stefan. "Sounds good to me." He shrugged and looked at Adam. "Where do you want me?"

Adam laughed. "Well, actually I want you on your knees with my dick in your mouth, but I'll go for your skinny butt in that chair." He pointed to the comfortable recliner in the corner.

Anton liked that about Adam. The man didn't give a rat's ass who he was, what kinds of abilities he'd once had. Adam treated him as an equal, not as the undisputed pack alpha, though now that he thought about it, his role might quickly become disputed if things didn't change.

Anton took a seat, had another sip of his cognac and set the glass aside. Then he leaned his head back against the cushion. Adam stood behind him, pressed his fingers to Anton's temples, and went perfectly still.

It was strange, really, to think of what Adam was doing. Anton knew the man was taking a walk through the cells of his brain, but there was no awareness of anything. Not of Adam's physical presence inside his skull, and certainly not anything mental. All Anton felt was the steady pressure of Adam's big, warm hands against the sides of his face.

He concentrated on the strength of those fingers, on the calluses and scars from all the physical labor Adam did around the place. Amazing, that a man who was at home repairing a carburetor could so confidently, yet gently, crawl inside someone's head, but Anton had seen Adam at work before. Had tagged along on his medical journeys through cells and veins and even into Tia's womb during her daughters' delivery.

He wondered if he'd ever get that chance again. If the ability to join Adam's amazing mind would be his once more. His hands were so gentle, the night so quiet that Anton lost track of the time. Might have even dozed off a bit. He'd been sleeping so much since that night. More than he'd ever slept in his life, but when Adam pulled away, Anton was startled enough to know he'd been on the edge of sleep at the very least.

He was even more startled to see that Liana had, at some point, joined them. She'd been inside his head as well, it appeared. He wondered if it had worked and tried to reach out.

Nothing. Shit. Answered that question. He smiled at her. "Hello, Liana. Any luck?"

She shook her head. "I see the problem, but there's nothing we can do to rush things. You're going to heal. I'm almost positive the damage isn't permanent, but you took a terrible blast to your brain when you pulled in so much energy."

"That I did. In fact, if AJ hadn't linked with me, I don't know if I would have survived it." Stefan refilled his glass of cognac. Anton took a small sip. The others had pulled up chairs and sat facing him. "Afterward, I had what felt like a visitation from Eve. She said something about AJ having what I needed. That I would know when I was ready to take it back."

"Ah! That would explain it." Liana smiled and glanced toward Adam. "I told you it felt as if something was missing, but I couldn't figure out what it was."

Anton frowned. "Missing? You mean something physically gone from inside my head?"

"Yes and no." Liana spread her hands wide, palms open, almost as if she reached for the answers she needed. "We are each unique, with our own abilities, our own way of thinking, of reacting. It affects everything we do, every decision we make, all our choices and beliefs. Even our fears. It's, for want of a better word, our spirit. Your mind is intact. Your brain has suffered a definite trauma. There is evidence of some swelling, even what looks like bruising, though nothing life threatening. However, the part of you that fires your thoughts, that gives you your unique signature and makes you who and what you are—that part of you was not evident. I searched, but I thought the fault was mine for not seeing it. Now I'm wondering if AJ has it for safekeeping. If, when you are stronger, he will be able to return it to you."

"How long do you think that will be?" He glanced down at his hands cupping the glass of cognac and saw that his knuckles had gone white. He relaxed as much as he could. The last thing he needed to do was shatter a glass of good cognac. Stef would never let him forget it.

"I would imagine a couple more weeks. We heal so quickly. Your injuries aren't that severe, especially considering what you accomplished. The amount of power you pulled in from all of us must have been tremendous. Even Adam and I felt some of the backlash."

Stefan chuckled. "I think we all did. It's got to take a lot to shut down the entire city of San Francisco. Everything from cell phones to lights and cable cars. Between the attempt on the president's life and the power going out, it was a big news night."

Anton slowly shook his head. "I feel sort of foolish, now. At the time, I was afraid of not having enough power to shut down the auditorium. It was a minor miscalculation."

"Minor, my ass." Laughing, Stefan turned to Liana. "So what now? What do you suggest?"

She cocked her head and stared at Anton. "Have you shifted since this happened? Sometimes shifting will help speed the healing process."

"No. I had such a hell of a headache the first couple of days, and . . . Well, really, there just hasn't been time." Even Anton realized his excuses sounded feeble.

"Try it. I want to see if you're still able to shift."

"Now?" He really didn't want to try. At least by not attempting a shift, he could maintain the illusion that he was still able to do it. Even if he couldn't.

"Now, Anton. Please. No need to disrobe. Just see if the mechanism is still there. If the process of shifting from man to wolf is still a natural act for you."

He gazed into Stefan's amber eyes and felt the fear in the man who loved him. There was no need for telepathy to recognize Stef's love—or his concern. Maintaining eye contact, Anton reached for the simple process that should turn him into a wolf.

And found absolutely nothing. It was almost as if that slate had been wiped entirely clean. He remembered how to shift, but when he reached for the workings in his mind that directed the change, there was nothing there. He didn't say a thing. He didn't have to. Everyone in this room recognized his failure.

Each of them mourned with him. He bowed his head and begged the Goddess for some kind of word, anything to encourage him, but there was no sense of Eve tonight.

He raised his head after a moment, almost done in by the compassion in the eyes of those here with him. He would have to tell Keisha. Have to make her believe his abilities would eventually come back.

First he had to convince himself. If he couldn't be the man he'd always been, he was nothing. Nothing at all.

"Well, that sucks." Adam's droll comment caught him by surprise. "Guess that means running and fucking's out for tonight."

Anton glanced at Adam and caught the twinkle in his eyes. "I'm doing it again, aren't I?" He shook his head, but he managed to dredge up a smile. "What can I say? I'm a glass-half-empty kind of guy."

"Well, I'm not." Stefan grabbed Anton's hand and pulled him to his feet, but he spoke to Adam. "Keisha and Xandi are sleeping in our room. That leaves either Anton's or yours. You okay with that, Liana? Think you can handle all three of us?"

"You're kidding, right? Have you seen Ig naked?" Chuckling, she grabbed Adam's hand and dragged him toward the door. "C'mon, boys. Potential mommy here. I can't drink but bring the bottle."

"I'm really gonna miss that guy." Adam sighed, reached for the half-full bottle of Hennessy, and trailed out the door behind Liana muttering, ". . . hung like a damned baseball bat," as he left.

Stefan squeezed Anton's hand. "No argument. You're coming with us. You're going to get naked, and for tonight, at least, forget how screwed up things are and do a little screwing yourself. You all right with that?"

He thought about Stefan and all he'd been through, trapped for so many years as half man, half wolf. What Adam had endured when he lost his mate, and how much Liana, a woman who had once been an immortal goddess, had lost. And then he thought of what each of them had gained—love. A life much richer than they'd ever imagined.

He thought of how much he still had, even if his abilities were lost forever—the love of his pack, the love of his mate, and the love of his perfect daughter. He grinned at Stef, aware this time his smile was real. Then he grabbed his glass of cognac and headed for the door, tugging Stefan along behind him.

"Yeah," he said. "I am all right. And I'm coming with you and I plan to get naked." He stopped and looked into the eyes of a man who could have been his brother, who was, in many ways, all things to him. "But I realize now that there is nothing I need to forget. Things really aren't as screwed up as I thought. Not as long as I have you guys. Thanks for reminding me what's really important."

Stef grinned at him. "I did that? Damn. Be sure and tell Xandi I finally got something right, would you?"

"Fuck off, Stef."

"You too, sweetheart."

Together, they headed out of the house and across the snowy drive to Adam and Liana's room above the garage.

Chapter 15

Anton lay in a sweaty tangle of muscular arms and hairy legs. Liana had long ago chosen retreat over valor—she'd left hours ago to sleep with Xandi and Keisha where she said the testosterone wasn't quite as invasive and overwhelming.

Anton might have laughed if she hadn't been right, if his body hadn't been totally sated. And if his mind hadn't been buzzing with all that he'd learned from her and Adam tonight.

Thank goodness his cognitive abilities didn't appear to be impaired. He might have lost the ability to shift and to mindtalk, to link with his mate or his lovers, but he could still think. Still reason.

Still ask questions.

And damn it all if he didn't have a million more questions for Liana. He'd been under the impression she'd lost all of her Chanku knowledge in the mindlink she'd had with Eve, but it appeared Liana had given up only the basics. Eve had taken the knowledge of what a goddess needed to know to function within the astral plane, to connect with the Mother. She'd only taken what she needed in order to be their Goddess.

Liana had retained her knowledge from thousands of

years of actually living through Chanku history. She still remembered what she'd learned of their physical and mental abilities.

All Anton had to do was ask the right questions, though it was Adam who had answered one tonight. He'd learned some amazing things during his mating bond with Liana, and this was something Anton had long suspected but never known for sure.

The Chanku life span appeared almost limitless.

While Chanku weren't actually immortal, they could be very long-lived. That was something they'd have to address at some point, when humans around them aged and they didn't. He'd seen it in Millie West the last time they'd been together. When he'd first met Millie, she'd been a youthful-looking woman in her mid-fifties. Now she looked like a thirty-year-old.

Not only was she not aging, she was getting younger-looking by the day. Essentially, it appeared the aging process paused at an individual's prime, and if the first shift to Chanku came at a later age, as it had with Millie, the body appeared to rediscover those prime years. For most men, it seemed to be mid to late thirties. The women all looked younger, when he thought about it. Late twenties at most. He wondered where Millie was going to end up. She was already beautiful.

Fascinating. Something he'd wondered about but really hadn't considered, at least not seriously.

Adam snored and rolled over. His muscular arm stretched over Anton's chest and his warm body pressed close along his left side. Stefan stretched in his sleep and shifted his position. He ended up with one long leg across Anton's thighs, his nose buried in his chest hair. Stef's fingers idly tangled in the thick, dark hair at his groin. Anton sighed as his once-flaccid cock slowly rose.

He couldn't possibly be horny. Not after hours of sex with these two, but then Stef's fingers wrapped around his erection. Stef was still sound asleep, but his dreams must have been vivid as he slowly stroked Anton's full length from root to crown.

Any other time, Anton would have slipped inside Stefan's sleeping mind. He would have shared the dreams, known what his friend was seeing. What he was feeling and thinking.

In a way, it was almost more arousing to imagine. Looking at Stef's face, at the half smile on his lips, the frown lines that came and went across his forehead, Anton felt his desire grow. Wondering what Stefan thought, imagining his dreams

Even without the mental link, Anton felt their connection, and in that moment of enlightenment, he knew the first positive awareness of his own healing. Maybe this was what Eve meant. Maybe it was a matter of learning to accept, of finding what was truly important in his life.

Stefan moved beside him, turned, raised his head, and winked at Anton. *Bastard.* He wasn't asleep after all! Then it didn't matter. Stefan wrapped his lips around Anton's cock and worked the sensitive spot beneath the glans with the tip of his tongue.

Anton groaned. Stefan sucked him harder, deeper. Cupped his balls in the palm of his hand and lightly rolled them between his fingers, until the exquisite sensations, the warmth and the connection that could only be physical, for now, took Anton over the edge. He climaxed silently, loath to awaken Adam, selfishly taking the pleasure Stefan gave him.

The wild, buzzing thoughts in his mind went quiet. Stefan lay his head on Anton's belly, but he seemed to have fallen asleep for real, this time, still suckling softly on Anton's cock. Stef's fingers were lax, lightly cupping his balls, and Anton might have laughed if he wasn't so touched by Stefan's thoughtfulness.

By his amazing love. He was maintaining the only kind

of connection Anton could truly experience for now. Not because Stefan needed to feel the link. No, he must have realized how very much Anton would need it, now that it was missing.

Stef nuzzled close, still softly sucking Anton's penis between his lips. Anton sighed, relaxed, finally. At peace. It was good. So very good, to feel at least a sense of that familiar connection once again.

Anton awoke at the first pale hint of dawn. Adam's room was shadowed and dark. Both Adam and Stefan slept soundly. Crawling out of the tangle of arms and legs, Anton went into the small bathroom and quickly showered. He grabbed his clothes, slipped on his dark pants, shoes without socks, and his plain white T-shirt. Then he wadded up his wrinkled dress shirt with his dirty socks and tucked them under his arm.

Quietly he left the room and headed down the stairs, around to the front door. He slipped in, planning to sneak into his room and maybe surprise Keisha with a kiss and a more sincere apology. He'd had plenty of time to think last night, and the only conclusion that had been entirely inescapable was the fact he'd been acting like a class-A jerk.

"Dada!"

He spun around in time to see Lily racing down the hallway, chubby little legs flying, her favorite stuffed wolf in one hand and her blanket dragging behind her. Keisha was hot on her trail. Anton knelt down and caught Lily against his chest and hugged her tight.

But it was Keisha he watched. Keisha who stopped a few feet away, almost as if she feared what he might say. Lily was babbling about her "woofie" and telling him something very important, and he knew he should listen to her, knew that Lily, being Lily, would expect an answer to whatever she asked.

Instead, he risked a toddler-size meltdown, swallowed

his pride, and focused on his mate. "I've been a damned idiot. More so than usual. I am so sorry, Keisha. Will you forgive me?"

Keisha sniffed and crossed her arms over her chest. Her hair was in tangles from an obviously restless night, and she was wearing his ratty old bathrobe, the one she wouldn't let him throw away. "I don't know. I can't feel you, so when you're rude and when you say things that hurt me, I don't know what you're thinking. Before this happened, you could be a self-centered jerk, and I still felt your love. I can't feel it, Anton."

She shook her head so hard her curls bounced. "I know this is a terrible thing that's happened to you, but it's happened to me, too. The man I love, the man who is always in my heart, isn't there. Instead I've had this stranger who says terrible, hateful things to me and expects me to understand. I don't understand because I only hear words. I can't hear your heart."

He stood up, holding Lily tight to his chest. Her little arms went around his neck and she kissed his cheek. She smelled of peaches and cereal and her favorite shampoo. He shifted her to his hip and held her firmly with one arm so he could pull her mommy into his embrace.

Keisha came willingly, wrapping her arms around Anton and Lily and holding them close. Anton nuzzled her hair and sighed. "It's the isolation that's hardest," he said, trying to explain how his world had changed. "I'm so used to being part of your thoughts, hearing you as you go about your day. Slipping in and out of the minds of our packmates as if they're all an extension of my own thoughts, my own world."

"I know." Keisha raised her head and kissed his chin. "I miss the sense of you. The feeling that you're always with me, no matter how far apart we are."

He took a deep breath. "I can't shift anymore. Liana had me try last night. I couldn't do it."

Keisha nodded. "She told me, but she said she believes that once you're healed, you'll regain all your abilities. Shifting, mindtalking, everything. You just have to be patient." She planted a kiss on Lily's nose and her daughter squealed and giggled. "Patience is not your strong suit."

"It's not yours, either, m'love." He raised one eyebrow and stared at her.

She grinned. "This is true, but we will get through this and you will get better. What can I do to help?"

"Just love me. Don't give up on me. Tell me when I'm acting like a horse's ass." He chuckled and kissed her. "I know you can do that. You're very good at cutting me down to size."

She kissed him back. "That's because you don't scare me. You make me madder than . . ." She glanced at Lily's wide eyes and said, "Madder than a really grumpy mommy, but I'm never afraid of you." She sighed. "Only afraid for you."

"Why don't you let me have the rug rat this morning and take some time for yourself. I need to adjust to this new reality, and I figure a dose of Miss Lily will remind me what's really important."

Keisha laughed and kissed him soundly. "You've got her. She's all yours, and if you take a deep whiff of that diaper she's wearing, you'll know exactly why I was trying to catch her. Mind Daddy, Lily. Be a very good girl."

She spun around and headed down the hall to their room. Anton took a deep breath and realized his mate hadn't been kidding. With Lily tugging on his long hair and giggling, Anton headed to the nursery in search of the diapers. He was smiling by the time he'd stepped into his daughter's brightly colored room. Smiling and actually feeling hopeful, in spite of the silence. Maybe Lily was the key. Lily and her perfect giggles, her sticky kisses and warm, snuggly hugs.

If he couldn't feel connected with that kind of attention, his problem went far deeper than merely his ability to mindtalk or shapeshift. There was nothing like a not-quite-two-year-old to remind a man what was truly important in life.

Bay rolled over in bed and pulled Manda into his arms. She grumbled and snuggled close, but he knew she was awake. "I dreamed last night," he said. Just mentioning the dream brought it back. It had been so amazingly clear, as if he'd really stood in a beautiful meadow and chatted with Eve.

Except she was different than the Eve he remembered. Something about her eyes . . .

Manda rose up on her elbows and frowned at him through her tangled hair. "And your point is?"

He couldn't help himself. He leaned close and kissed her. "My point is, I dreamed of Eve, and it was as clear as if I was standing right next to her. We talked about her new role as our Goddess, about your pregnancy." He kissed her again. "Yes, she said you are definitely pregnant. And then she said we need to go to Montana. That Anton will need us in two weeks. She didn't say why."

"You sure it was just a dream?"

He shook his head. "No. It was more. Much more. I think we need to wrap things up here and make plans for a trip west. Besides, that's about the time Tala and Lisa's babies will be due. I want to be there to meet my nieces and nephew."

Manda lay back down, across his chest this time. "If I'm really pregnant, I may be at the puking stage by then. You sure you want me along?"

"I wouldn't dream of going without you."

There was a soft knock on the door. Shannon poked her head in. "I thought I heard you guys talking." She glanced over her shoulder. "Told you they were awake." She stepped into their room, tugging Jake along behind her. "Tell Baylor what you just told me."

Bay and Manda scooted back to sit up against the headboard so they could give Jake and Shannon room to sit on the bed. Jake sat cross-legged near the foot with Shannon leaning against him. "I think I spent some time with Eve last night."

Bay glanced at Manda and they both burst out laughing. "Let's see," Bay said. "Shannon's pregnant and you need to go to Montana."

"How'd you know? Oh. You saw her, too." Jake grinned at Shannon. "But, yeah. We're going to be parents. You, too?"

Manda nodded. "I think so. Shannon? Are you sure?"

Shannon's grin nearly split her face. "I've been thinking I might be. I mean, I know it's way too soon, but I just feel different. My breasts hurt and I feel sort of sleepy and weepy."

Jake and Bay shook hands. "It's gonna be a long nine months, Bay. She's already had one crying jag this morning."

Manda punched Bay before he could say anything stupid. He probably owed her a thank you for that. Instead, he said, "Then we definitely need to plan a trip to Montana. You can both see Logan, get checked out, find out if you need anything like vitamins or stuff. And even though it's not convenient, I want you to think about delivering there, too. I like the idea of the others helping you share the pain from labor."

Manda chuckled. "What he really likes is the idea of the *other women* helping share our labor pain. Can you see either of these guys sharing the pain the way Tinker did when Tia was in labor? That man is a jewel."

Jake pressed his hand over his heart. "Are you casting aspersions on our character?"

"Just telling it like it is, sweetie." Shannon kissed him. "You wouldn't know an aspersion if it kicked you in the butt."

Bay laughed. "She's right, you know. And I really don't see either one of us dealing with labor pain. I talked to Tink after the babies were born. He said it felt like someone was trying to rip his balls right out of his sac when Tia had a really strong contraction."

Jake went a little green and turned slowly to pin Shannon with a hard stare. "You're definitely going to deliver in Montana. With as many of the pack there as we can get." He stared at Bay. "Maybe if we offer to pay Tinker . . ."

"I want the kids to come with us this time. Are any of your people capable of watching this place for a week or so?" Ric leaned over Millie with an arm on either side of her, effectively pinning her to the comfortable chair in her office at the wolf sanctuary. She glared at him.

He grinned back at her. "Deacon, Matt, and Daci need to get to know the rest of the pack better. They should have a chance to hang out with others of our kind, younger people. Not just a couple of old farts like you and me."

Millie raised her eyebrows. "If you think this is how to coerce me with your sweet talk, Ulrich, referring to me as an old fart is not a particularly effective way to go about it."

He shrugged. "I shouldn't have to coerce you. It's a chance to see Adam and Manda, so I know you want to be there, but it's also Lisa and Tala's time to deliver, and the kids are close to Tala. Hell, they saved her life. We are not going to leave them here babysitting your flock."

"A flock of wolves. I've never heard them referred to in quite that way." She looped both arms around his neck, dragged him close and kissed him. "It's all taken care of. I talked to Manda this morning and she said she would love to see Daci again. I checked with the day manager and he's willing to break up the shifts so that someone will be here at night while we're away. The kids are already figuring out what they need to get done before we leave. For your information, the High Mountain Wolf Sanctuary is entirely under control, and we will be ready to make the trip in two weeks."

Ric straightened up and glared at her. "You do this to me on purpose, don't you?"

She laughed. "Of course I do. Someone has to keep an old fart like you on his toes." Standing up, she grabbed his hand. "C'mon. I haven't had lunch yet. Let's go back to the cabin so I can get a bite to eat."

"And?"

She ran her palm over the growing mound at the front of his jeans. "And maybe a little cardiovascular workout?"

"That can be arranged." He tilted his hips forward as Millie pulled her palm away. Groaning he stepped out of her way.

She shut down her computer and closed the door. Daci was at the front desk, already working out the schedules for the time they'd be gone. "I'll be back in about an hour, Daci."

She smiled at Millie and then winked at Ric. "Take your time. I'll be here."

"Why do I have the feeling that everyone knows more about what's going on around here than I do?" Ric waved at Daci and followed Millie out the door.

"Because everyone around here *does* know more about what's going on than you do." She gave Daci a saucy wave and headed across the snow-covered meadow to the trail leading to their cabin.

Grumbling under his breath, Ric followed close behind, loving every minute of her teasing. Millie's trim hips perfectly filled out her tight jeans, and her blond hair, grown longer now and tied back in a ponytail, swung side to side with each step she took.

It was all he could do to keep his hands to himself, and knowing she wanted his hands all over her made it even harder.

Made him even harder.

Millie opened the door to the cabin and Ric followed her inside. They'd left the woodstove going this morning, so the place was still warm. Walking straight through to the kitchen, Millie opened the refrigerator and pulled out the leftover lasagna from the night before. She slipped the pan into the oven, turned it on to reheat, and set the timer.

Then she looped her arms over Ric's shoulders. "Think you can entertain me for about twenty minutes while that heats up?"

"I imagine that can be arranged." He swept her up in his arms and carried her out of the kitchen, down the short hall, and into their bedroom. Then he set her on the edge of the bed and knelt at her feet to slip her heavy hiking boots and socks off.

She unfastened her jeans, but Ric pulled them off, tugging them down her long legs along with her panties. He left them in an untidy heap on the floor. Why was it, he wondered, that he found her so unbelievably erotic this way, still wearing her warm sweater and vest, yet naked from the waist down?

His cock ached, but he wanted the taste of her on his tongue more than her heat around his dick. At least for now. He spread her thighs with his big hands and ran his tongue between her legs. She was already moist, her labia beginning to engorge from her arousal, and she lay back on the bed with her legs hanging down, completely open to his touch and taste.

Threading her fingers through his thick, white hair, she

hung on while he pleasured her with his mouth, licking and suckling until she squirmed and wriggled in his grasp.

He licked deep, spearing her with his tongue, and then latching on to her clitoris with his lips, pleasuring all her sensitive parts until she whimpered, alternately pushing him away and then pulling him close. He felt her body convulse as she reached orgasm, and licked deeper, taking long, slick strokes with the flat of his tongue.

When she was lying there, gasping and shivering, he unzipped his pants and shoved them down to his knees, lifted her buttocks in his palms, and slid his full length into her with one long, smooth stroke.

She groaned. So did he.

He paused, buried deep inside while her vaginal muscles rippled and pulsed the length of his cock. It was always like this with Millie, this terrible fight to keep from coming, but after a moment, he felt as if he had things under control.

Then he began to move, sliding in and out, deeper with each thrust, burying himself entirely within her wet heat. His balls brushed over her buttocks on each downward thrust and his fingers tightened around her smooth hips, holding her close, finding that perfect rhythm with the rock and sway of his hips, the muscles in his buttocks tightening with each penetration.

There was something so primal about this, fucking Millie in the middle of the day with sunlight streaming through the bedroom windows, his pants shoved down, bunched around his knees. Millie, naked from the waist down, yet still clothed in the sweater she'd worn to the office. The one she'd wear back there when this lunch break had ended.

He felt like a damned kid, sneaking away from school for sex in some girl's house while the parents were gone, something he'd done so many years ago with more than one nameless sweet young thing. Those long-forgotten young women had wanted him as much as he'd wanted them. Wanted him for only one thing—the pleasure he gave them, the illicit joy two teenaged kids could find right under their parents' noses.

It was like that with Millie on days like this, sneaking away from work even though Daci and her guys knew exactly what was up in the little cabin next to the sanctuary. Still, the fantasy was fun, the pure carnal joy they both took in the act, the fact it was a workday and the rest of the world was out there, people going about their business while he and Millie were holed up in this warm little cabin, fucking like randy teenagers in the middle of the day.

He gloried in the heat of her, the tightness of her sheath, and the hard mouth of her womb as he passed over it on every downward thrust. She had a perfect body, all taut skin and smooth muscles, firm breasts and trim waist. They might make jokes about their age, but he knew the truth. He'd seen it with his own eyes, confirmed now by both Adam and Liana.

They weren't growing older. Not at all. They were growing younger with each year that passed. Settling into their prime, finding that perfect age. He'd already found his since mating with Camille so many years ago, but Millie amazed him. She'd been a beautiful woman in her late fifties when he'd met her.

Now, almost sixty, she looked more like a thirty-year-old, and she grew younger looking, younger feeling, every day. If all went according to what they'd learned, she would soon look about the same age as Daci, like a woman in her mid to late twenties.

And he loved the fact that he'd done this for her. He'd been the one to bring her over, to show her the truth of her heritage. His Millie, his love.

She cried out, reaching for him as her climax peaked once again. The joy on her face, the love in her heart, and her soft cries of pleasure pulled him along as well. He felt the rising tide of his climax, seminal fluids boiling up out of his balls, racing the length of his damned cock, and bathing Millie deep inside, filling her as he'd done so many times before.

Each time fresh. New, as if they'd just discovered how this amazing act was played. And he realized, as his legs went weak and he lay forward, covering her body with his on the edge of the big bed, that they would be able to play this same scene over and over again, for more than a mere lifetime.

They weren't reaching the end of their days, not as he'd once thought. He remembered when he'd found Millie, when they'd first come together and he'd realized that he'd been lucky enough to find love once again at an age when so many men had given up. He'd felt blessed to think he could have this wonderful love for at least ten or twenty more years.

That short span had seemed like such an amazing gift. Now he knew he could love her for what amounted to many lifetimes—yet even that wouldn't be enough.

The timer went off in the kitchen. Lunch was ready. He pulled out of Millie and left her lying on the edge of the bed, legs hanging down, toes barely touching the floor. Hitching up his pants, he went into the bathroom, found a clean washcloth, rinsed it with warm water, and went back to the bedroom.

The timer continued its rhythmic *ding, ding, ding.* Ric bathed their combined fluids from between Millie's legs, helped her dress, tied her boots. Only then did he leave her to go to the kitchen and shut off the timer. They still had half an hour before she'd told Daci she would be back to the office.

Plenty of time for lunch. Smiling, Ric pulled the lasagna out of the oven and set the table. When Millie finally joined him in the kitchen, her hair was freshly combed, her clothes neat and tidy, and she smiled at him as if he'd hung the moon.

Tala sat on the couch in the sunroom upstairs, staring out the big window that faced the Pacific. Mik sat on one side, AJ on the other. Igmutaka lay on the floor at their feet. He'd become such a constant presence in their lives, Tala hardly noticed him anymore. He was just there, a big cougar who turned into a very sexy guy at mealtime and sat with them at the table.

She knew he missed his mountain home in Montana, but he insisted he had no intention of leaving Tala. The girl child she carried, Mik's daughter, was his charge. He claimed it was his destiny to protect her. That much he knew, and he had no intention of walking away from his duty.

Which Tala figured could come in really handy when she had two toddlers to chase. Tia's twins would be walking soon, and they were already wondering how she was going to manage, especially since Nick and Beth had, with Luc's sincere blessing, decided to take the job in Washington.

Tala almost envied the two kids. What amazing things they were going to see! Protecting the First Family would take them all over the world. At least she knew they'd keep in touch. There was no way they could ever totally abandon their packmates.

"Wow." AJ's soft exclamation startled Tala out of her daydreams. He wrapped his arm around her shoulders and hugged her close. "Look at that sunset."

Tala smiled. "Red sky at night, sailor's delight."

Mik nodded beside her. "Should be a gorgeous day tomorrow. How are you feeling?"

Tala shrugged. "How would you expect any itty-bitty pregnant lady full of two huge babies to feel? Like I've got a soccer team running across my bladder. Like my boobs are tired of sitting on my belly. Like I'm wondering how in the ever lovin' *hell* I let you two bozos talk me into this."

She flashed him a bright smile. "That's how I feel. Sorry you asked?"

"Never." Mik laughed and kissed her cheek. Igmutaka grunted and rolled over on his back. Tala snorted. "See? He's the only honest one around here. You two are afraid to speak your mind."

"No, sweetie. Just afraid." AJ's solemn comment had Tala spinning around to stare at him.

"Why? I'm in great shape. Even Logan says I've carried these two longer than he'd hoped. In fact, we need to make up our minds whether we're going to deliver here or in Montana. I really want to go up there if you don't mind. That's where Lisa plans to have her baby."

"Are you up to the trip?" AJ caught her face in his palms and stared into her eyes.

He was just so damned pretty he still took her breath. "Of course I am. Anton promised he'd send the jet. We can be there in a couple of hours."

AJ raised his head and looked at Mik. Tala felt the tension in him. She turned and smiled at the big guy. "Let's call Anton and go tomorrow. I know the others aren't planning to come right away, but they've all promised to be there as soon as they can. It's easier. There's more room and I really want Baylor and Manda there when I have the babies."

AJ grinned at Mik. "How does she do this?"

"What? Always get her way?" Mik kissed the top of her head. "Beats me. But it looks like we need to call Anton and then go pack. And, AJ? Maybe he's ready to take back whatever it is you ended up with."

"Shit. I sure hope so. I'm so tired of eavesdropping where I don't belong." AJ stood up and helped Tala to her feet. "C'mon, Ig. We're going downstairs to pack. Time to go back to Montana, even if it's just for a visit."

The big cat grunted and slowly stood.

Tala's mind was buzzing with all the things she needed to do if they were going to try and leave tomorrow.

She'd call and make sure Tinker and Lisa were up to the trip. And Logan, Jazzy, Tia, and Luc and the twins. It would be so cool if everyone could be there.

Tia had started a nice tradition when she'd asked them all to attend the birth of the girls. Tala didn't want anything less for her babies. She wasn't really due for a few more weeks, but her body was changing. Things were beginning to shift around inside. Maybe her babies were trying to tell her it was time.

Igmutaka was certainly sticking close. She walked with one hand on the big cat's shoulders, glad to have him nearby. As nervous as her two guys already were, she'd feel a lot better with the whole pack around to hold the boys up, but having the spirit guide close certainly helped.

Chapter 16

Tala wandered down the hall to the kitchen. She heard Alex and Lily giggling and figured maybe she'd find Xandi and Keisha. At least they'd be able to offer a little sympathy for her swollen ankles and aching back without going into panic mode.

Damn. She loved the boys to bits, but AJ and Mik were driving her absolutely batty. AJ, of course, had his own reasons. He'd really hoped Anton would have figured out how to get everyone's voices out of his head, but neither Anton nor anyone else had a clue.

It didn't seem fair that AJ had an ability Anton would give anything to get back, but they'd all decided it must be because he wasn't quite ready, that maybe the wizard had more healing to do.

She'd hoped that by coming to Montana they'd be able to relax a little bit, what with the babies so close to coming and all, but between AJ worrying about giving whatever he'd gotten from Anton back to Anton, and her not having the babies yet, it had been a bit tense. Thank goodness for the little ones—Alex and Lily had practically glued themselves to Mik and AJ.

Now that had been a hoot, but in such a wonderful way. She'd gotten to see even more of the guys' ability to relate to kids. They were already comfortable with Tia's little girls, but Alex and Lily were older—just beginning to talk. In fact, Lily had babbled on forever to AJ, as if she was carrying on a real conversation with him.

She heard Lily squeal and remembered when she'd first seen AJ. She'd crawled right up into his lap, put her little hands on both his cheeks, and kissed him on the nose. Then she curled up against his broad chest, patting him on the cheek with one little hand, chattering away for the longest time.

Tala asked AJ later what she was talking about. He didn't really know, but he thought she kept saying something about "Dada's smile." He figured she was telling him that daddies really needed to smile a lot.

Whatever she'd said had certainly helped improve AJ's frame of mind. For a while, anyway. But, as the days had passed and Tala'd done nothing more exciting than get bigger around, both Mik and AJ had taken to hovering over her like a couple of old grandmas.

After almost two weeks of waiting for something to happen, even Igmutaka was beginning to get on her nerves. She could have kissed Adam when he'd dragged all three of her manly protectors off to town today to pick up some stuff at the hardware store.

"Good afternoon, Tala."

"Anton!" She stopped dead in the doorway, fighting a case of giggles, but even after she got them under control, it took her a moment to get her breath. "My goodness! How are you?"

"Dada! Hold still." Lily stopped whatever she was planning next and put her hands on her hips. Tala's first thought was that the little minx looked exactly like her mother when Keisha read Anton the riot act.

The man in question grinned at her from his spot on the kitchen floor. His long hair was tied up in clip-on rollers and bows, and Alex was busily adding more. Lily appeared to be drawing an entirely new face on him with what looked like permanent markers.

"We'll chat later," he said, glancing toward Tala. Then he clamped his lips firmly shut as Lily scowled at him.

"I can hardly wait. This is definitely a new look for you. I hope Keisha approves. It may be with you awhile... that looks like permanent ink." She opened the refrigerator, found a soda without any caffeine, and carried it over to the kitchen table. Then she took a seat and tried her best to keep a straight face while Lily and Alex had their way with the pack's leader.

Anton could be so damned intimidating that seeing him like this, at the mercy of a couple of precocious nineteen-month-olds, gave Tala an entirely new appreciation for the man. Even though he was still dealing with some major issues since the assassination attempt, he seemed to be handling them well.

She wasn't sure how she would react, suddenly learning she could no longer shift, but even that paled beside the fact he'd lost his ability to link with his mate, to mindtalk with his pack. The intimacy of their telepathic communication was so much a part of their lives that the loss must be devastating for him. She rubbed her hand over her belly, aware of the subtle connection she already had with her babies. She'd been aware of them as thinking, independent individuals for weeks now.

What would it be like not to have that link? Not to know they were healthy and alive and growing perfectly within her womb?

"Anton! Oh, good Lord."

Tala glanced up. Keisha stood in the doorway, eyes wide, fingertips covering her mouth. It was impossible to tell if she was furious or trying not to laugh.

Maybe a little of both?

"See, Mama? Dada's purty."

Laughing, Keisha swept into the room. "Oh, he's definitely purty, sweetie. Time to put the colors away and come help Mommy. You, too, Alex. It's almost naptime." She knelt and began helping the kids clean up the bows and markers, but she shot a quick glance at Tala. "Just wait, darlin'. Someday you, too, will have a pair like this."

Tala laughed. "It's daunting, that's for sure. I'm just wondering how Anton's going to get those purty colors off his face."

Anton sighed as he stood up. "The original plan was simple. I figured I'd just shift and they'd all go away. Then, I realized . . ." He shrugged and reached for a paper towel. "Anyway, guess it's going to have to be plain old soap and water."

Keisha held up one of the pens, a bright green one Lily seemed to like best, if the scribbles around his eyes were any indication. "Read this, m'love. The word *permanent* is not there as a marketing ploy. It really is permanent."

Anton got the towel wet and scrubbed at the ink on his face. It didn't even smear. He glanced at the clean paper towel. "Well, then I guess I'd better hope you like the look."

Keisha finished cleaning up the toys and stood. She pointed both kids toward the doorway. "Mama Xandi's got the tub full. Better hurry before the water gets cold."

Squealing, Lily and Alex took off running. Keisha set the basket of toys and pens on the counter and carefully removed all the ribbons and curlers from Anton's hair. Then she looped her arms over his shoulders. "I love the look, and I love you, but I have a feeling we're going to have to resort to spot remover for this mess." She kissed him.

Even Tala felt the love Keisha had for her mate.

Love, as well as her sadness. A sadness so deep, so visceral, Tala's eyes blurred with tears. She sniffed. Stared at her swollen ankles and then bit back a groan as one of the babies planted a foot firmly atop her bladder. It came to her so clearly then—she had absolutely nothing to complain about. Nothing at all.

Because even though they were separated by many miles, Tala still felt both her guys in her heart. Still sensed Igmutaka's watchful mind and knew she wasn't alone. She never would be alone, as long as she and Mik and AJ shared their link.

And, as long as Igmutaka watched over his charge. It was something that just was, something she now accepted as one of her senses, never dreaming it could be lost.

She watched as Keisha and Anton left the kitchen together, laughing softly, arms around one another. She hugged herself, and decided the guys had been gone long enough.

Bay awoke with the sense he was being watched, blinked his eyes, and looked directly into Manda's. The moment his opened fully, she smiled.

"Good," she said, kissing him way too fast. "You're awake. We need to leave today."

"Leave? Where?"

"Montana, you doofus. It's time."

He rubbed his palms over his eyes and tried to scrub himself more alert. "Is someone in labor?"

Manda shook her head. "I dreamed last night that we needed to go today. It was Eve. I'm almost positive she was here in this room." She frowned. "Or maybe I was somewhere with her. I'm not sure, but I am sure we need to leave."

Bay lifted himself up on his elbows and slipped one leg over Manda. When she didn't try to get away, he eased himself entirely over her body until he covered her from toes to chest, until all he had to do was lower his head in order to brush her lips with his. "I guess we can go today. It's a little earlier than we'd planned. That's not a problem. But not right now. Maybe just a little bit later?"

She didn't actually answer him, but she wriggled a bit beneath him. Her legs parted and his slipped into the gap between. His cock was suddenly stretched up over her mound, pointing toward that perfect little belly. His balls pressed tightly against her sex.

She was already moist, her labia swollen and slick. Ready for him. He felt the rush of blood to his groin, the wonderful sense of fullness as his cock engorged and stretched along her belly. He thrust against her, his balls pressing close against that wet heat, feeling the brush of her curled pubic hairs tickling the underside of his shaft.

Groaning, suddenly needy and wanting, he tilted his hips, lifting high enough to slide his shaft down between her legs. Not entering her, instead, rubbing against those wonderfully damp lips, sliding the full length of his erection over her clitoris.

She whimpered, a surprised little sound that had him wanting more of her. He dipped his head, suckled one nipple between his lips, and ran his tongue over the hard little tip. She whimpered again and arched beneath him, rotating her hips in a fruitless effort to lure him inside.

The heat between her legs drew him. The slick fluids made him crazy and he fought himself, fought the powerful desire to thrust deep and hard, to fill her completely. It would be so easy, just a simple lift of his hips to raise his butt up just so, and he knew his cock would act like a heat-seeking missile, finding her warmth without any hesitation at all.

But the torture was exquisite. The sense of her so close, so ready for him. The knowledge he could enter her at any time while forcing himself to wait. To slide slowly up and down, that slow, slow drag of thick, long shaft over her swollen bud, the subtle tug against his foreskin, her thighs clasping his hips, her breasts rubbing over the thick mat of hair on his chest.

He slipped into her thoughts as easily as he knew his

penis could slide inside her pussy. Slipped in and found himself, found the fine edge of control where she balanced so precariously, almost painfully aroused, unwilling to let him force her over the edge.

He shared her arousal and all the sensations taking her higher, shared the way his shaft slid so easily over her clit, the smooth slide of his glans parting her folds, coming so close to penetrating and then moving beyond. Back and forth, over and over again, keeping that same, torturous cadence until she breathed in and out with each gentle sweep, until her heart beat in sync with his.

Then, without warning, he twisted his hips and plunged deep. Filled her full and hard, slipping his arms around her waist and rising up on his knees. She wrapped her long legs around his waist and cried out, tilting her head, arching her back until her long, blond hair swept the rumpled bedcovers. Their link was complete, an absolute binding of one mind to the other, of Manda's body to Bay's.

If they hadn't loved in the gentle light of morning, if the room had instead been bathed in darkness, he knew they would have seen flashes of light, energy rippling between them, so powerful was their connection, so intense their shared desire.

Manda screamed. She clutched his shoulders and tightened her legs around his waist, and her scream tipped Baylor over the edge. Her vaginal muscles clasped him, milking him with each ripple and pulse until his hips no longer thrust forward and his balls ached from the power of his climax.

Blowing as if he'd run a mile, Bay lowered Manda to the bed and wrapped his arms around her. He held her close. Their bodies were still connected, their hearts and minds linked as one.

He felt her tears on his chest. After a moment she raised her head and stared into his eyes. He'd expected to see the look of a satisfied woman, but she looked bereft.

"What's wrong?" He kissed her. "Did I hurt you? Did I...?"

She shook her head and pressed a finger to his lips, interrupting him. "Never. You would never hurt me, but at the height of our climax, when we were so completely together, I thought of Keisha. How it must be for her, to make love with Anton without that amazing connection. How lonely it has to be for both of them. We need to go today. Not just for your sisters. Somehow, we have to help make Anton whole again."

Keisha set the phone back in the cradle on Anton's desk, crossed her arms over her chest, and stared out the big back window. Anton played in the snow with Lily, while Stefan pulled Alex around on his little sleigh. Such a beautiful peaceful scene, and yet she felt so fragile she was surprised she hadn't shattered.

The isolation was the worst of it. Surrounded by people who loved her, and yet the connection that should have been strongest, the one between her and her mate, had practically disappeared.

They'd made love this morning. He was a skilled lover and he'd satisfied her over and over again, made her body sing and her heart soar, but when they both lay there in the big bed with their hearts thundering and lungs straining for air, she'd realized she'd never felt so terribly alone.

He hadn't been in her mind. His soft words of love, whispered against her ear, had meant the world to her, but she'd reached for him, reached for that amazing connection that was so much a part of their loving, and hadn't been able to find it.

She'd tried explaining herself to Xandi, but she'd ended up feeling like a fool. Xandi's soft comment had almost killed her.

He's alive. He could have died that night. You could

have died that night. Wouldn't you rather have this much of him, rather than not have him at all?

Xandi's words had been rattling around in her head all day long. They made her feel small and unworthy, as if she didn't have the sense to be satisfied with how much she had, how blessed she truly was.

But she'd known paradise in Anton's arms. She'd flown with him, been touched by that amazing mind of his, sharing his wisdom and his love, his fears, the things he could never speak aloud . . . He'd shared those things with her in the intimacy of their bond.

And she missed it. Dear Goddess, how she missed it.

At least everyone was finally on their way here. For some odd reason, the various members of the pack had each decided to come earlier than planned, and she was so terribly grateful. Keisha always felt stronger when the pack gathered. It was especially wonderful to come together for a birth, but to have three babies almost ready to make their arrival was nothing short of miraculous.

She needed wonderful right now. Needed that miracle, needed something positive, something to give her hope. Knowing their home would be filled to bursting for the next few days was a good thing—good for her and good for Anton.

Luc and Tia and the twins, Lisa and Tinker, and Logan and Jazzy were flying in later this afternoon. Tinker had taken on a lot of Pack Dynamics work following the assassination attempt, and his duties had meant that he and Lisa hadn't been able to come with Tala and the guys. Lisa was due within the next couple of weeks, though, and Logan hadn't wanted to leave her without access to medical care.

After Tia's delivery, everyone realized the importance of a doctor or healer who understood their unique physiology, who could, if an emergency occurred, go inside to treat the unborn child. Adam and Liana were here for Tala. Logan had chosen to stay with Lisa, which meant

Jazzy stayed in San Francisco. There was no way she was going to be separated from her mate.

Keisha hadn't realized how much she would miss the two of them, but it had seemed terribly quiet here without Logan and Jazzy. She was so glad they were finally coming home. The entire crew from Colorado was on the way, too, but they were driving. She'd expected them before now, but the call she'd just gotten from Millie put them about two hours out.

The Maine pack were flying in about the same time as the group from San Francisco, which was why Adam and Stefan were taking two of the big SUVs to the airport and hoping they could fit everyone inside. The only ones missing were Beth and Nick, but they were in Washington, DC, for at least a few more years. What a wonderful opportunity they'd been given!

She would always feel a special bond to Beth. She'd been so terribly troubled when they first met, but Beth had faced her fears and come through them stronger than ever. Keisha admired a spirit like Beth's. Sometimes she wished she had more of that daring herself.

Just then, Anton raised his head and caught her looking at him. Keisha smiled. He grinned and waved. Then he grabbed Lily up in a big hug and swung her around. Anton's deep laughter, Lily's high-pitched squeals, the sounds of Stefan laughing, and Alex's funny little giggles should have left her smiling.

She couldn't bear to watch. Sighing, feeling isolated and alone, Keisha turned away from the laughter and went back to the kitchen. She might as well start something for dinner. They'd have a houseful tonight. And maybe, just maybe, somehow, someone would help right her world once again.

Adam and Liana cleared the table after dinner. Daci and her guys offered to help with cleanup, and Keisha followed the rest of the group into the big family room. Lisa took a big, overstuffed chair near the window and Tinker sat at her feet. Tia and Luc sat together on one of the couches. Tia's babies were already asleep after a long day of travel.

Ulrich, Millie, Manda, and Baylor sat at the card table in the corner so Millie could show off some old albums she'd brought with her. Mei and Oliver leaned over their shoulders, checking out old photos of Millie as a child.

She'd looked exactly like Manda, and Keisha thought it must be bittersweet for all of them, to see what Manda might have looked like if she'd been able to grow up like a normal girl instead of one trapped between wolf and woman.

Jake and Shannon, along with Logan, were the only ones who'd gone for a run, but Keisha didn't expect them to be gone for long. Everyone was fairly subdued tonight. She wanted to think it was because of the travel, but she couldn't help but feel the concern the pack had for Anton.

He seemed oblivious to their worry. He'd been laughing with Ulrich and teasing Daci, and every once in a while he'd look at Keisha and wink. She wished she knew what he was thinking. His thoughts had often been blocked to her, but she could always invade them, always figure out what was on his mind.

Not now. Now she was merely one of many wondering what the wizard was thinking. He sat in his big recliner and pulled her into his lap. It was always better when they at least touched. She didn't feel nearly as alone then.

AJ and Mik sat on the couch with Tala between them. The poor girl looked ready to pop, but Igmutaka insisted the babies were not ready yet. He'd solemnly promised to let everyone know as soon as they told him it was time.

Like Tala wouldn't be able to figure it out? The spirit guide took his cougar form most of the time now, hunting during the day, and showing up in the evening to be with Tala. Now he lay on the floor at her feet, a big, beautiful tan-colored cougar stretching a full nine feet from his nose to the tip of his tail.

Lily and Alex raced into the room, all freshly bathed and warmly dressed in their fuzzy footie pajamas. Xandi and Jazzy followed close behind, both of them soaked through from bath time. Alex ran straight to his daddy, but Lily went to AJ. She crawled up into his lap, and once again she patted his cheeks and chattered away.

Anton laughed. "Ya know, Tala. You might want to watch her. She's really flirting with your man."

"I noticed. And whatever she's saying, she's really serious. You be careful, AJ."

AJ grinned and nuzzled Lily's belly. She giggled and shook her head. "No. No, Unca AJ." Then she patted his cheeks again. "Dada's smile. Unca AJ got Dada's smile."

Tala frowned. "I wonder what she means by that? She's been saying the same thing ever since we got here."

"What's that?" Keisha wasn't quite sure what her daughter had said, though her speech was getting clearer by the day.

"Something about Daddy's smile. That AJ has Daddy's smile."

Liana stepped into the room. "I heard her saying that yesterday. I wonder . . ." She walked across the room, stepped over the big cat, and knelt beside AJ. "Lily? Where is Dada's smile?"

Lily's eyes lit up and she let out a big breath. She patted AJ's cheek again. "Here. Unca AJ got Dada's smile. In here."

"Well, I'll be damned." Liana shook her head. "Anton? Come here. Can you fit beside AJ?"

"I think so." He lifted Keisha off his lap, crossed the room, and squeezed in beside AJ and the padded arm of the sofa. "What's going on in that ex-goddess brain of yours, Liana?"

"I'm not really sure. Lily? Sweetie, this is very serious. I want you to try something for me. Can you talk to Dada without using your big-girl words? With the quiet, secret words you keep in your head?"

Lily stuck her finger in her mouth and stared at Liana. Keisha held her breath for what felt like forever, until Lily solemnly nodded.

"Good girl. I want you to say, 'I love you, Daddy,' but don't use your noisy words. Use your quiet words."

Lily turned around and tumbled into Anton's lap. He picked her up and settled her on his chest. She leaned close and put her little hands on his cheeks, just as she had done with AJ.

A moment later, Keisha saw tears at the corner of her mate's eyes. She didn't realize she was holding her breath until Anton raised his head. His expression was one of dazed disbelief, but he smiled at her. "I can hear her. I can hear Lily. But how?"

Liana shook her head. "I don't know. The purity of a child's mind? I'm not really sure, but we're not done." She grinned. "Not by a long shot. Okay, Lily. Now, I want you to go to Uncle AJ and talk to him with your quiet words. I want you to go and get Dada's smile. Can you do that?"

Again Lily's fingers went in her mouth, but she nodded very seriously, crawled off Anton and back on AJ. He looped his big hands around her tiny little bottom and held her on his lap. "Hey, sugar. Can you find Dada's smile?"

Lily giggled and fell forward, slapping her little hands against his cheeks. Then she frowned, as if she was dragging up every single bit of her ability to concentrate. A moment later, she sat back on AJ's lap. He blinked, as if confused and maybe a little disoriented, but Lily didn't seem to mind a bit. She leaned forward and kissed his cheek, crawled off his lap, and went back over to her daddy.

The room had gone absolutely still. Adam, Daci, and the guys stood in the doorway, watching quietly. Even Igmutaka was sitting up, staring with solemn cat's eyes at Keisha's baby girl.

Keisha wondered if anyone else could hear her heart pounding. The damned thing felt like a set of drums beating in her chest as Lily hugged her father, and then looked to Liana for directions.

"Daddy wants his smile back, sweetheart. Can you give it to him?"

"Okay."

Keisha reached for Liana's hand and hung on for dear life. She glanced at AJ and realized he still had a dazed expression on his face, and she couldn't help but wonder what her baby girl had been able to do that would leave a grown man so spaced out.

Lily patted Anton's cheeks. Then she did something different. She stood up on his lap and leaned her forehead against his. Her black curls corkscrewed this way and that, a curly version of her daddy's hair. Her beautiful café au lait skin seemed even darker against the fairness of Anton's. His hands circled her little waist, holding her upright as she pressed her forehead to his and held her palms against his temples.

She stood that way for what felt like a very long time. Then she slowly pulled away and yawned. Anton folded her into his arms and held her the way he'd first held her at birth, snuggled into the crook of his arm as her amber eyes slowly shut, as her perfect lips bowed into a tiny smile.

"Is she okay?" Keisha leaned close to make sure she was breathing, that everything was working.

She's just very tired, my love. That's all. She's perfectly okay. Our little girl carried my smile from AJ back to me. That's quite a responsibility for a nineteen-month-old baby.

Keisha shoved her knuckles against her mouth to keep from sobbing. She didn't want to cry. She might frighten Lily, but she felt as if she might burst with all the emotions inside. "How?" She stared at Anton, at the huge smile that split his face. Then she turned to Liana. Tears ran down Liana's cheeks.

"Good." Keisha's laughter turned into a sob. "You can cry so I don't have to, okay?"

"Sure." Liana sniffed and reached for Adam. In two steps, he was by her side, grabbing hold of her. "Any time you want."

AJ blinked and shook his head. "What happened?" He glanced around him, down at his hand trapped in Tala's as if she held him in a vise. "That was just weird. I felt Lily's thoughts in my head, and then nothing. She sounded so clear. Not baby talk at all. Very weird." He stared at Anton and frowned. "It's gone. Whatever I got from you that night, it's gone. Lily?"

Anton nodded. "Dada's smile. That's what she was calling that part of me that you had. What'd you call it, Liana? My spirit or essence or whatever?"

Liana nodded and sniffed. Grinning broadly, Adam handed her a tissue.

Anton stared at his daughter, now sleeping soundly in his arms. "How the hell did a baby do that?"

"That's twice now she's saved you."

Stefan's solemn reminder had Anton nodding. "You're right. When Keisha and Tia were attacked, when I was so badly hurt. Lily was just an infant then. Her mind must be . . ."

Stefan laughed. "A very scary thing."

"She's definitely her father's daughter." Keisha couldn't take her eyes off Lily, couldn't keep her thoughts away from Anton. Feeling him, actually soaking up the connection that had been missing for the past two weeks.

It felt like forever, and she was almost afraid to ask, but she did, anyway. "I wonder if you can shift?"

He closed his eyes a moment and smiled. "I can. It's all there. The way it should feel, the things my brain and body need to do. It's as if there was a big blank spot in my mind, and now it's full. I don't understand any of this. Liana? Do you have any idea?"

She shook her head. "Not really, though when I was listening to Lily with AJ, I could tell there was more going on than just a toddler's babbling. I wasn't sure, but . . . AJ? How are you feeling?"

He chuckled and wrapped his arm around Tala, resting his fingers on Mik's shoulder. "Like me again. I don't know how you stand it, Anton—all those voices in the background. I couldn't figure out how to filter them out. When Lily wakes up, I need to tell her that Unca AJ owes her big time."

"So's her daddy." Anton slowly stood up without waking the baby in his arms. "I think she's worn out. I'm taking the princess and putting her to bed." He glanced at Stefan. "Looks like Prince Alex is out like a light, too."

"Hey, it's a rough job, keeping up with Lily. Give the little guy credit."

Keisha watched Stefan and Anton leaving the room with their toddlers in their arms. She turned and caught Xandi watching her, tears flowing. Xandi held out her arms. Keisha stumbled into her embrace and they both burst into sobs.

Tinker suddenly leapt to his feet. "Are you sure? But . . ."

Lisa nodded. "I'm sure."

"But . . . but Tala's the one who . . ."

Smiling serenely, Lisa shook her head. "Trust me, Tink. A woman knows when she's in labor."

"Oh, shit." Tinker swung around and glanced hopelessly at the rest of the pack. Lisa merely smiled and rubbed the huge mound of very pregnant belly.

Tala groaned. "This is so not fair." She stared at Igmutaka. "If I find out you've got anything to do with these babies staying in the oven longer than I expected, I swear . . ."

The big cougar dipped his head and lay down. He rolled over on his back in a show of total submission. Tala glared at him.

The door to the back deck slid open. Logan, Jake, and Shannon stepped into the room. Shannon was looking down, concentrating on tying the belt of her bathrobe around her waist. Jake and Logan had each put on the sweats they'd left on the deck when they shifted.

Jake was the first to glance up and catch the eyes of everyone in the room staring at them.

"Hey, guys," he said, grinning broadly. "We miss anything?"

Chapter 17

Tinker paced. He wondered if he was wearing a trail in the floorboards, but after Tia's long labor, Lisa's appeared to be moving quickly and without any drama at all.

At least, as far as everyone else was concerned. The women had finally told him to leave. He'd argued, but they'd won—only because they could take Lisa's pain away better than he could, but hell, he hated sharing that burden. Damned women wanted to share everything, but Lisa was his mate, having his baby.

Luc caught up to him and threw an arm over his shoulders. "They run you out?"

Tink merely grunted. He really didn't feel like talking. He should be there with Lisa, damn it all, but she seemed happier with the other women around.

"I think it was the groaning, if you want my opinion."

Luc kept pace with him as they reached the end of the hall outside the clinic and Tinker made another turn.

"Tia said Lisa couldn't concentrate. She was worried about you."

"What?" Tinker spun to a stop and stared at Luc. "Why the fuck should she be worried about me? She's the one having our baby. Going through all that pain. I mean . . . shit, Luc." His shoulders slumped. "I should be with her."

"I agree." Luc grabbed his arm and dragged him toward the clinic door. He didn't even knock. Just opened the door and walked in.

It looked like a blasted hen party. Jazzy and Xandi sat in the corner drinking wine. Mei, Daci, Liana, and Millie had chairs pulled up close to the bed. They had serious expressions on their faces, like they were really concentrating hard. Then Millie smiled at Lisa and wiped the tangled hair back from her forehead.

"That was a good one, sweetie. How're you doing?"

Lisa glanced up and saw Tinker. She smiled. "I'm doing great. You guys are much quieter when you deal with the contractions than someone else we all know and love."

"Who? Me?" Tink grinned at her and sat on the edge of the bed. Maybe Luc knew what he was talking about. "I tried to keep quiet."

"But you don't know how to share." Liana leaned close and kissed his cheek. "We know to take only as much as we can tolerate without really hurting. You think you have to do everything yourself."

He shrugged. "Hey, it's a guy thing. As long as Lisa's okay." He leaned close and kissed her gently. So perfect, and so absolutely beautiful this way, with her hair in tangles and her belly swollen.

He could have sat there all night, just staring at her, thanking whatever fates ruled his life that had given him this perfect mate—but the fates had other ideas.

Her labor began to pick up. Jazzy and Xandi set their wineglasses aside and joined the other women. Tia, Manda, and Shannon arrived a few minutes later and the room practically vibrated with the strength of so many powerful women working together.

Tinker stepped aside when Logan and Adam showed up around four in the morning, with Keisha right behind them.

"Where's Tala?" It seemed everyone else had come, but not Lisa's sister. That didn't seem right.

Keisha kissed his cheek. "Logan told her not to. The risk of the shared experience throwing her into labor is too great."

Tinker shook his head, laughing. "She is going to be so pissed. That poor little thing wants to go into labor."

"I know." Logan glanced over his shoulder at Tink. "I practically had to have the guys restrain her. She's not very happy with me right now. Tink, you might want to get up on the bed behind Lisa. She's about ready to start pushing this little girl of yours out into the world."

"Oh, shit." Tinker scrambled into position, scrunching his big frame into the space behind his mate, supporting her as Logan directed him. The moment he wrapped his arms around Lisa, he felt the pressure in her womb, shared the sense of their daughter's journey into life.

Lisa clutched his hands and braced against him, using Tinker's body for leverage. The strength in her grasp amazed and terrified him. He was suffused with fear—for his mate, for his baby, for himself. Then fear fled, leaving him overcome with awe—with the sense that women were so much stronger than men ever imagined—and the knowledge that their power came from their willingness to share, to help one another carry the load, bear the pain, achieve the impossible.

The women standing together about the bed held hands with one another. Their combined energy built upon itself until it became a physical presence in the room, empowered by each of them so willing to work together. Tinker couldn't take his eyes off his mate—the concentration on her face, the power and strength of her as she pushed their daughter into the world.

Logan caught their little girl. All Tinker registered was a dark cap of black curls and their daughter's look of pure indignation at being thrust out of her perfectly warm womb. And then she was taking a deep breath, her tiny lungs expanding.

He kissed Lisa and carefully crawled off the bed. Standing over Logan, Tinker waited for his daughter's cry, but she was quiet as her big eyes seemed to focus on all the faces in the room. He knew she couldn't actually see anything yet, couldn't really distinguish features, but when Logan had finished tying off the cord and wiping the afterbirth off her tiny body, when he finally handed her over to Tinker, Tink took his perfect little girl in his arms with a heart so full he felt as if it might break. She settled easily into his embrace and her dark eyes fastened on his face.

She stared at him, unblinking, for what felt like forever. And just like that, Tinker knew he'd lost his heart to yet another woman. Slowly he turned and sat on the bed beside Lisa. She reached out and touched their daughter, and then her fingers went straight to Tinker's heart.

She pressed them against his chest. "I love you. She is so perfect. I hope she's exactly like you."

He shook his head, bemused by the emotions racing through him, the changes rushing over him. *Father.* He was this beautiful little girl's father, and the responsibility, the joy, and the sense of completion was overwhelming.

Shaken, he handed her to Lisa. The others crowded around, each of them wanting to touch, to see, to experience this latest addition to the pack. The door slammed opened and Tala rushed in, followed by Mik and AJ. Anton stood in the doorway behind them, smiling at the crowd in the delivery room.

Tinker glanced up and caught Anton's benevolent grin. He stood and walked over to the doorway, shook Anton's outstretched hand. "Pretty mind-blowing experience. I still can't believe she's here."

Anton laughed. "No one can tell you what it's going to feel like, not until you hold your own perfect child for the very first time. There is nothing to compare. Nothing." He nodded toward Lisa. "How'd she do?"

"Wonderful." Tinker chuckled. "Probably much better after they ran me off."

"They merely suffer our presence," Anton said, gesturing toward the women. "They really don't need us once the breeding's done."

Keisha slipped between Tinker and Anton and wrapped her arms around her mate. "Yes, we do. You can reach stuff on the top shelf, carry heavy things." She kissed his chin. "However would we make it without you?" She grabbed his hand and tugged. "Come see. She's absolutely beautiful. I'm thinking maybe we need another one of these. What do you think?"

"What?" Anton shot a startled glance at Tinker and followed his mate.

Tinker's gaze settled on Lisa and their daughter. No longer merely a man and his mate—he was now the head of a family. His very own. He stood outside the gathering and watched them all—the smiles, the laughter, his beautiful woman with their baby girl in her arms. He realized that, while he stood outside and observed, he was still very much a part of this amazing group.

He couldn't help but think of the changes in his life, the difference between the man Ulrich Mason had hired right out of the military so many years ago and the man he was now.

There really was no comparison. He'd lived his life apart from the rest of the world, never feeling as if he belonged, not really sure just who or what he was. Now he knew. There was no doubt who Martin "Tinker" McClintock was—he was Lisa's mate, this gorgeous little girl's father.

He was Chanku, and very much a part of the pack.

Tala crawled into bed between Mik and AJ. The sun was high in the sky, but they'd been up all night while Lisa labored and everyone but Tala got to be part of her special night.

It didn't seem fair, damn it all, even though she fully understood Logan's reasons for keeping her out of the birthing room, but that didn't make her like it any better.

She was just so tired of being pregnant and it didn't seem fair that Lisa had sailed through the whole process with a perfect pregnancy and a really wonderful delivery, while she was still fat and ungainly, with her swollen ankles and the never-ending need to pee.

And on top of that she was horny. She lay there between two of the sexiest men on Earth, two men who loved her and wanted her as much as she wanted them, and she couldn't touch! While Lisa and Tinker had been able to fuck like teenagers up until just a couple of days ago, she'd been cut off for a couple of months because of spotting.

Having not one but two mates who were hung like a couple of bull elephants probably didn't help, but Logan had told her she needed to lay off sex altogether. No climaxes. He didn't want her uterus undergoing any strain at all.

Well, hell. What about frustration? That couldn't be good for a pregnant lady, could it? And Goddess knew, she was frustrated as hell.

But were the guys? Hell, no. They had each other—all the time. She'd had to lie there and take it when they'd had sex for hours, the two of them making her even more frustrated. There was nothing worse for a woman in her condition than lying there and watching two absolutely gorgeous guys giving each other one orgasm after another.

No consideration. None at all for her condition. And her condition was definitely pissed. Very, very pissed.

She lay there on her back with her arms folded across her chest, while both babies practiced their soccer goals on her bladder. Her brain was absolutely boiling.

Then she heard Mik chuckling. And what sounded like

AJ choking on something. Blinking, she glanced from one side to the other. "You guys okay? What's wrong?"

Mik let go with a snort and AJ just lay there and laughed. Damn it, they'd been eavesdropping.

She was going to kill them. Definitely—no doubt in her mind. Mik and AJ were dead meat.

Tala didn't remember falling asleep, and she wasn't really certain exactly what woke her. Then she realized she was sleeping in a puddle. *Oh, crap. I didn't wet the bed, did I?*

How embarrassing. Mik slept soundly and so did AJ, but she'd have to wake them so they could change the sheets and . . .

Holy shit!

Tala's entire body went rigid as the first hard contraction slammed across her midsection. Igmutaka scrambled to his feet and stood with his front paws on the bed. He sniffed Tala's middle and stared at her with those beautiful cat's eyes. *It is time. I'm going to call Logan.*

Then he threw back his head and cut loose with a full-throated panther scream. Mik and AJ exploded out of bed.

"What the fuck?" Mik was on his feet, hands curled into fists, staring about wildly.

AJ tangled in the covers, fell off the bed, and ended up on his butt beneath Igmutaka's back paws. "What's wrong?"

Igmutaka cut loose with another powerful cry.

Tala wanted to laugh. Damn but she really wanted to laugh, except she felt another strong contraction rip across her belly. This wasn't how Lisa's labor went at all. Her sister said she'd had hours of nice, easy contractions that built slowly into a smooth and practically pain-free labor.

This hurt like holy hell!

The door flew open and Stefan stood there, bare assed and buck naked, his hair flying in all directions. "What's wrong? What's going on?"

Mik shook his head. "I think Ig's trying to tell us Tala's in labor. Honey? Are you okay?"

AJ touched the wet sheets. "Looks like her water broke."

Tala sighed. The contraction was over. She wasn't sure if she was more relieved about that or the fact she hadn't peed in bed. Suddenly another strong contraction slammed into her. She grabbed Mik's arm and AJ's hand and curled into the pain.

And then, just like that, the pain was gone. Keisha and Xandi stood in the doorway. Keisha was tying her robe. Xandi had on a flannel nightgown that looked like something out of *Little House on the Prairie,* but both women muscled their way past Stefan and stood beside the bed.

A moment later, they each let out a huge breath. Keisha glanced at Stefan and grinned. "Want to find some pants, big boy?" Shaking his head, Stef chuckled and left. Keisha brushed Tala's tangled hair back from her face. "How do you feel? Like you have to push? Are you that far along yet?"

Another contraction hit before she could answer, and again Keisha and Xandi caught the pain, shared it and eased Tala through it. When she could catch her breath she nodded. "It feels like one of the babies is ready to come already. But I just started contractions! They can't be coming so soon."

"Actually, they can." Adam walked calmly into the room. Liana was right behind him.

Tala took one look at him and giggled. "Batman boxers? Adam! I never would have guessed."

"Liana's fashion sense needs some help." He placed his hands on Tala's round belly and closed his eyes. Then he shot a quick look at Liana. "Grab some clean towels out of the bathroom."

Mik and AJ were both slipping into sweatpants when Anton stuck his head through the open doorway. "I've called Logan. He's on his way. Hey, Tala! Looks like you're going to be the first to christen a guest room."

"What?" Her voice cracked on the word and she knew her eyes had to be as big as saucers. "Shouldn't I be in the clinic?" She felt another contraction coming, and this time there was no doubt in her mind about pushing. Mik crawled up behind her as Tinker had for Lisa. AJ hung on to her hand. Igmutaka had shifted and stood near the foot of the bed. His eyes were closed, his hands lifted before him as if he might be praying.

Jazzy, Shannon, and Manda showed up, all of them pushing tangled hair from their faces, tying their robes, taking her pain. With Adam directing, Mik helped her into a squatting position. It seemed more natural to her, like she actually knew what she was doing.

Fat chance of that, but she felt a need to bear down and she did, and it was Igmutaka who was there beside Adam, his big hands surprisingly gentle as he caught her first baby.

Mik's daughter. Adam cut the cord while Igmutaka held the tiny little girl and then Jazzy helped wipe away the afterbirth. Her baby opened her mouth and cut loose with a loud cry.

"Ohmygod." Tala almost forgot to breathe. "Mik, just look at her!"

Mik stayed where he was as Igmutaka carried their daughter to the bedside, but before Tala even got a chance to get a good look at her little girl, she felt the next one coming.

Logan arrived as she cut loose with a curse. His hands on her were gentle as she pushed, and then pushed again, and it felt like there had to be blood vessels breaking all over her body as she strained to deliver the second of her twins.

"Tala." Logan raised his head and stopped her with a glance. "Back off a little. I need to turn him. He's got shoulders like a damned linebacker."

Huffing and panting, Tala fought the horrible urge to push. She glared at AJ. "You are so gonna pay for this!"

AJ's eyes went wide but he didn't say a word. Tala figured that was probably his smartest course of action as Logan reached between her legs. She felt his hands working at something, felt pressure, but the pain was far away and she realized the crowd had grown and even the men were linking hands now, holding on with their women, all of them helping this next baby into the world.

"Now, Tala! Push! You can do it." Adam grabbed AJ and pulled him over to the end of the bed. Logan moved aside, and it was AJ catching the little boy with those big shoulders, AJ holding his son in his arms. He cuddled him close against his naked chest, oblivious to blood and afterbirth, as Logan cut the cord and tied it.

Tala got a glimpse of coal black hair and fair skin and then Mik was helping her to lie down, and Logan was doing something else between her legs that didn't interest her at all. Not when Igmutaka was putting her baby girl to one breast and AJ was putting her son to the other.

Mik still held her cradled in his lap with one arm supporting his daughter. Ig had moved to the side of the bed, where he sat and stared at the baby girl, and AJ supported their baby boy as he rooted and snorted in search of Tala's nipple.

She watched him for a moment, then studied her daughter. Their little girl had latched on immediately and suckled peacefully. It took a moment longer for her new son to find his first meal, but when he finally got his little mouth around her nipple, she felt the suction all the way to her toes.

She laughed and leaned her head against Mik's chest. "He's like a little wolverine! Listen to him."

He snorted and squirmed, sucking for all he was worth. Tala looked up and caught AJ staring at the baby with tears coursing down his cheeks. She tilted her head back so she could see Mik. His face was suspiciously damp as well. Even Igmutaka appeared slightly stunned.

"You ever seen a baby born before, Ig?"

He shook his head. "No. Never. She truly is a miracle." He raised his head and looked directly at Mik. "Your grandfather is proud, Miguel. He knows of this child's birth. He blesses both this perfect little girl, and all of you. She will be as a star in the heavens. She is destined to be a woman of great promise."

Tala smiled at her daughter. She already knew her name. "I want to name her Mikaela Star." She tilted her head back and smiled at Mik. "Is that okay? Mikaela for her daddy, but we can call her Star?"

Mik nodded. "I like that." He shot a sideways glance at Igmutaka, but the spirit guide was totally engrossed in watching the baby nurse. Mik grinned and shook his head. "What about this little guy? AJ? You have any preferences?"

"Tala first. Have you thought of a name?" He chuckled softly and ran his fingers through his son's coal black hair. "I can't believe we never really talked about names."

Tala smiled at him. She wasn't about to tell him she knew exactly what AJ wanted to name his little boy. "You were named after your father and grandfather, weren't you?"

AJ shrugged. So noncommittal. Tala almost laughed, and then she realized where his mind was going.

"I'm not about to name him after my father," he said. "The bastard abandoned my mother. Probably why she killed herself."

He looked away, and the pain in his expression made Tala's heart hurt. She knew how he'd found his mother, dead in the bathtub where she'd slit her wrists. He'd been about three at the time.

"Your mother's father was named Jackson, though. Jackson Temple. I'm thinking of Jackson Miguel. Is that okay with you guys?"

AJ spun around and looked at Mik, not at Tala. "Is that okay with you, Mik? We could call him Jack."

"Jackson Miguel Temple?" Mik grinned at AJ. Then he leaned across Tala and kissed his mate. "Works for me."

Igmutaka slowly stood up. It wasn't until he rose to his feet that Tala realized everyone else had gone, giving them this time as a family. "Ig? You don't have to go." She grabbed his hand. "You're family, too."

He leaned over and kissed her cheek. "Thank you. You honor me. My cougar needs to go into the forest. I want to give thanks to both my gods and your goddess. They have blessed us today."

Tala squeezed his fingers. "You're right. They have." She stared at the two babies, both sleeping now at her breasts. Star and Jack. She could get used to both names, really easy. "Thank you, Igmutaka. For watching over us. For being there when we needed you."

He bowed his head. "I will always be here. Always." Then he shifted, and the big cougar slowly walked out of the room.

Tala got the giggles and it took a minute before she could catch her breath.

Both AJ and Mik were looking at her like she was nuts.

"I just realized he was naked. Ya know, now that we've got kids . . ."

Mik looped his arms around his family. AJ sat on the bed beside him. "I am not wearing Batman boxers," he said. "You've really got to draw the line somewhere."

Tala nodded. "I wouldn't think of it. That is so not you." She relaxed against Mik's big, solid body and hoped AJ wouldn't find the packages from her trip to town last week with the girls. Not until she had a chance to bring him around.

SpongeBob SquarePants didn't have a thing to do with Batman. Not a thing.

* * *

Anton curled up behind Keisha and drew her into his embrace. Three new babies, all healthy, all perfect in every way. He thought of their futures, the futures of all their children, and realized how much better their lives would be than the lives of their parents.

Instead of growing up as outcasts, as misfits in a world that didn't understand them, they would always have the strength of the pack behind them, the love of parents who knew what it was like to be Chanku.

And these three were far from the last. Logan was going to be busy. Shannon and Manda were both expecting. Liana's pregnancy had been confirmed as well, and now Keisha and Xandi were talking about having more.

Which led him full circle to thoughts of his amazing daughter. Not even two years old yet, and already Lily had saved him twice. She'd pulled him from the brink of death when he'd almost given in to the lure of peace across the veil, and now she'd given him back his soul.

There was no other way to describe it. Lily had found and retrieved "Dada's smile," and then she'd given it back to him. Sort of like taking precocious to an entirely new level.

His mate rolled over and kissed his chin. "Ick. Bristles. Somebody didn't shave today. That's not like you."

He chuckled and rubbed his scratchy chin against her shoulder until Keisha giggled and tried to pull away. "Not fair. Maybe I'll let my legs go for a while and see how you like that."

He kissed her, carefully this time, cautious of the whiskers and her tender skin. "It was a rather hectic day. Three new babies, three new pregnancies. And you and Xandi dropping your little bombshells. Are you sure you're ready for another one already?"

"I'm not getting any younger. Neither are you."

He held her close and sighed, but it was a sound of pleasure. Of his pure and utter contentment. "That doesn't appear to be a problem anymore. At least from what Liana says. Even Millie thinks that, should she want to, she could get pregnant again. We are truly amazing creatures."

Keisha laughed and nuzzled the dark mat of hair on his chest. "And if you'll recall, Millie said it would be a cold day in hell before she considered having another baby. I don't want to wait too long, get too comfortable with my life. I'm afraid that a day will come when I actually remember life before Lily."

"I know. It was wonderful, having you all to myself, but I can't imagine a world without Lily in it. Nor do I want to."

He let that thought hang in the air for a while. Lily amazed him in so many ways. What would another child of theirs be like? With Keisha as their mother, he could only imagine any child she bore would be wonderful.

Keisha was silent. He let his thoughts caress hers and found what he'd expected. She'd fallen asleep in his arms, but it had been a rather long and hectic couple of days, and helping Lisa and Tala with their labor pain had to have been exhausting.

But for Anton, sleep would not come easily tonight. For the first time in weeks, he was complete, his mind free to take him beyond the four walls of their room. He let his thoughts wander through the quiet house. First he checked on Stefan and Xandi. Stefan's thoughts were of Xandi's wish for another child and his own desires as well. He was much too excited to sleep.

Anton hovered a moment, enjoying the wonderful world of Stefan's mind. Who would have thought that a man like Stefan Aragat would take to fatherhood so well?

But then, who would have figured Anton as father material? He moved on and found Baylor and Manda, Jake and Shannon, all sleeping together in one of the guest rooms, their minds at rest and bodies sated. Millie and Ric slept in another room, just the two of them. He bade them well and slipped on through the night. Mei and Oliver, Adam and Liana, Daci and her two guys. Tia was up with one of the twins, softly humming a lullaby while Luc slept with his other daughter curled beneath his chin.

Jazzy and Logan were making love. Anton lingered for a few moments, caught in the quiet passion of the two of them, but as Jazzy reached her peak, he moved on, unwilling to intrude more than he already had. At least they'd not sensed his presence.

Tinker slept beside Lisa with their daughter swaddled in soft blankets, asleep on his chest. They'd decided to call her Anna Marie, after Tinker's adoptive mother. A beautiful name for such a gorgeous little girl.

Lisa's fingers were tightly clasped in Tinker's hand, and there was a smile on the big man's face that matched the one in his heart. Anton paused there for a long moment, enjoying the unusual sense of peace in Tinker's thoughts. He'd truly found exactly what he wanted—a family of his own.

Tala slept soundly with Mik on one side and AJ on the other. Their babies were in the small crib beside their bed, sleeping close together. He was surprised there was no sense of Igmutaka. Anton figured the spirit guide would stay close to his new charge, but maybe he hunted tonight. The stars were bright and the night clear.

His last stop was the nursery. Alex slept in a tumble of blankets and stuffed toys with a little toy car clutched in one hand. Anton's thoughts hovered a moment before he moved on to Lily, expecting to find her sound asleep.

She sat up in her bed with what appeared to be a stuffed cat in her hand, chattering away as if it was the middle of the day.

Lily? Lie down now and go to sleep.

Dada? He felt her smile. *I waiting to say good night, Dada.*

Good night, Lily. I love you. Thank you for finding my smile.

You're welcome. It was lost, but Unca AJ took good care of it for you. Good night, Dada.

It wasn't the nature of cats to run for the joy of running, but Igmutaka knew that if he didn't race the wind tonight he might never sleep again. He had to run, had to do something to contain the joy that had practically burst inside him today.

The child he'd watched over, almost from conception, the one he had protected, and then had the unbelievable privilege of catching as she slipped from her mother's womb . . . that perfect child was his.

He ran on, thinking of the way she'd looked, all red and wrinkled with her thick, coal black hair and those tiny toes and fingers, and he tried to imagine her as a grown woman, with her dark hair cascading down her back. Would her eyes be amber, like her parents? Would she be small like her beautiful mother or tall and strong like her father?

He had no way of knowing. Not yet, but the years would pass swiftly, and one day he would see her as she was meant to be—grown and beautiful—and his.

He reached the peak of the nearest mountain. Not as high as the others, though high enough to be bare of trees. It was rocky and frozen this perfect winter night, but he found a place where the wind had swept the snow away, and he shifted. Standing tall and naked to the frozen night, he raised his hands in thanks.

It was a perfect night. The winter solstice—powerful and filled with magic and the promise of spring not so far away. Chanting the ancient words, as much a song of joy as a prayer of thanks, he called on the old gods to bless this child, to protect Mikaela Star and shower her with gifts. He asked for wisdom and grace, for strength and a strong heart. And he asked for beauty as well.

Might as well go for whatever he could, right? She was, after all, his charge. And while he was at it, he called for the same blessings for her brother, and for the child born to Tinker and his mate. They were good people. Strong, honest people, all honorable and loving, and they deserved no less.

Then he turned his voice to the Goddess of the Chanku. When he called on Eve, she answered him, which made him wonder if the old gods still had their power. They'd been silent for so long. It was good to know the Chanku Goddess was alert and watching over her charges. It hadn't always been this way, but he loved Liana in spite of her failings.

Loved her enough that he might return to her bed tonight and give Mikaela Star's family time alone to adjust to the new members of their little group.

The wind whipped over and around his naked body and his long hair tangled and twisted on the currents of air. He was a timeless creature, one who had lived for many thousands of years, but he knew he was going to be tested.

And it wouldn't be a battle-hardened warrior who would push him to his limits. No, he had a feeling it was going to be one very precocious, very beautiful young woman.

His young woman. His Star. He would be patient. It wasn't going to be easy, but he would give her room to grow, to experience life. To find the path she was meant to walk.

But when she finally took that path, he planned to be waiting right there in the middle of the road. Planted dead center along the way she traveled.

The wind died down. Igmutaka bowed his head for a

final word of thanks. Adam and Liana's warm bed was sounding better all the time—better than a cold night alone in the forest.

With that decision made, he shifted. The cougar screamed into the night, claiming this place as his own. With a swish of his long tail, he headed down the mountain, away from the barren piece of rock where he'd stood as a man—a man who had looked into the future and found his destiny.